CREATURES OF MYTH AND LEGEND

Three of the men reached one large van, all scrambling together to open its passenger door, all battling to be the first inside.

A peculiar "whoosh" of sound came from above them, growing quickly louder. The men paused in their struggle to look up.

A form swept down at them out of the blackness. Dimly seen in the growing dark, it seemed at first to be a huge bird. But as it approached, it quickly resolved into something much more terrible.

It was a flying monster, with the man-sized body of a raven, a huge span of blue-black wings, a cat's clawed feet, and a man's head on a scaled and serpentine neck.

The creature swooped in, hovering a moment just above the horrified men, vast wings flapping to hold it suspended there. The thing's human eyes glowed with a reddish fire like two hot coals. A forked tongue, also seemingly aflame, flicked out at the three cowering men. . . .

Be sure to look for these other titles from Bantam Spectra:

By Gillian Bradshaw
  Horses of Heaven
  Hawk of May
  Kingdom of Summer
  Winter's Shadow

By Kenneth C. Flint
  Otherworld

By Katharine Kerr
  The Bristling Wood
  The Dragon Revenant
  A Time of Exile
  A Time of Omens

By Angus Wells
  The Books of the Kingdoms
    Wrath of Ashar
    The Usurper
    The Way Beneath

  The Godwars
    Forbidden Magic
    Dark Magic
    Wild Magic

LEGENDS REBORN

Kenneth C. Flint

BANTAM BOOKS
NEW YORK · TORONTO · LONDON · SYDNEY · AUCKLAND

LEGENDS REBORN

A Bantam Spectra Book / December 1992

ISBN 0-553-29919-0

Published simultaneously in the United States and Canada

Bantam Books are published by Bantam Books, a division of Bantam
Doubleday Dell Publishing Group, Inc. Its trademark, consisting of
the words "Bantam Books" and the portrayal of a rooster, is
Registered in U.S. Patent and Trademark Office and in other
countries. Marca Registrada. Bantam Books, 666 Fifth Avenue,
New York, New York 10103.

PRINTED IN THE UNITED STATES OF AMERICA

RAD   0 9 8 7 6 5 4 3 2 1

DEDICATION

To my wife and best friend, Judith McCormick Flint, whose Irish heritage and interest in Ireland first awakened my own fascination with that most ancient country.

"This," they spake, "portendeth death to us,
    If we fly not swiftly from our fate!"
Self-conceited idiots! thus
    Ravingly to prate!
Not for base-born higgling Saxon trucksters
    Ring laments like those by shore and sea!
Not for churls with souls like hucksters
    Waileth our Banshee!

For the high Milesian race alone
    Ever flows the music of her woe!
For slain heir to bygone throne,
    And for Chief laid low!
Hark! . . . Again, methinks, I hear her weeping
    Yonder! is she near me now, as then?
Or was but the night-wind sweeping
    Down the hollow glen?

From "A Lamentation for the Death of Sir Maurice Fitzgerald, Knight of Kerry, who was killed in Flanders,
1642." Translated from the Irish by Clarence Mangan.

BOOK ONE

STRANGE ENCOUNTERS

1

Six warriors battled against one in the depths of the fall-tinged forest.

The woods were shot through with slanting rays of clear dawn light, asmoke with drifting dust motes, striking down from half-bared treetops to cast pools of glowing gold on the leaf-strewn floor. Light and color created a hazy texture, imparting an oddly dreamlike atmosphere to the scene of wild combat.

All seven warriors were lean, tall, well-muscled men, clad in short tunics and long tartan cloaks fastened at their throats. They were unarmored, armed with round shields and supple, slender swords.

The polished black blades glinted with light as they slashed through the sunbeams, whipping the dust motes to a frenzied dance. The air was filled with the din of iron on iron. A fight of both beauty and savagery it was as the six moved with graceful, powerful fighting techniques to attack the seventh.

But the seventh still held them all at bay.

That one man—of bold feature and piercing blue-grey eye—battled heroically, a mane of bright gold hair swinging at his back. His fighting style was a blend of great agility, amazing strength, and astounding skills.

With sword, shield, and body he wheeled and struck about him, so swiftly he seemed a constant blur. A shield

blow slammed back one man. A cut took down another. A
thrust sent a third staggering away.

When a fourth missed his own slash and instead found
his opponent's blade splitting through his heart, the final
two warriors determined they'd had enough. They turned
and scampered away into the trees.

They left the winner standing amid the slain. He
watched after the runners as he yanked his weapon from
the last victim. He stood for a moment, poised, guard up,
looking keenly about for any sign of new attack. He was
panting heavily from his exertions and his sinewy body
was laced by streams of blood from a dozen minor
wounds. But the fierce glow of his aroused battle energy
all but blazed out from him.

There were no more sounds or movements in the trees
around. Save for the dead, he was now alone in the once-
more peaceful woods. He swept his gaze over the bodies
of his attackers. It stopped abruptly on the chest of one.
Here gleamed a strange device hung on a chain.

He leaned down and tore it free of the man's neck with
a quick yank. He lifted it to examine closely.

The device was a large circle of silver, enameled with an
image. The artist's skill had rendered it with great realism
—the sharp peak of a jagged mountain thrusting up
against the sky.

A light of triumph lit the warrior's eyes.

"You have made your mistake this time, Brasal," he
growled.

His eyes lifted from the amulet. He turned and looked
away, up across the treetops toward the west.

There, above the forest, that same mountain, but the
real one this time, loomed up starkly and ominously
against the sky.

"Mount Corcsa," he said. "*Now* I have you."

"The warrior's arm reached upward, his hand grasping
at a small outcrop of rock.

"With this tenuous grip he drew himself upward, feeling for a toehold on the wall of stone. Then he repeated the process, pulling himself yet higher.

"Another fingerhold. Another toehold. But the tiny bit of rock gave way suddenly beneath his foot.

"He slid backward, dangling for a moment by one hand, scrabbling at the nearly smooth rock face with free hand and both feet. At last a spot was found to support his weight, and the hold was secure again.

"Catching his breath, he glanced downward. It was a sheer drop of several hundred feet that now lay below him.

"He looked above him. It was a climb of many hundreds more up a cliff even more sheer to reach the opening of the cavern just below the mountain's peak.

"He struggled on, his clothes torn to rags, his flesh scraped raw by the crawl upward over the rock face. He seemed very near to exhaustion now, the muscles of his limbs drawn taut, shuddering with strain, streaming with sweat. Still his face was set in lines of determination.

"Some way higher, he reached a ledge, a narrow lip cutting across the cliff. He threw an arm up to catch its edge, drawing himself up, rolling himself over and onto the flat space.

"He lay there for a moment on the secure place, resting, chest heaving with his labored breaths. His eyes dropped closed as if he meant to sleep.

" 'Rury O'Mor,' said a voice from nearby, 'what was it took you so long?'

"This brought him sitting up with a start, instantly awake, his hand reaching for his sword. But he stopped then, for he saw who it was who had spoken.

"Not far along the narrow ledge stood three men. One was very boyish in look, towheaded and slender of frame. A second was tall and elegant with hawkish features. A third was massive, thick and muscular, with coarse hair and rough-hewn features.

"All were dressed much like the one called Rury, wearing the short tunics and the long, colorful cloaks. All had long hair tied or braided at their backs. And all were armed with long swords and round shields.

"Rury rose to his feet as they came toward him, greeting them with great surprise.

" 'Kevan!' he said to the little one. 'Owen!' he called the tall. And 'Angus!' he named the third as he shook hands with each in turn. 'What is it you're doing here?'

" 'The Sidhe magic let us keep a watch on you through your long journeying,' said Owen. 'We saw you in great jeopardy here. Are you really meaning to go against the evil Brasal by yourself?'

" 'It's my own wife Etain that that monster stole from me,' Rury replied. 'Seven years I've searched for him to get her back. Yes, my friend, I'm surely meaning to go.'

" 'Then you'll die,' Kevan said simply.

" 'That I may do. But it's my own honor and my great love for my wife that have brought me here. They give me no other choice. Even so, I'll not ask any other to risk himself in this.'

" 'You are our chieftain,' Angus said stolidly. 'You are one of us. You are our friend. You won't keep us from going with you.'

"Rury smiled at the words and nodded. 'I thought that would be the way of it. Join me and welcome, my old comrades.' He glanced upward at the still faraway cavern. 'But how will we all get up there unknown?'

" 'Why, in the same way the three of us came here!' Kevan announced with a flourish, and waved his arms upward over his head.

"At once a radiant cocoon of silver light appeared around each man. It grew to a translucent cloud, concealing him except for the vague shadow of his form within. But that shadow began rapidly to change, seeming to grow fluid, altering radically, then shrinking down to take on a new, small shape suspended within the glow.

"At last the glow faded, the concealing screen of silver

thinning away to reveal that the four men had now become four majestic hawks.

"Immediately they began to flap their great spreads of wing. They soared out, making a graceful sweep about the ledge, then began to fly upward, heading for the cavern high above.

"The shadows of them flickered against the smooth grey face of the sheer cliff as they soared out of sight."

"And so it was," the rolling, deep, commanding voice continued in its Irish brogue, "that after so long a searchin' through the whole length and breadth of Ireland, into each deep rill and over each rocky tor, Rury O'Mor, that great chieftain of the Sidhe folk, went off to face the treacherous Brasal and rescue his captive wife."

Firelight shifted in a flicking patchwork of red-gold and grey shadow against the high, sheer wall.

This wall—not of living rock but of cut, whitewashed stone—rose upward toward an arched, elaborately beamed ceiling thirty feet above. The narrating voice echoed in the vast space as it went on.

"It was in that cavern deep within the cursed mountain that the brigand leader waited. He of the sharp tooth, the darting eye, the lean and hungry face. A wolf in its lair was he, his pack of cutthroats behind him. And at his side a greater danger yet: his evil druidess, Darvrack, spinning out her black spells, brewing up her foul potions, cackles of mad delight issuing from her toothless mouth."

The illuminating firelight came from flaring torches set in iron sconces lower in the wall. Their flames gleamed against displays of medieval weapons filling the space below, and cast a ruddy glow across the floor of the huge room.

"That rough cavern Brasal had turned to a palace for himself," the voice boomed on, "with every richness in tapestry and ornament of gold, with finest plates and goblets picked from the vast booty that his pillages had brought. A place of wealth and comforts it surely was, save in one corner, where bars of cold, black iron closed off a small chamber hacked from the damp stone.

"Here languished the gentle, comely woman called Etain, wife of Rury O'Mor. She, the white, frail-limbed woman of bright gold hair and soft red cheek, lay on her bed of straw, imprisoned, punished for her long rejection of the ruthless villain's love."

The huge room in which the speaker's voice echoed was the banquet hall of a castle—a single, large chamber in true medieval style. In its center, a fire of massive logs burned in a wide, round hearth, sending a plume of grey smoke up to the chimney hole high above. Around the hearth were rows of tables in four concentric rings, occupied by perhaps two hundred folk, the remains of an elaborate meal spread before them.

It was at the center of the rings that the speaker stood, moving about in an open area between tables and fire, gesturing as he spoke, his voice carrying out clearly over the crowd.

"The four hawks flew straight up to Brasal's den. They flew down the rough tunnel, past his score of guards, and into his chamber, catching the villain by surprise. There it was they shape-shifted back to fighting men right before his astonished eyes."

The speaker was an elderly man, but still hale and powerful, tall and straight. As he moved, the firelight shifted upon his grey-bearded face, casting the lines on cheeks and forehead into deep crevasses, highlighting a most marvelously rugged landscape created by age and weathering. And that landscape altered constantly with high animation of his storytelling.

He wore a simple costume of long hooded cloak over woolen tunic and trousers. He swung a long blackthorn stick around him in broad strokes for emphasis as he continued, his bright gaze sweeping the crowd.

"It was that wicked druidess Darvrack who used her powers upon the heroes first.

"With her magic she raised up lightning bolts to strike them, and caused torrents of burning rain to pour down. But the magic of the tall one called Owen, a high druid of the Sidhe, countered her.

"He called up thick, black clouds to hide the four. He threw a wall of ice up in a dome above to shield them. Then he sent a sharp sword of blasting wind to strike the sorceress, lift her, and cast her back to smash against the rocks. She fell to the cavern's floor, beaten, her wretched, bony form broken to bits."

The crowd about the speaker listened intently, silently, completely rapt by the masterfully told tale, like children upon their parents' knees at storytime.

The remnants of the meal before them were forgotten in their concentration. It had been typical medieval fare—chicken halves now gnawed mostly to bone, bread torn from huge round loaves, raw vegetables and fruits. The table settings too were of the middle-age—pewter goblets and plates, ornate copper flagons and serving bowls. The only eating utensils were short, daggerlike knives.

The trappings of the medieval were also evident among the banqueters—leather jackets, cloaks, feathered hats, even crowns on one elderly man and woman. But along with these, there were also objects that, in this setting, seemed jarringly strange.

Here at one man's elbow sat an Olympus 35mm camera with its length of telephoto lens. There in another man's hands was a compact video camera, whirring softly, a red light blinking rhythmically as it recorded the scene. Amid the medieval garb could be glimpsed printed sweatshirts and spandex shorts and logoed baseball caps. And the crowd itself was certainly not one typical of the western medieval world. Mixed with the Caucasian faces were those of Arabs, Orientals, Africans, East Indians, and more.

"Brasal then ordered his army of brigands to attack," the storyteller was going on. "A hundred savage fighters swarmed upon them. This time it was Angus and Rury who countered. Standing back-to-back, the giant warrior and his chieftain battled the attacking host."

At one of the tables of the inner ring, closest to the fire, sat a dozen men. Most wore the uniform of the modern ruling class: conservative, sedate-colored and expensive business suits. Like the rest, all were listening intently to the bard so masterfully spinning out his tale.

All, that is, but one.

This one was a well-built, handsome man of around forty. He had a square-jawed, tough, tenacious look that also held more than a hint of arrogance.

Just now, however, his look was also one of incredible boredom mixed with irritation. He fidgeted with his knife, digging at the untouched chicken. He sipped at his goblet, stared about him, completely disinterested in the thrilling tale the bard was continuing.

"What a battle it was then! The two warriors swung about them with their blades so swiftly it was like windmills they seemed. Like scythes they were, winnowing the ranks of their enemies, piling up the dead about them, making rivers of blood run on the floor. Until at last no brigand was left to stand against them."

The impatient man looked pointedly at his watch—a top-of-the-line Rolex. He sighed loudly.

The man seated next to him looked sharply around to him, frowning disapprovingly. He was an elderly, distinguished-looking man, his neat hair and mustaches silvering, his vested suit of the tweed variety. His bearing and manner announced "old-world gentleman."

"Only Brasal was left," the bard went on. "A villain he was, but surely no coward. He faced Rury in single combat. The two fought long and ferociously. Brasal made more than a single wound upon his enemy that day. Still, it was Rury's avenging sword stroke the brigand chief finally felt through his evil heart."

He paused there a moment to heighten the effect before going on.

"Yet even then, Brasal was not to be denied his own revenge. With his last strength, he cast his sword to strike Etain, the woman who had denied his love so long!"

The immense emotional impact of this tale upon the crowd was very clear at this point. The bard had worked them up and was now wringing them dry. Their faces were sorrowful, stricken, as they were drawn into the tragedy. A number of women, and even a few men, had tears glistening in their eyes as the speaker built to his heart-wrenching climax.

"With his bare hands, Rury tore those prison bars apart. With great tenderness he lifted out his wife, cradling her, drawing the lethal blade out from her smooth, white breast, leaving her crimson lifeblood to flow, unstoppable.

"The woman he had loved so much, so long; the woman he had sought and labored and battled for; the woman he at last had found and freed was dying in his arms, her strength ebbing away. And great was the mourning voice he raised over her!"

The bard's voice dropped, taking on the intense, soulful voice of the hero.

" 'Ah, my fair Etain, it's a cursed man I am,' he keened, 'without mirth, without light, but only sadness and grief, not to ever more see you, but only remembering your ways. Och! my grief pierces through me.'

"And she touched his hand and spoke with the last of her breath, saying: 'It was the best hero, the finest man, the greatest love you always were to me. You were my happiness, Rury O'Mor. And I am happy to see you this one last time.' "

The bard again paused dramatically here, letting those of his audience feel her sorrow fully in the great silence that fell. There wasn't a cough, a rustle, a breath of sound from them. Finally he looked around at them, concluding in slow, somber tones.

"It was then she died there, in her husband's arms. And it was there they buried her, beneath a great cairn of stones on that very mountain's top. A cairn you can see in that lonely, windswept place until this very day."

At this, a single, pointed word came back to him from the crowd.

"Bullshit!"

2

At the single blunt word, the bard wheeled in surprise to look.

Its speaker was the man in the throes of such great boredom. He had apparently made the remark to himself, but had done it loudly enough to be quite clearly heard by people for some distance about him.

These people, like the bard, looked around to the critic, clearly shocked and irritated by the crudeness that had so roughly broken the bard's spell.

The distinguished man seated beside him seemed especially affronted, and commented sharply: "Mr. Kean! Please!"

The one addressed glanced around him at the frowning faces. But if he realized he had been somewhat out of line, he gave little evidence of it in his scant apology.

"Sorry, Lord Roderick," he said in a clipped American accent. "I just couldn't take any more of that. We've wasted too much time here already."

He looked to the other men at his table. "Come on, boys. Time to move."

He rose. With instant obedience, all those with him rose too. Only Lord Roderick rose with less alacrity, clearly not liking the notion of being ordered about.

As the others moved away from the table, Lord Roderick paused to give the insulted, glowering bard a little sorry-but-please-just-let-it-go wave and shake of the head. As that man stomped off, the lord turned and followed after Kean.

Behind him, a young woman in elaborate medieval gown moved out quickly to introduce a new act to the agitated crowd.

"Ladies and gentlemen, I'd like now to bring in for your entertainment our own Turfmen—one of Ireland's finest traditional music groups."

A half-dozen men trooped quickly into the space around the fire, carrying fiddles, Irish pipes, flute, drum, and harp. They made no delay in taking up a lively Irish jig, the bright music filling the room.

It brought the attention of the crowd back from Kean's party, which had been drawing dark looks as it pressed its way out through the rings of tables to the hall's main doorway.

The music faded away behind the suited company of men as they passed out the doorway and strode down a corridor to massive double doors of thick timber, now standing open. Moving through this opening brought them outside and onto a plank drawbridge. It was an affectation now, as the moat it had been meant to cross had long since been filled in. They crossed it to a broad, graveled yard enclosed by a stone wall. The yard surrounded the castle that loomed above—a square, fortified tower house of grey stone blocks, reaching up some six stories to a battlemented roof. Close around its base a dozen ancient cannon squatted, browsed over by a score or so of tourists busily posing, snapping photos, and recording videotape.

"Look here, Mr. Kean, I certainly wasn't intending to waste your time," Lord Roderick was explaining as they all matched Kean's brisk pace across the yard. The lord's own cultured Irish accent was only slightly softened by his brogue. "The Minister of Tourism 'requested' that I show you my park and guide you about the area. I only thought you might like to see some of what we already do here to entertain our visitors."

"Entertain?" Kean said derisively. "Is that what you call

that old guy boring us to death? Hey, remember: I'm here to bring in the new stuff, not to see the old."

"But, it's very popular," the lord said defensively. "The storyteller is a very old tradition in Ireland."

Kean gave a scornful laugh. "Yeah, sure. And you really think people would *choose* to listen to him telling a story? When they could watch it on a sensoround, 3-D, wrap screen?"

They had by this time reached a gateway through the outer wall, and they moved out from the castle yard into the surrounding grounds.

Just outside the gateway they passed a large sign proclaiming Duncovey Castle and Folk Park.

The folk park, through which the men now marched on a meandering path, was a most pleasant—if low-key—place. There was very little to it but the single path winding its casual way through a collection of rustic cottages representing different periods of Irish history. Here was a tiny, single-room, mud-walled hut such as might have huddled in the hundreds around the castle during its heyday. Over there was a squat, whitewashed fisherman's house with a net over its thatched roof to keep the straw in place before stiff sea winds. And just beyond was the long, low, neatly stuccoed house of a wealthy Golden Vale farmer.

About and within the cottages and their various outbuildings a number of craftsmen and artisans plied their age-old trades. A leather-aproned blacksmith fashioned horseshoes and fire spits, his pounding hammer sending up showers of sparks from the red-hot iron. A beshawled woman rocked and knitted at a cream-white Irish sweater beside a turf fire whose pungent smoke scented the garment's wool. An elderly man rethatched a cottage roof with straw, weaving the new, golden stuff into the weathered grey.

"Sheamus is one of the last ones with the old thatcher's skill," Lord Roderick explained as they passed by. "It's dying away, along with the last of these old cottages."

"Great," said Kean. "Then he fits right in here."

"And just how do you mean that?"

"Well, it's this whole little folky park thing of yours, Fitzpatrick. Great for the geriatric set, and that's about it." He waved about him. "I mean, people just walk around and look at these old huts? Way, way too static, pal. You want to get them involved. You want to grab 'em! Hold 'em! Make 'em yours!"

"I beg your pardon," the lord replied with some indignation, "we do have over five hundred thousand tourists visit here each year."

"What I'm doing will bring millions," Kean shot back. He looked to a man behind him. "Right, Lance?"

The one addressed was a prim, young, officious-looking type, bespectacled and most scrupulously dressed. He instantly consulted a small, computerized notebook, tapping in some data on its keyboard, then consulting the LCD readout as he replied briskly: "More, sir. Projections are six million five hundred thousand per, prorated over the first ten years of operations."

"There ya go," Kean said, grinning smugly at the lord. "You see? Over ten times more. That's *real* business."

They were now approaching a long, low building, whitewashed and thatched like the cottages, but clearly of more modern construction. A sign above its open doorway declared it the gift shop.

"Only way in and out is through the touristo-trap store, eh?" Kean declared as they passed inside. "That's one halfway decent merchandising gimmick you've got anyway."

The shop's interior was a single room lined with shelves and counters all crammed full of Irish souvenirs. There were maps, posters, sweaters, ashtrays, toys, and trinkets galore; most of it emblazoned with the orange, white, and green Irish flag or a shamrock; much of it cheap.

Once inside, Kean stopped and turned to another of the men in his group. This one was a close-cropped, sturdily built man of steely, darting eyes and highly energized manner.

"Frank," Kean said to him, "call the cars to pick us up."

Frank immediately pulled a compact transceiver from within his coat and spoke briskly into it.

"Stony? Mr. Kean says to bring the limos up now."

Kean looked around to Lord Roderick. "Frank Garvey's a good man," he explained. "Head of my security. Ex-Secret Service. Don't leave home without him."

He turned away and began to browse idly over the souvenirs while he waited. He picked up a small, plastic leprechaun with rosy cheeks, curled coattails and shoe tips, and a pot of gold in his hands.

A smiling, dark-haired young saleswoman approached him, speaking cheerily. "And may I help you, sir?"

"Just take a look at this crap," he said, disgusted. "All you do here is dream about the good old days and the damned fairies. Jesus. No wonder Ireland's a century behind."

The young woman's smile was wiped away. She cast a dismayed look from Kean to Lord Roderick, and beat a hasty retreat.

Frank Garvey stepped up behind his boss.

"The cars are here, sir," he announced.

Kean nodded and at once headed for a door labeled Exit. But he paused at the doorway to stop yet another of his men.

This one was Bill McBride, a fortyish, pudgy man with a rather florid complexion, thinning red hair, and a pleasant but weary old-basset-hound look.

Kean handed him the leprechaun. "Say, Mac, why don't you stay here. Pick up a few little things—you know, for the office girls?"

The other man looked somewhat taken aback at being saddled with this menial task. He opened his mouth as if to protest. Then he closed it and only sighed resignedly.

"All right, Michael," he accepted. "If you want."

"Good boy. Don't go overboard. Five bucks a pop should do it. I'll have you picked up later."

With that Kean went on out, leaving McBride looking after him morosely.

Outside, three very large, very black Mercedes limousines had been drawn up close by the door, effectively blocking anyone else trying to get to it from the parking lot.

As Kean approached the first car, a man leapt from behind its wheel and moved to open the rear door for him. He was an immense, massively muscled, totally bald man clad in a chauffeur's kit that strained at the seams when he flexed any part of his bulging form.

"Thanks, Stony," Kean said as he reached the door. He paused there to look back toward the castle looming up beyond the gift shop. He shook his head. "What a goddamned waste of real estate. Boy, is it time to wake this country up." He looked around to Lance. "So, where's my site?"

"On the coast, sir," Lance replied. "Somewhere northwest of here."

"I'd best direct you," volunteered Lord Roderick, though with no evident willingness. "It's a somewhat complex route."

"Fine," said Kean. "You ride with me." He looked around at the rest of his group. "Okay. Let's roll!"

The men quickly divided and piled into the three vehicles. Lance and Frank Garvey also rode with their boss. As the vehicles pulled away, Lord Roderick spoke to the driver—separated from the passenger section by a pane of glass—through the intercom.

"Take the road north please, driver."

The big man nodded and wheeled the heavy limo easily out of the parking lot and onto the narrow, barely two-lane road.

"Your chauffeur is a most . . . impressive man," the lord said, sitting back beside Kean.

"Jack 'Stone Man' Starski," Kean said with a touch of

pride. "Marine, mercenary, boxer, wrestler, bouncer, and now my private driver-bodyguard. Found him in Chicago. Never seen anyone take him down anywhere. That's how he got the nickname."

"Sounds a most amiable fellow," commented the lord dryly.

"He's loyal," Kean replied. "That's all I want."

Lord Roderick continued to give Starski directions as the cars rolled in caravan along the narrow road.

They passed through an idyllic and seemingly endless countryside of rolling meadows, quaint cottages, picturesque ruins, and grazing cattle herds.

The road was extremely sinuous, and it became even narrower as they progressed. At last it slowed the cars to little more than a crawl between stone walls and hedgerows, vegetation often brushing the sides of the massive vehicles.

As the progress became slower and slower, so did Kean become more and yet more irritable.

"Christ! This is crazy!" he burst out with at last. "Where in the hell *is* this site?"

"It's only thirty miles from Shannon Airport, sir," Lance swiftly provided. "Actually very near to many of the existing tourist attractions. It should be very convenient."

Kean peered out the window at a wall of piled stone only inches away. "Not on *this* goddamn road!"

"Uh . . . Mr. Kean, what's that ahead?" came the voice of the driver through the intercom.

The passengers all looked. They were approaching a crossroads. Five narrow lanes divided from the first, wandering away in various directions into the landscape.

Lord Roderick stared, looked left and right and ahead, obviously perplexed.

"Would you just stop here, please?" he asked the driver.

Starski nodded and slowed the car to a stop. The other limousines pulled up behind it. Lord Roderick pressed a button and his passenger window hummed down. He craned his neck out to look up at a signpost.

Kean poked his head out beside the lord's and also peered up at the marker. Its slender support was topped with over a dozen signs in bristling array, so many it seemed amazing the thing could stand. All were labeled with town names—some in English, some in Gaelic, some in both. They pointed off haphazardly in all directions.

"Never seen a road sign that made things *harder* to find!" Kean exclaimed.

"There are those who say Irish road signs are this way in case we're ever invaded," the lord said with amusement. "Any enemy who comes here will find himself hopelessly lost."

No sign of responding amusement showed in Kean's face at this.

"I suppose they're one of your 'traditions' too?" he asked.

Lord Roderick's smile faded. "Yes, in a way, I suppose they are."

Kean shook his head. "Man, you people really love to wallow in it right up to your necks, don't you? So, which way? That is, if *you* even know."

"To the left," the lord told him coldly.

"Left, Stony," Kean relayed to his driver. And as the cars rolled on again, he turned to Lance.

"Make a note," he said briskly. "Get permission from the Irish government to ram through a real highway right from Shannon to my site. Four smooth, straight lines of concrete. No—make it six."

"Yes, sir," said Lance, tapping the information into his computer notebook.

Kean looked back to Lord Roderick, smiling gloatingly, slapping the man's knee. "When I get through, Rod, you'll see this whole countryside developing. Houses, offices, strip malls, businesses everywhere."

"Oh, really?" said the lord, but unenthusiastically.

He turned from Kean to look out the still-open window. An especially lovely, sun-drenched, unspoiled scene of meadow and vine-covered ruin was just sliding by. Lord Roderick stared at it, deep misgiving in his eyes.

A new landscape now lay spread out before the eyes.

Meadows dotted with stands of woods swept down in gentle swells from a high ridge to the ocean shore a mile or more below. Beyond the shore, the silver-blue glimmer of the sea was visible.

Along the top of the ridge's crest, the three limousines were pulled up in a neat line. The men were out of them, some consulting maps and architects' renderings, some gazing down on the countryside with large binoculars.

Just beyond the limousines, several vans and a contractor's trailer were drawn up. Some two score surveyors and workmen were unloading and setting up surveying gear.

By the first limousine stood Kean, Lord Roderick, and Lance. Garvey and Starski stood not far away, keeping watch over their boss and the surroundings with keen eyes.

Lance had a large portfolio opened on the car hood. It was opened to an artist's color rendering of a hotel and amusement park complex.

The seaside hotel was a massive, soaring, overblown monument to glitzy bad taste, designed in a mock Gothic castle motif. The rides and attractions that sprawled upward on the slopes behind it were festooned with colored lights and signs. The flamboyant label in one corner of the drawing dubbed the whole creation KEAN'S IRISH WORLD.

Lance was bent down over this drawing, examining it intently, looking up and down from it to the landscape as he endeavored to identify and point out the locations of the various future constructions. When he did, his boss and Lord Roderick examined the spots through binoculars.

"The main hotel complex will be down there, of course," Lance said, pointing toward the seashore. "Twenty-six hundred rooms. No real beach yet, but we're making arrangements for the sand. From Spain, I believe.

Theirs is supposed to be of the finest grade. Tentative plans are for the Old Irish Village attractions to be on that rounded hill—there, down to the left, about five hundred yards."

Kean and Lord Roderick turned their glasses to look. They focused on a low, neatly rounded hilltop covered in lush grass.

"Good choice," said the lord. "Quite likely that actually was a hill fort two thousand years ago. Might be able to find some original foundations, some artifacts. Even restore the . . ."

"We don't restore, Rod," Kean told him impatiently. "Who the hell cares what some crummy little fort looked like two thousand years ago? All that gets bulldozed. We do our version. The movie version, you know? Spectacular kind of stuff. All animatronics."

"I'm sorry," said Lord Roderick. "Anama . . . what?"

"You know. Robots. The happy natives, living, playing in their village, just like the real thing. Like Pirates of the Caribbean, only a hell of a lot better. It may not be as big as Euro-Disneyland, but on the attractions I'm gonna make those Disney people look damn cheap."

"Just beside the village we'll have the Irish Heroes Gallery and Games Arena," put in Lance.

Kean lowered his glasses and looked to the lord. "Wait'll you see that!" he said proudly. "All your old-time heroes strutting around, having battles, fighting monsters, going on adventures. I've got state-of-the-art computerizing there. Interactive games so real you'll think you're right with those guys."

"How . . . nice," said Lord Roderick guardedly. "And just how much of the area below us will be taken up by this entire complex?"

"Why, it will fill up the whole thing," Lance supplied. "Right up to here."

"The whole thing," the lord repeated in regretful tones.

"Don't sound so concerned, Rod," Kean told him. "It's

just a chunk of empty ground. We're not tearing out historical sites or your mom's house or anything."

"Not too many places like this one left," piped up a voice suddenly from behind them.

They turned to look. An elderly Irishman in the typical farmer's garb of worn tweed jacket, baggy pants, and battered cloth cap was just striding up to them. He looked in his sixties, but that was hard to tell for certain, so lined and leathery had his skin become by years of wind and sun. But his expression was cheery, his manner easy, and his grey eyes glittering bright.

Garvey and Starski gave him a hard once over as he moved toward their boss, bodies tensing as if they were ready to leap on the unknown interloper should he make a suspicious move. But Lord Roderick intervened, quickly making introduction to Kean.

"Mr. Kean, allow me to introduce Jimmy O'Brien. He's the one who sold you most of this land." He looked to the newcomer. "Jimmy, this is Mr. Michael Kean."

Jimmy shook hands with Kean, eyeing him with interest.

"Himself, is it? Well, sir, it's surely a fine piece of sod you've bought here. Been in my family well over a thousand years, so it has."

"You're kidding," Kean said.

"That I am not. That's the ruin of our own old family keep just beyond there . . ."

He pointed, and Kean turned to look at the ragged top of a half-ruined tower house poking above the crest some half mile farther north.

". . . and the rath of our first homestead is just beyond. Back in St. Paddy's time, that was."

"All that time and you've never developed this?" Kean asked in amazement. "Never farmed it or anything?"

"Parts of it, certainly. But never this bit here. Didn't seem right, us never feeling it was ours." He leaned closer to Kean and added in a more hushed tone: "Left it for the 'Others' you see."

"Others?" Kean said blankly.

"Them. The Hidden Ones. The fair folk. Ah, you know what I mean." He straightened, speaking out more loudly and with great conviction. "It's Their own piece of country about here, isn't it? Always has been. Why, didn't Sheamus Mahoney see Them dancin' in the ruins one Samhain eve? And wasn't I myself chased by a great ball of wool that must surely have been some *shoeugy* beast of Theirs?"

"Uh, yeah. Sure," said Kean. "Will you excuse me?"

He stepped away a few paces, sharply signaling Lord Roderick to follow. As the lord joined him, he whispered irritably, "What's with this old guy? Is he crazy, or is he just skinful of Irish booze?"

"He is neither," Lord Roderick said indignantly. "There are still many in Ireland, especially older ones, who maintain a sincere belief in the ancient superstitions."

"Not more of that 'tradition' crap!" Kean fumed. "Well, sober or not, just keep him away from me, okay?"

He turned and signaled Lance to him. The young man all but leapt to his side.

"Lance boy, how much longer we gotta be here?"

Lance considered. "We just need to check over a few details with the surveyors, Mr. Kean. A half hour at the most."

"Look, you can take care of that, can't you? I think I want to take a stroll around, kind of get a feel for the place, get the old brain cells percolating. Maybe I'll come up with some new ideas. Okay?"

"Whatever you say, Mr. Kean."

"Good boy. You just give me a blast on the horn when you want me back."

Lance bustled off to talk to the surveyors, who by now had most of their equipment unloaded and were setting up. Kean looked back to Lord Roderick.

"And you, Rod . . . maybe you'd better break it to our man Jimmy there that his old family ruins aren't long for this world, huh? See you later."

With a parting smirk and a jaunty wave at the frowning lord, Kean set off, heading over the crest and down the hillside at a brisk clip.

Starski and Garvey, noting his departure, both started after him.

"Mr. Kean," Garvey called, "don't you think you should have some company?"

"No thanks, Frank," he called back carelessly. "You boys stay here. I think better alone." He waved around him at the peaceful countryside. "Besides, what's here that can do anything to me?"

Bodyguard and security head stopped on the crest. They exchanged a look and a shrug. Then they stood watching as their boss went striding on, crossing the soft swell of a small rise just below and passing out of sight.

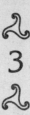

3

Kean continued on downward through the meadows and the trees. He looked about him in a calculating way as he went, his shrewd mind working out the details of just what might go where, and how it would all look when transformed to his world of concrete, glass, plastic, and electronics.

At high points in the ground he would pause and glance back up the hill to reset his bearings, noting the spot on the ridge where the cars sat, noting the tip of the ruined tower house just north of that. Then he would continue on, always moving downward, toward the sea.

It was a soft, drowsy, golden afternoon. And little by little his pace began to slow as he walked along, as if the gentle atmosphere was having some tranquilizing effect on him.

He began to look around him with more curiosity, actually noting what was there, rather than what he would put there. Bright-feathered birds soared above, filling the air with trilling song. Startled rabbits hopped away, bobbing white tails flashing in the sun. The hum of insects created a soothing background.

Patches of colorful wildflowers caught his eye. He took in deep breaths of air made sweet by their fragrance. The long grasses of the fields swished about his legs and the soft breezes rustled in the tree leaves over his head. Gradually his hard, mercenary look gave way entirely to a softer, meditative one.

Was it possible that as he progressed, the atmosphere about him became gradually more hazy? Taking note of this change himself, he glanced skyward. A scrim of clouds did appear to have risen from somewhere, from nowhere, covering the sky, diffusing the sunlight into an even, subdued white glow.

He only shrugged and went on. Clearly the odd change didn't matter to him. He seemed by this point to have become content to just drift on along, carried by the breezes, gliding farther and farther into the timeless, endless landscape that enfolded, engulfed, entrapped him in its most gentle clutches.

So obviously pastoral had his mood become that he even stooped to pluck a bright yellow wildflower and sniff appreciatively at it.

As he straightened, the flower still in his hand, he glanced idly around. Then he looked again, more sharply. His bemused expression was swept away abruptly by a bewildered one.

The landscape about him was now radically changed. There was no glint of ocean visible below him. There was actually no "below him" anymore. He was in an open meadow edged all about with woods. The higher crest with its parked cars and its ruined tower was nowhere visible.

"Where in the hell am I?" he said aloud, casting his searching gaze over the strange surroundings.

As if in answer to his question, the sound of a voice rose suddenly in the quiet. It was a woman's voice, soft, distant, but quite clear and most melodious.

Kean cocked his head to listen, turning slowly, then stopping as he located the direction. It was coming from the woods nearby.

Without hesitation, he moved toward it, plunging into the trees.

He threaded his way along between thick trunks of ancient oaks and yews, their branches interlacing to form a dense canopy above that blocked the light and plunged him into a grey gloom. He felt his way along, pushing through underbrush, clambering over fallen trunks and limbs, but always moving closer to the voice.

It was growing steadily louder as he went. The words had become audible now. The voice sang a lilting ballad tinged deeply, delightfully with the rich shades of the Irish soul. He began to listen to the words:

> "The purple heath-bells, blooming fair,
> Their fragrance round did fling,
> As the hunter lay,
> At the close of day,
> Down by the haunted spring."

He made his way at last to a final screen of brush. There seemed to be more open ground lying just beyond. As he forced a way toward it, the singing continued:

> "A lady fair, in robe of white,
> To greet the hunter came;
> She kiss'd a cup with jewels bright,
> And pledg'd him by his name."

He found himself out of the woods again, under the odd, hazy silver sky. He stopped there, gazing at the new scene ahead.

He was looking into a small valley, closed in by the woods. Below him, down a grassy slope, a lively little stream burbled and flashed along through a rocky bed.

On one of the large rocks at its side a woman sat, combing her hair and singing as she combed:

> " 'Oh, lady fair,' the hunter cried,
> 'Be thou my love, my blooming bride—
> A bride that might well grace a king!
> Fair lady of the haunted spring.' "

Kean stared down at her, most obviously intrigued. She did indeed make a quite striking picture there, in this wild, secluded place.

Her slender body was clad in a simple sleeveless shift of a softly glowing green cloth. She sat with legs curled under her, looking down at her rippling reflection as she drew the comb smoothly through her hair.

It was long, flowing waves of hair she had, colored like autumn-touched leaves with the sun through them, or red-gold after it's been rubbed. As she combed, she sang in rhythm with her smooth, even strokes:

> "In the fountain clear she stoop'd
> And forth she drew a ring;
> And that bold knight
> His faith did plight
> Down by the haunted spring."

He started to move forward again, this time as if drawn by some irresistible force, making his way down the slope toward the stream and the woman as she sang on.

> "But since the day his chase did stray,
> The hunter ne'er was seen;
> And legends tell he now doth dwell
> Within the hills so green."

Kean reached the stream edge just across from her. As he did, her song ended and she looked up from the water to him, smiling in bright welcome, speaking in light and graceful Irish accents.

"Hello to you. So, you've found this place at last."

"You expected me?" Kean said in surprise.

"I saw you up above, with the rest. I saw you going off alone. I arranged that I should meet you here."

If something in the normally very rational, very calculating mind of the man was telling him to be wary, it was overwhelmed by the enrapturing aura of this place and this woman. He crouched down at the stream side, staring at her in fascination.

She was young, looked in her early twenties at most. Her form was supple, her bearing one of unstudied natural grace. Her face and arms were of a whiteness and smoothness like a night's snowfall in the purity of next dawning. She was a fresh, bold-featured beauty, and a glow like that of a bright moon seemed to shine out of her face. There was a high, proud arch to her eyebrows and a dimple of delight in each of her cheeks. Her full lips were red as the berries of the rowan tree. Her eyes were a blue more deep, more brilliant than the clearest sky and a light like warmth, affection, trust, and fullest honesty gleamed in them.

"You arranged to meet me?" he said to her. "Why?"

"Because I watched you, and I was . . . well, I was quite taken by you." She looked down, a flush coming into her pale cheeks at this. "I'm sorry. I'm being too bold now."

"No, no!" he said quickly. "I really like a woman who says just what she thinks. Saves a helluva lot of time. So, what's your name?"

She looked up to him again. "Caitlin. Caitlin Bawn. And may I ask your own?"

"Michael Kean."

"Michael. It's a good, strong name." She stared intently into his eyes. "Are you a good, strong man, Michael Kean?"

He met that penetrating gaze, and he spoke out the truth it seemed to demand from him: "If you mean at doing business, no question." He then swiftly shifted the subject. "But, look, are you from someplace around here?"

"I live nearby," she said vaguely, then shifted subjects herself. "What is it you and all those others are about?"

Once more Kean was surprised. "You don't know? But you must have heard."

"I don't get about in the world much. It's not allowed."

"Not allowed? Hey, you look like you're over twenty-one."

She looked puzzled. "Twenty-one what?"

"Years old. I mean, you look all grown up."

"Oh, I am, yes. Certainly. It's just that my people like keeping to themselves."

"Well, if they live near here, they'll still hear about what I'm doing soon enough. I'm going to build a world-class hotel and Irish theme park."

"Theme park?" she repeated blankly.

"You know, like Disney World."

She shook her head, at a loss.

"Boy, you really are out of touch!" he said. "It's an amusement park. You know? Rides, games, concessions."

"Do you mean, it's like a fair?" she ventured.

"Yeah, I suppose. But a whole lot bigger than any fair you've ever seen."

"I've never seen one, to say the truth," she said. "I've only heard of them. Still," she added in an awed way, "a thing so grand as that must be a wondrous sight to see! And you say it's you who's going to build it. Won't it take many men, and great riches?"

Kean dropped into his usual casually bragging tone. "Oh, there'll be a few thousand in the crews. And the tab's going to be two point eight bil. That's at minimum."

Caitlin looked awed. "I'm not certain what these 'bills' are you speak of. But, so many men! You must be a very high chieftain indeed!"

Kean laughed. "Some would say too high. Especially a lot of the little Indians."

"Your speech is strange sometimes," she said, eyeing him curiously, "and your accent is as well. You're not of Ireland, are you?"

"American. I'm from New York."

She gave him that quizzical I-don't-know-what-you're-talking-about look again.

"New York," he repeated. "The city."

"City. Oh, like Dublin?"

"I guess. A lot bigger, though."

"Actually, I've never seen Dublin either," she admitted. "I can't begin to imagine what your city must be like, except that it must be wondrous."

For a moment Kean didn't reply, just contemplating again this so young, so unspoiled-seeming woman who now stared off into some fantasized distance of her own, her face all but beaming as she spoke yearningly of things so strange to her.

Finally he spoke, and in a voice of intense earnestness for him declared: "I'd love to show it to you."

She looked back to him most eagerly. "You would?"

"Well, sure! Of course! I mean, you ought to see a city. You can't spend your whole life stuck away out here."

At this she became a bit defensive. "I'm very happy here. It's all my life."

"How do you know?" he argued. "There's so much out there to see, to do, to get your hands on."

"Do you really think so?" she asked, her eagerness returning.

"It's my motto. What a waste not to go for it all, not to take some risks, have some thrills. Look, since I was ten years old, I've been—"

The blaring sound of a car horn came from the distance, interrupting him. The young woman leapt up like a startled fawn, looking around toward the harsh noise in alarm.

Kean rose too. "It's okay," he assured her. "Just the boys calling me back."

The horn sounded insistently several more times. He looked about him, finally locating the direction.

"It's from over there," he pronounced. "At least I can find my way out of here." He looked back toward her. "Look, Caitlin, why don't you come up with me, and we—"

He stopped abruptly, staring. The rock where she had stood was now empty. In that instant she had somehow vanished.

He looked around him again at the vale and woods, his

expression deeply puzzled. Just where could she have gotten to so fast?

The car horn sounded again, more urgently. No more delay, it was saying, or they'd be down beating the bush for him.

He shrugged and began to turn, preparing to start away. But he paused, noticing the wildflower he still clutched in one hand.

He stared at it as if it were something he'd never seen before, then tossed it down into the stream. He turned and strode off, climbing the slope toward the now steadily, rhythmically beeping horn, vanishing once more into the masking band of woods.

Behind him, the flower he had thrown away floated down the little stream, only to be drawn into an eddy. It spun slowly there a moment before a slender hand reached down and plucked it to safety.

Caitlin straightened with the flower. She gazed at it, lifted it to sniff its fragrance. Then her eyes rose after the departed Kean.

"So much to see . . ." she said musingly, "to do, to . . . to feel!"

As she stood there, considering, Kean was pushing out through the shadowed forest, using the continuing signal of the horn to guide him ahead.

The closer he came to the sound and the louder it became, the more his expression became puzzled, as if the bizarreness of the whole experience were beginning to dawn on him.

He caught his expensive suit coat's sleeve on an oak's broken branch, tearing it, and cursed the old tree soundly.

"Goddamn jungle," he said, the hardness returning to his voice again. "It'll be a pleasure ripping it out of here."

He fought his way past a particularly clinging bush and abruptly found himself on open ground and in sunshine once again.

The odd haze was gone, the afternoon sun blazing down from a cloudless blue sky to brilliantly light the scene.

That scene was once more the familiar one—the sloping land that ran upward from the sea, glittering away below. And above him, not more than a few hundred yards distant, was the ridge at the slope's crest, the tip of that ruined tower sticking up clearly above it.

Astonished, he turned to look back the way he'd come. He got another shock. The dense band of woods he had just come through wasn't there.

Oh, there were trees, yes—a small grove of them, thin and widely spaced. He could easily see right through them to the meadowland beyond. They certainly masked no vale.

He shivered as if a sudden gust of cold sea air had swept him. He turned around and started on toward the honking horn, moving with increasing speed until he was all but sprinting up the slope.

It was only moments later that he was coming over the crest to where the limousines and trucks sat.

Starski stood by his car, a hand in through the open window to honk the horn. He stopped as he saw Kean, turning to Lance and Garvey who stood beside him.

"There's the boss now."

They moved immediately to meet Kean. Garvey looked both relieved and irritated.

"Jesus, Mr. Kean. Where were you? We were going nuts up here." He noted the torn coat. "And what happened?"

"Nothing," Kean assured him brusquely. "It's okay, Frank. I was just . . . just a little lost. That's all."

"Lost?" Garvey said with some disbelief. He looked down the relatively open slope to the sea, then around to the clear landmark of the tower. "Here?"

"You can get kind of mixed up going through the trees," Kean said by way of excuse. "Just drop it, okay?"

"Mr. Kean, I've told you you can't go off like that," Garvey began in a stern lecturing tone. "You don't know what can happen—"

"I said drop it, Frank!" Kean said sharply, cutting him off.

Not willingly, but obediently, Garvey did so, nodding and stepping back.

"Everything's been worked out, Mr. Kean," Lance now volunteered. "The surveyors know what to do. Is there anything else you want checked out?"

"Let's just get out of here," Kean snapped. "Let's go now."

"Yes, sir," said Lance, and moved at once to pass the word to the others.

Within the minute, the businessmen were piling back into their vehicles. Kean went to his own, where Lord Roderick stood waiting.

Starski opened the car door to let his boss in, but Kean paused there, looking back toward the scene spreading below, a strange expression on his face.

"Something wrong, Mr. Kean?" the lord asked him.

"Oh, no. No," Kean said bluffly. "Just giving it a last look." He clambered in, adding to the lord, "You should do that too, Rod. You may never see it like this again."

Lord Roderick said nothing, just climbed in after him.

As Kean settled himself, he noted Jimmy O'Brien standing not far away, looking after the hurriedly departing men with an amiable smile.

"Didn't you tell him the bad news?" Kean asked the lord, pointing to the man.

"I did," said Lord Roderick. "Oddly enough, he didn't seem the least concerned."

"Why should he be?" Kean said. "He got enough dough for the spot."

Lance and Garvey entered the limousine.

"All ready, sir," announced Lance.

Kean gave the order to go, and Starski started the car. As it pulled away, the other limousines following, Jimmy O'Brien lifted a hand to wave a cheery good-bye.

Kean looked after him, then turned around to the lord.

"Say, Rod, you don't know of a Bawn family living around here?"

"Bawn?" repeated the lord, considering. "Why no. But then I'm not that familiar with all the families hereabouts. Why?"

"No real reason," Kean said, looking out the rear window at the rapidly dwindling scene. "Nothing important at all."

Back on the ridge, O'Brien dropped his waving arm and stood looking after the cars as they rolled away along a narrow lane. Not far away, the workmen and surveyors had set about their task of measuring and laying out the site.

All but Jimmy O'Brien were too occupied to note an odd little ball of silvery light rise from somewhere down the slope, flit upward, loop, spin, and then set out in a blurred line of speed after the limousines.

Only Jimmy saw it, and he looked up to the departing will-o'-the-wisp with a smile of knowing on his time-weathered face.

"So," he said, "that's it then. It's started again."

4

Streamers of colored light flickered across the waters of the black pool as the long rod of glowing crystal rhythmically stirred it.

Two voices hummed out eerie, sharply undulating tunes with the rhythm, the two entwining thorny vines of sound like the strident skreels of twin bagpipes in last torment.

The two women who created this somewhat discordant noise both knelt at the edge of the small, circular pool. They were in a low, cylindrical chamber rough-hewn from grey rock striped through with glinting veins of gold.

The woman who wielded the stirring rod was the elder, her long silver hair drawn tightly back from a face already made severe by extreme gauntness, pointed chin, and hawkish nose. The one beside her seemed more of middle-age, her loosely plaited hair a warm brown, her features plump and pleasant and made quite ruddy now with excitement and chagrin.

Both women wore long shiftlike gowns of rich brocade, covered by luxurious cloaks of bright-hued wool. They disregarded possible damage to the fine materials as they knelt upon the hard stone floor to peer intently at the colors that shifted like an aurora borealis upon the midnight-black of the water's surface.

From its initial wild roiling, the mingling streams of color were slowly settling, forming, seeming to take on less abstract shapes that defied the disrupting influence of the rod.

The older woman ceased to stir. Both stopped singing. They sat motionless and silent, their breaths held, watching expectantly as the last ripples faded and the wavering images became clear.

They were looking at a picture of a forest vale, so sharp and bright of color the pool might have been a window onto the scene. It was a secluded place, deserted save for a single figure kneeling on a boulder beside a stream.

The figure was Caitlin Bawn.

And as the two women watched, the whole scene that had taken place in that vale not long before was reenacted, exact in all detail. From the trees above the vale Michael Kean appeared. He walked down to the girl, knelt, and the two spoke. But no words of theirs came to the women by the pool. The image was a completely soundless one.

"There, Lady Aisling!" said the younger woman, pointing emphatically. "That's the same man the both of us watched from this very pool when he first came here with his men. Watched his every move Caitlin did."

"She was so taken with him?" said the older in brusque tones. "And yet you let her go out to meet him?"

"That I did not!" the other defensively replied. "Well, she'd sent me away before, hadn't she? She said it was to fetch her some handwork she was meaning to do. But when I returned, she was nowhere to be found." Her voice took on a steadily more distressed note as she went on. "I searched and searched for her. I swear I did! Well, you know she has a way of wandering off, mooning about out in the glade, and—"

"Enough, Caoimhe!" the one called Aisling said sharply. "Just tell me what happened then."

"Well, I saw her here, in the pool, just as you're seeing now. And I saw her following him away. That's when I ran for you."

"Yes," said the other thoughtfully. "Let's look at it again."

She drew the rod's tip through the image, forming a rippling figure eight. The shapes at once were swept away to tatters, but quickly re-formed.

This time they showed a scene of Kean's limousines pulling away from the crest and driving off along the road toward the south.

"You see," said Caoimhe, "there's no doubt. He drove off with the rest in the belly of those strange, metallic beasts."

"And no doubt that she did go after him," said Aisling, watching the ball of silvery light that rose up to fly off in pursuit. She shook her head irritably. "That foolish, head-strong girl."

"They are such strange men," the younger woman mused. "Not warriors, surely. And their clothes so plain and dull. I've never seen the like. Just who are they?"

"The better question is, where did they go?" said the other. "My poor powers won't bring this imaging pool to see beyond our own little domain. Someone must go out there and find where she's gone. And that's something none of us here can do. There's no one hale enough left."

"Who then?"

"You know that as well as I," Aisling said grimly.

"Not him!"

"It must be. He'll have to know anyway. And there's none in Eire so capable of finding out." She looked back down at the pool's image where the strange spot of light could be seen just vanishing into the distance. "Yes, he'll discover where they went . . . one way or another."

The jetliner roared in toward the runway, wheels and flaps down, throttled-back engines assaulting the air, a thousand tons of sound and fury and metal settling to the earth.

It landed smoothly, taxiing along, sweeping past the terminal topped with giant green letters to proclaim it SHANNON AIRPORT.

It swept on past the gates as it braked down, past other big planes parked to load and unload.

One of these planes was a 747 jumbo jet, and it was at the moment a scene of great activity. A gang of ground crewmen swarmed about it like drones eagerly servicing a queen bee. They were fueling it up, stocking it with supplies for its passengers' needs, feeding luggage onto a conveyor belt running up into the gaping maw of its round belly.

The logo of a four-spired castle was emblazoned on its side, and beside that, in flamboyant Gothic script, were the words "Kean Castle Enterprises."

By the boarding stairs leading up and into the plane, security chief Frank Garvey stood with a female flight attendant, his eagle eye scrutinizing a list on a clipboard in her hands as she checked off passengers moving up the stairs. These were the last of Kean's business associates, ready to head home.

In the parking area outside the terminal, the three limousines, now empty, were drawn up, their use by Kean's people terminated. The big chauffeur/bodyguard named Starski was taking the last of the luggage from the trunk of the vehicle his boss had used. It was a matched pair of large, leather-sided suitcases.

He set them down a moment as he checked the trunk, making sure it was empty and then shutting its lid. While thus occupied, he didn't take note of a small ball of silver light that shot down from the sky.

It struck against the side of one case, just at the crack of its closing. It smashed against the spot like something of thick liquid, entering the crack and oozing through to swiftly vanish within.

The last finger of the liquid light sucked through and out of sight just as the big man, still unsuspecting, turned back to the cases. He lifted both. One came up easily. The other he heaved up only with an effort, looking down at it in surprise.

"Jeeze!" he muttered irritably. "What's the boss packing now? A set of weights?"

Shrugging his broad shoulders, Starski headed off. Through the terminal's main concourse, through a cursory customs check, out the boarding gate, and across the tarmac to the plane the big man toted the cases, manfully disdaining a luggage cart even though the one case obviously caused him a bit of strain.

He stopped at the bottom of the boarding stairs to check in with the attendant. Frank Garvey eyed him curiously.

"That the chief's stuff, Stony?"

"Yeah, the last of it."

"You're not going to have them stow it with the rest?"

"His suit got screwed, remember?" the big man pointed out. "He said he was going to change. Wanted both of these."

"Yeah, okay," the security chief allowed. "You can take them on up. You need help?"

Starski smiled contemptuously at the suggestion. "Are you kidding?"

Pointedly showing no sign of his strain, he toted his load on up the stairs, stooping to get his big form through the door and into the plane.

The interior of the jumbo jet had been structured as part passenger plane, part business office. It had rows of ordinary airplane seats in the forward half, but from midsection back, it turned into a well-appointed work space with desks, computer terminals, and a long conference table of polished burled oak surrounded by plush chairs.

Kean and some of his associates—including Lance and the one called Mac—were now seated about this table, having a last-minute conference before the takeoff. Lance was at the moment succinctly finishing up his own carefully prepared report.

"So the surveyors will be concluding their work in just ten days. Then the crews will move in and start the clearing out. Equipment begins to arrive at the site in two weeks. Exactly on schedule."

Kean was not really listening to this. He was staring away into space. It was as if images of some sun-washed, flowery glade hung before his eyes to cover the true scene, and the sound of a lilting song filled his ears to drown out Lance's lecturing drone.

"By precisely four years from the next May Day," Lance was continuing, "all construction should be completed . . . all according to our schedule. We will be ready for your grand opening, Mr. Kean."

Getting no reply to this, he looked up from his report to note Kean's distraction.

"Ah . . . Mr. Kean?" he repeated.

The voice recalled Kean to reality. He shook his head and looked around at Lance blankly.

"What?"

"Are you all right, Mr. Kean?" Lance asked him.

"Of course I'm all right," Kean brusquely replied. "Now, what's the status on the surveyors' completion time?"

Nonplussed, Lance looked around at his fellows. They too all seemed clearly taken aback by Kean's most unusual lapse.

"Ah . . . Mr. Kean . . . I already went over . . ." Lance hesitantly began.

But he was saved from this awkward moment by the arrival of Frank Garvey, who approached the table to announce: "Excuse me, Mr. Kean. We're all set. Everyone's aboard. The pilot's ready for takeoff. Shall I give the go-ahead?"

"Yeah, sure, Frank," Kean told him. He looked around at the others. "Okay, end of meeting, boys. Find seats for yourselves."

They all immediately began to rise, gather up papers, and move toward the rows of seats.

"Look, I guess I am a little tired," Kean said as he rose too. "I'm going back to grab a little rest. See you all later."

He moved away to a door behind the office area and toward the ship's tail. Lance looked after him, then turned toward the one called Mac, once more clearly surprised by his chief's unusual move.

"Kean? Tired? He actually rests?"

Mac shrugged. "I guess he's human too. Hope you're not too disillusioned."

Kean passed on through the doorway, shutting it behind him. This rear section of the plane had been done up as a private suite whose poshness rivaled that of a four-star hotel's finest room. It was fitted out with king-size bed, desk, sofa, easy chairs, even a fully stocked bar.

Starski was there, having brought the two cases back and set them in a luggage rack. Now he approached his employer.

"I got your stuff, boss. You want me to unpack?"

"Not now, Stony. I just want to rest. You can go on out. We're going to take off."

The big man nodded and left the room. Kean removed his suit jacket, pausing a moment to look musingly at its torn sleeve before tossing it down on the bed. Then he sat down in a lounge chair bolted to the deck and fitted with a seat belt, strapping himself in.

In moments the private jet was taxiing away from the Shannon terminal.

As it moved out onto the runway, Kean sat staring off into space again. As it turned to assume position for its takeoff, he began to hum. The humming was so soft as to be unintelligible at first. But as the sound of the revving engines gained in volume, he hummed louder, the tune becoming recognizable as that the girl had sung.

The plane roared down the concrete strip and lifted away. The green lands of the Shannon estuary with its glinting blue-silver band of river dwindled behind. Then Ireland itself began to grey with distance as the plane flew westward toward the sea, its engine noise subsiding into a steady background drone.

Still, Kean hummed on.

A Fasten Seat Belts sign on the suite's wall flicked off. Kean unbuckled his belt and got to his feet, still humming.

He crossed to the little bar and fetched himself a healthy belt of Scotch, pouring the amber liquid from a cut-crystal decanter to a cut-crystal glass. As he did, his humming slowly transformed into words. He was actually singing a verse of the song:

> "A lady fair, in robe of white,
> To greet the hunter came;
> She kiss'd a cup with jewels bright,
> And pledg'd him by his name."

He lifted the glass toward his lips at this point, his eyes rising to fix on his own image in the mirrored section of wall behind the bar.

His gaze froze there as another figure came into view over his shoulder, appearing suddenly in the room behind him.

It was the girl named Caitlin Bawn.

He wheeled, Scotch sloshing from his glass at his speed. He stared at her in astonishment.

"Michael Kean," she said with a warm voice and a matching smile, "it's surely a fine job you're doin' with that air."

Kean managed to find his voice, but barely. "Wha . . . what are you doing here?"

"Ah, well, I'm taking up your offer," she casually replied, "to show me your New York."

"But how did you get here?"

"My clansmen were all busy watching after what your people were about," she said, beginning to move slowly toward him. "They never even noticed my going away."

"I mean, how did you get onto this plane?" he asked more insistently. "Through customs! Through security!"

She moved closer, her shoulders giving a little shrug.

"That wasn't much trick at all for me. Having no idea how to find your far city on my own, I decided to go with you."

"But you can't just . . . sneak on here. Do you even have a passport?"

She stopped, eyeing him quizzically. "A pass . . . what?"

He shook his head. "That's what I figured. This is crazy!"

She smiled again. "Wasn't it you who spoke of 'taking risks'?"

"I didn't mean breaking the law. At least, not this kind. Sorry, but I've got to tell them you're here."

He started to turn away toward the cabin door. But she moved more swiftly. She leapt lightly forward to grasp him in her arms and draw his lips to hers.

Taken off guard, Kean was drawn into the kiss. He then began to pull away, trying to regain control. But her arms tightened, holding him, and as the kiss continued, it appeared to have an effect on him. He began to actively, then avidly return it, lifting his arms to encircle her.

As he did this, her hands lifted upward. They slid up his arms, over his shoulders, and on up to his face. The fingers caressed softly, stroking, sliding higher, finally touching his temples.

They touched there lightly, then suddenly pressed harder.

Kean gave a low grunt—mixed pain and surprise. His head dropped limply back.

The drink glass fell from his instantly nerveless hand, thudding to the thick carpet, its brown liquid spraying out in a fan across the pearl-grey wool. She deftly swiveled Kean's suddenly sagging body about and plopped him down onto a chair. He lay there motionless, eyes closed.

Caitlin stood over him, looking down at the still form. There was a touch of regret, but also a great determination in the expression of her young face.

"Sorry, Michael Kean," she told the unconscious man. "But I've gone too far for you to stop me now."

And his private plane sped on, heading on into the beginnings of a red-gold sunset, soaring on into the rising cloak of nighttime and the western land that lay far beyond.

The sun was setting beyond the western rim of the sea in a spectacular display, casting a ruddy glow up the coastal hills of Ireland and striking crimson flares from the contractor's vehicles parked on the hillcrest.

The surveyors were packing up their equipment. Already they had marked out sections of the site with scores of flagged stakes. They were scattered down the hill, marking out its wild, natural precincts in neat mathematical shapes, ready for shovel, grader, and plow.

As one truckload of men and equipment pulled away, a pair of the surveyors stood looking out on the western scene.

"It's a most beautiful sight, is it not, Seamus?" asked a lanky, long-faced one.

"Yes," agreed the other, a stocky, bald, and round-faced man with a sadly musing expression. "I wonder what it'll be like all paved over with concrete and lit up by a million electric lights?"

"Now, Seamus," said the first in a scolding tone. "It'll be bringing a great, new wealth to Ireland. We've no right to be criticizing it."

"Haven't we?" asked the other. "There just may be some things not worth doing only for the gain of money, Conor O'Flynn." He shrugged resignedly. "Ah, well, it's little enough that we can do in any case. Let's go."

They turned and started walking back toward their trucks. But they stopped abruptly as a voice sounded from behind them: "Caitlin Bawn."

Startled, the two wheeled back around, staring in surprise.

At the edge of the crest, a strange figure had suddenly appeared.

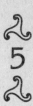

5

Silhouetted against the setting sun, no detail of the dark figure could be clearly seen. A long, voluminous, and hooded cloak fluttered about it, further obscuring the form's nature, save that it was definitely massive and most certainly ominous.

The two disconcerted men stared at the being who seemed to have popped into existence from nowhere. Finally the lean surveyor named Conor found his voice: "Who . . . who are you? What do you want?"

"Caitlin Bawn," the figure repeated in a low rumble of voice. "I want to know where she's gone."

"We don't know what you're speaking of," put in the round one called Seamus. "We've never heard the name."

In response the figure made a swift move forward. A hand shot out from within its cloak to grab the second man by his jacket front, hauling him up onto his toes. The figure looked down at him from a height nearly a head taller. Eyes seem to gleam out with a hard silver light from within the blackness of the hood.

"She followed after the man who came here and left," the voice grated. "Your chieftain he must have been. Where is he now?"

Conor tried to pull the figure's hands from his helpless comrade.

"Here, let go of Seamus, you! You can't be doing that. Who d'ya think you are?"

The figure swung out with its other hand, the light backhand blow still enough to lift and toss the surveyor away some feet and slam him down hard on his backside. Seamus began to scream out in fear.

"Help! Help!" he shouted out. "We're being attacked!"

This cry caught the attention of one who was gathering tools close by. He was a worker, much more burly of build than the surveyors, and he moved at once to intervene. Grabbing up a thick and heavy iron rod, he rushed to help, swinging it up to threaten the dark figure.

As he approached, the figure cast the seized surveyor away. Then, in a single move of incredible speed, it drew out a longsword from beneath the cloak. The blade swung out in a blurred fan of light, contacting the iron rod to produce a flash of brilliant blue-white.

The metal rod was cut in two as if it had been a slender stick of wood. The worker stopped in his tracks, staring at the stub in his hands in shock. Then he looked to the figure.

It was fully dusk now, darkening rapidly. The figure was reduced to little but a mass of black. But the sword in its hand showed clearly, the keen length of blade luminescent with an icy glow.

The workman turned and ran.

The two surveyors got to their feet and ran too, shouting out a warning: "Help! Look out! It's a madman. A madman!"

The dark figure strode after the fleeing men. A dozen other surveyors and workmen who were still laboring to pack up their trucks heard the frightened cries. They turned to see the running men approaching, the shadowy figure in relentless pursuit.

They all began to move forward, clearly meaning to give aid. Some grabbed up shovels, rods, stakes, and the like as makeshift weapons.

"Oy, lads! What is it?" one of them shouted to the running men.

"He's trying to kill us," Seamus shouted back as he and

his fleeing companions rushed on through the others without slowing.

"We'll see about that," another worker replied. He lifted a sledgehammer above his head, preparing to strike out as the dark figure reached him.

But an immense hand shot in from behind him and grabbed the hammer. An enormous fist closed over and completely swallowed the head. The tool was torn out of the man's hands.

Astounded, the workman and his fellows turned to see a second figure—dark, massive, seemingly bearlike—looming up a good two heads over them. Its one hand still grasped the hammer, now lifted high above. And within the darkness of a hood that also hid its face, white teeth gleamed in a maniacal smile.

Then the teeth parted, and the sound of a loud, savage snarl issued from between their rows.

With yelps of fright, the men all bolted, scattering in various directions, making for the trucks.

Three of them reached one large van, all scrambling together to open its passenger door, all battling to be the first inside.

A peculiar whoosh of sound came from above them, growing quickly louder. The men paused in their struggle to look up.

"Look there!" one of them cried in a panicky voice.

A form swept down at them out of the blackness. Dimly seen in the growing dark, it seemed at first to be a huge bird. But as it approached, it quickly resolved into something much more terrible.

It was a flying monster with the man-sized body of a raven, a huge span of blue-black wings, a cat's clawed feet, and a man's head on a scaled and serpentine neck.

The creature swooped in, hovering a moment just above the horrified men, vast wings flapping to hold it suspended there. The thing's human eyes glowed with a reddish fire like two hot coals. A forked tongue, also seemingly aflame, flicked out at the three cowering men.

Then the being soared back up and away, gliding back out into the swallowing night.

The men looked at each other in disbelief.

"HolyMarymotherofGod!" gasped out one. "Just what was that?"

"I'm not staying here to find out!" declared another.

With that, the three recommenced their mad scramble, all finally managing to squeeze into the truck. One of them clambered behind the wheel, fired its engine up, and clanged it into gear.

As the van began pulling away, it shot by five more men in their own battle to scramble over a tailgate and into the back of another truck. The immense black figure lumbered toward them, holding the big sledgehammer right way 'round now, clearly intent on mayhem. That provided the men an especially fine inducement to hurry.

The last of them was just climbing over the gate as the truck started up and began to roll away. He was caught there, balanced on the gate and carried off screaming, his legs flailing out behind.

The black figure, just nearing the truck, swung out at him. But the truck shot ahead to safety, the sledge's head only just catching the edge of the truck's fender, though still caving it in.

By this time, the surveyors Seamus and Conor had reached their own small van. The figure with the glowing sword still stalked after them, slowly but most determinedly.

The two men climbed into the van, Seamus getting behind the wheel. He started the engine, flicked on the headlights, and drove the van away, eschewing the road and bounding the vehicle right out over the bumpy meadowlands in his haste to escape.

But then yet another figure loomed up in the way ahead, appearing so abruptly it seemed to have risen up right from the solid sod.

It stood square before them, caught in the twin yellow cones of the van's headlights. It was a very tall, very lean figure, rather scarecrowlike in its gawky stance, clad also in a long and hooded cloak.

"There's another of 'em!" Seamus shouted out.

"Run the bastard down then!" Conor replied.

Thus prompted, the round man gritted his teeth and shoved the van's gas pedal to the floor. He steered right at the figure planted in the way.

"Yaa, yaa! We'll get him!" shouted Conor in savage delight as they roared in.

But as they came near, the figure abruptly raised both its arms high. From the fingertips of both hands flares of sapphire lightning shot out, twining and combining and forming two thick, crackling beams of light.

These twin rays shot down to explode at one spot in a great blinding ball of light right before the speeding van's front wheels.

The driver screamed and jerked the wheel over violently. The van skewed sideways, tipped onto two wheels, and heeled on over, carried by its momentum, crashing down on its side and rolling onto its top where it came to rest, tires still spinning.

For a moment the two men inside lay motionless, stunned, crumpled against the cab roof. Then a hand grasped the outside handle of the passenger door. A single heave wrenched the door free of its hinges with a squeal of rending metal.

Other hands reached in and grabbed Conor, hauling him out, leaving the whimpering Seamus within the van.

Conor was lifted upright by the shoulders and slammed against the side of the upturned car. The hapless surveyor, groggily shaking his head and looking around, found four dark figures hemming him in. The being they'd met first, the one who held the sword, now grabbed him tightly by the throat.

The tip of the glowing blade lifted to touch his chest. The figure spoke slowly, carefully, but with great force: "Now, little man, you are going to tell me just what I want to know!"

"I will. Yes, I will!" the other gasped. "Anything you
want to know."

"Then tell me, who is the man who was here?"

"Kean is his name. Michael Kean."

"And what clans is this Michael Kean the chieftain of?"

"Clans? I don't know what you mean. He . . . he's our
boss. The owner of our business. Kean Castle Enterprises.
That's what it's called. Here . . . this is it."

He pointed to a patch on his jacket breast. It was a
round, embroidered badge of cloth bearing the name of
the company around its edge and a stylized version of the
four-spired castle logo.

The shining gaze of the dark figure fixed upon it.

"What is this?" said the voice.

"His company. That's it."

"But where is it?" the figure demanded, shaking him,
rattling his body against the van. "Where is he? Where has
he gone now?"

"New York. New York!" cried Conor desperately. "He
was going straight back there. Tonight! That's where he's
gone! I swear!"

"New . . . York," the figure repeated slowly, considering each word. Then its hand moved from the surveyor's
throat to his chest, gripping the logo. A quick tug ripped it
free, along with half the jacket front.

As the freed surveyor sank down in exhaustion, the figure turned from him toward the other dark forms, its voice
booming out: "This place is where *she* must be too! Come
on!"

And the four moved swiftly away to vanish into the
gathered night.

The night's vault of clear, black sky was speckled thickly
with the cold white dots of stars.

A massive object swept across them, moving from the
east, its birdlike shape showing in outline against them as
it flew on. Their faint light glinting against its shiny metal
skin was enough to reveal the flying object's true nature. It

was the jumbo jet of Kean Castle Enterprises still cruising along on its way back toward its home.

Inside the plane, most of the passengers were asleep, although most without much comfort. They lay awkwardly or stirred fitfully, attempting with little success to configure a human body to the inhuman seats.

However, the one called Mac seemed to be having little trouble, looking like a contentedly snoozing old family hound draped across its master's best sofa, snoring away. The half-dozen tiny and drained bottles of gin discarded on the empty seat beside him might have provided some reason for that sound repose.

As he shifted slightly, finding a better way to pillow his head on his arm, a hand moved in to grasp his shoulder, shaking him gently.

He shifted, snorted, but stayed asleep. The hand shook harder. This time he gasped, blinked, turned his head, and looked up in groggy irritation to see just who had dared disturb him.

It was young Lance who stood bent over him, his expression a concerned one.

"McBride," Lance said insistently, "McBride, wake up!"

"Christ, kid, what do you want?" Mac grumbled. "What the hell time is it?"

"One-thirty A.M. Irish time."

"Then go away!" Mac told him. He tried to recompose himself for sleep, but the other wouldn't have it, shaking him again with more force.

"Wake up, you sot. It's important."

"Important?" the other repeated, sitting up more fully awake this time.

"Yes!" Lance shoved aside the pile of empty bottles and sat down in the empty seat. "It's Mr. Kean. He's been in his cabin since we left Ireland. We'll be landing in New York in just an hour."

"So he's been sleeping for five hours!" McBride said irritably. "So what? The man was tired."

Lance continued fretting. "But it's not like him. Shouldn't we wake him?"

"Why?" Mac countered. "Look, just wait 'til we land. Give him the extra hour. Relax." He spotted a female attendant moving down the aisle past them. "Have a drink, okay?"

He leaned out past Lance, pushing him back, to flag her down.

"Hey, Sheila," he called, "another gin on the rocks."

As she nodded and went off, Lance's nose wrinkled in disgust.

"I don't see how you can drink that poison at this time of the day."

"Got to. My mind works way too well when I first wake up. Got to anesthetize it real quick. Thoughts, you know. Very dangerous things. Now, if you're not drinking with me, just go the hell away. And leave Mike strictly alone 'til we get home!"

The disgruntled Larson rose and began to move away. Then he paused, glancing back toward the door to Kean's suite. He was clearly contemplating checking on his boss despite the warning. McBride saw his look.

"If you wake him up," he warned, "he'll have your ass, my friend. Wanna risk it?"

Clearly Lance did not. He turned the other way and went back to his own seat.

McBride looked after him, muttering under his breath: "Shoulda let the yuppie sonofabitch get himself fired!"

Then the attendant was beside him, offering up a glass and a gin bottle that he gratefully accepted.

A scene glowed on the black surface of the circular pool.

It was a nighttime view of the hill's crest. But the normally dark and empty landscape was alive with shifting lights. A dozen cars marked with the Guarda label of the Irish police and a pair of ambulances were parked there, the beams of their spinning red and blue lights crisscrossing through the night.

Some two score uniformed men swarmed about the crest and the meadows behind it, the beams of their torches scouring the ground for clues. White-garbed ambulance attendants treated a battered Conor and Seamus while other policemen looked over the wrecked van and took the two men's statements, exchanging glances of open disbelief at the weird tale.

Within the cylindrical cavern the two women turned from the scene in the pool to confront the four dark-cloaked figures who now stood lined up beside them.

"You've aroused them," the one called Caoimhe said in a worried way.

"They'll find nothing," the gaunt one named Aisling responded curtly. "And if they move down from the crest, you know the power will lead them Astray. What was done was necessary."

"I suppose," the younger woman conceded. She looked to the four cloaked ones. "You did discover where the man has gone."

"Yes," answered the one who had earlier wielded the sword. "To this New York."

"And where is that?" asked Aisling.

"I think I know." This came from another figure, the slightest of the four, whose high and pleasingly musical voice issued rather incongruously from within the hood of the sinister form. "It was years ago, when I was out awandering the lands, that I met a fellow who said he had been there. A new town he said it was. Far away in the new land out beyond the western sea."

"Indeed?" said Caoimhe. "I thought there was nothing lay beyond that."

"Not so," corrected Aisling. "I myself have heard the tales of one of those they call a saint who sailed his little curragh to the very spot—oh, hundreds of years ago, it was. A most wild place, filled with forests and savages."

"It doesn't matter how far or how wild a place it is," the first figure said in a most determined voice. "If this one called Michael Kean carried Caitlin away to it, it's where I mean to go."

"Then you know that we'll all go too," came a rumbling voice from the most massive of the four.

"Yes, I knew that would be the way of it," said the first. "We all go then. But how? Shall we sail there as well?"

"We'll do nothing so slow," said the tall and lanky figure in a dismissing way. "I'll raise a force to carry us as if we were motes of dust before the highest gale. Like rays of light we'll travel, shooting across this sea and to the very place you seek. Once Caitlin is found, we'll bring her back the same way."

"We put ourselves in your hands, then," said the first. "But let's go at once."

"Wait now," said Caoimhe. "And are you so certain that Fionnbharr will agree to this? To go into their world, so far away from home . . . it will be dangerous."

"He would never deny my going," the first cloaked one replied. "He knows what it means to me."

"Still, he might be against it," the lanky figure said gloomily. "You know how he's become about any contact between ourselves and *them*."

"But he's also kept a greater watch on their world than any of us," the little one put in. "He knows much about them that he might tell us, if we asked him for help."

"We can't take the risk," the first one said firmly. "To rescue Caitlin from the foul clutches of this one who has stolen her, I will do whatever must be done. I'll not allow even Fionnbharr to stop me."

"Aye," said the massive figure heartily. "We four have dealt with the most monstrous of villains before. We can surely deal with this one alone."

"Then, come on, my friends," the first dark figure said, gesturing to the other three.

The four turned away from the pool and trooped single file out through the one narrow opening in the cavern's wall.

The two women looked after them. When they had gone, Caoimhe looked accusingly to Aisling.

"'Stolen' is it? So you didn't tell him that it was Caitlin who followed the man away?"

"We don't know the truth of that," Aisling hedged. "He might have put some power on her that forced her to run away."

"It was her own interest in him that took her, and you know it," the other said. "She made no secret of that. It was her own choice to go."

"Maybe. But I thought it best not to confuse the thing. She must be recovered, and safely, no matter what. Those who go after her should be clear on who is the wrong one here."

"You lie again," the younger woman said with surprising audacity, boldly meeting Aisling's eye. "It's Caitlin's interests you're protecting in this, and your own as well!"

"Very well then," Aisling admitted, but with great haughtiness. "I've tried to save my daughter from her own foolishness. And is that wrong?"

"I hope not, Aisling," the other said misgivingly. "I most truly do hope not."

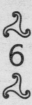

6

Kean's airplane touched down on the lit runway of New York's J.F.K. airfield.

It taxied in to the gate of a private terminal whose several hangars were stamped with the Kean Castle logo. As it pulled up, a ground crew similarly branded hustled to run out a passenger ramp.

Inside the plane, Kean's people were gathering briefcases and carryons, preparing to disembark. But they all turned to look as the door to Kean's private cabin suddenly flew open.

He came out in a somewhat unsteady lunge, looking disheveled and groggy after six hours of unconsciousness. He stopped and stood weaving, staring around him, clearly fighting to regain his orientation. His people stared back at him in various puzzled ways.

"The girl," he said in an odd, half-dazed voice. "Where's the girl?"

Lance immediately moved toward him. "Girl, sir?"

"Yeah! The girl, dammit!" Kean said irritably. "Where'd she go?"

While Lance seemed to be taken at a loss, McBride stepped in.

"Michael, what girl are you talking about?"

"A . . . an Irish girl," Kean said, rubbing his head. "She must have snuck aboard."

Frank Garvey had joined them by this time. "I went

over this plane with a tweezers myself before we took off, Mr. Kean," he assured. "There wasn't anybody aboard but us."

"I'm telling you she was with me"—he gestured behind him at his cabin door—"in there!"

Instantly Garvey was stepping past Kean and into the suite, face taking on a grim and cautious look. With one hand inside his coat he moved cautiously but swiftly about the room, checking inside bathroom and closet, looking under the bed and behind the furniture. Then he moved back to Kean, shaking his head.

"No sign of anyone, sir."

"That's impossible," Kean snapped. He looked around at the curious faces massed behind him at the door. "Didn't anyone see her? See anything?"

They exchanged blank looks. They shrugged or made negative noises.

McBride, glancing in through the cabin doorway, noted the dark fan of the spilled whiskey on the carpet and the empty glass still lying on the floor nearby. He turned back to Kean.

"Are you certain it wasn't a dream, Michael?" said McBride. He nodded toward the stain. "A bit too much of the ol' sauce perhaps?"

"You would think of that, Mac," Kean returned.

"Look, I'll go over everything again if you want, Mr. Kean," the security man volunteered.

Kean was by now returning to fuller consciousness. He looked around him at the odd stares of his employees, his face showing his realization of just how ridiculous this looked. Quickly he took hold of himself, reestablishing firm control.

"No, Frank," he said dismissingly. "Just forget it. Mac's right. It was just a dream. A screwy dream."

"All right, people," Lance said officiously, clapping his hands. "You heard Mr. Kean. Get on with your deplaning please."

The group obeyed, breaking up and moving away with

Lance herding them. But McBride lingered, looking at his boss in a musing way.

And Kean, not noting him, lifted a hand to lightly touch his fingertips first to his lips and then to his temple, turning to look back into his empty suite.

A white stretch limo rolled out of the J.F.K. parking lot and drove into the city.

Starski, as before, was at its wheel. Lance, McBride, and Garvey rode with their employer in the back.

McBride rode a jumpseat and poured out a stiff drink of Scotch at the limo's posh bar. Kean sat staring out a window at the passing night streets and fuming loudly.

"I can't believe I slept the whole way back. What a goddamn waste of time. And now I'll be wired and up all night."

McBride handed him the drink and looked around at the others.

"Anyone else?" he asked.

Lance and Frank Garvey shook their heads. McBride shrugged and poured out a generous straight gin for himself.

"Well, maybe you can use the time to do a few odd jobs around the house," he commented dryly as he plopped in some cubes of ice. "You know, fix a faucet or something."

Kean gave him a sharp look. "Watch it, Mac," he warned.

McBride only smiled and settled back to quaff his gin.

The limo went on through the streets, plunging ever deeper into the neon-lit canyons wending between the towering ranges of skyscrapers.

Ahead, beyond a ragged crest of lower structures, one peak thrust up much higher to loom startlingly above. It was a simple soaring rectangle of a building, its sheer walls of glass and marble stripes glowing white in the light of countless floods. From the four corners of its top, round, slender, and peaked turrets thrust yet higher up. They were intended to create a stylized castle look. Instead, they seemed more like a battery of missiles ready to be fired.

The limousine made its way to the base of this building, turning off the main street into an alleyway. Halfway along it, the car turned again to roll down a ramp leading to an underground parking garage beneath the skyscraper. A plaque beside a closed metal door read Kean Castle—Private Parking Garage—Security Key Cards Needed.

The car paused there while Starski opened his window and inserted a plastic card into the slit mouth of a small device set on a thick post beside the ramp. The device hummed and sucked on the card awhile, then spat it back out like something unpalatable. But the tasting must still have satisfied it, for a red light on its top flashed off, a green one beside it flashed on, and the metal door smoothly and soundlessly slid up.

The limo rolled through into the garage beyond. It was a vast cavern of concrete, its low roof propped by rows of massive square columns.

The limousine pulled into a wide spot whose stenciled wall proclaimed it as Reserved for Michael Kean. Starski leapt out and opened the door for his passengers. The four got out and walked from the car to the nearby door of an elevator. It too was labeled, as Mr. Kean's Private Elevator. Penthouse Access. RESTRICTED!

Frank Garvey whipped a plastic card out from within his coat and inserted it into a slot beside the door. The elevator immediately whispered open. Kean, Lance, and McBride stepped in. Garvey glanced up to a small surveillance camera peering down from above the door. He gave it a wave and then followed the rest in. He punched a button and the door slid closed.

With his boss seen safely on the way, Starski moved to the car's trunk. He opened it and began the task of unloading the mass of luggage crammed within.

Meantime, far above him, the express elevator was shooting toward its destination. The long rows of lighted floor buttons by its door indicated the meteoric nature of the rise, blinking in seconds up through a hundred numbers, slowing as the car came to final rest at 105.

With a faint ding the door slid open. Kean and his companions walked out into the king of this castle's most private domicile.

The penthouse took up the entire area of the building's top levels. Its paneled ceiling was a full two stories above its plush carpeted floor. Most of its decor was a clean and classy modern version of art deco, with lots of smooth curves, grey tile, chrome, and glass.

It was largely a single space, with wide, round-arched windows in the center of each wall framing a kitchen area, a conversation grouping, and a huge bar. In all four corners were circular metal staircases winding up into the turrets rising directly above. Doors at each stair's top allowed access from each turret to the roof.

For a pleasing counterpoint to the room's rather stark effect, the center of the floor was an oasis of green—a miniature forest of potted plants and trees replete with graveled walks and oak benches. Above it a large skylight poked its pyramidal peak of glass high into the night.

Kean strode out into the room, looking around him at his high keep.

"Home again," he commented.

"Home is the hunter," added McBride.

Kean eyed him sharply. "What do you mean?"

"Just something from a poem, I think," the other answered, a little taken aback. "It popped into my head. I didn't mean anything."

Garvey, meantime, had gone directly to a massive desk that was clearly Kean's personal control station for his vast operation. It was elaborately equipped with three computers, a variety of communications gear, several monitors, a security control panel, and an intercom system. The security chief slipped yet another card into a slot on the intercom, thus prodding the machine to give out a small, sharp beep.

He spoke briskly into its mouthpiece: "Mr. Kean is in his quarters. Go to green-level security."

In a row of variously colored lights on the control panel, the glow switched from a blue to a green bulb in response.

Garvey nodded in satisfaction and turned to face his employer.

"All set, sir."

"Good enough," Kean replied. "Well, you boys want to stay around a little while? There's no need for you to rush off."

"I'm really sorry, Mr. Kean," said Lance with apology, "but I've got to get some rest. You know I don't sleep well at all on a plane. And I've got to be alert tomorrow, sir, don't I? Lots of work! You do understand," he asked with some anxiousness, "don't you?"

"Yeah. Sure. Okay," Kean assured him. "I always want my top people fully rested." He waved him away. "Take off."

As Lance beat a grateful retreat, Garvey also made his excuses. "And I've got to go too, sir. I have to check out the security. Be certain they've been on top of things while I was gone."

Kean snapped him a mocking salute. "Right, General! You're dismissed."

Garvey wheeled smartly and followed Lance into the waiting elevator. The two looked back toward McBride. He waved them on.

"Go ahead, guys. I'll hang around awhile."

Garvey punched a button and the elevator closed. Kean turned to his last companion.

"I figured you'd stay around."

"Sure. You know me. Nowhere else to go. And the booze is free."

He crossed at once to the graceful sweep of polished bar, passing behind it to reach the racks of bottles, stocked in numbers and varieties vast enough to shame a good-sized saloon. He filled a large tumbler with ice from a dispenser and pulled out a bottle of Tanqueray gin.

"Want one?" he asked Kean.

"Not right now."

Kean eyed McBride as the man filled the big glass with gin. His expression showed a flicker of concern.

"Don't you think that's a little too much?"

McBride grinned carelessly. "You can never be too thin or too rich. Hell, you should know that, Michael lad! But, too sober? Well, that's another thing."

He took a deep draught of his gin and ice. Kean opened his mouth as if to comment further. But he was interrupted as the elevator door opened once again and Starski came out, carrying Kean's suitcases.

"Sorry, boss. Just passin' through," he said, and wheeled the cart on across the room.

He skirted the central jungle and moved toward a partition of translucent glass bricks curving out from the opposite wall to form a bow. This partition, some eight feet high, formed the only closed-off space in the penthouse. A single wide door gave the only access to the area beyond.

Starski passed through it, wheeling his cart. What he entered was the bedroom of his chief. It was appointed in the style of the rest of the penthouse. Its huge bed was positioned before the outer wall's huge window so that its occupant, if sitting up, might easily gaze out on the city spread below, like a ruler gazing out on his domain.

Without delay, Starski lifted the cases off the cart, lining them up beside the door. Then he backed out, closing the door behind him.

Almost at once, a glow rose within one case, first shining out through the whole crack around it in a thin bead of silver, then beginning to swell out from a spot on one side in an iridescent bubble.

Outside, Starski was moving away, completely unaware.

"It's all in there, boss," he said as he pushed the cart back across the floor toward the elevator. "Good night. Be seeing you."

"Right," Kean answered. "Good night, Stony. See you tomorrow."

He watched the big man go into the elevator, then turned away, moving to the window behind the bar to stand staring out.

McBride plumped himself down on a bar stool, took another swig of gin, and eyed his employer curiously. After some moments of this, with Kean neither speaking nor moving, he asked, "You okay, Michael? You seem kind of . . . odd."

"Odd?" said Kean, not looking around.

"Yeah. Distracted. Jumpy. You've been like that since before we left Ireland."

"Have I?"

"Hey, you know it. Is something bugging you? I mean, we could talk about it. We used to talk, back in the old days."

Kean stayed staring out the window, not replying at first, seeming to consider.

"It's hard to say what it is," he finally answered in a careful way. "I do feel a little odd, I guess. Sort of . . . disconnected, maybe. I don't know. I've never had a feeling like it before. Like . . . like there's something missing."

McBride shook his head. "Michael, I think you work yourself too hard. You've got to relax. Do something else besides business. Get yourself a hobby."

Kean gave a little laugh and turned toward his friend.

"What, like fixing faucets, I suppose?"

"At least that's got a direct purpose to it," McBride said defensively. "There's a real, down-to-earth effect to your laboring that you can see. Surely there's a virtue in that."

"Some virtue," Kean said. "Getting covered with dirty water and stinking muck. I'll pay somebody else to do that, thanks."

McBride took another stiff belt of gin.

"Then maybe you should pay someone to see to those Morristown apartments," he said, the liquor making him both drunker and bolder. "It's certainly well past time for that."

"Christ," Kean said irritably, "are you calling me a slumlord now?"

McBride slid off the stool to stand, weaving slightly. "I'm calling you a guy who only knows making money and doesn't give a damn how it affects anyone else," he replied in a voice now growing slurred. "You feel disconnected. Well, that's it, my lad. You pulled the plug on yourself a long time ago."

Kean stepped in to face him squarely, his own voice hard. "That's just the gin in you talking now. Even so, I wouldn't let anybody but you get away with talking to me that way."

"Why?" McBride shot back. "Because I'm your old family friend? Because I knew you when?"

"I'm not sure there's any other reason to keep you on," Kean said harshly.

Clearly stricken by this, McBride drew himself up.

"Well, I'm not sure I want the charity," he answered with great indignation. "Good night to you, Mr. Kean!"

And with that he turned and stalked proudly, if a bit unsteadily, away. Setting his emptied glass down hard on the bar as he passed, he made his way to the elevator and punched its call button.

The door obediently slid open at once, and he stepped inside.

"Can you get home all right?" Kean called after him.

"What do you care?" McBride told him, and hit the down button.

The door closed on his drink- and anger-flushed face. Kean stared irritably at the door a moment, then walked to the desk intercom, snapping it on.

"Security?" he called.

"Yes, sir," a crisp voice responded.

"Mr. McBride is coming down. See to it that he gets home all right. But no fuss. Know what I mean?"

"Yes, sir. We've seen to it before."

Kean snapped off the intercom, gave an exasperated sigh, then moved back to the bar.

This time he went behind it, taking a glass and pouring a drink of neat Scotch for himself. He walked to the window and once again stood there, taking small sips of the drink as he stared out into the night.

The lights of the city made a twinkling abstract pattern across the images of himself and the room behind him reflected in the window glass.

He ignored the reflections, his gaze concentrated on the lights below.

At least, he did at first.

But then a movement in the image of the room brought his focus shifting to it. He watched a figure slide into his view.

He wheeled in shock.

Once more he stared at Caitlin Bawn.

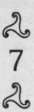

7

"**Y**ou're here?" Kean gasped out.

"Of a certainty I am, Michael Kean," she replied with great gaiety. She looked about her. "And this must be your high chieftain's palace!" She spun around with a dancer's easy grace, her long skirt billowing out about her slim white legs. "Ah, what a fine place it is."

"H-how?" Kean got out, still stunned by his shock. "You couldn't get in here."

"Oh, of course I could," she said dismissively. "I snuck in with your clothes, if you want to know." She began moving around the room in sprightly, sweeping movements, pausing to touch this or stare at that, taking all of it in with awe. "Such great wonders! Grander even than the Dagda's Sidh."

"'Sith'?" he repeated blankly, then shook his bewildered head. "Look, never mind that. How in hell could you sneak in? And hide on the plane? It's impossible."

"Not if you've the gift," she said, tossing him a wink and a mischievous grin as she swirled on. "Grandfather had it stronger than any druid. My mother passed on some of the powers to me. Nothing great you know, but . . ."

"'Powers'?" he said, trying to keep his gaze on the flitting form.

"Magic, you know. For the hidin' especially. Oh, our people have always been very good at that." She stopped finally to examine more closely the room's central green space. "Ah. And you grow living things inside. We do so as well"—she fingered the spiky leaves of a palm—"though nothing so strange as this."

"I can't handle this," he said, exhausted. He strode back to the bar, pouring out more Scotch for himself. She noticed this and came over, most interested.

"Drink, is it?" she said. "And could you spare a bit for me? I'm after being of a frightful thirst from so long a voyage."

Without speaking, he went around the bar to fetch another glass.

"It's a long, long way your city must be from my own land," she commented as he did.

"Three thousand miles," he said, dropping ice into the glass from the dispenser.

The clinking caught her attention, and her gaze fixed on the glass as he set it upon the bar. Before he could pour Scotch into it, she snatched it up, staring in fascination at the glinting objects within as if they were precious gems.

"Marvelous things," she breathed. She took up one of the cylindrical pieces, remarking in surprise: "Oh! It's so cold!"

"Ice usually is," he said. "You . . . uh . . . know about ice, don't you?"

"I see it in winter, shimmering on lakes and dangling in glittering icicles from the trees. Not captured in neat bits like these."

She dropped the piece back into the glass and stirred the lot of them with a finger, looking delighted at their musical tinkling.

While she did this, he gazed searchingly into the bright eyes in the so fresh and so ingenuous face. "Look, are you for real," he asked, "or are you just a dream?"

Her eyes lifted from the glass to meet his, probing far into their depths. Her voice took on an odd intensity. "As real as anything there is, Michael Kean. Maybe more real than many things in your own world. There's a likeness in the two of us, you know. You've said to me that you've had much of life, but you've missed some great part of it, as I have. I see the longing for that part burning in your eyes. I felt it pulsing in your blood when I touched your temples."

She lifted her hands as if to repeat this act. But before her fingertips could touch his face, he grabbed her wrists, gently but firmly pushing the hands down. "Let's not have that one again."

She looked hurt by his move, eyeing him now with some uncertainty. "You're not . . . angry with me?"

"Angry?" he said sardonically. "You stow away on my plane. You . . . you knock me out somehow. You sneak in here. Why should I be angry?"

"You invited me," she said defensively, taking up the Scotch bottle and filling her glass to near the rim. "It was you who made the offer, quite of your own free will. I only accepted it."

She lifted the glass and poured back the Scotch, draining most of it in a single draught as Kean stared wonderingly. She set the glass down, smacking her lips in consideration.

"Refreshing," she declared. "Not bad at all, though maybe a bit sharp. You must taste some of our drink sometime. A full-bodied honey-mead, sweet and warm as a fine spring day."

She left the glass and moved away to the window by the bar.

"This is where you were standing when I first came in," she said. She lifted a hand to run across the window's surface. "So smooth and chill. Though not so cold as ice. A mirror is it? But what are all those bands and squares and dots of light that seem to float in its depths?"

"You're looking out a window on the city at night," he explained. "I forgot. You've never seen one."

"If that's what this is," she said raptly, "then a city is far more wondrous even than I had imagined it. So beautiful, so glistening, so pure it seems, like the moon and stars glowing out in the clear night." She turned to him, adding with childlike excitement, "And will you show it to me in daylight too?"

The question recalled him to the realities of the situation. His response was brusque. "I'm not doing anything with you except to figure out how to handle your being here without the feds getting involved."

Her look changed to a puzzled one. "What? I don't understand. I thought you meant to help me."

"Not to violate immigration laws," he said, moving toward his electronics-laden desk. "Uncle Sam's been real touchy about me since that little inside trading thing three years ago."

He reached the desk, flicking on a computerized Rolodex. "A lawyer," he said, punching in a code number. "That's what I need first."

"You can't do that," she said with great dismay. "I came all this way."

"Well, somehow you'll have to just go all the way back," he said. The number came up on the Rolodex screen. His finger descended toward the button that would have the phone dial it.

"But I can't go back," she said, now with despair. "You can't let them get me now!"

He paused, looking toward her.

"Them?" he asked.

"My people. It would be very hard."

He turned away from the desk to face her. "What do you mean? Are you in trouble?"

"I . . ." she paused, considering, then continued, first hesitantly, but gaining conviction as she went. "Well, you could say that I am. Yes. In great trouble. You see, I ran away from them. No one's done that before. It's not something that's allowed."

"You make it sound like you're a prisoner."

She nodded. "It's true. All my life I have been one. I've never been able to do anything or go anywhere outside our own lands. I've never even talked to anyone from the outside—from your own world. You were the first. And you made me your offer. You promised me help. You showed me a chance to escape."

"Escape?" he repeated.

"Yes, to escape. To be free. 'You can't spend your whole life stuck away . . .'" she echoed in a good mimicry of his own voice. "Isn't that what you said to me? And would you betray me now?" A mix of fear and indignation sounded in her voice. "Would you take back your offer and leave me to face their anger all alone?"

"Would they be that hard on you?"

"It's most fierce indeed that their anger would be," she assured. Tears were now welling in her bright eyes. "Bad enough that I left them. Much worse that I'd revealed anything of myself or of them to you." Her shoulders began to shake from the sobs that rose in her, breaking up her words: "Death itself . . . would indeed . . . not be too harsh . . . a punishment . . . for the likes of me."

The crying was too much for him. He stepped up to her, lifting his arms toward her.

Then he hesitated. A frowning, what-the-hell-am-I-getting-into-here look crossed his face. But it was only an instant before the sight of this helpless, frightened girl standing before him with tears glinting on her pale cheeks took total sway over him.

He was drawn in. He moved close to her. His lifting arms continued up, sliding around her.

She let him pull her gently against him as his arms encircled her comfortingly. She rested her head against his shoulder.

"All right," he said soothingly. "Take it easy now. I'm not going to do anything that would get you hurt. I promise."

Her sobbing faded. She lifted her head to look up at him, sniffing back the tears. "Do you mean that?"

"I do. I'm not making any moves until I know exactly what's going on."

"And I can stay here until then?" she asked with a renewed hope.

"Here?" he said, suddenly aware of the ramifications of all this. He released the warm body pressed so close against his and stepped back.

He looked down at his watch. "Hell. Too late to get anything done now." He looked back to her. "Looks like you'll *have* to stay here, at least for the time being. Can't have anyone else knowing about you until I'm sure I'm . . . that is, *we're* in the clear."

She was beaming delightedly once again. "I'm most grateful to you for that, Michael Kean."

"Just call me Michael," he said, assuming a most brisk, businesslike air about the thing. "You can sleep in my bedroom."

"Oh? And what about you?" she asked with a most innocent tone.

"I'll find a spot out here," he said curtly. "Don't worry about that."

"I just don't wish to be any trouble to you."

"You're already plenty of that. Have you got any things?"

"Things?" she repeated.

"Did you bring clothes with you? Pj's? Anything?"

"Just myself."

"It figured," he said. "We'll take care of that tomorrow too. You'll have to fake it tonight." At her puzzled look, he quickly amended, "I mean, I'll find you something you can wear."

"And will you also show me your lovely city tomorrow?" she asked eagerly.

"We'll see," he said guardedly. "Here, come on. I'll show you where things are."

He began to lead her toward the bedroom door, then paused and looked back to her.

"Say, you really are over twenty-one, aren't you?"

"No question of that," she told him. "Why?"

"I just want to be sure I'm not violating the Mann Act or something like that. I don't want anything else happening to make this whole mess worse!"

The vagrant stirred uneasily beneath his makeshift shelter of cardboard.

He pulled tighter into a fetal position, drawing his ragged overcoat around as much exposed body as possible against the chill wind that swept down the alleyway.

A blue-silver light flared suddenly into being not far away. A much sharper gust of wind rose with it, blasting the cardboard cover from the sleeping man.

He sat up, lifting an arm to partly shield his gaze against the brilliant light flooding the alleyway. He blinked his red-rimmed eyes and peered into the glow, his sagging and stubbled face drawing into rigid lines of fear. A dozen yards away, four columns of shimmering light were settling to the worn bricks of the alley floor. They were like small tornadoes formed of flickering lightning strokes drawn into tight coils. Their rapid spinning generated a force of wind that swept up the litter and cast it violently away. The hapless vagrant ducked down as a flurry of paper scraps swirled over his head.

The four columns touched down. At once the vortexes of light that formed them began to dissipate; the speed of their spinning began to slow; and the winds they generated began to die away. But as the glowing cylinders faded, the forms concealed within them came into view. And those forms were no less terrifying to the watching man.

When the lights had gone completely, they revealed four things of man size and shape, but only vaguely so. Their true nature was shrouded by strange hooded gowns of a deep black that seemed to billow about them like thick smoke stirred by a breeze. It made them appear more as wraiths than living beings.

The four masked heads moved as the figures looked around. The sharp glint of four pairs of eyes showed out from the black depths within the hoods, swinging around as their gazes swept the area.

The vagrant cowered farther back into the dark corner where he lay as the eyes swept over him. But he lay against a blank wall at the dead end of the alleyway. The gazes passed above him and went on.

The four figures turned to face the other way. On either side of the narrow corridor, black, windowless walls lifted up like sheer cliffs for some dozen floors. But fifty yards down the alley in that direction, there was a sharp turning, and a brighter light spilled into the darkness from beyond.

The four figures looked to one another and nodded. Then they moved away, their black forms seeming to glide across the ground.

The vagrant watched them turn the corner, passing out of sight. He laid back, breathing in relief. After that he pulled a half-full wine bottle from within his coat and drained it to its last dregs in a single pull.

Beyond the corner, the four ominous forms had passed into an area of both more space and light.

It was still a canyon between the massive buildings rising on either side, but a much wider one here. And far ahead, the way seemed to open into an even larger space.

But there was something else between the four figures and that opening that brought them to a halt. On the outthrusting concrete platform of a loading dock, a group of two dozen figures was gathered under the glow of a security floodlight.

The doors at the back of the dock had been violently forced. The sledgehammers and crowbars that had done the job lay scattered around. Cases of a dozen different kinds of liquor had been carried out from the building's insides and opened up. Those of the group, clearly unconcerned at the threat of apprehension, were brazenly partying at the crime scene, guzzling their loot.

They were all in their teens and twenties, and all in full gang dress—lots of leather and jewelry, lots of bared muscle, lots of elaborately coiffed hair. Their identifying colors —a brilliant red—were proudly displayed in jackets, vests, shirts, scarves, and headbands.

One of the group noted the four newcomers and passed the word to the rest. Their loud talk and laughter died as they all turned toward the dark figures. There was no sign of surprise or fear in their hard young faces at the sight of the strange four. Only challenge.

"Hey, who the fuck you think you are?" asked one muscular young man of long raven hair. He jumped down from the dock and strode boldly toward the interlopers, a whiskey bottle in one hand. "This is a private party."

"We don't wish to fight you," said a low voice from one of the figures as it moved out before the rest. "We only wish to pass."

"Well, you shoulda thoughta that before you were dumb enough to put foot on the Bloods' turf," the young gang-leader answered.

" 'The Bloods'?" the figure repeated. "Is that your clan, then?"

"Clan?" said the youth. "I don't know what you're talking about. Blood's our color, Bloods's our name, and blood's what you're gonna be pumping on the pavement any second, sucker. Now just what the hell are you freaks hiding there? Let's see!"

In answer, the lead figure shrugged its shoulders. The move threw off the enshrouding gown, the strange blackness of it fluttering down in shreds to vanish away.

Even the hardened gang youths had to stare at what was revealed.

It was a tall, lean, and sinewy man who confronted them now. His features were boldly chiseled. Golden hair streamed in rippling bright waves about his face, and his blue-grey eyes flashed out like sun from ice.

Beneath the black garment he was clad in a crimson,

knee-length tunic edged in golden trim. His muscled legs were bare, his feet shod in leather boots strapped about his calves.

Around his shoulders there hung a long, four-folded cloak of rich wool, patterned in a brilliant green-and-yellow plaid. A large golden brooch with an intricate curlicue design of bright enameling fastened it at his throat.

A silver-studded belt about his waist supported a sheathed sword with jewel-studded hilt and silver-banded scabbard. On one arm hung a round shield of black leather banded with a thick iron rim.

"Jeeezus Kee-rist!" another of the youths breathed.

As one, the three other forms shrugged off their own enveloping gowns of black.

Three more men were revealed. One seemed little more than a boy, closer in age to many of those in the facing gang, very slim of form, freckle-faced, and tow-headed. Another was also slim, but very tall, almost gangly, with huge hands and feet, features outsize for his long face, and a red mop of very curly hair. Between them stood a figure most massive indeed, topping all his fellows by nearly a head, bull-like in his breadth. His bulging arms and muscled chest were sheathed in a thick leather vest. Coarse black hair was plaited loosely at his neck.

All three were clad similarly to the first, in tunics, boots, and cloaks. But only the big one was also armed, wearing sword and shield and clutching a short, thick, barb-headed spear as well.

The raven-haired leader of the gang looked unmoved by their rather exotic look.

"Hey, you don't think that Halloween costume shit scares us, do you?" he declared with bravado. He cast the whiskey bottle down, shattering it on the bricks. He gestured to the youths behind him. "Ready, guys?"

The group was suddenly bristling with its own instantly produced weapons. It was a formidable array, including bats, chains, knives, nunchakus, and more than a gun or two.

"Okay," their leader said, a large commando knife flashing into view in his own hand. "Let's take 'em down!"

The whole gang, grinning savagely in anticipation of the coming massacre, advanced on the four men.

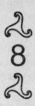

8

The massively built man stepped up beside the other armed one. He lifted his spear while the blond man drew his longsword, the blade leaping from the scabbard in a sweep of light.

The slender blade glowed with a bluish luminescence. But this odd effect slowed the gang members no more than the men's weird appearance had. They stalked ahead, spreading out as they closed in.

Halfway to their goal, one thick-bodied youth gave a shrill battle cry and leapt forward from the rest, charging at the huge warrior with an upraised machete, eager for the glory of drawing the first blood.

The big man stood his ground, unmoving, shield down while the youth approached. His expression was one only of boredom. Then, in an almost casual move, he thrust out with his spear.

The strike was too swift to see, much less to evade. The attacking youth gave a sharp cry as he jerked to a stop, the spear head rammed deep into his chest. The machete dropped from his hand, and he toppled backward, the cruel barbs tearing out of his chest as he pulled free of the spear.

His comrades paused as they reached his body, staring at the bright and gushing blood.

"Youfuckinsonsabitches!" their leader shrieked at the four men, and led his fellows on.

Caught in the battle heat now, all of them followed, voicing savage war cries of their own, flushed by rage and a thirst for revenge.

As they swarmed in, the two warriors struck out. The sword of the blond one drew broad arcs of light, back and forth, as he scythed through them. It flared brighter as it struck and slashed through weapons, sizzled as it swept through flesh and bone.

So fast did the lethal blade move that no enemy could draw close enough to strike. The gang leader himself took a deep cut across a shoulder as he angled in to make a blow, dropping his knife and staggering back. His fellows fell all around him like chopped trees.

Beside the blond man, the giant one was holding his own lot at bay, thrusting with great vigor and accuracy, knocking away counterblows with his shield as if he were swatting flies. The drum and clang of combat echoed in the alleyway.

A few of the youths gave up on the battling pair. They moved around and past them, going in at their unarmed companions.

Three of the gang charged at the small, seemingly most defenseless one. But as they neared, his form grew suddenly hazy with a silver light. In an instant he was enveloped, and his shadow began to alter within the glowing cocoon. In an instant more the shadow had swelled upward, the surrounding shroud of light shredding away to reveal a ghastly form that towered three stories high.

The youths stared up in terror at a scaled beast with taloned claws and lion's head. It glared upon them with red and baleful eye. It bared sharp, saliva-dripping teeth.

They turned and ran.

Meanwhile, those who were attacking the gangly, red-haired man were faring no better. As they approached, he lifted both hands high above his head.

Seemingly in response, the security light on the loading dock suddenly dimmed as if its power were being sucked away. At the same time, for half a mile around the spot, lights flickered and momentarily paled. A watchman in the nearest Consolidated Edison substation saw a monitoring dial's needle dip drastically, then pop back up to its normal place. He shrugged and went on reading his *Field and Stream*.

Meantime, the drawn-off energy appeared to have coalesced in the ruddy-haired man's hands, forming a blazing ball. He hurled this down to smash before the astonished gang lads' feet. Its power crackled up across their bodies in twining tendrils of blue fire. The youths staggered back, scorched and twitching from the shock, then turned tail and took flight.

The rest of the gang, already half-decimated by the brief but ferocious fight, had had enough too. Most of the remaining members still capable of walking began a hasty retreat, their erstwhile leader at the fore. But a foolhardy young man, finally seeing a clear shot, lifted his large automatic pistol toward the blond warrior as he advanced.

The youth fired, the explosion of his gun near deafening in the confined space. His nervous aim was wide, the bullet just clipping the iron edge of the warrior's shield and zinging harmlessly away.

Before he could fire again, the blond one struck back. One sweep of the blade took off his forearm, sending it and the gun flying away in a spray of blood. He had not even the time to react to his pain, for a return blow took his head.

The rest of the gang was by now in full rout, pouring out of the alley into the street beyond.

A police car just happened to be cruising by. Its two officers observed the band of youths erupting in panic from the alley mouth and scattering away. They looked at one another, shrugged, and kept their car rolling on.

In their mad flight the gang members had abandoned their downed comrades. Half a dozen lay sprawled in grisly attitudes of death. Three more, alive but too badly hurt to move, lay moaning on the filthy bricks. Their spilled hot blood steamed up from the cool stones into the night.

The blond warrior stooped to wipe his blood-smeared sword on the coat of a fallen one and returned it to his scabbard.

"Poor sorts of warriors they have here," he commented emotionlessly. "Hardly worth a fight."

"And puny as well," the big one said in a rumbling voice. He prodded another corpse with a foot. "You suppose mortals have been growing smaller all these years? That there are no real fighting men left?"

"A sad world it would be then," said the other. "No challenges. No chance for glory."

"Some of their speech is surely strange," the big man said musingly. "I wonder, now, just what a 'fokinsunsabeeches' is?"

The towering creature had by this time metamorphosized back into the small man's form. He moved forward, taking up a fallen aluminum baseball bat to examine curiously.

"They also have strange weapons," he put in. "But not so deadly as our own."

"Here's one that is," said the gangly, red-haired man, pulling the revolver from the severed hand by its barrel and holding it up. "This seemed to have a power not unlike mine." He looked to the blond one. "And that . . . that bolt it shot out could well have caused you grave damage, my friend."

The giant warrior took the gun from him, examining it curiously.

"I wonder how it works?" he said, prodding at its parts with a thick finger.

"Careful," the gangly one warned.

Too late. The gun fired again, its slug striking a wall and ricocheting away. The startled man dropped it clattering to the bricks.

"Best leave it alone now," the gangly one advised. "I hope we'll not be facing many more of those."

"If we do," said the blond one, "it'll be for your magic to shield us."

"If it can," the other replied soberly.

"We've a greater problem to be considering now," the blond man told his friends. "Look at this place we've come to. As we dropped down toward it, I saw below what seemed an endless city, its bewildering maze of lights and avenues and immense buildings running away to the world's rim in all directions." He looked accusingly to the little one. "I thought the man you'd once met said there was only a village here."

"Well, two hundred years ago perhaps there was," the other replied in a defensive way. "It seems that men may have shrunken, but their towns have grown vast."

"Aye," said the big one, looking up at the walls. "Like a thousand castles grown up around us it seems." He shook his head. "And just how will we find Caitlin Bawn amid all of it?"

"It won't stop me," the blond said stolidly, drawing himself up in a heroic pose. "Nothing will stop my saving Caitlin from her vile captor."

"Yes, yes. Of course," the gangly one agreed. "And we'll help, certainly. There's still the problem of just how to go about it."

There was a clattering noise behind them. They all wheeled. The blond and the giant raised their weapons defensively.

It was only the vagrant. In peering around the corner from his dead end to see what had caused the row, he had upset a trash can. Now, as the men turned toward him, he froze, white-faced in fear.

"Don't kill me, please," he cried, lifting his hands.

"We don't mean to," the blond assured him.

"You killed all them," the man said, pointing toward the cattered bodies.

"They attacked us," the blond warrior explained, and slipped his sword away. "You see? We mean no harm."

"Were these friends of yours?" the gangly one asked.

"Them?" The vagrant laughed harshly. "They were scum. Gang punks. Some of the worst."

Seemingly reassured that he was safe here, the man moved forward, looking over the downed youths. "God-damn Bloods," he said contemptuously. "Drug dealers. Thieves. Murderers. Good riddance to 'em."

"Brigands, were they, then?" the big one asked.

"I ain't sure what that means," the vagrant said, "but they were wors'n animals, I'll say that. Set people like me on fire . . . just for fun!"

He stopped by one corpse, giving it a kick. "This one here, he robbed me just last week. Nearly broke my arm off. Bastard!" He spat on the dead man.

"Then we're pleased we could have done a service for you," the blond told him.

"Yeah. You did a big one. Thanks," the vagrant returned.

He took note of the liquor on the loading dock then. His face lit with his rapture. He made a beeline through the bodies to it and grabbed up an opened vodka bottle, taking a long swig.

"Ah! That's good stuff!" he said with gusto, and belted back some more.

Thus fortified, he turned back to his new acquaintances, fully at ease with them now. He looked them over critically.

"You boys're from outta town, ain't you?" he judged.

"We're from a great distance," the blond man agreed. "We've come here searching for someone. Maybe you could help us. Do you know a man named Michael Kean?"

The vagrant considered, then shook his head. "Nope."

"A great chieftain, he is," the little one added. "Maybe even a king."

"King, eh?" the vagrant said. "Sorry, even that don't help. We got all kindsa kings and chiefs and grand poobahs and every other kind of big-time bullshit like them here."

The blond looked to his fellows. "Then we'll go out and search and ask others until he's found."

The vagrant shook his head again. "I donno, pal. You sure as hell ain't gettin' far that way. Not even in ol' New York."

"What can we do?" the tall, red-haired one asked.

"Look, you did me and mine a favor," the vagrant replied. "I can do one for you. I know a place I can get you some clothes. They won't be much, but just maybe they'll let you get by."

It was four most strange figures who made their way along the city streets.

All wore long, baggy, and very filthy overcoats that had seen a great deal of wear. On two the fit was almost passable. On one the coat flapped around the small figure like a tent. On another, the garment was stretched tight over a bulging form. The blond and redhead wore old fedoras pulled down over their long hair. The giant and the little one disguised their heads with ragged stocking caps.

The bare legs of the four were covered now by threadbare trousers. The weapons that the two fighting men bore were concealed beneath the coats, though not without creating obvious and very odd bulges. The shields, too big to hide, were being carried in plain view.

A strange sight they certainly were, but—thanks to the vagrant's help—now not strange enough to draw stares or even extra glances from what others they passed by on their way.

Not that there were many of these. It was into the early hours of dawn now, and the streets they traveled were relatively deserted.

They stared around them continuously as they went. Street after street of soaring buildings opened up before them, all looking much the same.

"That man's directions into the city's heart aren't of much help," the giant one said, looking up a sheer wall of glass looming above them. "We've turned corners so often, I've no way of knowing if we're going right."

"And the strange symbols on these signposts mean

nothing to me at all," said the gangly one, peering at a street sign.

"The stars might have been a guide to us," said the blond, lifting his gaze to the narrow, dead-black strip of sky visible above, "but there're none of them to be seen." He looked to his friends. "Well, the rising sun will show us a direction, anyway. Meantime, we keep looking as best we can."

"A thousand years of looking might not discover anything in a place so vast," the red-haired one grumbled. "Searching every vale and hill and forest in all Eire wasn't so daunting a task."

"Then we'll take two thousand years," the blond said determinedly. "Three. Four. Forever! But we'll succeed! Come on."

"It may not be we'll have so long," the little one put in. "With the rising sun, won't the inhabitants of these huge palaces pour out to swarm these streets? Will these pitiful disguises that we wear protect us then? Or will the mortals call us enemies and fall upon us?"

"Yes, my oldest friend," the big man said grimly, putting a hand on the blond one's shoulder, "consider this. It's great dangers we've faced and survived in the past. You and I have fought back-to-back against the strongest warriors and fiercest beasts that mortal and immortal worlds alike could throw against us. But have we now come into a time and a place where what we are and know and do means nothing anymore?" He cast his gaze up and around at the hulking structures hemming them in, at the glowing lights and flashing signs and signals, at the strange metal vehicles parked or rolling in the streets. "I tell you truly," he said in a slow, strained voice most unnatural to him, "for the first time in all the years I've lived, I feel afraid!"

"I feel fear too," the blond one said. "I know what a dangerous and impossible task we face. But I have to go on. You know what this means to me."

The big man nodded. "Yes, of course I do. And if you mean to go on, I'll go too."

"And I," said the little man.

"And I," added the gangly one.

"We should be moving then," said the blond. "We're attracting notice."

He indicated a rather stocky woman in an exotic and unpleasantly revealing outfit who had stopped on the street nearby to eye them suspiciously.

"Hey, what are you?" she called out. "Fuckin' perverts?"

The four exchanged glances, then turned and headed away at a brisk pace. They left her to stare after them, shaking her head and muttering, "Christ, they're going in teams now!"

"More of that strange speech," the big man said. "I'd like to find out what it means."

"Perhaps you wouldn't," the blond replied.

"Is that one of their females, then?" the gangly man said, glancing back at her and grimacing with distaste. "It seems that comeliness has left these people along with their strength."

"And their modesty as well," the little one said. "A fine, full gown would have done that one some good."

The four continued on, wending their way through the seemingly endless canyons of the city, seeking some clue to the whereabouts of their quarry without success, until . . .

. . . the blond man suddenly brought his comrades to a halt with a lifted arm.

"Look there!" he said in an excited voice, pointing ahead. "See that tower!"

All looked toward where the square spire of a glowing white building lifted high up from beyond a line of lower structures. Their gazes traveled up its smooth sides of glass and marble to a roof where four corner turrets thrust yet farther up into the night like gigantic spears.

"What about it?" the big man said.

"I know it," the blond said.

He thrust a hand beneath his overcoat, searched around

within, then drew something out. He held it up for the others to see.

It was a patch torn from the pocket of the surveyor at Kean's Irish worksite. It depicted a stylized version of a four-spired castle logo.

A light of triumph lit the blond warrior's eyes.

"You've made your mistake this time, Michael Kean," he growled.

His eyes lifted from the patch. He looked away, up across the rooftops to where that same four-spired castle, but the real one this time, loomed up starkly and ominously against the sky.

"Kean's own tower," he said. "*Now* I have you."

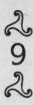

9

Morning-bronzed sunlight streamed in through the eastern windows of Kean's penthouse palace, flooding the interior with a warm and ruddy glow.

The relentless shower of cheery light was clearly too much for a hungover Bill McBride. He sat hunched defensively on a stool at the kitchen's eating bar, a cup of steaming coffee before him. His soft face was drawn into frowning lines by a tight squint as he watched his boss busily making pancakes.

"I just cannot see how this girl could sneak over here on the jet," Mac said in a voice still thick with a too-early rising.

"I can't say how she did it, but she did it," Kean responded, a spatula in one hand expertly flipping a cake up from the Jenn-Air's griddle to flop onto a plate held in the other.

McBride noted the easy move and shook his head. "Do you know how weird it is seeing you do something for yourself again? Don't you have cooks or maids or valets for that?"

"I gave 'em all a day off," Kean said, flipping another done pancake onto the plate. "Nobody's coming up here today."

"Michael Kean . . . homemaker!" McBride said sardonically. "Boy, this girl really has affected you."

Kean flipped a final cake onto his stack. He fetched a

syrup jug and sat down at the bar across from the other man. Mac watched as he poured a golden syrup stream across the high stack and shuddered in revulsion.

"Sure you don't want some?" Kean asked him as he dug in with a fork.

"I can barely stand to smell them," McBride said, looking away and sipping at his coffee. "Look, Mike, aren't you afraid that somebody's still going to find out about this? I mean, there are laws . . ."

Kean cut in. "I thought about the laws too. Then I decided I don't care about them. It's her, Mac. It's just what's best for her. She's in trouble and she needs help."

"So, when's that ever had an effect on you? Unless there was money in it, I mean."

Surprisingly, Kean didn't strike back at this sharp jab. Instead, he looked around toward the door to his bedroom. A warm and very wistful smile played across his face.

"Maybe you're right, Mac," he actually agreed. "Something's different this time. There's just . . . something about her."

Jolted by the strange tone in his boss's voice, McBride wheeled on the stool to look back at him. He stared at Kean's mooning expression searchingly. Then he shrugged in acceptance.

"Okay, so she touched a heartstring you forgot you had. So you took in a stray. So, what am I doing here?"

Kean looked to him, meeting his gaze. "You're the only one I can trust with this, Mac," he said earnestly. "The rest'll think I'm pulling some kind of scam, or that I've just gone crazy."

"Hey, I'm not sure that I think any different," Mac cautioned.

"But you'll still help me, won't you?" Kean pressed. "You're still my friend. You may not like me sometimes, but you won't betray me. Anybody else, they might use this somehow."

"What, you don't trust your eager buddy boy, Lance?" McBride said sarcastically.

"Least of all. The things that make him a top assistant— the drive, the cunning, the ruthlessness—also make him the most dangerous."

"Takes one to hire one," Mac pointed out.

"Look, you wanna cut the cheap shots?" Kean said, some of his old testiness resurfacing. "Now, are you going to help me or not?"

"Just let me think about it," Mac hedged. "This whole thing's too far out. Just let me get my head back first. It's still bouncing on the ceiling." He sipped the coffee, then looked at it in distaste. "And this damn coffee's no help at all."

He set down the cup, climbed from his stool, and headed for the bar with all the booze.

"I need someone to check her out," Kean called after him. "Very, very discreetly. Not through any of the company channels. Nobody should trace anything to me or have the slightest clue she's here. And *especially* our press pals can't know."

" 'Tycoon Hides Beautiful Illegal Alien in Penthouse,' " Mac quoted the fictional tabloid headline as he moved behind the bar. "Okay. You said that she's in trouble. So what kind?"

"I don't know exactly," Kean said.

Mac fetched a glass and got ice. "Yeah? How come?"

"She hasn't said too much. I haven't really pushed it. I think she's pretty scared. All I know for sure is that it's her family."

This lifted McBride's eyebrows. "What, are you talking about abuse?"

"I don't know. She only said they kept her hidden away, like a prisoner. She was really afraid of them finding her again. She doesn't seem like a victim. I mean, there're no marks on her, and she's so cheerful . . ." Kean shook his head. "Still, I suppose it could be. You know the old stories about backwoods types, cut off from the normal world.

And, believe me, *nobody* could be more cut off than this girl's bunch. Hell, anything could be going on."

"I suppose it could," Mac said darkly. "These days it's easier to believe the worst than the best." He took up his gin bottle from the night before, still sitting on the bar. "Thanks for leaving this out."

"That's why it's especially tricky," Kean went on. "If I'm going to help her, I can't make a move 'til I have something really concrete. Otherwise, the Powers That Be will just ship her back home."

"Not to mention tossing you in the slammer for abetting."

"I said I didn't care about that," Kean said sharply. "Right now she's safe. I don't care what I have to do to make sure she stays that way. Are you going to help me?"

"Goddamn. This woman really does have you under a spell, doesn't she?"

Before Kean could reply, he was interrupted by a buzz on the intercom. He went to his desk and answered it.

"Yeah? What's up?"

"Security, Mr. Kean," said a voice. "We've got a delivery man here. He says he has stuff for you. A lot of stuff."

"Right," Kean replied. "Have it brought up."

There was a pause, and then the voice said hesitantly, "Ah, Mr. Kean, are you sure? I mean, this stuff . . ."

"What about it?"

"Well, it's . . . ah . . . all women's clothes."

"That's not your problem, pal," Kean said brusquely. "Send it up."

"What's that about?" asked McBride.

"Just a few things I ordered. For her."

"For her, huh?" the other said expressionlessly, unscrewing his gin bottle's cap.

"Yeah. Well, she didn't bring anything to wear," Kean explained.

"Gee, that must have been entertaining," Mac said dryly, pouring out a glassful of gin.

"I mean, she had clothes. Some dress kinda thing.

Looked like my great-grandmother's. Poor kid's probably never had a chance to get anything new. So I ordered." He eyed Mac challengingly. "So what's wrong with that?"

"Nothing at all," Mac assured him, taking a pull on his glass. "It's just fine."

"I know what you're thinking, pal," Kean accused. "Just knock it off. And why don't you try knocking off guzzling the gin too? I want you sober if you're gonna help me."

"I haven't said I would yet," McBride reminded him with a smile, and took another drink.

With a faint ding the elevator arrived, its door sliding open to reveal a uniformed security guard. He peered into the room hesitantly, then wheeled out a big cart loaded with several scores of boxes.

"Here it is, sir," the guard said to Kean. "Where do you want it?"

"Leave it there," said Kean. "I'll take care of it."

"You will, sir?" the guard said with surprise. "But . . ."

"I said leave it," Kean said sharply. "And thanks."

The guard retreated. The elevator went down. Kean moved to the loaded cart to check the boxes. An impressed McBride watched him from the bar.

"Did you say 'a few things'?" McBride said. "She must be some impressive piece. I haven't seen you spend like this since you got involved with that bimbo who called herself an actress. And she had a set of assets like I . . ."

"This is nothing like that," Kean said irritably. "She's not like any woman I've ever known. She's not like any I thought I'd ever find. It's like she's . . . well, she's from a different world."

Once more Mac stared at his obviously rapt friend with incredulity.

"I have just *got* to meet this little charmer," he said sincerely. "Just when's she making an entrance anyway?"

"I was letting her sleep in," said Kean. "I think she was pretty tired." He checked his watch. "But it is late. I guess she should be up by now. Maybe I should peek in on her."

"Yeah, maybe you should do that," said McBride.

Kean went to his bedroom door and eased it open. He peeked through. The room seemed empty, quiet.

Mac peeked into the room past him.

"You are sure she's in there," he said. "Remember last time."

Kean looked around to him. "You don't think this was just another dream?"

"Even if it's not, she did disappear once before," Mac pointed out.

A frown of doubt crossed the other's face. "She's got to be here," he said.

As the bed faced the big window, its broad headboard blocked them from seeing if she was there. Kean moved through the doorway, stealing softly forward. Then he realized that Mac was stealing in right behind.

"Just keeping you honest," Mac whispered to Kean.

They crept up to the headboard. They paused. They listened. There was no sound. Kean exchanged a look with McBride, then cautiously leaned forward to peer around the edge. His face was tensed in expectation of an empty bed.

But she was there, and awake too.

She sat upright, staring ahead of her at the scene spreading out so far, so spectacularly beyond the big window. She seemed frozen there, captivated by a mix of awe and apprehension that shone clearly in her open face.

McBride peered around past Kean at the girl, and his own face expressed wonder at the sight of her.

"Caitlin," Kean said softly.

She gave a little start and her head jerked around toward him. Then she gave an embarrassed little laugh.

"Oh! Sorry. You gave me a turn. I was so caught up in staring out there." She looked back to the window. "It's the first thing I saw when I awoke. I never imagined what it was like out there last night. It's so beautiful, but so frightening as well. Are we really so high up as it seems?"

"Over a hundred stories," Kean said.

"It made me feel a bit giddy," she explained, "as if I

were going to fall." She looked back to him. "But I feel quite safe now, with you here." And she beamed so brightly at him that her whole face seemed to light with it.

Then she took note of McBride. "And who's this, may I ask?"

"It's my . . . my friend," Kean replied. "Bill Mc-Bride."

Her warm smile took him in too. "Well, friend of Michael, I'm most glad to meet you."

"Just *seeing* you's a real treat for me," Mac said, and there was no hint of facetiousness in his tone.

"But the day must be well along now," she said. "And I've no wish to be missing any moment of it."

She threw back the bed covers, revealing that she still wore the long, shiftlike gown.

"Did you sleep in that?" Kean asked.

"Well, I tried that shirt and the trousers of the fine silken cloth that you gave me," she said, and pointed to the pair of Kean's Chinese-print pajamas draped on a nearby chair. "And very good to the touch they were, but very awkward in the wearing, always twisting about me and sort of wriggling up in the most uncomfortable way. So I went back to sleeping in my own, having none else."

"Not anymore," Kean said. "You just wait here."

He started away, then paused and looked to Mac. "You stay here too, huh? Keep an eye on her?"

"Gotcha, boss," Mac said.

Kean headed out of the room. Mac looked back to the woman as she climbed from the bed and stretched her lithe body in a graceful move. He watched her closely, scrutinizingly, and a little warily as she moved to the window, barefooted, and stared straight down. Her fear of the height seemed to have vanished now.

"You've never really been up so high?" he asked her.

"I've never been more than a hillock's height above the rest of the world," she said.

"And you've never seen a city? Any city? Or anything else outside your little piece of Ireland?"

She looked around to him. "Michael told you that, did he? Well, it's the truth. There're rules in my world, you know. Very strict rules."

"Doesn't sound like much fun."

"They're meant to keep us safe," she told him, "or so they say." She looked back to the scene below and added wonderingly, "But to keep us from knowing about such things as these now seems most cruel to me."

"Downright illegal, I'd say," McBride said.

She turned to him again. "And what about you . . . Bill McBride, was it?"

"You can call me just Mac."

"But 'McBride,' " she said, intrigued. "That's a name of a kind I surely know. Is it of Ireland you are?"

"Not me. That goes back to granddad's time."

"Ah. And have you gone back to visit your clansmen there since?"

McBride smiled. "I don't have any idea where my 'clansmen' would be now, if there were any still alive. My family stopped being Irish a long time ago."

"Ah, you never can stop being Irish, so long's the blood's in you," she said. She went toward him, moving so lightly across the floor she seemed almost to glide. She stopped before him, staring into his eyes. "And it is strong within you, Bill McBride. That I can see. A hundred years or ten thousand, and there's still its hold on you. That binds us in a way."

"There is something," he said, transfixed, staring back into the lustrous depth of her eyes as if there were some image there. The words came from him as if tugged forth by a power he couldn't stop. "My grandmother . . . I remember her. Yeah. She told me how it was. The green hills. The flowered fields. The sounds of harps and pipes. The scent of sea and sod and growing things in the winds. She pined after those things to her dying day. I can hear her voice now. It was . . . it was like yours."

Kean reentered the bedroom, breaking the spell. She

turned from McBride toward him. The pudgy man blinked and recovered, as if wakened from a reverie.

Arms laden with boxes, Kean moved to the bed. He dumped the load of them down and began opening one.

"A lot of these are the same thing in different sizes," he explained, pulling a dress out. "I wasn't sure exactly what size you were, so I had 'em send a range."

As he brought the deep blue garment into view, she gasped and swooped in, taking it from him.

"It's most lovely," she said, holding it up. "I've never seen a cloth with such rich texture or bright hue."

"I went for colors I thought would look okay on you," he said, a bit uncomfortably. "I'm no expert about that, but I hope there's something you'll like. The choice is up to you." He indicated some boxes. "There's shoes in those." He waved at some smaller packages. "Those have all the . . . the other stuff. Pick what you want."

"You're far too generous to the likes of me," she told him.

"Hey, it's no big deal," he said carelessly. "I own the store." He turned to McBride. "Come on, Mac. Let's go outside and leave the lady to this."

As the bedroom door closed behind the two men, Caitlin moved to the bed, looking down curiously at the smaller packages.

"Other . . . 'stuff'?" she said, picking one of them up and opening it.

She pulled out a brassiere, looking at the small garment of lace and straps with a bewildered eye.

"Now, what do you suppose . . . ?" she said.

Outside the room, Kean headed toward his communications desk, where the phone was ringing with persistence.

Kean answered it. "Yeah?"

"Mr. Kean? Is that you?" said a concerned voice. "It's Lance Larson. We hadn't heard anything in the office from you yet, and . . ."

"So you thought you'd bother me here?" Kean finished curtly.

"Well, Mr. Kean, it's nearly ten A.M. You've never not been in here before nine. We thought . . ."

"That I'd died in my sleep or something? No such luck. I just decided to take the day off. That's all."

Lance's voice filled with astonishment. "Day off?"

"I think I can decide to do that if I want. I'm going to stay at home." He tossed McBride a grin. "Got some handyman jobs to do."

"Mr. Kean, you could still have called in to tell us," Lance said, now in a scolding tone.

"You're not my mother, Larson," Kean shot back. "I'm telling you now. And don't you or anyone bother me up here again."

He slammed the receiver down.

In his corporate headquarters office some dozen stories below, Lance hung up his phone too. The young assistant's look was very troubled.

"Stranger and stranger," he muttered. He considered a moment longer, then lifted the phone again.

"Mrs. Hartley," he said briskly, "please get me the chairman of the board."

Up in his boss's penthouse, meantime, Kean was in the process of laying out a safe game plan for Mac.

". . . and I'll give you some names of contacts here and there who'll help you," he was saying, "no questions asked. You check the girl's family out, and that place she came from. We've got to know everything we can—and fast."

"And while I'm out doing this, what will you and she be doing?" McBride asked, returning to the bar and retrieving his drink.

"Well, for one, I'm going to take her out and show her around the town."

McBride nearly choked on his sip of gin. "Are you crazy? You can't go out with her. You said you didn't want anybody to know about her."

"They won't. We'll go in and out the private way. I'll make sure that not even security will know."

"People will see you."

"So? Out there we're just two more fruit flies swarming on the Big Apple. I've spent a lot of money keeping my face off of *Entertainment Tonight.* Nobody'll pay any attention to me."

"What about if you run into somebody you know?"

"Then I'm just me escorting another good-looking young woman around. They won't know I'm hiding her out here."

"It's not safe," Mac persisted.

"I'm taking Stony along as usual. Him I can trust too. And, just for you, we won't even get out of the car. I'll just give her a driving tour. Is *that* okay?"

Mac shook his head, unconvinced. "It still seems like a real stupid idea."

"Well, maybe it does, a little," Kean agreed. "But I made her a promise, Mac, and I've got this feeling . . . this weird feeling like I don't have any choice but keeping it. No matter what, I'm going to go along with her—and I'm going to like it."

Mac looked toward the bedroom door and nodded. "I think I know what you mean. And I haven't felt anything like this since the eighth grade."

"What the hell does that mean?" Kean asked, looking quizzically at his friend.

"I guess it means I'm going to do whatever it takes to help her out," Mac said. He eyed the drink in his hand and then pointedly set it down. "And I guess it means I'm going to do it without this."

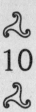

10

At an outside table of a cafe across the street from Kean's soaring building sat three of the oddly garbed figures trying, with only very modest success, to look inconspicuous.

It was the blond man, the gangly one, and the small one who sat crammed in around the little table, nearly full coffee mugs in front of them. Across the street, meantime, the fourth member of their crew paced slowly up and down before the main doors of Kean's castle, eyeing the people going in and out.

"It'll be my turn to take his place soon," the blond one commented.

"Just how long do we have to be doing this?" asked the little man.

"Yes," said the gangly one. "Wouldn't it be better to go in there and seek out where Caitlin is?"

"How can we go into a place so vast as that?" said the blond. "Why, man, without knowing where she is, we could wander about in the place for days, and we'd bring the whole power of that evil one's warriors down upon us surely. And before all that, we don't even know if she's in there."

"How will sitting here tell us?" the little one challenged. "If she's a prisoner, he'll not be letting her come out."

"Maybe not her, but mustn't he come out himself, sooner or later, to go about his own work in the world?"

"Maybe," the gangly one allowed. "But how will we know him at all? We've never seen him."

"Won't a chief so high have a grand host of his court people following him?" the blond countered. "Won't we know him by the immense to-do when he emerges from his great stone dun?"

The other two exchanged a glance and then gave nods of agreement for this logic.

"Then for now, we wait," the blond concluded.

So they took up their vigil again, not aware of the white-jacketed waiter who emerged from inside the cafe behind them. This young man—who by expression was already not much thrilled with his menial lot in life—delivered a hearty breakfast to a portly pair of dark-suited business-men, then stopped to look at the odd and overcoated trio.

His look was a testy one, and growing more testy as he watched them sit, all but immobile, over the unemptied coffee mugs. Finally giving a snort of exasperation, he stalked up to them.

"Can't I get you . . . 'gentlemen' anything else?" he asked tightly.

"No need," the little one said cheerily. "We still have these drinks you brought us."

"Yes. It's a brew rather bitter to the taste," the gangly one added sourly. "Hard to get down. Was it 'coowa-fee' that you called it?"

"Yeah, coffee," the waiter said. "But look, guys, like it or not, you can't sit here nursing one cup all morning. We're busy, the boss's getting mean, and I'm losing tips. So I think you should either order something more, or pay up and move on."

"Pay up?" said the blond.

"Yeah. You guys owe me three bucks." A look of appre-hension filled his face. "Jeez, you can pay that, can't you, guys? Please tell me you can pay."

"Pay?" said the little one. "With what?"

"I knew it," the waiter said angrily. "Damn! I never shoulda let you sit down. But no! I'm a nice guy. I'm a sucker. I'm a—"

"Would this pay for it?" the gangly one said calmly, pulling something from inside his coat and laying it on the table.

The waiter stopped in mid-tirade at seeing the large, glinting disk come into view.

He picked it up. It was a coin of a softly gleaming gold, roughly circular, of silver dollar size, embossed with a picture of a spear-wielding warrior astride a running horse.

The waiter eyed it curiously. "What's this?"

"It's an Armorican stater, I believe," the gangly one said. "You see we're from . . . out of town."

"I guessed something like that. But this isn't a currency exchange. I don't know what this is worth." The waiter turned it back and forth and weighed it in his palm. "Heavy thing, though. What is it, brass?"

"It's gold, of the purest kind," the gangly one said. "From the treasure hoard of High King Brian Boru himself."

An avaricious glint came into the waiter's eyes. He looked again at the coin and again at them. "Let me just check a minute," he said and hustled away inside.

The gangly one looked to his friends and shrugged. Then all three turned gazes back across the street.

Here another potential problem was clearly developing. The big man's pacing before the Kean building's door had caught the eye of a pair of foot-patrolling policemen.

They moved up behind the huge figure as he made a turn. The big man came around to find himself confronted. He stopped cold.

"Could I ask you just what you're doing hanging around here?" the older, thicker of the two officers asked. His younger partner stood just behind him at one side. Though both were a foot shorter than the one they faced, they showed no sign of fear, but their nightsticks were clutched ready in their hands.

"I . . . I'm . . ." the big man said, nonplussed.

"Don't know, eh?" the officer pressed. He pointed at the shield. "And what's that you're carrying. A trash can lid?" He peered closer at the thick, black, iron-bound circle. "Or, what, didya steal a manhole cover?"

"No . . . it's . . . I'm . . ." the big man stuttered. He cast a desperate gaze across to his fellows, as if asking what to do.

"Just what're you dressed for here?" the officer said. His suspicions now fully aroused, he looked up and down the huge form more carefully. His eyes stopped at the tip end of the man's sheathed sword, sticking out a half foot below the frayed hem of the overcoat.

Instantly he stepped back, putting a hand to his gun.

"I'm going to ask you to please show me what you've got under there," he said in a hard, slow voice. "And do it very, very carefully."

The big man looked back to his comrades, now standing at the table to watch. He was clearly stymied by uncertainty as to what to do.

The older officer took the hesitation as a sign of possible hostility. He decided to take no chances.

"Dan," he said to his partner, "call for backup."

And as the younger officer took hold of the microphone of his mobile radio, the older began to draw his gun.

The full potential for a problem was quickly realized.

With his sword bound away beneath the tightly drawn coat, the big man had few choices of response. He seized upon the simplest, swinging out with his shield.

The heavy circle slapped across the older policeman's side, the blow's force casting him sideways to collide with his fellow. As the two were slammed down hard to the pavement, the big man turned and ran.

If the three watching from across the street expected a panic to ensue among the passersby, they were surprised. When the two officers thudded down and lay there, stunned, most pedestrians kept moving on by, looking away, picking up their pace a bit to get clear of the scene. Only one man went to the officers' aide. And no one at all tried to interfere with the departing perpetrator.

"Come on," said the blond man, and the three abandoned their table, heading off in pursuit of their fleeing comrade.

They didn't heed the call of the young waiter, who had reemerged from within the cafe, his manager at his side.

"Hey, you!" the waiter cried after them. "Your coin!"

"Christ, where're they going?" the manager said. He held up the gold coin. "This thing's gotta be worth a couple hundred at least. Don't they want change?"

The waiter snatched it back out of his grip. "We'll just call it a tip, okay?" he said with a grin.

Meantime, the big man had reached the corner of Kean's building and had turned it, vanishing from sight. Behind him, the two policemen were just getting to their feet, seeming unhurt, but looking around them in bewilderment. Their assailant had vanished.

Seeing that no pursuit from the law seemed imminent, the three others turned the corner after their friend.

They moved into an alleyway between the skyscrapers that was not much wider than two cars. The big man was nowhere in sight.

The three walked forward slowly, looking around them for some sign of him. Halfway along the alley a ramp sloped downward to vanish into a shadowed cavern beneath Kean's building. As they moved past it, a voice came up from the darkness below.

"Hello there. I'm down here."

They stopped and peered down the ramp. The big man moved out of the shadows below into sight.

"Is it safe?" he asked.

"It seems to be, for now," the blond said.

"I came down here to hide," he said, walking up the ramp to them. "It's some kind of man-made tunnel. But there's a door of metal at its end. I felt trapped there. I was certain they'd catch me." He shook his great head. "I hated that, more than anything in my life. To have to run! To hide!"

"I'm sorry for that," said the blond, putting a hand to his friend's shoulder. "Still, your running was the best choice. We can't be battling the full might of this city's fighting men." He gave a little smile. "Even you and I would lose."

"We also can't stay about here," the gangly one pointed out, looking apprehensively back toward the alley's mouth. "They may yet organize some pursuit."

"But to go where?" the little one said. "There'll be no more hanging about out there at the front. What can we do now?"

As if his words were triggering a response, there came a clattering sound from below. Startled, they all looked down the ramp.

"It's that metal door," the big man said. "It's opening!"

And as they watched, the long hood of a vehicle poked out into view.

"Hide!" said the blond, and the four scrambled to take shelter behind a trash dumpster parked on the far side of the alleyway.

They were just out of sight as a nondescript blue car rolled up the ramp and into the alleyway. The four peered back out toward it as it went past, eyes wide in their surprise.

"By Good Danu, look there!" the gangly one breathed. "The fates are with us yet!"

For through a window, Caitlin Bawn could be seen in the car's back seat.

The blue car had pulled up at a curb.

The disguised four, looking more than a bit out of breath, peered out at it from the cover of a truck parked a half block away.

"Thank the powers they've stopped," the little one gasped out. "I don't think I could've followed much longer."

"Are you in such poor shape as that?" the big one asked.

"And aren't my legs half as long as your own, you great elk?" the other shot back. "I've been running twice as fast."

"I think the press of all those other metal chariots on the roads has saved us," the blond said. "At times we can walk faster than they can roll."

"Our luck's holding, but only so far," said the gangly one morosely. "They've ridden about through half of this city already. How much more will there be?"

"Something's happening," the blond one said.

The driver's door had opened. The four men watched expectantly as the figure of Jack "Stone Man" Starski emerged.

"Well now!" said the big one, impressed. "So not all the men of this time are shrunken, then. The Dagda himself would find that one a fair match."

"Could that be him?" said the little one. "Could that be this Chieftain Kean?"

Starski moved around to the rear door and opened it. Out stepped Caitlin, to stand looking about her with a smile.

"It is her, surely," said the blond.

"What's that she's wearing?" said the gangly one. For she was clad in a pert, modern, bright green dress that barely reached her knees. "Shocking it is. It must have been forced on her."

"Yet she doesn't seem unhappy," put in the little one.

"And I see no chains," added the big.

Michael Kean emerged right after her. The two stood talking, apparently quite pleasantly, while he pointed around them at various buildings. Starski stood deferentially at one side.

"*That* must be the one," said the blond, his jaw tightening. He unbuttoned his overcoat. "Well, I'll go see to the villainous beast right now."

But as his fist closed upon his sword's hilt, the staying hand of the gangly one fell upon it.

"Hold on, now, my lad. You can't just charge out there."

"And why not? She's all but alone with him."

"Aye. That one other man's no threat," the big one added confidently.

"How can both of you be so sure?" the gangly one countered. "Doesn't it seem to you a bit too easy? Would such a man of power and ruthlessness be such a fool? I don't think so."

The blond one looked around. "You think he has more protection?"

"I think we can't know if a thousand warriors might descend from everywhere were you to show yourself. I think we can't know if he has magic forces at his beck and call. Remember that strange weapon from before? There are too many things here we don't understand."

"You're right, of course," said the blond, buttoning the sword back out of sight. "It would be foolish to act without knowing more. But how do we get more?"

"They're off again," said the little one.

Kean and Caitlin were moving away from the car along the sidewalk. Starski fell in a dozen paces behind, gazing constantly around him warily.

"At least they're on foot," said the blond. "Let's follow."

The four moved out, staying well back in their quarry's wake. Kean led his companions up the sidewalk along a wall of stone. When they reached an opening, they turned to pass through the wall and out of sight.

The following men moved more cautiously as they reached the opening. On guard they passed through it. Beyond lay a path through a screen of trees. They crept forward along the path, ready to leap for cover should they see the others stopped ahead. But soon they reached the end of the narrow band of woods.

A large, open area lay before them. A great patch of countryside it seemed, lifted from there and dropped here amid the buildings that soared up on every side. Green meadows stretched away, dotted with gardens and shrubs and stands of trees. Down a slope ahead, the blue-silver glimmer of a lake could be seen.

They stopped behind the cover of the last trees to peer out at the green space.

"Wonder of wonders," the little one said. "It's like a bit of home."

"Likely stolen and imprisoned here," the blond said harshly. "Like poor Caitlin."

Caitlin and Kean were, at this point, about a hundred yards ahead, strolling a path down toward the lake, Starski still guard-dogging from behind.

"Shall we keep after them?" asked the little one.

"It may be a bit too risky here," said the giant. "The four of us, going out in the open. I say we'd be noticed for sure."

"I've got to talk to her somehow," the blond said, frustrated. "It may be I can find out something of what's going on that way. There may not be a better chance to get to her."

"I have a way," said the gangly one. "It'll mean your having to go out there alone."

"Tell me."

The gangly one reached inside his clothes and drew out a tear-shaped pendant of crystal hung on a gold chain. He breathed upon it, then rubbed it vigorously between his palms.

The crystal began to glow with a soft, red-gold light. The man held it out to his blond friend.

"Here. Take this. Get as close to her as you dare. If you see your chance to speak to her, slip it on. For a brief time it will make you invisible to all mortal eyes. But keep your own eye on it," he added warningly. "When its light begins to fade away, your concealment will be fading as well."

"I'll remember," said the other, taking the stone. "All right then, you three stay here. Try to find some good concealment in the woods. We've no need for more unpleasant encounters with these people."

His companions moved off into the shelter of the trees. Face set in grimly determined lines, he moved out into the open, after the other three.

Caitlin and her escorts had by now reached the lake and were walking a path that skirted the shore. Kean was still indicating various points of interest in the city around them.

"And over that way is the Metropolitan Museum of Art," he was saying. "I've given them a mil or two over the last few years. I could set up a private tour there."

"Really? What's it like?"

He shrugged. "I've never really gone there myself. But there's a lot of famous art, I guess. It's something you might like."

"All the places you've spoken of would be most exciting to see," she said. "Still, I'm glad you brought me to this place. All those buildings. All that metal and glass and stone. All those people hurrying who knows where. And all that noise! It becomes a bit too much, all at once. This is more like the piece of world I know. It's peaceful and very soothing here."

"Don't come at night," he said. "I wouldn't even be here in daylight if it wasn't for you."

"Are you saying you lead the whole of your life inside?"

"I like the inside, especially if it's my own inside. I build it, I control it. Climate, lights, landscape, the whole shooting match. It's all just the way I want. It's a little tougher to do that with nature. But I'm learning."

They passed a pair seated under a tree—a man and a woman, both looking most ragged and forlorn. Their faces sagged expressionlessly, and there was a blankness in their eyes.

"I've seen a great many like those," she commented. "They seem like those who've been touched by the Fool."

"The Fool?" he repeated.

"Yes. In my Ireland there is a . . . a man. The Fool of the Forth, he's called. He haunts the old places, and his touch will steal your wits. They say there are many who've been touched by him."

"Those bums back there may be 'touched' all right," Kean said, "but it wasn't any ghost who did it to them. Oh, they'll blame everything for being losers but themselves, but it was their own weakness and failure and just god-damn stupidity that put them there."

There was so much sudden venom in his last words that she looked at him strangely.

"You sound as if you hate those poor, miserable people," she said.

"I don't hate them," he said, defensiveness coming into his tone. "I just have complete contempt for anyone who can't make something of himself. What's wrong with that?"

"Not all are as strong as you," she said. "Maybe they need help to change their lives, just as I got from you. Maybe they need support and protection. Maybe they need . . . love."

He looked around to her at that, but she'd turned her face away, hiding the flush that had crept into her pale cheeks.

Just ahead of them several swans glided majestically across the surface, ducking their graceful necks to snap at underwater objects that might be food.

"Swans!" she said with delight. "I never thought to find such creatures here."

"You like swans?" he asked.

"In my land, they're thought to be creatures of great beauty, but of great sadness as well. We've a story of four children of a great man named Lir, much beloved by him, who were changed to swans by a jealous stepmother." Her voice took on a soft, faraway tone. "For hundreds of years they were trapped in the birds' forms, carried about Ireland by the winds from pond to pond. Their father grieved for them and searched for them, refusing to give up. In the end it was love that broke the spell on them. And though they died soon after, they died free."

"Amazing what people will do for love," he commented.

She looked at him. "Oh, yes? What would you do?"

"I'm not sure," he sidestepped, meeting her eyes. "I don't think I've ever really been in love . . . before."

Their gazes locked. Once more a flush came to her cheek, but this time she didn't look away. Instead, their contact was broken by a loud honking from close by.

They looked around to see the swans gliding in toward them, long necks stretched out as if in supplication.

She smiled. "Perhaps they know me," she said, holding out a hand.

One of them gently touched it with a beak.

"More likely they want to be fed," said Kean, indicating a small boy nearby who was throwing them popcorn while a young woman watched him from a bench.

Caitlin turned to Kean eagerly. "Might I feed them too?"

"Sure," he said, smiling at her childlike delight. He glanced around. A popcorn vendor was visible another hundred yards along the lakeshore. "I'll get you some," he said, and indicated another bench close by. "Why don't you wait here?"

He turned and signed to Starski, mouthing the words "watch her." Then he started off toward the stand at a brisk walk.

She sat down on the bench and watched the swans. Thirty feet behind her, Starski stood spread-legged, ready, keeping a lookout.

A figure moved up along the bank, coming into her view. She looked toward it, seeing an odd, worn-seeming person in old overcoat and slouch-brimmed hat. A small object dangling at his chest gave off a ruddy glow. She stared at him curiously.

One of his hands lifted and removed the hat. Her eyes widened and she sucked in a sharp breath.

"Rury O'Mor!" she said in astonishment.

11

The blond man moved toward the astounded young woman.

"Yes, it is me, Caitlin. I've come here to rescue you."

She managed to recover enough of her wits to speak: "H-how did you find me?"

"Ah, it was the help of your mother and the word of some of that villain Kean's own henchmen that told us where you might be. And it was the magic of Owen the ard-druid that swept us across the sea."

"Us?"

"I've come with my best comrades. Besides Owen, I've little Kevan of the shape-shifter's art and great Angus the finest warrior of the Sidhe with me."

"But you can't be here," she said most urgently. "Not in this place. It's far too dangerous."

She looked around. Kean was just reaching the popcorn vendor. Starski was still standing by, looking around constantly, wary but at ease. His gaze passed across the blond-haired man without a flicker of change.

Surprised, she looked back to O'Mor. "That man should see you. He's a guard."

"He can't see me," said Rury, reaching the bench. He indicated the glowing amulet. "This shields me from all mortal eyes. Now, tell me quickly, for there's not much time: how much danger are you in?"

"Danger?" she repeated. "Why, I'm in none."

It was his turn to be surprised. "He's done nothing to threaten you? Then how is it you're his captive?"

"I'm not," she said.

He shook his head. "Then I don't understand this, Caitlin Bawn. Come away with me right now."

She drew herself up and looked directly into his eyes. Her voice was calm and sure. "That I will not."

His eyes met hers searchingly, bewilderment filling them. "What's wrong with you? It sounds like madness you're speaking now."

"There's no madness in it," she replied. "I simply like it here. I will not go."

"You're bewitched then," he told her. "You must be. What power is it that he has over you?"

"None at all. It's my own choice."

"I don't believe that!" he said with force. "How could I?"

"Believe this is a world like I've never seen before," she said. "Like I never knew existed."

"I won't listen to this. It's not you speaking."

"It is. Life is very exciting here. And it's new! Not like the life of eternal sameness I was trapped in back there."

"You couldn't say that if you weren't under his spell," he said with certainty. "He's made you forget how fine a life you had."

He sat beside her, placing a hand upon her arm. His voice filled with a compelling intensity.

"Listen to me now, Caitlin. How can you forget the wonderful country that is ours? Here the people are ugly and small and loud and cruel. In our realms the people are beautiful and without blemish. Their hair is the color of the flag-flower, their fair bodies as white as snow, and the hue of the foxglove is on every cheek. Here the life seems vile and short. There the young never grow old; the fields of crimson flowers are as pleasant to be looking at as the speckled blackbird's eggs; warm sweet streams of mead and wine flow through the countryside. I see misery on every side here, but in our lands there is no care and no sorrow on any person."

"I haven't forgotten those things," she told him.

"Then come back there with me," he pleaded. "Oh, fair lady, come back to our proud people and it's the flesh of pigs newly killed I'll give you for food; it's new milk and mead I'll give you for drink, and it's a crown of red-gold that you'll wear in your glowing hair."

A faint flame of doubt, of regret, of longing flared up in her eyes then. But it flickered out, replaced by a determined blaze.

"I know what you're feeling, Rury," she told him with great force. "I know what you mean for me. But it's freedom I want right now. My spirit's crying out for it. And if it is a true love for me you have, you'd give my desire to me."

"No!" he said stubbornly. "I can't believe it's anything but his voice speaking in you. Freedom? How can living in this terrible place be that? Like a great prison itself this city is, with its buildings like high walls of stone and the streets like narrow, filth-blackened cells trapped in between them. But I will truly free you. Somehow, I'll make him give you up."

"Don't do that, Rury, please," she said. "Go back. There's nothing more to do. He is a most powerful man. You'll only come to harm."

"That fear won't stop me," he said fiercely. "I won't lose you. Not this time."

A pulsing in the light of the amulet brought his gaze down to it. The glow of it, after the warning flare-up, was slowly beginning to fade.

"The time's up for me," he said, "but only for now. I'll come back for you, Caitlin," he vowed. "You mark my words on that. There's no power on this earth that can keep me from you."

He rose from the bench at that, pulled on his hat, and started away from her at a brisk walk. The light of the amulet was fading quickly now, and he got only some dozen paces away before his form began to come back into view, as only a faint ghost at first, but swiftly taking on more solidity with every step.

This transition time was still long enough to conceal him from the shifting gaze of Starski, whose eyes didn't swing to him until he had fully materialized some fifty feet away. But it didn't save him from being observed by Kean, now on the way back from the vendor with a popcorn box in each hand.

From forty yards' distance, he watched the odd figure fading into view as it moved away. His eyes widened in surprise. He picked up his pace to a trot, uncaring of the loose popcorn that bounced out on either side. But by the time he reached Caitlin at the bench, the overcoated figure was a good distance from them.

"Who was that?" he asked her.

"Who was what?" she asked him innocently.

"There was a guy just here." He pointed. "That guy."

She glanced after the departing man, then shrugged. "I don't know. I didn't see him here."

"I did. He was just walking away from you." He looked around to Starski, calling out: "Stony, didn't you just see that guy here?"

He moved toward them, looking puzzled. "No, boss. I didn't see anyone there."

"Jesus Christ, how could you miss him?" Kean said frustratedly. "Weren't you watching her?"

"Well, I wasn't actually looking at her so much as I was checking out the layout around," the big man admitted. "Still, boss, I woulda seen anyone close by. That bum there never got closer than fifty feet."

"Are you kidding?" said Kean. "I swear he was just a few steps away when he . . . when he was . . . ah . . ." He faltered here.

"When he was what, boss?" asked Starski.

Kean, who'd been about to say "fading into view," thought better of it. He shook his head. "Never mind. The sun off the water must be playing tricks on my eyes. He was probably farther away than I thought."

"You want me to go after him, boss?" Starski volunteered. "Check him out?"

"No, that's okay," Kean said, glancing after the man. "Anyway, it's too late. He's gone now."

The overcoated figure had indeed vanished back into the shrubbery by this time. Unnoted by Kean, Caitlin breathed a small sigh of relief.

"Well, anyway," Kean said, trying to bring things back to normal, "I got the popcorn." He held out the two boxes to her, realizing they were now half-empty. "Or what's left of it anyway. Shall we feed the swans?"

"I don't know," she said. "Suddenly I'm feeling rather tired. I think we should just leave."

"Leave now?" he said, taken somewhat aback. "But I was hoping we'd sit here awhile, toss some of this to the birds, talk . . ."

"I know," she said, "and I'm sorry." She got to her feet. "But I am very tired. It's been a day of great excitement for me, don't you know. I really would like to go back to your home now, if you don't mind."

"Oh, well, no," he agreed quickly. "Not if you're tired. Sure. Let's go."

She moved off at once, heading back toward the car. He stared after her, at a loss over her quick mood change. He looked at Starski, to find the man was eyeing him peculiarly.

"Here, have some popcorn," Kean said, thrusting both boxes into the big man's hands. Then he started off after her.

A white, dovelike bird swooped in easy, slow circles above the glass pyramid skylight on the roof of Kean's high tower.

The bird glided down lower over the big window. Its sharply glinting little eyes focused down through the glass panels to the interior of the penthouse below.

Kean was clearly visible there. He was pacing the graveled walks of the little indoor forest right below the skylight. No one else seemed to be with him in the room.

It was beginning to grow dark far down in the city's streets. The sun sinking behind the high cliffs of the buildings brought a premature twilight to the depths of the crisscrossing canyons. Already lights were coming on.

The big superfloods that bathed the walls of Kean's Castle suddenly flashed to life, catching the bird in their beams and making it gleam bright like molten silver. Startled, the bird wheeled sharply away from the blinding light. Once free of the glare, it began a spiral down. It was headed for the narrow avenue beside Kean's building that gave access to his underground garage.

There, behind the same dumpster that had hidden him before, waited the blond warrior named Rury O'Mor. Waiting with him were the gawky, red-haired magician he'd named as Owen and the giant warrior he had called Angus. All three sat silently on empty trash bins, staring broodingly into the gathering shadows.

This lasted until the bird swept down from above and came in for a graceful landing right before them.

A familiar sheath of light encompassed it, swelling quickly larger. The form shrouded in the light swelled too, rising up and taking a manlike shape. In seconds the glow was fading, and the sprightly little man called Kevan was revealed.

"Back finally, eh?" the gangly Owen said testily. "And did you find anything out at all with all your great flapping about?"

"More than you would have, for all your magic power," the little one shot back. He looked to the blond. "His grand throne room is at the very top, Rury, just as you supposed. It's our good fortune there are immense windows up there. I'd have taken a year if I'd had to peek in through each of those thousands of smaller ones below looking for him. But up there I could see nearly all the

inside. This High Chieftain Kean's in there all right, b
life, trodding about."

"And Caitlin?" asked Rury.

Kevan shook his head ruefully. "I don't know about
It's a very big place though. She could surely be the

"Then I say we storm the place," said Angus. "W
right up there and force this man to set her free."

"As we did with Brasal?" said Rury. "We can't do
This man might be a thousand times more powerful, f
we know, and a thousand times more ruthless too. I'l
risk losing her as I . . . as I did before through some
act."

"We could use some trickery," said little Kevan. "
Owen's powers and my own, we might be able to stea
away."

"But there's this spell he seems to have on her," p
Owen. "It's not of a kind I've ever heard of before.
very strong indeed it must be to so control her. Even
were to win her from him, there's no certainty tha
own powers could free her of it. Her body would r
with us to Eire, but her mind might remain forever

Rury looked up at the soaring tower, so arrog
agleam in its bath of light. For some while his face
drawn in the frown of heavy thought. Then he looked
to them again.

"I must talk to him," he said determinedly. "We l
that Brasal was wholly evil, but we know nothing o
man. I must find out. Perhaps, if he has any hono
might face me man-to-man and give me a chance to
her. Perhaps he's a man of reason I might convince
her go. Perhaps I could buy her. Or maybe a threat w
set her free."

"A threat?" said Kevan. "From just the four of us'

"Why not?" said Rury. "If we know almost nothi
him, it may be as true that he knows no more of us. I c
play out a bluff on him."

"Unless under his spell she's told him the truth of
we are and how much we can do here," put in Owe

"I'll have to take the chance," Rury replied. "For all his seeming power, he might be as reluctant to enter an all-out war as we."

"The whole scheme's madness," Owen said bluntly.

"Still, I'm going to try it," Rury said.

"Then we'll go with you," Angus volunteered.

"No," Rury told him. "Thank you, my old friend, but not this time. I won't risk you in this. But I'll be safe. Owen can renew his amulet. If I'm threatened I can vanish and escape. Right, Owen?"

Owen sighed. "I suppose so," he said reluctantly.

"And just how will you get up there?" asked Angus.

"The same way as our little friend," Rury said, smiling and clapping a hand to Kevan's shoulder.

The bell dinged softly, signaling the arrival of Kean's private elevator.

Kean stopped his pacing and turned as the door slid open, allowing Bill McBride to step out.

He looked a bit harried, more than a little fatigued, and much more rumpled than usual. He moved down to the central green space on seeing Kean there and plumped himself down heavily on a bench, breathing exhaustedly.

"Jesus Christ man, don't ever ask me to do anything like that again," he said, pulling out a handkerchief to wipe his sweating face. "I've been in places so clandestine that I felt like I was a goddamn foreign spy."

"Never mind that. Just what did you find out?" Kean demanded.

"Well, I've had her checked out as far as I could," Mac said. "And guess what, me boyo: no record of her at all. No record of a family called the Bawns either. Nothing! Hell, there's no record of anybody living anywhere around the place where you met her except for the family of some old guy named O'Brien who you bought the land from."

"Yeah. Jimmy O'Brien," Kean said thoughtfully. "I met him. Family'd been there for a thousand years he said. And I remember I also asked that Lord Roderick Fitzgerald about a Bawn family at the time. He told me he didn't know of one."

"There you go," said McBride. "Pretty strong evidence she doesn't live there. But, you know, she might have run away from somewhere else before you saw her. She could have come from anyplace in Ireland."

"Okay, then just check out the name nationally. Track down every one in Ireland."

Mac gave a scornful laugh. "Oh, right. That'll be easy. There can't be mor'n a few thousand Bawns scattered all over who knows where. Providing that Bawn is, in fact, her real name. Face it, Michael, you just know way too little about this girl. That whole line she handed you could just be bull."

Kean gave him a sharp look. "Do you really think that?"

Mac considered, sighed, shook his head. "I don't know. That face, those eyes, that voice, can make you believe about anything. But still, you've got to figure—it could be a con. You're a rich, rich guy. There're lots of ways that hooking up with you—"

Kean cut this brusquely off. "No. I don't believe that. She's in some kind of trouble, Mac. I know it. And I think something else happened today. She's been hiding out in the bedroom since we got back. She says she's resting, but . . . I don't know."

"I told you not to take her out," Mac reminded him.

"Yeah, I know. I've been cussing myself out for it all afternoon." He gave a sigh, considered for a time, then spoke again exasperatedly. "Hell, hell! I guess I really can't take more chances here. So tomorrow, Mac, if you can't get anything else . . . well, it looks like we'll have to bring some lawyers in. I'm not selling her out yet, but I'm sure going to protect my ass."

"Yeah, fine. Tomorrow," Mac said wearily. He stood up and stretched. "But right now I'm going to get some rest. Been a long day. Been a lotta years since I worked, or stayed sober, for this long." He started for the elevator, throwing back over a shoulder, "And your other little helpers sure haven't been much help."

"What do you mean?" Kean said, following him.

"Sorry, I forgot you've been playing incommunicado up here in your marble tower. Well, Frank Garvey's on a real rampage. Says you went out unauthorized, violated security. Wants to know why. Stony's stonewalling him. And your faithful boy Lance's been buttonholing me whenever he had a chance, trying to get my opinion on whether you've gone nuts or what. A real tizzy that one's in."

"What'd you say?"

"I just told him you needed a day off to rest. Bad head cold. All that Irish damp. So just sneeze a little when you talk to him, okay?"

"I don't give a damn what that little sycophant thinks," Kean said harshly.

"You'll give one if he gets the whole board riled up over your slacking off," McBride said. They reached the elevator and he pressed the button. The door immediately slid open. "He's been calling every one of the Old Boy Bunch who'll listen, including Mr. Big. You were right, Michael . . . he can't be trusted at all."

"I can take care of him, Mac. You just go on home to bed. But, remember, get those new feelers out for me as soon as you can."

"Right, chief," Mac said, tossing him a mock salute.

He stepped into the elevator, lifted a finger to the button, but then paused, looking back to Kean. His face grew solemn, and his voice turned serious.

"Michael, you just be careful here. I've a feeling, a most terrible feeling, that you're diving headlong into a kind of danger like you've never known before."

On this ominous note he punched the button, and the door slid closed. Kean stood there, staring at it, his own expression a very thoughtful one.

12

The ringing of his phone recalled Kean from his meditative state.

He moved to answer it, speaking curtly.

"I said I wasn't taking any calls."

"It's from the chairman of the financing board, Mr. Kean," said an apologetic woman's voice. "He insisted I put it through."

"Christ," he swore. "Okay. I'll take it."

A male voice came on the line. "Mike boy, is that you?" it asked in gruff, clipped tones.

"Yes, Arnold. It's me."

"Sorry to disturb you there. Had to speak to you. Some damn-fool assistant of yours has all the members in an uproar. What's your problem, Mike?"

"Nothing to worry about, Arnold. Just a cold."

"Still damned unusual for you. Never knew you to miss a day of dealing from a cold. And not even to keep in touch . . ."

"It was a pretty bad one," Kean replied, getting a little testy. "But you're sounding like my teacher. Do I need a note now if I stay at home?"

"Course not. But, damm it, you know how jittery everyone is. Lots riding on this, boy, for all of us."

"Yes, Arnold, I know."

"All that backing," the voice hammered on. "Three billion in loans. Commitments. Guarantees. Touchy negotiations with the Irish government. Five years of planning. And it's all on you now, boy. We've put all our faith in you to pull this off."

"It won't go wrong," Kean promised. "I've got everything in control."

"I hope so." The voice took on a harder edge of threat. "But I'm still warning you to be very careful here. You get enough of these people doubting you, and you'll see a rout of your troops that'll make Iraq's stampede out of Kuwait look like an Easter Sunday stroll. Your name may be on that company, Mike boy, but there're still a helluva lot of other folks who say whether or not you control it. Is that clear?"

This last admonishment pushed Kean's temper over the edge.

"I don't take lectures, *sir*, from anyone!" he said with heat. "Good-bye!" And he hung up the phone with considerable extra force.

"Old son of a bitch," he growled to himself. "Who the hell does he think he is?"

He stomped back toward the parklike central area, but stopped, looking out a window. Beyond it, night had fully fallen now.

He glanced toward a clock. It read 8:10. He looked around to the door of the bedroom, still closed.

He stood considering a moment, then said, "Well, she's got to eat." He headed for the door.

He knocked at it softly. "Caitlin? You all right?" he called.

"Yes," came her voice from beyond. "I'm fine. Come in."

He opened the door and stepped through. She sat in the darkness of the room, on a chair pulled up beside the window. She'd been staring down at the city, but looked around to him as he moved toward her.

"It's dinnertime," he told her. "I thought maybe you'd want some food. I didn't bother you, did I?"

"No," she assured him. "I was just looking out."

He pulled up another chair and sat down beside her in the darkness, looking out too. The city lights had created their abstract, cubistic patterns in the dark below, the frantic winking of a thousand signs and signals and the start-stop streams created by the headlights of a million cars giving evidence of the vast, bustling, and ofttimes desperate energy of modern man that was behind it all.

"It really is fascinating to look at," he said. "I've never paid much attention to it before."

"It's most exciting," she said, "and most beautiful as well . . . from up here. Like some bejeweled wonderland. Like something bright from a fair dream."

"I guess it would seem a lot more that way to you," he said.

"And yet," she went on, "how it seems to be, that's not really the truth of the thing, is it?"

There was an odd, subdued quality to her voice, and he looked closely at her. "What do you mean?"

"I was told that here, in your land, there is great misery, great ugliness, great pain. I wouldn't have believed that last night, looking down upon your city as I am now. But tonight . . . well, I don't know. Going down there with you today, seeing so many poor, so much filth, such great contrasts with the life you lead up here made me wonder."

She turned to face him squarely. "I've no wish to be so hard with you, but this must be said," she announced determinedly. "Among my people, a chieftain who lived so while his people suffered would be called a tyrant."

He stared at her in bemusement for a moment, gazing into those bright eyes challenging him. Then he put out a hand to lay on one of her own, and answered with great earnestness.

"Caitlin, please understand—I'm not their leader. I've got nothing to do with them unless they work for me. You're confusing a company boss with a politician here. See, we live in a democracy. You must know what that is. Everybody's supposed to look out for themselves."

"Then you mean you've no leaders? No kings or chiefs or anything at all?"

"Well, sure we've got leaders," he said, "if you can really call them that. But I don't think they're much more interested in solving the world's problems for it than I am. They're mostly protecting their own ass . . . uh . . . tails."

"But you could still choose to give your help to others, couldn't you?" she said.

"Why should I?" he asked uncompromisingly. "None of them ever did anything for me. I had to take what I got. I had to be tough and strong. If they're not strong enough, why should I give up what I've got for them?"

She put her other hand on top of his. She leaned toward him. A great intensity gleamed in her eyes and poured out in her voice. "Out of kindness. Out of love. Out of the goodness I feel penned up within you. Ah, you've the power to make life a paradise for many others, Michael Kean."

"You make it sound very easy."

"So it is."

"Just give up everything I worked so hard to get."

"And are you happy with all that you have now?"

He considered her thoughtfully once again. He shook his head. "I thought I was. Two days ago I was certain. Then I started wondering. Right after I met you."

She looked flustered by the implication of this. "What is it you're saying to me?"

"I'm saying that you've had an impact on my life. I'm admitting—and it's not an easy thing for me to do—that you've done something to me."

"Something?" she echoed softly, leaning yet closer. "And just what something is that?"

"Something," he said, "that simply mystifies me."

And he leaned forward, pressing his lips to hers.

Without a hesitation she responded. For a long, warm moment she held the kiss with him, but then pulled back. They both looked a bit flushed now.

"It's a lot better when you don't knock me out," he said.

"That's the last thing I would ever wish to do," she said.

"Good," he said, leaning toward her again.

But this time she sat back, pulling her hands away from his.

"You just wait now, Michael Kean," she said in a suddenly prim tone, drawing herself stiffly upright. "It's already much too great a liberty that I've let you take with me."

"Let *me* take!" he said in surprise. "But before you . . ."

"That was in necessity. This is in . . . in something else. Yet, it's barely a day I've known you. Not nearly long enough for any such intimacy. Why it was two hundred years—"

She broke off suddenly.

"Two hundred years?" he repeated in puzzlement. "For what?"

"Never mind that," she said briskly. "Just know that with my people, it's a very long period of proper courtship we go through before there's any kind of . . . of touching being done."

"Just what the heck is it with your people, Caitlin?" he said, frustrated. "All these weird customs. All these old-fashioned rules of theirs. Look, isn't it time you told me some more about them? If you really want me to help you . . ."

Something flashed up past the window suddenly, drawing their attention. They caught a flash of a large, dovelike bird, flaring silver in the light from below, as it swept upward to disappear.

Caitlin gasped in alarm and jumped forward into Kean's arms, throwing her own about him.

"Hey, isn't this unauthorized touching?" he asked in surprise.

But her body trembled. She clearly felt real fear. He hugged her tight.

"It was just a pigeon," he assured her.

"No," she gasped out. "It was more!"

"*Now* what do you mean?" he asked. "Everything you say is so damned cryptic."

"Please, I'm sorry," she said contritely. "Believe me when I say there are good reasons. There are things I . . . well, I just can't tell you. Things you would never believe."

"Has life really been that rough for you?" he asked.

She lifted her head and looked up to him. "Michael, you said to me before that if someone wasn't strong enough to help themselves, you wouldn't give help to them. Well, *I'm* not strong enough for what I wish to do. Will you help me?"

"I told you I wouldn't let anything bad happen to you," he said.

"That might take a great sacrifice. Greater than anything you know. Are you ready to make such a thing for me?"

"I'll do everything I can," he told her. "I promise you. Nobody's going to make you do something you don't want."

She sat up and moved back to her own chair. Her spirits seemed much buoyed. "I couldn't wish to hear better," she said. "I won't be afraid again."

"Okay," he said. "Then what about some food? Come on out and I'll whip something up."

She glanced toward the bedroom door. She looked back to the window. Some of the anxiety resurfaced in her face.

"I think that, for now, I'd like to stay in here. I feel much safer here, in this smaller and more sheltered place."

"Okay," he agreed, "if it makes you feel better. So why don't I get something and bring it in? We can both eat in here. Maybe then we can talk. There are a lot of things I'd like to talk to you about."

"That's fine," she told him. "I'd like that."

"Be right back."

He rose and crossed to the bedroom door. But he

paused there and turned to look back to her. In the darkened room she was only a dim silhouette against the city glow from outside.

"You want me to turn on some light?" he asked.

"No, not yet. I want to keep on gazing out. I want to make as bright a memory of its beauty as I can, so I can remember it forever."

"Oh, sure. Fine," he said, and turned back to the door, but her voice made him pause again.

"Michael, whatever happens, be careful. There are things that even with your power, you might find most challenging."

He turned back. "That's the third warning I've had from someone in a half hour," he said. "And I'll tell you the same thing I told the other two: don't worry. If there's one thing I love, it's a good challenge."

He went out, closing the door behind him, leaving her alone in the dark room. He started across the main room to the kitchen.

"So there you are, Michael Kean," said a man's voice, coming from above.

Startled, he stopped and looked up. At the top of one of the circular staircases that led up to the corner roof turrets, there stood a man. A cloak of green-and-yellow plaid was draped about his shoulders and hung nearly to his feet.

Though taken by surprise, Kean showed no fear. He recovered quickly, snapping back: "How did you get in here?"

"I have ways."

"I'm sure my security people would love to know what they are."

"It wouldn't help them. I've some powers, Kean, that go beyond even yours."

"Is that a fact?" Kean said. "And can I ask just who in the hell you are? Seems fair, since you seem to know me."

"I'm from a land that's far removed from yours, in many ways. My name would mean nothing to you."

"Try me anyway," Kean urged.

"Very well, if you wish it," the man said, starting down the stairs. "Rury O'Mor is my name. I am chieftain of the clan of Mor, son of Mor MacGaible and Ainge, grandson of Gaible O'Dearg, and a great-grandnephew of the High Chieftain Dearg Curoi himself!"

Kean watched the man move down toward him. His wary eye took in the long, loose plait of white-gold hair that hung at the man's back. It observed the gold brocaded red tunic beneath the cloak and noted the fact that the man's sturdy legs were bare.

" 'Darrig Koo-roy' himself, huh?" Kean said, sounding wholly unimpressed. "And a high chieftain, yet. I suppose that's some other traditional Irish nobility thing. Is that why the . . . ah . . . kilt bit?"

O'Mor reached the base of the stairs and stopped there, repeating in puzzlement. " 'Kilt bit'?"

"The short skirt and the tartan plaid," Kean explained, beginning to move, most casually, in the direction of his desk. "Is that your formal visiting costume?"

"These are my clan's colors, if that's what you're meaning. So you do know that I'm of Eire?"

"Hard to miss with that accent."

"Then you must know as well why it is I've come to you."

"Geez, no. I haven't any idea," Kean said, reaching his desk.

"That is surely a lie," said O'Mor, stepping toward him.

"Hold it, pal," Kean said, lifting a hand above a button. "One press on this and a whole army of armed security boys will come rolling in here like oranges. Just stay put."

Mor did so. "I had hoped you were enough a man of honor to face me and have this out alone," he said contemptuously.

"Hey, I've got as much honor as any guy," Kean responded with indignation. "I'm not afraid of you. I've taken care of myself for a long time." His hand moved

away from the button and he turned to face O'Mor hea
on.

"If you had true honor, then you'd not lie to me," t
other said. "Caitlin Bawn is here. I know it. She was se
with you. She was seen coming here. I know that sh
somewhere within this great tower."

"Somewhere, huh?" Kean's gaze shifted for an instant
the walls of his bedroom. Its glass walls were dark. Th
looked solid. Nothing showed beyond. He looked back
O'Mor. "Yeah, well, even if that were true—and I'm
saying it is, understand—what about it?"

"I have come to get her back, either with your will or
necessary, without it."

"That sounds like a threat to me," Kean said, steppi
boldly toward the other man. "I don't take threats fr
anybody. Especially not from just one guy . . . in a sh
skirt."

"It's not one man you'll be facing, Kean, if you wo
deal with me. I've a force of my own as a chiefta
Through my family and friends I've a greater power y
And if need be, I'll raise the whole might of my peo
against you for this great wrong to us."

"You really think you can cause that much trouble
me?" Kean challenged.

"Do *you* really wish to risk going to war with u
O'Mor countered. "Just how much are you willing to lo
Michael Kean, for the sake of this one girl?"

The defiant gazes of the men locked in a hard star
match for several moments, as if their two strong, st
born wills were locked in mortal combat. It was Kean v
broke first.

"Now wait a minute," he said in a more conciliat
tone. "Just take it easy. There is a lot at stake here, for
and for your country. Let's not go completely nuts
screw it up. Like you said, it is just the one girl, after
There's got to be some way to work things out with
bringing in outsiders."

"There is," said O'Mor. "You could simply give her up to me."

"Yeah, yeah. I know. But I guess I'd rather not do that."

"No, I thought you would not," said O'Mor. "Well then, just how brave a man are you? Would you be willing to contend with me for her? Just the two of us. Alone. Face-to-face."

"Contend with you?" said Kean, clearly intrigued by the option. "You mean a contest of some kind?"

"As you'd wish," said O'Mor. "I'm making challenge to you. It would be your choice."

"If I won?" asked Kean.

"If *you* won?" said O'Mor with raised eyebrow, as if this possibility had never occurred to him before. "Why, then, I suppose that Caitlin would have to remain here. There's nothing more I would do against you."

"And if I lost?"

"Then she would return to Eire with me. That would be the end of it."

Kean considered. "Sounds fair. I love a good scrap, with proxies or with fists. And I've won both kinds every time. What do you have in mind?"

"We could fight it out here and now," O'Mor said. He threw his cloak back behind his shoulders, revealing the sheathed sword hanging at his side. "Single combat. Swords, spears, axes, or some weapon of your own. As I said, that choice is yours."

"You go a long way with this tradition crap, don't you?" Kean said, eyeing the sword. "So what if my choice is for something less lethal?"

"If you fear straight combat, I'll not say you can't choose some other, less deadly contest," O'Mor said, but with a touch of scorn. "My people have resolved many a dispute with a game. Chess is used often. It's my own favorite. Do you know that game?"

"Sure. It's a little old-fashioned and a lot too slow for me though." Kean eyed the warrior thoughtfully, shrewdly, calculatingly, like a carnival huckster eyeing a real rube.

"But, you know, you just gave me an idea. You seem to be into that old martial arts stuff, and you say you like a good game. How would you like to try something that's a little of both?"

"Explain."

"I'll do better. I'll show you. Why don't you come with me?"

He turned and headed for the elevator. O'Mor hesitated to follow, looking after him suspiciously.

"Can I trust you?" the warrior asked.

Kean looked back to him. "Hell yes!" he assured. "Believe me, I wouldn't miss a chance like this."

His voice dripped solemn sincerity, and the warrior was too far from him to see the glint of devious light in his eyes.

"Mr. O'Mor," Kean said, "I promise I'm gonna take care of you all by myself."

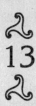

13

The elevator car slipped downward with a soft hum and a faint vibration.

Kean noted O'Mor looking around him with open wonder.

"You like my elevator?"

"Aye. It's a most interesting little room." He peered at the light flicking down through the floor indicators. "But, what exactly is it doing?"

"Let me guess," said Kean. "You've never been in an elevator before."

"El-ev-ay-tur?" O'Mor repeated. "No. That I have not."

At that a superior little smile played across Kean's lips. O'Mor didn't notice it.

A ding sounded and the car came to a stop.

"Well, here we are," Kean announced as the door slid open. "Come on with me."

They stepped out into a broad corridor running away through the center of the building. Doors lined it on either hand. O'Mor looked up it in great surprise.

"Just where are we now?" he demanded suspiciously. "What's happened to your great hall?"

"We're ten stories below the . . . uh . . . 'great hall' now," Kean explained, leading the way out. "The 'little room' here lowered us to it. Follow me.

"This floor and the five below are mostly for R and D, Research and Development, that is," he explained as they moved along. "The wonder boys invent all the technical stuff here."

They strode past doorways labeled Computer Graphics, Robotics, Imaging Systems, and Human Interface Technology.

"These markings haven't a meaning for me," said O'Mor, peering at the doors.

"I had a feeling," said Kean smugly, then added quickly: "I mean, it doesn't matter. Nobody really understands it but the experts. I know I sure don't. But I still love to play with the stuff. That's why I've got this room here. My private playground."

He stopped before a doorway at the end of the hall. He inserted a card into a slot beside it. A small camera fixed above it immediately swiveled down to point its lens at them. A voice came out of nowhere.

"Mr. Kean? That you?"

A startled O'Mor grabbed his sword hilt and stared searchingly around.

"It's okay, Security," Kean assured, looking up at the camera. "Just going in for some recreation."

Far below, in the surveillance office on the street level of the building, a uniformed young security man peered at one of the monitor screens in a bank of dozens. His eyes narrowed as he stared intently, trying to make out the rather oddly garbed figure standing behind his boss.

"Who's that with you?" he asked into his headset microphone. "I've never seen him before."

"He's just a friend of mine. A visitor," Kean replied. "From out of town. *Way* out of town."

"I should check with Mr. Garvey."

"Look, just forget about Garvey. I don't want to be bothered by him tonight. My friend and I are only going to play a game. That's it. Now let us in."

"I don't know, sir. It's regulations . . ."

"I know," Kean said curtly. "I made them. Garvey works for me and so do you! Now let us in there, and make sure that we're left alone. Got it?"

"Yes, sir!" the voice snapped. The door instantly hummed open.

"There," Kean told O'Mor as they passed through, "just like I promised." The door hummed closed. "You and me, alone."

He punched at a panel by the door and the room lights flashed on. They revealed a large space all but crammed with a bewildering plethora of objects. There was a wall of monitor screens, audio and video equipment. Counters were lined with computers of many kinds, and complex electronic toys crowded shelves above. Rows of arcade games shaped like cars, spaceships, fighter planes, and other vehicles made the floor like a crowded—and very eccentric—parking lot.

Kean led on through this into another area beyond. On entering it, O'Mor stopped abruptly, hand going to his sword once again.

He suddenly found himself facing a massed company of creatures and men.

A huge, snarling wolf rubbed shoulders with a sleek horse and a fat bull. Men in staid Victorian dress were ranked with those in flamboyant Renaissance garb. One pair was in full medieval armor. Another couple was clad in only loincloths. All stared ahead, unmoving.

"Who are these?" O'Mor demanded.

"It's okay," Kean assured. "They're not alive."

"Is it frozen they are?" the warrior asked. He moved closer, peering into the faces, noting the stiffness of the features and the glassy eyes. "And what kind of evil spell was it you used on them?"

"They're not even people," said Kean. "They're robots. Machines. Animatronics, we call them. Here. I'll show you."

He stepped over to a computer console nearby. He flipped switches and power came on, lighting up the board. He began punching keys.

"Watch that one there," he said, pointing to a dim figure in a shadowed cabinet behind the rest.

Lights within the cabinet came on. A massive form was revealed. It was almost as much ape as manlike—thick-bodied, coarse-featured, and hairy—roughly clad in a bear skin. He towered above O'Mor, his head nearly touched the twelve-foot ceiling.

His eyes blinked and rolled. His mouth opened in a snarl. A growl of rage issued from his throat. One huge arm rose up, lifting an immense club.

O'Mor jumped back, his sword whisking out from its sheath this time. He planted himself and prepared to receive the attack.

"Whoa," said Kean. He swiftly punched a key. The huge figure went immediately dark and silent, its arm dropping down.

"It's only a robot, like I said," Kean explained. "Just a quarter million bucks' worth of aluminum, plastic, and wire."

"That you can bring to life so?" said O'Mor, shaking his head. "This is beyond my ken."

"God," Kean muttered to himself as he shut the console down, "this'll be almost too easy. Poor sucker."

O'Mor moved in toward the immobile, giant figure, but still with caution, his sword out. He peered close at the face.

"Just who is this fellow supposed to be?" he asked.

"Oh, he's for the Irish folk heroes display," Kean said, moving to join him. "We've got a bunch of your guys from way back in the fairy tales. That one's called . . . ah . . . Finn McCool, I think."

"Finn MacCumhal?" said O'Mor in outrage. "Why, this thing's an insult to his name. MacCumhal was a noble, proud chieftain of Eire, not such a loutish beast as this. He led the mighty band of the Fianna and was a great warrior —for a mortal man. He was fine of dress, fair of hair, handsome of feature, and most surely no giant at all. Why he barely came up to my own height."

"Oh, yeah?" said Kean with a smile. "A close personal friend of yours, I suppose."

O'Mor moved away from the giant figure to a group of contrastingly small ones close by. They were under three feet tall, with freckled cheeks, red noses, pointed ears, and curling hair and beards of a flame-red. All were clad in green suits with curled tails, green shoes with curled toes, and green derby hats decorated with white shamrocks.

"And just what are these?" O'Mor asked, peering at them.

"You ought to know that," Kean said. "Hell, they're as Irish as Paddy's pig. They're leprechauns."

"What?" O'Mor looked quizzically to him.

"The little guys. You know. From St. Patrick's day? Crocks of gold. Wishes. All that crap. They're like . . . gnomes, or something."

O'Mor continued to look blank.

"God," Kean said in exasperation, "don't you even know about *them*? They're part of your own country's traditional stuff, for Christ's sake."

"Well, it may be I've heard something of them in more recent years," O'Mor allowed consideringly. "But I'll tell you right now that they're only creatures made up by some foolish bard. They're beings of purest fantasy for certain. My own people know of no such like them in Ireland"—he looked down at the absurd little caricatures in disdain—"nor would want to."

Kean only shrugged dismissively. "Hey, who cares what you think over there? I had a top-rated research team on this, and these guys are what they came up with. Americans think that they're just Irish as hell, and they're what's going to go. McCool and his little buddies here will suck in more tourist kiddies than the Bear Country Jamboree."

O'Mor looked at him blankly. "I know that you and I seem to be speaking that same Sasunnach language, Kean, but there are many times you seem to be using another tongue entirely, for all the sense it makes to me."

"Sorry," Kean said. "I keep forgetting that modernity hasn't reached your neighborhood. Okay, come on with me. Let's just get on with the main event."

He indicated another doorway in a corner. O'Mor sheathed his sword and followed him, entering an odd room of a long, rectangular shape. It was some twenty-five feet wide and some seventy-five feet long. The room was totally empty of floor and bare of wall, save for one place in the center of one short wall. Here there was another computer and a rack filled with equipment.

"And just what is this?" O'Mor asked.

"V.R.S.," said Kean. "Virtual-Reality Simulation. In this empty room I can create a video game like none you've . . . well, like none anyone but the inventors and I have ever seen. Super-cutting-edge stuff. Way past state of the art."

He went to the console, patting it proudly. He continued in a voice that was openly bragging now. "Sure, there are things like it, but nothing to touch what I've had developed. Took multimillions and years, but when that park's done, this baby's gonna be drawing them in from everywhere in the world."

The Irishman looked bewildered once more. "I don't understand."

Kean smiled his smug little smile again. "Right. Sorry. So, never mind. All you need to know is that this room's going to be the playing field for a game between you and me. A game that should be right up your alley. A battle in an Irish forest, just like back at home."

"In here?" O'Mor's gaze swept the bare room.

"That's right," said Kean. "With these."

He took down a pair of ponderous goggles, shaped much like a scuba diver's mask, with a thick circle of glass for either eye.

"Through these you'll see the scene in these two little TV monitors"—he indicated the glass circles—"in full color and 3-D." He put down the goggles, taking up a pair of large gauntlets. "With these you'll touch, feel, and hold things as if they were solid." He pointed to a row of rubber suits—some blue, some red—that hung upon the rack. "And in one of those you'll feel things that might touch you." He looked to O'Mor and smiled. "And you don't know what the hell I'm talking about, do you?"

O'Mor shook his head. "You well know I do not."

"Just believe me: you put these on, and you can fight me, sword-to-sword, right to the death even, without either of us getting hurt. Are you still game to try?"

"I've said the choice of the contest was yours," O'Mor said stoically. "Though this seems like your wizardry, I'll not back away from it. I'll dare anything to win Caitlin away from you."

"Good boy," said Kean. He turned away to hide a now wide and triumphant smile. He took down one of the red suits and turned back to O'Mor, looking sober again. "Then, let me help you get into all this." He indicated the sword. "You don't mind taking that off first?"

O'Mor hesitated, then nodded. "Very well."

He unbuckled the sword's belt and set the weapon aside.

"Now you'll have to strip down."

"Strip down?"

"Take your clothes off," Kean translated, lifting the suit. "To get into this. Down to your underwear, anyway."

"Underwear?" said O'Mor. He unfastened his cloak and tossed it aside. He whipped off his tunic to stand unbashedly naked save for his boots.

He was a very hard and very hale-looking man. His muscled limbs and sinewy body were marked with the white lines of many old scars.

"You're in good shape," said Kean, helping him climb into the close-fitting suit. "Looks like you've had some rough spots here and there."

"I've been in more fights than I could ever count," O'Mor answered. "I thrive on that. It keeps the vigor in you. Keeps the blood warm. Too bad it's been so quiet these past years."

"Yeah. Where's a good war when you really want one?" Kean said dryly, zipping the suit closed.

It was now Kean's turn to strip. He shucked his pants

and slipped off his shirt, leaving himself in T-shirt and boxer shorts. He hesitated, eyed O'Mor, then pulled off his T-shirt as well. His own figure, though unscarred, was also taut-muscled and lean, his flat abdomen hard-ribbed.

"You're very fit as well," O'Mor observed.

"I keep in shape," Kean said casually as he pulled on another; blue-colored suit. "Not too many hand-to-hand battles, but you need lots of energy to fight a corporate war."

He got the suit on and zipped. He took up two pairs of goggles, handing one to O'Mor. "Now for these. Just do what I do."

He donned the goggles slowly, demonstrating how the straps went over the ears and around the head, and how the goggles were settled over the face. O'Mor followed suit, finding his vision of the room was now clouded by the thick glass of the lenses. Kean became a hazier figure before him.

"Now the gloves," said Kean, passing some over. "Just slip them on."

The gloves were donned easily. The two men stood facing each other, looking more like a pair ready for an underwater expedition.

"Are you ready?" Kean asked, voice muffled by the mask.

"Better for you to say that than I," O'Mor replied. "I feel half smothered by all this."

"Are you sure you want to go through with it?" Kean asked. "I mean, this really isn't necessary."

"For me it is," the other said inflexibly. "I only want to have Caitlin safe home again."

"You know, I didn't kidnap her or anything," Kean said. "She chose to come with me. I think she's afraid of you."

"So you would say," O'Mor replied coldly. "But I know of the evil spell you've put on her, poisoning her mind. I trust it'll be part of our bargain that you'll remove it, after I beat you."

"Remove my spell?" said Kean. "Why sure, pal. I'll do

whatever you want . . . *when* you win. So shall we start?"

"As soon as possible."

Kean ushered O'Mor to a spot at one corner of the triangle base, positioning him on a line there. He moved back to the computer console and brought it to life.

"When I activate," he explained as he typed the keys, "the computer will read the signals from your goggles. It'll know where you're looking, and it'll create a 3-D image as you go. You'll see trees, rocks, sky, birds, all kinds of things. Like they were really there. And with the suit and gloves you can interact with them."

"I think I understand that," said O'Mor.

"Just treat it like the real thing," Kean advised. "That's the easiest way. The rest'll come naturally. If you're really good with that sword, you'll have it made. You'll have one in the game. Not real, of course, but it'll seem the same. All you've got to do is go forward 'til you get to the far end. To the far wall down there. You'll meet me there, and we can have it out."

"So simple?" said the warrior. "Move there, and then we fight?"

"That's it. You ready?"

"Yes. Let's begin."

Kean punched in a two-player mode on the keyboard. He set the game for "fantasy scenario number five." On the screen the computer asked, "What level of skill?"

Kean grinned and typed in the single word "expert."

He moved away to the lower corner opposite O'Mor, taking up position on his line. As he did, the small screens within the goggles began to come to life.

Within seconds, the wondering Irishman was watching a scene fade into view, superimposed on the blank room. Soon walls and ceiling seemed to fall away into a limitless forest landscape.

Tall pine trees rose ahead. Sun slanted down from the sky above in columns of gold, speckling the needle-strewn ground. He looked up. Fat white clouds drifted against the blue. He looked around. The woods surrounded him. He focused on detail. Tree limbs swayed in a light breeze. Birds fluttered from branch to branch. The only gap in the illusion of reality was the absence of sound. No bird song, no hiss of wind, only total silence.

"Great magic indeed," O'Mor said in awe.

He looked down at his hand. He now held a weapon there, a long sword, its slender blade seemingly formed of a silver light. He swung it around experimentally.

"Amazing," he said. "It's not truly there, yet I feel it. A good weight and balance too."

"Thanks," said Kean.

O'Mor looked to him. Kean's computer-generated version appeared slightly more as an animated puppet than the real man, but it was very close.

O'Mor now became aware of a row of square dots across the bottom of his vision, superimposed upon the scene. Below this was printed the flashing words "Ready to Start."

"What are those symbols?" he asked.

"Hey, illiterate too, huh?" said Kean. "They just say that we're ready. All you have to do is take a step forward to start."

O'Mor took a step forward.

From the ground right before him, a monster suddenly sprang up.

An immense, sluglike being burst upward from the earth in an explosion of sod, lifting its long body high above, then arching down to strike at him with its head.

Caught totally by surprise, O'Mor had no time to move. He could only stand and look up into the wet, gaping cavern of the huge thing's pulsing mouth as it dropped down over him.

His vision went black. Wetness enveloped him. He stumbled and dropped down.

A few seconds later his vision cleared again.

He shook his head and looked around. He was on his knees, still in the same sunlit spot in the forest. The thing was gone, the spot in the ground it had burst from healed as if never there.

Shaken, he turned to see Kean grinning at him.

"Oh, gee, sorry," Kean said in a mock-apologetic tone. "I guess I forgot to tell you one thing. Before we can meet down there, we have to pass through some obstacles to reach the spot. Every encounter will sap some of your strength, more or less, depending on how well you do. That row of dots at the bottom will shrink to show you what you've lost."

O'Mor looked at the row. From one end of the two dozen dots that formed it, three had disappeared.

"If your power level shrinks too low before you get to the end, you won't have the strength to do any harm to me. If my level stays high, it'll be easier for me to 'kill' you. And vice versa, of course. Understand?"

"I think so."

"That first little surprise is a warning. You don't lose much on that. But the opponents will get worse and the power drain higher as you go on."

"Worse?" said O'Mor. "Than that?"

"Just keep your eyes peeled for anything," said Kean. "Good luck then, pal. And one last piece of news," he added gloatingly. "I've played this game over a hundred times. I know every little trick of it now. I just can't lose!"

"That," said O'Mor grimly, "we will see."

And he strode boldly forward into the unreal woods.

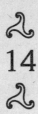

14

Kean started forward also, and he vanished from O'Mor's view as the two passed into the trees.

The rubber-clad warrior made his way cautiously forward, looking around him constantly for signs of another surprise attack.

But the next obstacle simply stepped out of the woods and stopped before him, awaiting his advance.

It was a giant, hairy, and menacing figure. It was also one he had met not long before, save that this time the fabrication of the outrageous being was even larger, towering over twice his height. As he moved in, it struck out at him with its immense club, swinging the weapon with an amazing speed.

O'Mor tried to sidestep, but he was struck a glancing blow across the shoulder. He actually felt a rush of warmth through the suit there at the impact of the blow and saw three more of the dots indicating his power level flash out of being.

Two more blows he successfully ducked. The next he tried to parry. But the club only swept through his blade of light without even slowing. There was a temporary disruption of the sword's power, as if the blow had damaged it. His power level dropped another point.

Clearly no match for the giant in a head-on fight, O'Mor resorted to strategy. He fell back. The attacker took a giant stride forward. As it did, O'Mor dived forward suddenly, dropping and rolling right between the giant's legs.

He came up behind the being. Seemingly confused by the move, it hesitated before it began to turn. That was enough time for O'Mor to set himself and drive his sword into the giant's back.

The blade flared with light as it struck the being and slid in to the hilt. The giant reared up as if in pain, shuddered, then stiffened and toppled forward to the ground like a felled tree.

As if it had, indeed, turned into wood, the form lay motionless there for an instant. Then it shimmered, turned to a shapeless mass of light, and collapsed into a glowing pool that faded swiftly away. Only O'Mor's electronically formed sword was left behind.

He picked it up, looking at the empty spot of ground.

"Sorry, Finn MacCumhal," he murmured, turned, and headed on.

Now a trio of birds swooped down on him from the trees. Like huge ravens they seemed, but made of shining black iron. Hooked, silver jaws like cruel pincers snapped at him. Curved, golden talons like wicked bailing hooks swept close overhead.

He ducked, he dodged, he spun to avoid the birds' attacks. He swung his sword up high to fend them off. He managed to slash one of them as it swooped by, taking off a wing. It spun wildly out of control, spiraling in to smash against a tree. There was a burst of light and the thing vanished.

The unexpected explosion momentarily distracted him. It gave another bird the chance to sweep in and rake him with its claws. He felt the streaks of warmth where he had taken the "wounds" across his face and neck.

A third bird then used this opening to make its own attack. It struck at him from behind, its claws tearing up his back. Six more points dropped from O'Mor's line of power.

The remaining two birds then swept out away from him, circled, and started back, one shooting in from either side. This time he neither ducked nor dodged them, standing fully erect and rock still between them, his sword down. Both birds arrowed in at the easy target on which their computer program had focused them.

At the last possible moment O'Mor went flat. The creatures, unable to stop, slammed together, bursting like a twin fireworks explosion as their powers collided, blossoming into great balls of sparks that spread thin and flickered out.

O'Mor arose, took a deep breath, and went on.

He pushed his way through some unreal underbrush that he could really feel catching at his legs. Beyond it was a clearing surrounded by tall trees.

Six warriors awaited him there.

All looked exactly alike, armed with swords and shields, clad in chain-mail shirts, elbow and leg guards, and helmets spiked with tall blue plumes. Their square-jawed faces were set in identical grim lines.

Walking in step they moved into a curved line blocking his way. He strode unhesitatingly toward them. In unison they charged at him from three sides.

Six warriors battled against one in the depths of the computer-generated forest.

The synthesized forest was shot through with simulated rays of clear sunlight, asmoke with randomly generated dust motes, striking down from electronically imaged treetops to cast spurious pools of glowing gold on the artificial floor. The man-made light and color created an unnaturally crisp and hard-edged texture, imparting a fittingly video gamelike atmosphere to the scene of wild combat.

The false swords flared brighter as they slashed through the false sunbeams, whipping the false dust motes to a frenzied computer-choreographed dance. The air was filled only with silence as blade struck blade. A fight of both much mechanical stiffness and of totally bloodless violence it was as the six 3-D illusions of warriors moved with rigidly calculated fighting techniques to attack the real seventh.

And that real seventh held all of them at bay.

The real man battled heroically, his real mane of bright gold hair swinging at his back. His own human fighting style was agile, powerful, and skilled. He wheeled and struck around him with his sword so swiftly that he seemed a constant blur.

Though the blades of the others inflicted several minor "wounds" on him, his response was unslowed. The attackers were felled by slashes and thrusts, winnowed away like blades of ripe wheat.

Until, finally, the winner was left standing alone among the rapidly fading flickers of light that marked the "slain." He stood poised a moment, guard up, looking about him for any new attack. He was panting heavily from his exertions, and his dots of power had been reduced to only four, but the fierce glow of his aroused battle energy all but blazed out from him.

"Not bad," said a voice behind him.

He wheeled to see Kean standing there, at the clearing's edge.

"I've been waiting for you. It only takes me a little while to get here," Kean said cockily as he strode forward, swinging his sword in a careless way. "I polished off my six boys ten minutes ago. They aren't really even a challenge anymore. Got twenty points left." He grinned at O'Mor. "Bet you've got less."

"I have four," the other admitted.

"Jeez. Then you're not going to give me much of a fight either, are you? I'm disappointed. I'd hoped for at least a little more of a scrap from you. Hell, you'll have to hit me five times more than I hit you to win. Why don't you just give it up right now?"

"I'll give it up when you have completely beaten me," O'Mor said tersely. "Not before. Let's get on with it."

And so they fought. And it was a ferocious, hard, ba
and-forth combat that they had. The truth of Kean's gr
advantage was demonstrated to O'Mor very soon. Thou
the warrior did strike successfully three, four, five tim
his opponent got blows home twice. At this rate of
change, O'Mor's time seemed about to run out. Ke
laughed in victorious glee.

"You're finished, pal," he said as he thrust in again,
blade "piercing" O'Mor's shoulder, destroying one m
point.

But his most desperate strait only seemed to galvan
O'Mor. In a sudden burst of powerful energy, he becam
savage storm, a vicious whirlwind, tearing about and i
Kean, running him ragged, spinning him dizzy, slamm
him around physically with body blows to keep him
balance while the flaring blade struck in again and aga

Four, six, ten times more Kean was struck. His sm
smile of easy victory was wiped away and he cried out
dismay.

"Hey, what? Wait. No! You . . . you can't. Ow! St
Whoa! Time out!"

But O'Mor would not relent, not let his foe regain eit
balance or breath. Kean tried desperately to make a co
terattack to save his last five points, but his assault v
parried and his guard easily beaten down. He fell ba
before a final, furious onslaught.

One, two, three, four more of Kean's points flicked av
before the warrior's flashing sword. The exhausted, d
perate Kean drove in to make a clinch with O'Mor, hop
that might gain him a respite. They locked together fo
moment in tight embrace.

"No good," Mor said then, shoving him backward.

Kean staggered back and fell. Instantly O'Mor was up
him, a foot coming down on Kean's wrist to pin his sw
hand.

Kean lay helpless as O'Mor's sword lifted high a
swung down toward his head. There was an explosion

brilliant crimson light that filled his goggle's lenses, and then all went black.

When a moment later his vision returned again, it was to a view of the V.R.S. room's bare walls. Only two flashing words were still superimposed on the sight. They repeated mockingly, "GAME OVER."

The now noncomputer-enhanced Rury O'Mor still stood over him. The man lifted his foot from Kean's wrist and stepped back as Kean got to his feet.

"Goddamn. Goddamn. Goddamn!" Kean swore. "I had you. I had the points on you. How could you win? Am I that bad a fighter?"

"You handled your weapon well," O'Mor said. "You have the skills and the strength to become a great warrior. But there's something else."

"Something else?" Kean echoed, pulling off his gloves. "Like what?"

"In a real fight, there's yet another thing needed. Skill and strength, aye. But you also need the spirit to win. You let these creations of your magic fight too much for you. Your own spirit's lacking."

"Yeah? And where'd all your goddamn spirit come from?" Kean asked, yanking the goggles from his head.

"From total desperation," O'Mor explained. "You see, Caitlin does not mean your life to you. Someday when *you've* something really worth fighting for, something that it's worth giving all else up for, maybe then you'll truly gain the will to win."

"Hey, I lost, okay?" Kean said bitterly, hurling the goggles to the floor. "It doesn't mean I have to listen to a goddamn lecture from you, pal. Let's get the hell out of here!"

The door to Kean's darkened bedroom softly, slowly opened to a narrow crack.

A bright, single eye appeared in the opening, peering intently out into the vast emptiness of the main room. The look in the eye was wary, worried. As she had done a dozen times since his departure with O'Mor, Caitlin was checking for some sign of Kean.

The eye's gaze flicked to the elevator as a hum arose from there, growing swiftly louder. Alarm filled it. It withdrew, and the door eased closed.

Just as it did, the door of Kean's private elevator slid open once more, letting the two men out into his penthouse. Both of them were back in their respective civilian clothes.

"So the room slides up and down a tunnel through the building," O'Mor said. "I begin to understand some of the marvels here. They're not magic. They're a kind of . . . crafted thing."

"Wonderful discovery," Kean said coldly. "Well, we're back here, O'Mor. So, now what?"

O'Mor turned to face him. "Very simple. Now you turn over Caitlin Bawn to me."

"Yeah. Well . . . it's just not that easy," Kean hedged, not meeting his eye.

"Not that easy?" O'Mor said suspiciously. "But why not? I've won her freedom from you. You say that she's here. Fulfill our bargain. Now!"

"I never said that she's here," Kean countered. "As a matter of fact she's not here. Not *right* here anyway. I mean, I've got her in a safe place."

"Then fetch her."

"Well, see, it's really complicated. I've got to go through all these . . . these guards and doors and things. Well, you saw what it was like downstairs. Tons of security. That'll take some time. And then there's . . . uh . . . there's that spell. Yeah. You wanted that spell taken off of her, didn't you? That means I've got to bring in a . . . a wizard or someone, and you just can't get a hold of someone like that in the middle of the night."

"What are you saying?" O'Mor demanded, eyeing him narrowly. "Is it excuses you're making now to keep her from me?"

"No. No," Kean assured. "Look, taking off spells and things takes time. You must know that. You want it done right, don't you? You want Caitlin all straightened out before she goes home with you."

"That I do," O'Mor admitted. "I want no trace of your dark influence left on her."

"Just leave it 'til tomorrow then," Kean advised. "I'll get her, have her all exorcised or whatever, and you can pick her up tomorrow night. Right here."

"I want to see her," said O'Mor.

"No. She's got to be asleep by now. You don't want to get her all shook up, do you?"

"How can I trust you?" asked the other, "after all your treachery?"

"I guess you don't have very much choice," Kean said, "if you want her back. I promised to turn her over, and I will, but it'll be on my terms. Unless you want to start your war after all?"

He met O'Mor's eyes challengingly. This time it was the warrior who wavered. "No. Not if there's another choice," he allowed. "Very well, Kean. I'll consider you as a man who does have honor. I'll trust that you will hold to your vow. Tomorrow night at this same time I'll come back to you. But," he added in a voice that now grew harsh, "if Caitlin is not here and ready to go with me, then not all the powers you have will save you from the wrath that'll fall upon you, even if it means destroying us both!"

Kean showed no sign of quailing at the threat. "I'll keep that in mind," he flatly said.

"Then I'll go now," O'Mor said.

"Great. Fine!" Kean agreed. "I'll show you out of here." He turned away and started toward his desk.

"Unnecessary," said O'Mor. His hand came out from within his tunic. It held the magic amulet, its crystal glowing. "I can find my own way out."

"My guest? Hell no," said Kean, reaching the desk. "I'll just call security and—"

His voice cut off abruptly as he looked around. The man was gone.

"O'Mor?" he said in surprise, his gaze searching around the room.

A faint whoosh came from above. He looked up to the top of the circular stairway where he had first seen O'Mor. The glass door leading from there out of the turret onto the roof was just swinging closed.

He ran up the steps to the door. He pushed it open, passing through onto the rooftop.

He looked around. From each corner the four pointed turrets, glowing white in the glare of spotlights beaming upward from the roof, soared five more stories higher into the night sky. From the roof's center the pyramidal sky-light thrust upward too, its glass gleaming softly with the light from below.

Besides these, the flat and open roof was empty.

Kean stared around again in bewilderment. "Where in the hell . . . ?" he muttered.

He shook his head and turned back toward the turret door.

But a flapping noise brought him around again in time to see a silvery, dovelike bird fly once around the roof, glide right overhead, do a neat wing-over, and spiral down to be lost in the dark below.

He went back inside, carefully locking the door behind him. As he started down the stairs, the bedroom door opened and Caitlin stepped into the main room.

Her face was pale, her expression fearful.

"It was Rury, wasn't it?" she asked him as he reached the floor.

"It sure was," he said, starting across toward her. "Looks like he's pretty hot to take you back."

"Yes, yes, I know," she said in distress. "I hoped first he'd never find me. Then I hoped you'd never know, that he'd see your great power, give it up and go home. I prayed to Danu that he would leave me alone to find my own way. But . . . my prayers weren't heard."

"No kidding," he said, stopping before her. "I think the guy is out of his mind. Believing in a few old traditions is one thing, but he's gone way over the top. I mean, all that talk about magic, not knowing anything modern . . . and that sword bit! What's the deal with him?"

"He's lived a life much . . . removed from your world, Michael," she explained. "Just as I have. But believe me, he's not mad."

"Then we'd better brace for trouble," he said, "'cause he's talking war if I don't let him take you back."

Dismay filled her face at that. She flung herself upon him, clutching him to her tightly, crying out, "Oh, Michael, you wouldn't give me up to him, would you?"

He wrapped her with his arms, hugging her tight.

"Hey, easy," he soothed. "No way would I just hand you over to him. We've come too far. I'll figure out something."

"It's just that I don't think now that I could stand to go back there," she said, "to return to my little life, tucked away, out of the world's ken. The freedom I've had here, with you, makes me thirsty to have more. I want to be part of the world. I want to walk out with you into it and not be afraid. I want to choose my way, my friends, my . . . my loves. It'd seem death itself now if I went back with him."

"And you won't, if I have anything to say about it," he vowed. "No powers I have can stop him, he says," Kean sneered. "Well, he's going to find out what he's really up against. No man says that to me."

She pulled back and looked up to him. "But I don't mean to bring on such a conflict between himself and you. I don't want anyone hurt."

"It's already started," he said. "And next time, I won't lose."

"I do believe the strength you have is great enough to win. Still, it won't be easy. In all his many years, Rury O'Mor has never known defeat."

"Just who is this guy anyway?" Kean asked. "He never

really said. What's he to you? Is he some kind of lawyer? A
relative? Some family friend? Or what?"

She hesitated, frowning. Then her eyes fell.

"It's something else I hoped never to tell you," she told
him softly. "He's my betrothed."

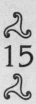

15

"Are you completely out of your mind?" Bill Mc-Bride said with great heat. "Why'd you even play a game with him?"

He sat on a bench in the penthouse's central arboretum, watching Michael Kean pace the graveled path before him.

"What can I say, Mac?" Kean offered. "It seemed logical at the time."

"Logical? Some stranger shows up here out of nowhere, and you and he decide to gamble over who gets the girl?"

"It wasn't a gamble," Kean said defensively. "At least, it wasn't supposed to be. Look, you just had to be here, Mac. He came across like the biggest, easiest mark you've ever met. Talk about a boy from the sticks. He'd never even seen a video game before. I just knew I had him!"

"And you couldn't pass up a chance to show him who was boss, right?"

"You make it sound like it was just some stupid macho thing," said Kean. "But it seemed like an easy way to put the guy off, at least until I worked something out for Caitlin. And that challenge thing was *his* idea, not mine."

"Yeah, well, it sounds to me like it was also *him* who hustled *you*," Mac said. He put on a high, mock-naive voice. "Gee no, sir, I've never played pool before. Just what does this stick do?" He dropped the fake tone, adding harshly, "And then the guy mops up the table with you." He shook his head. "I just can't believe you bought that crap. You, of all people. Mr. Shrewd."

"Enough. Enough," Kean told him testily. "Do you think I haven't been kicking myself since?"

Mac was unrelenting. "I've heard that before. And I've heard it a whole lot lately. Your mind's clouded, Michael. You're confused. This whole thing has made you . . . well, weird somehow. Just like she and this Rory O'More guy are."

"You sound like you're jumping on Lance's Kean-is-going-crazy bandwagon," his boss accused.

"No," Mac assured, "but he's sure gonna have extra loudspeakers out on it if he gets wind of this. You've got to get this thing resolved, Michael. It's getting messier by the minute."

Kean stopped pacing and sat down on the bench. "So, what do you want me to do?"

"It seems like you took care of that yourself last night. You made a deal. You lost. So pay up."

"Turn her over to him? Mac, she doesn't want to go."

"That's her problem, not yours. Let her go claim asylum or something if she doesn't want to go back. Find her a lawyer who can file a writ or whatever they do. Just, please, don't stay so involved with her yourself. That's big, big trouble. This is her family you're messing with. Her fiancé. It's up to her to work out her problems with them."

"So she's supposedly engaged to him," Kean argued. "So what? That wasn't her choice either. She told me it's one of the reasons she had to run away. Her family won't let her do anything. They make all her choices for her, including who she's going to marry. I'm telling you, Mac, those people are living in the dark ages. For all we know, they kept her locked up in a dungeon somewhere."

"She didn't say that?"

"No," Kean said, frustrated. "She still doesn't say much about her life at all. It's like she's afraid to. Like it'll be too horrible. That's why I've got to be sure that something's done."

"Where is she now, anyway?" asked Mac.

Kean gestured toward the bedroom door. "In there. I decided she should stay out of sight while I'm taking care of things. I think she's asleep right now. She said she didn't sleep too well last night, poor kid. I can sure understand why."

"Mike, you cannot play white knight in this," Mac insisted. "You've got to get out from in-between. Keep a low profile."

The elevator dinged, and the two men looked around. The door opened, and McBride stared in surprise as Frank Garvey, "Stone Man" Starski, and half a dozen uniformed security officers poured out. The uniformed men carried rifles and shotguns.

"All right, Mr. Kean," snapped Garvey. "What are your orders?"

"Get those men up on the roof," Kean said. "You might need more."

Garvey signaled the officers. "Move out. Up there."

"Armed men on the roof?" said Mac as the six headed up a stairway to a turret door.

"I want the entrance security beefed way up, and a cordon around the building too," said Kean.

"A cordon around the building?" Mac repeated in growing dismay.

"Check everything, Frank. I don't want a hole into this building that an ant could get through. And what about the helicopter?"

"Helicopter?" echoed a disbelieving Mac.

"One's on the way, Mr. Kean. But we'll need half a dozen if you want round-the-clock coverage."

"Get them then. Get whatever number you have to. I want one of them overhead all the time."

Garvey nodded and headed for the phone. Kean looked to Starski.

"Stony, I want you staying up here with me for now. That means sleeping up here too, if you don't mind using a sofa."

"No, boss," he said amiably. "Anything for you." He moved off a few feet to stand vigilantly by.

"You really are nuts," Mac exclaimed. "Low profile, I said, and instead you turn this place into a fortress crawling with armed men? Aren't you afraid *somebody* might notice?"

"I don't care who notices," Kean said with force. "Neither that guy O'Mor or any of her people are going to get in here again until I say so."

"If you want to keep hiding her, why not move her somewhere else?" Mac suggested. "Preferably to someplace you don't own. There must be one or two left."

"No good. Too dangerous. From what he said, they must be keeping close watch on this place. If she leaves here, she's too vulnerable."

"Okay, could be. But do you really need all this firepower?"

"He got in here way too easy somehow last night," said Kean. "He must have help. Maybe a lot. Maybe even a chopper. Well, he won't find it so easy getting back in here next time."

"So you welsh on your deal with him. So then he goes to the law . . . to the government . . . to, heaven help us, the press! He makes a big stink about her being up here and whammo! It's an international incident."

"I don't think it'll go that far. I get the feeling he's no more anxious to go public on this than we are. If she really was kept a captive, mistreated maybe, they'd want to cover up."

"The trouble is, you really don't know anything. You're doing all this to help one girl, and you can't even be sure she's telling the truth."

"I know she is."

"You *believe* she is. That's different."

Garvey returned from the phone. "All set on the helicopters," he announced. "I'll see to the building security myself. But, Mr. Kean, this is very irregular. What's going on? Is there some threat?"

"It's hard to explain," Kean sidestepped. "Could you just trust me on this and do it?"

"I could do it much better if I had some details," Garvey persisted. "To be blunt, sir, there've been a number of very strange things going on that I don't like. I was informed that there was an unauthorized person in the building last night. A rather peculiar person. In a security area. With you. Has that anything to do with this?"

"Knowing how thorough you are, I suppose you checked out the security camera videotape?" said Kean.

"Of course, sir."

"Then just keep a special eye out for anyone who looks like that long-haired dude."

"Not enough, sir," Garvey brusquely rapped out. "I think I deserve to know why."

"You do, Frank. And someday I may tell you. But for now, just humor me, okay? Let's just say that I want extra security up here for a day or two. That's it. No big deal."

From his expression it was clear that it was still a *very* big deal to the chief security man. Still, he obediently swallowed his misgivings, snapped, "As you wish, sir," to his boss, turned on his heel, and marched stiffly away.

"That is one disgruntled guy," said McBride, looking after him as he went into the elevator.

"Loyal, though," said Kean.

"Maybe not if he knew what was really going on. Michael, I'm pleading to you again: don't do this."

"If Caitlin had asked *you* for help, wouldn't you?" Kean returned.

"For her?" Mac considered. "Maybe. But then, what have I got to lose? You know how much it is *you're* risking."

"I'm not sure I do anymore."

"Then it's like I said: you have lost your judgment. You've let that woman get control of you. I think you've fallen in love with her."

"No," Kean denied brusquely. "She came to me in trouble. I'm only trying to help her."

"Bull. I see the look in your eye. I know. You've got her right under your skin. You're whipped, man."

"Don't try to get me mad, Mac," Kean said. "It isn't going to work."

"No." Mac sighed in resignation. "I don't think anything normal works on you anymore." He sagged defeatedly. Then his eye lit upon the bar and he perked up. "But I know something real normal that works just fine on me."

He went to the bar, grabbing up his favorite gin bottle and a tall glass. He poured a handful of fingers of the booze out neat.

"Come to Dada, pretty baby," he lovingly told the drink. "We missed you, the liver, the bladder, and me."

Before he could drink, Kean swiftly moved in, snatching the glass from him.

"None of that yet, Mac. Please. I still need you." He put a hand on his friend's shoulder. "Come on, Mac. You've got to help me. Help her. That guy who came here is a genuine flake. Who knows what he'll do if he gets ahold of her? We can't give her up to him. And we can't let the authorities get her either. It'll end up the same way. She's an illegal. They'd ship her home before they did anything else. Then what would happen to her?"

"Maybe," Mac allowed.

"All I want to do is be sure she's got some protection first," Kean argued. "That's it. We get a day or so extra time. We keep him out, make excuses, create delays. Meantime we keep checking out our options. No big deal, right? I mean, what can he really do?"

"You were quite mad to go against him alone," the man called Owen grumbled to Rury O'Mor.

The two of them and the big man called Angus were back hidden away behind the alleyway's dumpster. Angus sat by the corner of the metal bin, sharpening his spear's point on a whetstone while keeping a watch.

"It made sense to me then," O'Mor told Owen.

"Sense?" Owen cried. "What sense in going into the

ery den of this alien being, whose nature you don't know,
nd then challenging him to a *contest* over the girl?"

"I have never yet lost a contest, Owen," O'Mor said
defensively. "It was the best chance I saw at winning
Caitlin's freedom. What I encountered up there only
made me more certain that any attack by us would have
much less possibility of succeeding. And win or lose, it
would likely be of great cost to us. I couldn't risk you all in
something so dangerous as that if there was another
choice."

"So, you nobly risked just yourself again," Owen said
with a touch of sarcasm in his tone. Then he looked closer
at O'Mor. "Or was there something else in it? Could you
not pass the chance to prove yourself more mighty than
his great foreign chieftain in a single combat?"

"Of course it was not for that," O'Mor protested. "You
make it sound some prideful act of male rivalry. No, it
seemed the best way to save her, as I said. And after all,
the choice to accept a challenge was his own, not mine."

"More foolish yet," said Owen. "To play in some game
of his choice when all is so very strange to us here. You let
him talk you into what could well have been a trap for you.
And you, the one who they call Rury the Clever."

"Owen, your grumbling and fretting will be my death
long before some enemy's blade," O'Mor irritably returned. "It worked, didn't it?"

Owen's pessimism was unrelenting. "It will work *if* this
man Kean keeps to your bargain. But why think he will?
Why believe he's a man of any honor at all?"

"Because he could have destroyed me at any time. I am
certain that his warriors were always near. He chose not to
call upon them and dealt with me himself. Isn't that the
mark of an honorable man?"

"Or another fool like yourself," said Owen.

"The fact," O'Mor said tightly, "is still that he didn't
trap or kill me when he might have. Why not trust him
now?"

A familiar dovelike bird of white fluttered down from above and settled beside them. In moments it had transformed to the shape of little Kevan. He was most excited.

"Something's happening, Rury," he said, nearly breathless. "There are men, many men, up on the tower."

"Men?" said O'Mor. "Of what kind?"

"They wear grey garb that is all alike. They carry long, heavy things that, from the way they clutch them, I say are weapons. They stand guard on all four sides of the roof."

"Armed guards?" said Angus, who had stopped his honing to listen. "That bodes very ill."

A sound from up the alley brought his attention there. Several figures were visible just moving into that end of the alley's mouth.

"Someone's coming!" he warned.

All peered out. Four men in the uniform of Kean's security guard were stopped there. They paused a moment to examine the walls of the buildings on either side, then started up the alley at a brisk walk. They were searching around them as they came.

"They'll find us," said Owen.

"Quickly, out the other way," said O'Mor.

They moved along behind the dumpster to its other end. Angus peered out around its corner and drew quickly back. He had seen several other uniformed men there, also striding inward, scouring the alleyway.

"They're coming from that way as well!" he hissed to the others. "What now?" He lifted the sword still in his hand, asking eagerly, "Do we fight?"

"Not now!" said O'Mor. "We must get out of here."

"Run again?" the big warrior asked in dismay.

"We're here to save Caitlin," O'Mor said. "Fighting now will not help us to do that." He looked to Kevan. "Can you shape-shift us so we can fly away?"

"Birds will take too long," the little man said. "But I'll save us. Clasp hands with me."

They formed a tight circle, joining hands at its center.

Kevan muttered some words. A bright aura rose from him, flowing out his arms, across onto the others, enveloping them. In several seconds all were encased in the huge cocoon of light. And then the shadowy forms of the four began to change.

One of the advancing security guards, looking ahead, came up short, staring. He grabbed the arm of one of his fellows, pulling him up too.

"Look there, Pete," he said, pointing to the dumpster.

"What?" said the other, gazing at the spot intently.

"There was a light there, behind that thing. A kind of weird silver glow."

"I don't see anything."

"It's gone now. It sort of pulsed up bright for a second, then faded away," he insisted. "Didn't you see it?"

"I didn't see anything, Tom. It was just the reflection from a car or something. Come on."

They went on, but the one named Tom went more cautiously, staring hard at the spot, his hand on his holstered gun.

The two groups of guards reached the center of the alleyway together. Four of them searched the ramp down to Kean's underground parking garage thoroughly. The four others, Tom included, moved in around the dumpster to check it out.

"Nothing back here," said one man, looking behind the big metal bin.

Another lifted one of its lids to peer inside. "Nothing but trash in here."

"Maybe you should get in and poke around in that stuff," a third suggested, grinning.

The other wrinkled his nose. "Yeah. You first. Kean don't pay me *that* much. Anyway, who'd hide in this stuff?"

Tom's attention was drawn from his comrades by a rustling noise at his feet.

A jumble of litter piled against the dumpster's base was

moving. He stared at it in wonder, beginning to bend down. Then he recoiled in shock as four very large rats burst out from it, scampering right across his feet and away.

He wheeled around after them, whipping out his automatic pistol. He brought it up to level on the pack as they ran down the alleyway.

He targeted the fattest one. "Goddamn rats!" he cried. His hand tightened on the butt safety, squeezing it off. His finger began to press on the trigger.

A hand shot in to grab the pistol, pushing it down. A very stern face was thrust up close to his.

"You idiot! You can't shoot that thing here."

"Sorry, Sarge," Tom said contritely.

"What the hell were you doing anyway?" the other guard asked. "They're just rats."

"I went nuts when they scared me, Sarge," Tom explained. "God, I hate rats!"

The four creatures, meantime, had run free of the alleyway. They now scampered up a sidewalk mercifully free of pedestrians at the early, hour, still managing to panic the few they encountered.

It was their good fortune that only such a kind of beast, when so little, could still deter most humans from interfering with it. A small pug-faced dog walked by a very svelte woman did move to give challenge, but as the four large, determined-looking rodents charged unhesitatingly toward it, it thought better, dashing back behind its owner and nearly knocking the horrified lady down.

The rats raced on, crossing a main street. Three passed by a tail's length before the wheels of a speeding pizza delivery van. The fourth, the skinniest one, was caught beneath, barely missed by the undercarriage, but sent tumbling by the wash of air as it swept by. The rat jumped up, unhurt but shaken, and followed after the rest.

They passed another building, diving into the alley between it and the next. This was a much narrower, trash-congested space between the structures. They pushed back far into its depths until they had burrowed out of sight beneath the piles of filth.

There was no more movement for some seconds. Then the trash began to shudder and then to lift. Silver light began to shine out through the gaps in it. A mound of the glow rose up from beneath into view, the rubbish falling away as it swelled into a ball that filled the space from side to side. Within the globe of light, dark forms altered and grew, assuming man shape.

The light faded, leaving the four men of Eire revealed once again. This time, however, they were a bit worse from the wear.

Kevan picked strings of something wiry and wet from his hair, saying in his eternally cheery tones, "Well, *that* was a near thing."

"Rats!" said Owen disgustedly, looking down at his soiled cloak. "I can't believe that you turned us into foul rats!"

"It was the simplest thing I could think of so quickly," Kevan said in defense.

Angus spat something green, limp, and slimy from his mouth. "How shaming this is!" he bellowed. "What great insult! I'll stand for no more of this being heaped on me. Better to die in a hopeless fight, then run and hide as a craven rodent among this filth."

"Well, Rury, what do you think of this Kean's honesty now?" Owen asked, trying gingerly to pull a gob of something grey and sticky from his leg. "It would seem he's not going to welcome you back into his lair."

"No," O'Mor said angrily. "He only played that game out to be rid of me and bar the door behind me. You were right, Owen. He's a man of great treachery, and I'm a greater fool!"

"It'll surely make acting against him harder now," Kevan said. "He's been warned. He's going to be ready for us."

"Yes, and it's my own fault," said O'Mor. "I won't ask you to endanger yourselves for the likes of me."

"You won't have to," Angus told him grimly. "There's nothing would keep us from the satisfaction of striking back at that villain after this."

The other two nodded their heads.

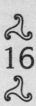

16

A helicopter chopped its way lazily through the sky above the turrets of Kean's high-rise castle. Its metal hide caught the light of the fading sun and glinted redly as it turned to circle back in its continuous patrol.

Below it a complement now risen to a dozen armed security men strolled the rooftop or stood guard at the turret doorways. And below them, inside the penthouse, "Stone Man" Starski lay stretched on a sofa avidly reading a *Smithsonian* magazine while on chairs nearby Kean conversed with a very harried McBride.

"Nothing. Nada!" the pudgy man was saying frustratedly to Kean. "It's all been checked out through every channel your boys could request, coax, threaten, or bribe information from. And I'll tell you, there are a lot of people out there getting very suspicious about exactly what you're up to."

"Screw them," said Kean. "I just can't believe you couldn't find anything at all."

"As far as the country of Ireland is concerned, Caitlin Bawn doesn't exist. There are no Bawn families anywhere that admit to being relatives of hers. And this Rury O'Mor? Same thing. No such guy."

They were interrupted by the arrival of the elevator. Frank Garvey exited it and moved to them.

"The building's completely sealed up, Mr. Kean," the chief security man announced. "Employees all gone home. I checked out everything down below myself. There are only you people here, myself, a dozen maintenance men, and a hundred security guards left inside."

"Good," said Kean. "Any signs of intruders? Anything suspicious at all?"

"Nothing, sir. Now I'm going up to check the men on the roof."

He left them, going up a staircase to a turret door.

"I don't like this," said Mac, watching the security man exit to the roof. "Not at all." He looked back to his boss. "Michael, something very, very strange is going on here."

"Why, because you can't find anything out about them?"

"That's part of it. But I've got a kind of . . . of spooky feeling about the whole thing. Her and that guy both popping in and out of nowhere. Their seeming so . . . well, so out of place and time. And there're some other things too."

"Like what?"

"One is a report I came across from your surveying crew on the site in Ireland. Seems they got attacked by a group of . . . *something*. They really weren't sure. It was right after we left them. That night." He shook his head over it, frowning. "A really strange report, Michael. Seems there were a lot of special effects going on."

"Special effects?"

"Yeah. Like fireballs exploding, monsters swooping around, giant guys dressed in black coming out of—and get this!—thin air."

"You've got to be kidding," Kean said.

"Not a chance. It was apparently a pretty wild night. Some equipment damaged, a few bruises, and a lot of guys shaken up."

"And just what did they say they got attacked for?"

"For information, I guess." Mac leaned toward Kean, fixing an intent gaze on him and saying the next words emphatically to heighten their dramatic effect: "It seems that one of this strange bunch was very, very concerned about finding you."

"Oh, yeah, sure." Kean laughed scoffingly. "It sounds more to me like the crew got ripped and got into a brawl, smashed up some stuff themselves and are covering with this crazy story."

"If they were, don't you think they'd come up with something less far out?" countered Mac. "Anyway, there was one other little detail that might interest you. They said the one asking for you was carrying a sword."

This did seem to catch Kean's attention. "Sword, huh? But they didn't see his face?"

"Nope. None of them did. But I picked up another piece of news today. It seems one of our hometown street gangs got into a fight night before last. Not a typical rumble though. Ten of them got wasted. Hacked up, most of them . . . by swords."

"Swords again?"

"Yup. The survivors swore they'd been jumped by a whole army of guys with swords. A couple of them also reported some special effects. Particularly interesting things too. Fireballs, a huge monster, a giant guy. And this time, they got a good look at the characters." Again he looked intently at Kean. "Just take a guess at how they were dressed."

"Minidresses and long plaid cloaks," said Kean.

"Got it in one. And very long hair, on one of them also very blond. Of course the cops are saying about the gang what you said about the surveyors—that the witnesses were just stoned and hallucinating. They think the punks got beat up by a particularly nasty rival gang. But I think we know better, don't we?"

"Do we?"

"Come on, Michael! How many people are running around dressed like that? Even in New York. And how many carry swords? It's the guy who was here that that gang ran into, along with a few of his friends. And I bet they're the ones who went after that survey crew too. They were searching for you, my friend, and they were not fooling around."

"That's a big assumption to make from two fairy tales," Kean said in most skeptical tones.

"Don't give me that," Mac said angrily. "You can't just ignore it all. This thing is getting way too serious. People are getting hurt. They're dying! And this stuff these freaks are doing, it's not natural. There's something going on here that we haven't even started to understand."

"So maybe this O'Mor knows a few tricks," Kean said, still unmoved. "He's not scaring *me* off with some Irish mumbo jumbo he uses on the peasants back in the old country."

Mac fought down his anger and frustration. In more patient tones he said, "Look, Michael, think about this. We really aren't doing very well here. That O'Mor guy was talking about a war. Well, maybe that's exactly what he means. Maybe that's how his people handle things. You know, pride, traditions, and all that? We've got to do something."

"Like what?"

"Like getting her out here and asking her some hard questions. Jesus Christ, man, you can't leave her alone while we're beating our brains out."

"I told you she doesn't want to talk."

"Your Mr. He-Man defense isn't doing her any good. Sure, keep her hidden away in your bedroom, and wait to see if some loony pack of Irishmen come rampaging into the lobby with swords during business hours. If she wants our help, she's got to help us. She's got to tell us something we can use."

This had an effect on Kean. He considered a moment, then nodded his head. "All right. I'll ask her to talk to us." He got to his feet. "But no rough stuff, Mac," he warned, turned, and headed for the bedroom door.

"At last," Mac said with relief. "Maybe we can get something settled around here."

·   ·   ·

The alleyway beside Kean's building was thoroughly barricaded. No vehicles or people could get in or out. Armed guards were posted at either side of the blocking line of steel fence. Another patrolled back and forth across the space between.

The guards were extremely vigilant. But vehicles and people were one thing, smallish rodents another, especially in the gathering shadows of evening. None of the men noted the four rats that slipped around a corner and past an end of the barricade and into the alleyway.

In very unratlike, cautious single file, the rats crept on along close to the wall, arriving safely at the ramp to Kean's underground garage. Safe from possible observation, they scampered down the incline to the heavy steel door that sealed the garage.

Here they formed a circle. The familiar light of the transformation surrounded them, and in moments they were four men once more.

"Rats," Owen said in revulsion. "I can't believe that we were rats again."

"It got us here unseen, didn't it?" Kevan replied with a grin.

"I still don't see why we couldn't all have flown up to the roof," Angus complained.

"I told you that," Kevan patiently explained. "I couldn't shift us back quickly enough. All those guards up there would be upon us before we had a chance."

"Kevan's right," O'Mor said. "And the main entrances to the building all are too heavily guarded as well. This doorway seems our best chance. If we can get in through here, unknown, we can work our way up to the top level somehow."

"Somehow," said Angus, looking up at the towering building with a doubtful frown. "A very long way to go."

"One thing at a time," said O'Mor. "First let's just get inside."

"But, Rury," said Kevan. "If we do get inside, and if we manage to reach this Kean's main hall, how do we get

Caitlin? We can't be certain that she'll be up there with him."

"If she's not with him or close by," O'Mor said grimly, "we'll wring the truth of where she is from him. This time, he'll give her up or die!"

Angus was prodding at the door with the tip of his spear.

"This is very thick," he said. "I'm not certain even our weapons could cut through. And the trying of it would make an unearthly row. They'd be upon us at once."

O'Mor looked to Owen. "What about your magic?"

"Given time I suppose I could generate enough power to blast it away, but that would raise an alarm with them just as surely."

"What's this thing?" asked Kevan, examining the key card opening mechanism on its post a few feet in front of the door.

The others went to it.

"Perhaps it's a lock of some kind," Owen said. "If I could open it . . ."

"Here, let me try it," said Angus, striding manfully in.

And before anyone could stop him, the massive warrior seized the machine by its head, twisted lightly, and wrenched the whole thing bodily from the ground.

There was a crackling and sparking from the torn wires left in the broken base. Angus looked at the now-dead device in his hands, looked to the motionless door, and shook his head.

"Nothing," he said, dropping the wreckage down.

"You great mindless bear!" Owen said with heat. "I might have used some magic to work the thing. Now you've ruined it."

"Sorry," Angus said contritely. "Every lock that I've ever seen could just be wrenched open. How could I know?"

"We have to act more quickly now," said O'Mor. "It might be that just damaging this thing will arouse them. Someone think of a way in."

"There's a little hole, just above the door," Angus said, trying to be of help.

They moved back to examine it. It was a square opening, some foot and a half on a side, covered with a heavy metal grate. Kevan had Angus lift him up so he could examine it more closely.

"It goes through to the inside, I think," he said as the big man set him down. "I see light shining through from not far away. Too small to get through, but only for beings of our size."

"Then transform us to something," said O'Mor.

"Of course," Kevan agreed. "And I have the perfect thing. We'll be mayflies. It's the simplest, most common of shape-shifting forms. The first one I ever learned. I can do it easily."

"I thought a rat was humiliating enough," Angus said.

"It can fly, can't it?" Kevan cheerily pointed out. "And it'll fit through that grate's holes."

"A most delicate insect," Owen gloomily noted. "It lives less than a day."

"Then it may be most appropriate for us," said O'Mor. "Make the change, Kevan. Quickly."

While they were moving into their close circle again, far above, on the roof, the walkie-talkie on Frank Garvey's hip was beeping to draw his attention.

He cut off his inspection of his men to answer it.

"Garvey here."

"Surveillance room, sir. We got a signal. Malfunction of key station at number one garage door."

"Malfunction?"

"It just went out. But there's no real problem. The door's still secure. So's the alleyway. I've already sent a maintenance team out to check."

"Send some security too," Garvey ordered. "Let me know if there're any irregularities at all!"

Back below, two overalled men were already past the barricade and walking along the alleyway. They reached the ramp and started down just as the last of four tiny, whizzing insects vanished through the openings in the grate above the door.

The mayflies—slender and round-headed insects with large, net-veined wings—darted along a grimy tunnel through the outside wall. It was a short one, providing some exhaust ventilation for the garage inside. They came out through another grate into the parking area. After buzzing around in the space a few moments to make certain it was empty of human life, they settled to the ground and formed a circle again.

Soon the restored Irishmen were examining their surroundings with human eyes.

"I see no stairways upward," said Angus as the four moved out cautiously across the concrete floor.

"Look there," said Kevan, pointing out a dark, nondescript sedan in a row of several cars. "That's the one we saw Caitlin being driven about in."

They started toward it.

"There, in the wall just beyond," Owen said as they drew near. "Isn't that some kind of door?"

O'Mor's gaze fell on the familiar-looking door, and then on the belensed little box of the surveillance camera affixed to the wall above it.

He put up his arms to stop his friends, hissing warningly, "Get back!"

They quickly withdrew to the inside of the garage door, examining the small door and its camera from the safe distance.

"Do you see that device over the door?" said O'Mor. "Well, I've seen one before. If we come up close beneath it, I believe Kean's guards will be able to see us, and hear us too."

"Then we'll have to stay well away from it," said Kevan.

"That we may not be able to do," said O'Mor. "That door the thing sits above looks just like the door to his little lifting room."

"Lifting room?" echoed Angus.

"Yes. It's a room that slides up and down a shaft through

the tower. That must be it. It would take him from here up to his grand hall at the top. If we could get inside, we could ride it up there. I think I could make it work. I watched him do it."

"Well, let's go then," Angus said eagerly.

"No," said O'Mor. "That guardian box would alert them before we got inside."

"Then we go in as mayflies," Kevan offered, "and change back once we're inside."

"We've still got to open it," O'Mor pointed out. "Kean used some kind of small, flat thing to make the door slide back. He put it into a slit on the wall by the door. See, there's one there too, on the left. In that square of metal at waist height."

Owen peered toward it. "It could well be like that thing we saw outside. A kind of keyhole. Maybe my magic can unlock it"—he shot a hard look at Angus—"so long as I can try it *without* help. Kevan, go ahead and transform us."

The little man quickly obeyed. In a few moments the four insects were hovering close before the door.

One buzzed in closer to the slot set in a metal plate beside the door. The mayfly hung inches from it for a time, its compound gaze intently examining. It landed on the plate, crawling about and feeling the edges of the slot. Then the insect boldly plunged inside. It wiggled its tiny body through the hole, vanishing from the sight of its fellows.

Inside it found the complex patterns of the device's circuitry. It saw the contact points and the scanning light for sensing the electronic pattern on the card's key band.

The insect studied the construction of the inner workings for some time while its fellows flitted about impatiently outside. Finally it crawled back to just within the slot and began to vigorously rub its front legs together.

The network of veins in the clear wings began to glow with a silvery light, making the whole of the wings iridescent. As this energy built up, it moved forward, along the slender body, over the round head, finally gathering in a tiny, glittering ball between the fly's front legs.

When the ball reached a size nearly too large for it to grasp, the insect hurled it forward, at the same time backing hurriedly away.

Outside, the others saw a bright flash within the slot. Light flared outward, and an object shot out too. It was the mayfly, blasted from the inside, tumbling out and down through the air, but recovering just before it struck the ground.

It flew back up, somewhat erratically, to join its waiting comrades. It was a bit scorched on the wing tips by the blast, but seemed otherwise intact.

Meantime, inside the slot, more was happening. The initial explosion seemed to have triggered more, causing a chain reaction that flared to a popping peak before culminating in a last bright spurt of flame.

Smoke trickled from the card slot. The flies turned expectantly toward the door. For a long moment nothing happened.

And then, slowly, the door slid back.

In the surveillance room the guard saw the new warning signal come to life on his board. He looked at the monitor for the garage camera. Nothing was visible there. He shook his head and went for his two-way radio.

Inside the elevator the four had already shifted back to human form.

Owen, clothing scorched and eyebrows singed, announced most irritably, "Well, *that's* something I'll never try again."

O'Mor looked at the floor buttons, ranged in several columns. "See here," he said, indicating the lowest left one, which was alight, "that's where we are." His finger moved to the topmost right one. "There's where we want to be." His finger punched the button. "Here we go!"

The door closed. The elevator started its express run upward.

"Oh, no!" Angus wailed as the sensation of gravity struck him. "I want my stomach to go too!"

Far above, Garvey was on his radio again.

"Looks like we've got another malfunction, sir," the surveillance room guard was reporting. "This time it's in the card key station down in the private garage. The thing just went out. Like a short circuit."

"You're sure that's it?"

"Must be, sir. Everything's still secure. And the monitor doesn't show anyone being down there. This has happened before. Just a bug in the system."

"Maybe," Garvey said, still unconvinced. "But check with that maintenance crew outside, will you? See if they found out what happened out there."

"Right away," the guard promised.

Inside the elevator, the four men grimly watched the light climbing swiftly through the columns as they rose through the tower. Angus clutched the short spear ready in his hand. O'Mor drew his sword.

In the penthouse, Caitlin Bawn was finally out of the bedroom and now sat beside Kean on a couch in the main room. She looked most distraught, wringing her hands, looking down at the floor.

McBride, seated on a chair across from her, exchanged a look with his boss. Kean shrugged. Mac sighed heavily, steeled himself, and plunged on.

"Look, I'm sorry to do this," he said to her. "But you can see from what I've said why we're worried. This O'Mor guy sounds dangerous. If we're going to do something, we have got to know who he is, who your family is, and who you are too."

"I understand," she said in a quavering voice. "It's just that it's . . . very secret."

"What's that mean?" McBride asked. "There's a conspiracy? A cult, maybe? Or some kind of criminal thing?"

She shook her head. "You will not believe me if I tell you."

"You have to try it anyway," Mac gently insisted. "Please, Caitlin. If you want us to help you."

She hesitated, then nodded. "Very well. My people are . . . different from yours. They have certain . . . powers. Once they did rule Eire, walking out freely on its sod, living as they wished. But then troubles came, and they chose to withdraw into a . . . a more private life. There are some of your world who still know of us. But not as they'd know about other people. You see, we're of a race known as—"

But she cut off as Starski jumped suddenly to his feet, standing tensely, head cocked.

"What's wrong?" asked Kean.

"The elevator, boss," the bodyguard said. "It's comin' up!"

They could all hear the rising hum of the machinery now.

"What in hell's going on here?" said Kean, rising too. "Nobody else has been authorized to come up. Check it out, Stony."

Starski nodded and strode across to stand before the door, ready to give challenge to its occupants. The others watched expectantly.

On the roof above him, Garvey was getting the report from his surveillance man.

"The maintenance guys say it looks like the thing got torn off, sir. Completely trashed. But no sign of anyone."

"Get some men down in that garage right now!" Garvey ordered, urgency in his tone. "I'm coming down!"

He headed at once for a turret door. At that same moment the nonstop elevator from the garage arrived.

17

The door slid open.

Caitlin gasped in shock as Angus charged out, spear in hand.

The bodyguard's hand dived beneath his jacket, going for a holstered handgun. Angus thrust out his spear in a lightning move, the barbed head flashing in toward Stony's chest.

But the ex-boxer's countermove was just as fast, his left hand sweeping up to knock the spear away. At the same time, his right hand brought a very large revolver clear of his coat, swinging it around to point its muzzle at the big warrior.

Angus's counter was of equal swiftness. His free hand shot out to slam the gun away. He dived in on Stony and the two huge, solid men collided, staggering back.

O'Mor and his other companions moved out of the elevator, spotting the three by the sofas and running toward them at once.

McBride cowered back, going pale in fear. Kean started toward his desk and the alarm button, but stopped as O'Mor came before him, the warrior's sword point lifted threateningly.

"No game this time, Kean," O'Mor snarled.

Caitlin, recovered from her first shock, lifted hands before her, mumbling something hurriedly. A faint golden glow began to show around her.

Owen quickly moved in, his own hands lifting to point fingertips at her. Her gold aura instantly faded away.

"No escaping that way," he told the dismayed woman. "Your frail magic's no match for mine. You cannot turn."

While O'Mor kept Kean covered with his sword, Owen and Kevan moved up to Caitlin, one grabbing each arm, pulling her to her feet.

"Please, don't do this," she said.

"Let her alone," said Mac, showing renewed courage at her distress. He got to his feet and advanced on them.

One of Owen's hands swung toward him. A lightning-like bolt flared from the fingertips to strike Mac's chest. It was small but still strong enough to fling him back, smash him down, and leave him lying stunned.

Not far away, Stony and Angus still wrestled together like two savage bears. The fight seemed equal, until Stony tripped backward over a cocktail table. He fell, Angus falling right atop him. The hefty warrior's weight drove the air from the bodyguard and made his head crack back hard against the ceramic floor. He was out.

Angus climbed to his feet. For the moment there was no more opposition visible.

"All right, we have you," O'Mor told Kean. "You'll release her and let us leave now or—"

"Hold it there!" cried another voice from above them.

They looked up to see Frank Garvey atop the stairs to one of the turret doors. The large bore of a heavy revolver was pointed down toward them.

"Just put down the weapons," he advised.

Angus instead lifted his spear to cast. The gun and his spear fired off simultaneously. The faster bullet reached the warrior first, tearing through the thick flesh of his upper right arm. But his own missile struck too, though with no greater accuracy, its barbs just raking along Garvey's side.

Angus was staggered but managed to stay erect. Garvey was spun around, colliding with the stair rail, dropping his gun to grab on and save himself from toppling over. His weapon and the spear that had grazed him clattered to the floor below together.

His threat was ended, but the sound of his gunfire had alerted those on the roof. Through the turret doors on all four sides, security men appeared, brandishing arms.

O'Mor swept his gaze around at them as they rushed down the stairways and spread out to encircle the room.

"You're not going anywhere," Kean told him with restored confidence. "Breaking and entering. Armed assault." He smiled. "I think we can let the law take care of you."

"What now, Rury?" Angus asked his chieftain, clutching his profusely bleeding arm to stanch the flow. "Do we fight?"

O'Mor eyed the strange, lethal weapons in the guards' hands with a look of hopelessness. "I'm afraid we must, if we can't escape."

"We can, Rury," said Owen, pointing to the central atrium. "There."

"Let's go then," said O'Mor.

He and Angus followed while Owen and Kevan urged a reluctant Caitlin ahead toward the parklike space. As they moved, the guns of the security men lifted to train on them. Safeties were clicked off.

"No!" Kean shouted, turning to address all his men. "No shooting! You might hit her! Garvey?"

The security chief had recovered, stoically pressing closed his own wound with a hand. He replied through gritted teeth, "Yes, sir?"

"You still in control there?"

"Yes, sir!" he said forcefully.

"Then make sure they don't shoot."

"Wise choice, Kean," said O'Mor as he and his party reached the square of vegetation. "Wiser yet to stay where you are."

The five moved into the center of the green space. Their figures became partially obscured now by the surrounding plants. Directly below the peak of the skylight pyramid, Owen stopped them.

"What are you doing?" Kean yelled in. "You're crazy if you think I'll let you leave with her. You can't get out of here. Why don't you give up?"

O'Mor ignored him, looking to Angus. "How are you?"

The big man lifted his hand for a quick peek at the wounds. They were the blood-oozing two ends of a tunnel the slug had plowed right on through his rock-hard biceps. He shrugged. "I've had worse."

O'Mor looked to Owen. "Well, *can* you get us out of here?"

"Of a certainty I can," the lanky one assured. "Mind her, then. And stand back just a bit."

O'Mor moved to grip Caitlin's arm securely. They all moved back to stand several feet from Owen. The magician lifted both hands above his head, holding them palm in, inches apart.

A first, small spot of blue-white glittering appeared over him. It began to grow rapidly larger. At the same time the room's lights began to flicker and fade.

"What's going on here?" said Kean, looking around him.

"Don't do this," Caitlin pleaded to O'Mor. "Rury, if you love me, let go. Get away. Leave me here."

"You're under a spell," he said uncompromisingly. "Don't worry. We'll find a release from it when we get home. I promise you."

"There is no spell, Rury," she said. "Please, listen to me!"

But he only stared ahead, jaw set grimly, unheeding of her now.

The ball of power grew ever larger, larger, Owen's hands moving apart to accommodate it. Already it was over a yard across, a globe made of intertwined tendrils of sapphire light, seeming to spin atop the magician's outspread fingertips.

As the ball swelled, the power within the building was further sucked away. Interior and exterior lights faded, making the vast, gleaming structure seem to vanish into the dark. Passersby in the street below stared in wonder as Kean's castle became only a towering patch of black.

Meantime, in the penthouse, the radiant ball had become the only light source, filling the room with its blue-white, flickering glow. The security men stared in wonder at the globe that had grown to six feet across. Kean stared in growing dismay.

"What are you doing?" he demanded. "O'Mor, what are you doing in there?"

In the center of the room, Owen looked to his friends. "Be ready," he said. "Look down."

His hands came together in a sharp clap. The ball shot upward, slamming into the top of the skylight's pyramid.

There was an explosion, as if the peak of glass had erupted, its glass splintering to tiny fragments that spewed upward, arched outward in a scintillating geyser, then fell back in a tinkling downpour to the roof.

In the patrolling chopper the pilot and his passenger gazed down in astonishment at the spectacular blast.

"My God!" breathed the pilot. "What happened?"

They watched the glass settle. Then he guided his helicopter closer to see, maneuvering the machine down and in carefully against the stiff wind that blasted eternally across the peaks of the city's cloud-scraping towers.

What had happened was obvious: a ragged hole some twenty feet across had been blasted out of the center of the skylight.

Directly beneath it, Owen looked up in satisfaction to the open night sky. "Now," he said, "I can take us home." He looked to the rest. "Move in closer."

The other four came in about him. He began to gesture above them with sweeps of both arms, around and around, chanting in unintelligible words. In moments the foliage about them began to move too, leaves tugged out horizontally, fluttering rapidly, as if a sudden breeze was sweeping through them.

The breeze rose higher, swirling around and around,

creating a miniature cyclone with the five people at its eye. More eerie illumination appeared in the rotating wind, like strands of luminous pearls strung on silver light, running around and up to form a coil. And the strands grew quickly thicker.

"What are they trying now?" said Kean, peering into the wind and glow. His gaze followed the coils up. They were rising higher, above the tops of the potted trees, stretching toward the hole.

Above, on the stairs, Garvey's radio came to life.

"Mr. Garvey," it said, "chopper five here. What the hell's going on?"

He answered it. "Get down here!" he said. "The bastards blew the roof. Move in and block 'em. And keep an eye out. They must have a rescue bird coming in!"

"Aye, aye, sir!" the pilot declared.

Skillfully he began to maneuver the chopper even closer. Battling now against the forces of both the constant crosswind and the rising vortex below, he kept control of the ship with great effort to drop it down amid the four turrets and bring it in to hang just yards above the hole.

"Keep an eye out for bandits coming in," he told his passenger.

The other man nodded. He slid open his window, cocked the heavy assault rifle cradled in his lap, and thrust its muzzle out. He was ready.

Within the penthouse, the whomp, whomp, whomp of the craft's blades became audible. All looked up to see the lit belly of the helicopter suspended close above the opening.

"They're caught now, Mr. Kean," Garvey shouted triumphantly to his boss. "They can't go out that way."

"He's right," Owen said in chagrin. "We cannot go up while that thing is over us."

The vortex created by his powers was swirling around with a vengeance now, its force stripping leaves from the surrounding growth and spinning them up toward the hole. But the coil of lights, blazing intensely, was stopped just below it.

"I'll see to this," little Kevan amiably volunteered.

Before his friends could stop him, he stepped through the wall of swirling lights and wind. Out of the vortex, he lifted arms and instantly began to glow.

"No, Kevan," O'Mor cried. "Don't risk it!"

"It'll be no trouble," the other called back in a carefree tone, his form already swallowed in the cocoon of light. "Just make yourselves ready. I'll clear the way for us!"

And with that, his shape swiftly altered within the glow, swelling upward and outward grotesquely. The light faded to reveal a strange creature already lifting toward the hole.

Kean and his men caught only a glimpse of a large, winged being as it flashed up and out into the night.

"Where did that come from?" Kean asked disbelievingly.

Above, the men in the chopper were getting a much better look at the thing. They stared in astonishment as it flapped out the hole, flew away to the roof's edge, turned, and circled around them. It was a composite creature of leathery wings, hawklike head, lizard body, and lion claws. In wingspan it was a good six yards across.

It gave them little time to observe it, however, for after making a sweeping circuit of the craft, it dived in right at the front windshield.

"Jesus!" the pilot swore as the thing shot toward his face. He turned the ship, wheeling it away. The rotor of his swinging tail nearly clipped one of the turrets, but he recovered, holding the ship in position above the hole.

The creature swept past, dropping down to avoid the big rotor, winging out past the edge of the roof and then turning to come in again.

"Give me a shot at it!" the armed man said.

"There's no room to maneuver here," said the pilot.

"Just gimme a shot at it!" the other demanded.

The thing swooped in at the chopper's front once more, looking fully determined to collide. As it neared, the pilot swung his craft sideways swiftly, bringing his passenger's gun around to bear.

The gunman fired off a burst. A tracing of bullets stitched across the beast's chest. It jerked and screamed in agony, dropping suddenly downward, sweeping under the chopper, all but scraping its bottom.

Beyond, it recovered before striking the roof. It lifted up, sweeping out past the edge to turn back again. But it moved painfully now. The wings flapped with great labor to bring it around. Red blood streamed from a row of wounds across its scaled breast. Still it circled about its metal adversary to bravely confront it yet again.

"Damn! What's keeping that thing up?" the pilot cried as the two faced off.

"Let it come in!" the gunman said. "I'll finish it this time!"

The creature started forward as before. The pilot again waited until it was near, then spun his craft sideways.

The assault rifle fired. The slugs struck home, ripping through body and wings, but this time without apparent effect. The determined being kept on coming in, arrowing right for the chopper's side.

"Get us out of here!" the shooter screamed.

The pilot tried to lift up, but too late. The creature slammed full on into the passenger window.

It grappled on to the chopper's undercarriage with its powerful claws. Its wings beat at the craft while its beak darted in through the opening, snapping at the gunman, tearing into his arm. He shrieked and jerked sideways into the pilot. The pilot lost control.

The tail swung around, this time striking a turret. Its metal boom ripped a gash through the turret wall, but its rotor was torn off by the blow as well.

Thus damaged, the chopper went crazy. Gyrating wildly, the creature still affixed to its outside, it stayed airborne only seconds more before slamming headfirst into the base of another turret.

There was an explosion, a huge fireball of ignited gasoine, wracking the machine, blasting through the foundation of the slim spire. The turret shuddered, tilted slowly, gracefully outward, and then toppled over the side, dragging along the machine and the creature tangled in its wreckage.

The whole, flaming mass fell in what seemed slow motion toward the street below.

There was no traffic directly beneath it at the time. One lucky cabbie, seeing the fiery avalanche descending before him, shifted his taxi into reverse and screamed backward out of the way, barely reaching a safe distance before the mass struck.

There was another, larger explosion on impact, filling the whole street. The lower windows of Kean's tower and the building across the street were blown out by flying debris. The entire neighborhood shuddered, and the vast sound reverberated far away along the deep canyons of stone and glass.

Inside, the turret's destruction had also torn out that corner of the penthouse. Debris had been scattered through the whole room, and the sparks from rent electric wiring flickered within a swirling cloud of dust and smoke. Several guards lay partly buried in the rubble of walls and ceiling. The rest of the room's occupants, though mostly unharmed, still appeared to have been paralyzed by the catastrophe.

Under the skylight, O'Mor and his comrades looked the most in shock. They had seen the collision of the creature and the machine. They had heard the explosion and watched as turret, chopper, and what had been their friend plummeted past the windows.

"Kevan!" O'Mor cried in anguish. "Not you!"

"We can't help him, Rury," Owen said. "We must go. Now!"

He gestured upward with his hands. The vortex lifted, stretching out to reach the hole. The whirling light strands coiled through it and on up into the night.

The circumference of the vortex tightened as its length

stretched, closing in on those within, catching at them, tugging their clothing, lifting their hair as if it was being charged with static electricity. The bodies of the four began to glow like the surrounding lights.

Caitlin attempted to break free. She jerked her elbow away from O'Mor and leapt for the spiraling wall, calling out desperately, "Michael!"

He heard the voice, and it roused him to act. He charged forward, heedless of risk, pushing through the vegetation toward the vortex.

He could see her ahead. O'Mor had grabbed one of her hands and stood stone-faced, gripping it tight to hold her back. She was stretched out, her taut body straining for the freedom beyond the wall, her face a sharp-etched mask of yearning and despair. Her fingertips just brushed the spiral's edge.

They stood in this tableau as the forces around them spun upward with a fiercer velocity, actually drawing their bodies along in the coils of light. They were glowing brightly now, the white luminescence making their forms grow hazy.

Kean tried to press nearer, hands stretched out as if he could yet grasp her and haul her free. But the blasting winds pummeled him and pushed him back.

He could see her, just faintly, again mouthing his name, but this time no sound came.

"Caitlin!" he shouted back, and tried harder to reach her.

Suddenly the whole vortex lifted upward, its base rising from the floor. Like a waterspout sucked back into its clouds, the shining coils slipped through the hole and out into the darkness.

The vortex rose up in a long tube of glinting light. High above Kean's roof it arched toward the east, then shot away to be swallowed by the night.

It was over.

Around Kean, his men began recovering. Starski was groaning and getting to his feet. Garvey was seeing to his

men. One guard was hunched over the still-unconscious
but still-breathing McBride. In the silence that had fallen,
the eerie sound of sirens could be heard as fire engines
rushed to the conflagration still raging in the street below.

Kean was unconscious of all of this. He stood where he
had ended, his face stricken, staring up through the skylight's gaping hole.

He stared up into the endless dark for a long moment,
and then his expression hardened to an angry and most
determined one.

"I'll find you," he vowed to the night through his
clenched teeth. "Somehow, Caitlin Bawn, I *will* find you
again!"

BOOK TWO

LAST CHALLENGES

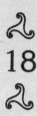

18

Lance Larson climbed from his taxi before the elegant, Georgian-facaded building.

He paid his driver, turned, and looked up to the sign that tastefully proclaimed the place the Royal Dubliner Hotel. Drawing himself up stiffly as if steeling himself for some contest, Larson mounted the front steps and pushed through the revolving door into the lobby.

It too was a study in Enlightenment elegance, cool and rationally balanced, with rows of marble columns flanking the length of polished marble floor that led to the front desk.

He approached the desk where a tall, slender, and aristocratically nosed young man was presiding. The man eyed him with an eyebrow arched in question.

"May I be of some help to you, sir?" he asked Larson, his carefully cultivated speech evidencing only the faintest hint of an Irish brogue.

"I'm here to see Mr. Michael Kean," Larson said. "What room is he in?"

"And may I ask who is inquiring, sir?"

"Mr. Lance Larson," he answered, matching officious manners with the desk clerk. "I am an executive assistant to Mr. Kean."

"Really?" said the man, monumentally unimpressed. "Is he expecting you?"

Impatience entered Larson's tone. "He should be. If he got any of my twenty messages."

"Might I just see some form of identification, sir?" the unflappable clerk inquired. "A passport would be most ideal."

With quick, irritated movements, Larson drew a wad of documents from within his coat, shuffled out a passport, and handed it to the man.

The clerk scrutinized it thoroughly, looking several times from the photo to the now-fuming real thing to verify the likeness before nodding.

"Very well, Mr. Larson." He handed the passport back. "I'll ring up to ask if he'll see you."

Larson stood fuming for moments more as the man stepped away, used a phone, then returned.

"You may go up, sir."

"Finally," Larson snapped. "So, where is he?"

"Mr. Kean has engaged our two top floors, four and five, for himself and his entourage. He himself is in the President Kennedy suite, in the south wing on floor five. It's our largest suite."

"Naturally," said Larson. "Where do I go up?"

"Elevators to the rear of the lobby, sir. Have a pleasant day."

"Not so far," Larson mumbled, and stalked away.

The elevator to five let him out in a corridor. It stretched away through the whole floor one way, but the other way went only a few feet to a door. A small, silver plaque upon it labeled it The President John Fitzgerald Kennedy Memorial Suite.

He stepped to the door and lifted a hand to knock, but the door swung open before he could do so, revealing the towering form of "Stone Man" Starski, glaring down at the much smaller Larson. His hand was meaningfully thrust inside his coat.

"It *is* you," Stony said, relaxing a bit and drawing his hand out.

"Of course it is," Larson said sharply. "How did you now I was out here?"

"I heard the elevator," said Stony. "I listen real close for nose now."

"Great to know. So, can I see Mr. Kean, or are you oing to frisk me first?"

"Sorry," said Stony, stepping back. "Come in."

Larson moved past him into the room. It was of large ze, clearly intended as a living room for the suite. But it ad been transformed into what looked more like a war oom.

The original, expensive and delicate Queen Anne furniure had been cavalierly pushed back to the walls, clearing ne central area for a half-dozen tables. On these were oread maps and books and documents and computer rintout sheets. A number of men and women worked round them, poring over materials or making phone calls n some of the score of phones that had been run in there. : all had the hectic feel of a stock market floor on a good ading day.

"My God!" said a rather astonished Larson.

He made his way forward, edging through the throng. t one table he saw Frank Garvey and some intense-lookag men checking over detailed three-quarter-inch maps f Ireland. Beyond them he spotted Michael Kean himself ent over someone at another table.

"Mr. Kean," he called.

Kean straightened and looked around to him. "Lance!" e acknowledged, more in a disapproving than a greeting ay. He waved Larson to him.

As the assistant moved closer, he saw that Kean stood ver Bill McBride, the man apparently none the worse for is run-in with a lightning bolt, but definitely seeming uch thinner.

"What are you doing here?" Kean asked Larson some hat curtly.

"Didn't you get any of my messages?" Larson asked in eturn.

"Messages?" Kean said awkwardly. "No. Well, I've been pretty busy"—he waved around—"as you can see."

"Apparently so," Lance said cautiously. "But, Mr. Kean, I need to talk to you. Very urgently. I've been sent over here by the board especially for that purpose."

"The board, eh?" Kean said. "So, you're working for them now?"

"I work for you, sir, as always. But I must insist on talking to you, now!"

Kean looked around at his people, some of whom were clearly bending an ear to this. "Okay," he agreed. "Then let's go into my private room." He gestured toward a door. "This way. Mac, you come too."

The three went through the door. Beyond was a sitting room, and through doors beyond that a bedroom furnished with a huge canopy bed.

A handsome Queen Anne desk, pressed into Kean's service too, was all but overloaded with a bank of telephones and a welter of file folders. Kean sat down behind it. Mac dropped into a chair beside him. Larson took a seat in front.

The assistant eyed his employer closely for the first time. The normally vigorous and self-possessed Kean looked harried and a bit haggard, his face drawn. He seemed jumpy as well, picking up a pencil to drum on the desk.

"So, what's up?" Kean asked brusquely. "I've got lots of work to do."

Larson took a deep breath and plunged in. "Well, sir, I've been sent out here to you because you seem incapable of answering queries or sending back updating reports on your activities."

"Oh, really?" The pencil drummed harder.

"There are a lot of questions back there, sir," Larson went on. "Not the least of which concerns your rather, ah, precipitous departure for Ireland. Many people think it amazing that you were even allowed to leave, considering the unpleasant circumstances just before."

"Hey, I was the victim there," Kean said defensively. "Why the hell should I be the one stuck in New York answering questions because some bunch of terrorists tried to get me?"

"*Were* they terrorists, sir? I mean, there have been suggestions that you had some idea who they were."

"That's garbage. I told the F.B.I. everything I knew. Some screwy cult or something threatened me. I didn't know who they were. That's for the lawmen to figure out. And I'm not waiting around forever while they do it."

"You could have alerted the authorities earlier, sir. You could have informed me or the chairman as to what was going on."

"What for? So you'd worry too? Lance, you know I get threats all the time. Every rich guy does. I put on extra security, but I didn't take it that seriously. So I got surprised when this bunch really busted in. So, sorry about that."

"The chairman still feels you shouldn't have pulled strings to get yourself clear," Larson persisted. "He says it looks bad. As if there's a cover-up. And there are some most bewildering things the investigation hasn't revealed. Like the power fadeout, the explosion, and the helicopter crash."

"So the federal boys haven't found anything?"

"Nothing more besides those remains of an unknown third man in the helicopter's wreckage. He was small, but otherwise he was too burned for further identification. The rest of the attackers have vanished completely. And that raises another question: how did they get off the roof?"

"Likely they had a chopper ready too," Kean said offhandedly. He threw the pencil down, adding with force, "Look, Lance, that's still got nothing to do with me. I don't have any answers. I'm over here now, and that's that."

"But *why* are you here?" Larson asked. "That's really the main thing the board wants to know. Why did you suddenly feel a compulsion to come back to Ireland only a

few days after you'd left? And what have you been doing
here for the past two weeks?"

Kean sat back in his chair. "I thought the Irish operation needed some more personal attention," he said
vaguely.

"But so far as we know, you haven't done anything
connected with it!" Lance countered. "And now the Irish
government wants to know what you're up to. You've been
stonewalling them, us, everyone; and everyone's beginning to get a little upset."

"What I'm doing is . . . well, it's delicate," Kean explained. "I'm feeling pulses, here. Picking up vibes. Real
P.R. stuff. Good for business. But it's got to be handled
with a very low profile, you see?"

"No," Lance said flatly. "Couldn't you just explain to
me?"

Kean exchanged a glance with McBride. McBride was
poker-faced.

"We could fill you in," Kean allowed. "It's complicated.
It'll take a while. But we'll get right to it . . . as soon as
I've got time." He got to his feet, his manner turning
brisker. "But for now, I've got to get back to it."

He moved round the table. Mac rose and followed him.
They closed in on either side of Larson's chair.

"Besides, you probably need rest, right, Lance boy?"
Kean said, clapping a hand to the man's shoulder. "Jet lag
and all that."

"I feel just fine, sir," Lance protested, looking up to
him.

"Nonsense." Kean exerted some pressure and hauled
him up. "Get a good night's sleep."

"It's ten A.M. here."

"A good day's sleep then. We'll talk later." He looked to
McBride. "Mac, you'll see about finding Lance a nice
room . . . somewhere?"

Mac smiled. "Why sure, boss."

"What about here?" asked Lance.

"Oh, they're all filled up here," Kean assured him.

He hustled Larson to the door, opened it, and gave him a hearty slap on the shoulder in parting.

"We'll get back together, real, real soon," Kean vowed. "And don't worry, Lance, it'll work out. Doesn't it always for me?"

"I . . . guess so, sir," he said as he was ushered on through the door.

Mac moved out behind him and the door slammed closed. Lance stood looking at it blankly, clearly nonplussed at his bum's rush.

"There you go," Mac said brightly. "Everything's fine. So come on, Lancy lad. We'll see about a room."

Larson looked to him, eyeing him up and down, a new question in his gaze.

"Just what is with you, McBride?" he asked. "You seem so . . . chipper."

That he certainly did. Besides his new thinness, he appeared to be much fitter. The sagging look of his booze-dissipated face was disappearing; there was a brightness in his eyes and a springiness in his manner.

"I've been doing okay," Mac said offhandedly.

"You know, I don't think I've ever seen you not drunk or hungover," said Lance.

Mac gave him a broad grin. "It's the Irish air, me boy," he said. He threw an arm about Larson's shoulders and began herding him toward the outer door. "Yes, it's just this lovely Irish air. You should try it. It has an intoxicating quality all its own!"

The two wraithlike figures in the fluttering cloaks of black moved out of the night-shrouded woods into the moonlight.

The white light from the nearly full orb in the clear night sky struck glinting silver from the dew-touched grass blades of the meadow they crossed now, making the eerie, black forms stand out starkly. They appeared to float rather than walk across the ground, gliding smoothly toward a large, rounded hill that showed ahead.

An elderly man in the worn jacket and cloth cap of a farmer was just making his somewhat unsteady way home from the nearby town's pub, cutting across the same meadow. He himself was giving the hill a wide berth, though it was adding much distance to his route.

He stopped stone still, staring wide-eyed as he saw the two figures sail by some distance ahead. He watched them in fear as they drifted straight toward the hill. Some yards from the base they began to shimmer, as if seen through a surface of rippling sea. Then they vanished, dissolving as they continued ahead, seeming to merge into the side of the hill.

Crossing himself often and vigorously, the man turned right around and strode quickly away, heading back toward his pub.

At the same time, the dark figures were sloughing off their concealing shrouds of black. This revealed that the wraiths were in fact Rury O'Mor and a lean, long-faced man of elderly look and thinning grey hair, clad in a robe of purest white.

They were within what seemed a great hall of a seven-sided shape. Each wall of the room, sheathed in softly glowing bronze, was pierced by a doorway. In the room's center, a seven-sided hearth of marble enclosed a bright wood fire. About the hearth, seven pillars of polished red-gold rose up to support a ceiling of burnished silver on the curved horns of seven capitals fashioned as rams' heads.

Scores of tables were drawn up about the fire, enough to accommodate several hundred diners. Now, however, only three others were in the room.

Two were familiar: the giant warrior Angus and the druid Owen. The third was a tall, broad, and handsome man in a cloak of deep red. He looked some few years older than Rury. His features were strong, his eyes a bright green, his hair a striking wealth of curling silver-grey. As he and the other two stepped forward to greet the newcomers, he spoke in a tone of bluff authority.

"Ah, Rury. Good to have you back here. And I see you've succeeded in bringing Matholwch with you."

"Aye, Fionnbharr," said Rury, clasping hands with the silver-haired man. "But a fair task it was, believe me."

"And why shouldn't it be?" the older man complained. "Many years it's been since I was forced to leave the comfort of my own Sidh. And it's a great nuisance traveling this way only in the dark."

"That's my own fault," said the one called Fionnbharr. "I insisted. It's much safer that way."

"All those strange things out there," said Matholwch, shaking his head. "I didn't realize how long it's been since I saw the outer world. All those roads crisscrossing over the land, and those creatures traveling on them, in hundreds, sweeping the way ahead with those light beams from their eyes. Most frightening!"

"Those things are called motorcars," the silver-haired one said. "They're just one of the reasons our own travel must be so secret now."

"Well, I'd not be traveling at all if it hadn't been Rury O'Mor who needed my help and my king who requested it," the older man told him. "Now then, where is the enchanted one?"

Owen spoke up at this. "She is in the guest house called Harp, under a guard, I'm afraid. This power is so strong on her that we feared she'd try to escape again."

"And there's nothing *you* can do, Owen?" Matholwch asked. "Your own skills are as great as mine."

"Not in dealing with spells over the mind," Owen said. "In such arts, no other ard-druid has so much knowledge as you."

The older man gave a small smile and bow of acknowledgment. "But I may well need your help. Will you accompany me to her?"

"I will gladly," Owen said, "this way."

He led Matholwch off toward a doorway, adding as he went, "Oh, her mother is with her. Rury fetched her here before he fetched you."

"We may have to get her away while we work," said the other as they passed out of the room. "Some of the effects of my counterspells aren't pleasant to see."

Rury, looking after them, caught this last remark. He looked in distress to Fionnbharr. "The druids won't hurt her, will they?"

"I'm certain they'll try not to," said the silver-haired man. "But we must give them a free hand. You do want your Caitlin returned to you free of the evil influence, don't you?"

"Of course. Can I go and see her as well?"

"No. I think that might only make her worse. Much of her anger is directed at you. She seems to see you as an enemy now."

"As if it were *you* who had stolen her away from her home," Angus said in disbelief. "A madness indeed."

"We'll pray to Danu they can help her," Rury told him. "But how are you feeling, old friend?"

"In the days you've been traveling, I've fully mended," the warrior said, showing him the arm that had been wounded. The places where the bullet had pierced it were marked only by two round, white scars now. "At this kind of healing, Owen has no peer."

"Too bad he had no chance to use his saving arts on Kevan," O'Mor said sorrowfully.

Fionnbharr looked thoughtfully on the two men. He allowed them a moment for their grieving, then said, "My two comrades, now that Rury's brought help and we have some time, I think we must talk about this quest of yours. You know I am much troubled by it, Rury. You should have come to me."

"And if I had, would you have told me to leave her in that treacherous man's hands?"

"I might have warned you of the dangers, made you consider how great a task you faced. I have kept a bit more in touch with the outside than most of you. I knew the changes in the mortals' world had begun to move at a headlong pace, making things strange and frightening.

Why do you think I have admonished that we must, more than ever before, stay separate?"

"If they invade our world, if they ravage it or steal from it, how can we just stay hidden?" O'Mor countered. "Haven't we the right to fight back?"

"Even if we put our whole people at risk? We can't go to war with the mortals, Rury. The cost is too great."

"Caitlin is my betrothed," O'Mor said stubbornly. "I have grown to have a deep love for her over these years. The great emptiness had at last faded from me. I've waited over fifteen of those mortals' centuries for that, my king. I could not lose her."

"I can understand your deep feeling, Rury," said Fionnbharr.

"Besides," put in Angus heartily, "we did defeat them, for all their magic and men. Maybe your concern over their powers is much exaggerated."

"You lost one," the silver-haired man pointed out.

"And I grieve for Kevan," said the big warrior. "But he died gallantly, battling great odds, as we all hope to die."

"Perhaps you're right," Fionnbharr said, but doubtfully. "I'm only happy that it's ended now. You entered their world and brought Caitlin home to ours. We're safe, and there's an end to it."

19

"I am not going to rest until I find those people and that woman again. Do you all understand?"

Kean looked piercingly around his sitting room as he said this. It was somewhat crowded now with over a dozen men and women, the key people of Kean's search effort, called together to collate the results of their efforts so far.

By their dour expressions, it was obvious those results were somewhat less than spectacular.

"We've hunted, gone through data, and sifted facts for days, Mr. Kean," one of the men said defensively. "We've done everything we can think of. It's just not getting us anywhere."

"He's right, sir," said another. "We've done everything to find these people but to search Ireland house-to-house. I'm afraid even you haven't enough money to pay for doing that."

"Don't make any bets on it," Kean replied curtly. He looked to his security chief. "Garvey, what about the secrecy angle? You're sure this couldn't be some kind of underground thing?"

"If it is, sir, it's a very well hidden one," Garvey replied. "I've been to some of the best sources that there are. I've talked to a lot of old friends and old contacts from my intelligence days. I've checked through our government, through Ireland's, and even through the U.K.'s. There's still nothing. These names you've given us just aren't

known to them. And there is no one in their files of terrorists, subversives, criminals, or anything else clandestine
that matches up."

"What about the techniques they used?" asked Kean.
"Couldn't that give some clue as to who they are? How
they operate?"

Garvey shook his head. "No one could even make a
good guess as to how they pulled those tricks off. Some of
them thought I was lying. One of them suggested we talk
to a magician. He wasn't being funny."

Kean sighed in frustration. "Damn! There has got to be
some way to identify them." He looked to a dark-haired
young woman. "What about the clothing?"

"We've checked on them from the descriptions you
gave us," she said, her accent identifying her as an Irish
member of the team. "We've discovered it's the traditional
clothing of the Irish Celtic tribes during a period from
about five hundred years B.C. to about five hundred A.D.
Apparently it was very authentic as well."

"Okay, then how about that historical angle?" Kean
said. "They got all that stuff from somewhere, didn't they?
And they must have had *some* reason for dressing up that
way."

"No good either, sir," said a red-haired young man also
of Irish accent. "We've spoken with every costumer, every
theatrical troupe and agent in the country. We've checked
every place that holds historical pageants, every site that
has people dress in period costume, every society, club,
town, and sect that reenacts historical events. No help
there."

"Damn. Damn. Damn!" Kean said, rubbing his forehead irritably. His haggard look was even more pronounced now. He seemed near to defeat.

"Mr. Kean," another man said, "isn't there anything else
that she told you? Or maybe something this O'Mor mentioned. Some casual remark? Something you overheard?
Something?"

"I've been over it and over it," Kean said. "Nothing comes."

"It could have been a name. A place," the man persisted. "Something you maybe didn't even understand. Something you might have disregarded."

"Didn't understand," Kean echoed thoughtfully. "Yeah. You know, I *do* remember. There *was* something she said, the first time she saw my place. She said it was grander than somebody's . . . I think it was 'sith.' "

"A what, sir?" asked Garvey.

"Or 'sif' or 'siv.' Something like that. I don't know what the hell she meant."

"The word does seem familiar," said the red-haired man. He considered and shook his head. "Very strange, but I believe that it was my grandmother that I heard speak of such a thing."

"You said *'somebody's* sith,' " said Garvey. "Whose, sir?"

"I'm trying to remember that," Kean answered, frowning in concentration. "Things were just a little confusing at the time. But it was . . . 'Dada'? Something like that. No. 'Dak-ta.' More like that."

"Not 'Dagda'?" asked the Irish young man.

"Yeah. That was it."

"Then I do know what she meant!" the other said with a note of triumph. "That's jogged my recollection. My grandmother told me tales as a child. I heard those words in them." He looked to Kean, his expression growing doubtful. "But, Mr. Kean, I don't see how knowing will be very much help to you."

"What do you mean?" Kean said impatiently. "Just tell me!"

"Well, it's only that these things that she spoke of, they're from our old Irish . . . well, what you would call our fairy tales."

"It's a most amazing tale you tell me, Mr. Kean. Yes, yes. A *most* amazing tale."

The man who spoke was short and broadly built, with a solid rectangle of a head framed by bushy hair and beard of deep black shot through with streaks of grey.

Just now he was standing precariously on a ladder, holding it with one hand while the other stretched far out to reach a book on a shelf.

That shelf was nearly the topmost one of a very high wall of books. A dozen feet below him, Kean and McBride sat on chairs before a massive, cluttered desk, looking up to watch him with some apprehension. Besides the desk and chairs, the decor of the room around them was very simple: floor-to-ceiling shelves on the other three walls, some long tables also cluttered with materials, and a few more chairs.

The man grasped his book—causing the watchers to release held breaths—and started down.

"I know it's amazing, Professor Connelly," said Kean. "That's why I'm hoping very much for your discretion in this. The people at Trinity College who recommended you said we could count on your having that. I hope they're right, because, frankly, there are people who might think I was either crazy or lying if they heard what I just spilled to you."

The man nodded soberly as he sat down behind his desk, fixing dark, intense eyes on his visitor. "Ah, yes. I can see where that might be. And I assure you the most generous fee you've offered for my research services will guarantee the confidence of a confessional from me."

"Good enough. But can you help me, Professor? I mean, can you shed any light on any of this?"

"If any man in Ireland can," he said without modesty. He waved at the hundreds of books around the room. "About you is one of the finest private collections of Irish historical and literary materials in the world. Researching into the old knowledge has been much of my life."

"Okay then. For starters, what about this Dagda character. You've heard of him?"

"Of a certainty. He's one of the most famous figures of the most ancient Celtic myths. One of the chief gods."

"A god?" said McBride. "Like the old Roman and Viking ones?"

"Somewhat." The professor's voice took on a scholarly tone, as if he were lecturing a class. "The Indo-European roots are possibly the same, but the gods of the Celtic tribes developed independently. The Dagda and his fellow gods go back to very ancient times, well into the neolithic age, several thousand years ago. Their origins are very obscure. Dagda himself was an earth god. His name can be translated as the 'Good God.' "

"So we *are* talking about some kind of supernatural being here?" said Kean, clearly disappointed.

"Why yes. Though, according to myths, he was a mortal once, as were all his people. They gained supernatural powers from a mystical queen named Danu before taking control of Ireland. That's why one name for them is the *Tuatha de Danann*, or 'Children of Danu.' "

"What happened to them?" asked McBride, clearly intrigued.

"They held Ireland for a while, but then a new race invaded the country. Its people were called the Milesians, a mortal race. They are the ancestors of those who inhabit the country to this day. You see, the de Dananns fought a war with them and lost it, despite their supernatural skills. After that they vanished. They withdrew into the secret places, whole magic kingdoms if you will, supplied to them by Queen Danu's immense powers. The folklore still persists that various mounds and hills all over Ireland are hiding the entrances to these places. *Sidhe*, they are called."

" 'Shee'?" Kean repeated, pronouncing the word.

"S-I-D-H-E is the actual Gaelic spelling," the professor said, "though the British, in their zealous attempt to anglicize everything Irish, did spell it as it sounds, S-H-E-E. And that finally became the popular spelling."

"Look, just what's the point of all this for me?" Kean asked.

"Well, that word is the plural of *Sidh*," Connelly explained, "that other name you heard. The immortals who lived in them became known as the *Aes Sidhe* or 'People of the Hills.' Finally this was shortened by the peasantry to the single word *Sidhe*, synonymous with 'fairy.' You see, with the passing years and the great changes in the world, the old ones' status as gods rather dwindled away. They were forgotten entirely by most civilized and Christianized men; and even among the simpler, rural folk who still believed in them, their nature degenerated both in power and size."

"You mean they're little? Like Tinkerbell?" asked Mac.

Connelly gave a little smile at that. "Yes. So more recent tales would lead you to believe. But a student of the old myths and legends knows them as a tall, fair, and handsome people of great nobility. In the modern world, however, the only popular survivals are such distorted creatures as the leprechaun and banshee."

"Banshee," said Kean musingly. "I remember hearing my mother use that word. A lady up the street used to always be screaming at her kids. Mom said she had a 'wail like a Banshee.' I never knew what it meant."

"I know," piped up Mac. "It's a ghostlike thing. Floats around your house moaning right before you die. Like in *Darby O'Gill and the Little People*, right?"

"Your knowledge of old Walt Disney flicks astounds me," Kean said dryly.

"A very crude parody of the original," Connelly said. "You know what the *Shee* means now. Well, the *Ban* is simply a simplification of the Gaelic *Bean*, meaning 'woman.' Thus, *Ban-Shee*, 'woman of the Shee.' It was their ancient penchant for warning Irish heroes of coming death that carried over to the grotesque figment that survives today. But a true Sidhe woman would be much like any other, save that she might be of especial grace and beauty."

He looked hard at Kean, adding most seriously: "But you might know that best yourself, Mr. Kean. If your tale is true, it seems as if you have met one."

"What the hell are you talking about?" said Kean.

"You don't mean Caitlin Bawn!" said Mac.

The professor nodded. "I do," he said earnestly. "Everything you have described to me could be attributed to the nature and abilities of the Sidhe. This strange, isolated glade where you met her is the kind of meeting place often described in the old tales. It is a kind of protected area of the earth where they may move about outside freely. These are the few small pieces of our world left safe to them. And their dress, their weapons, even these . . . these 'magic tricks' as you call them, are as the bards tell of them in tales two thousand years old." He leaned forward eagerly. "Mr. Kean, if what happened to you is true, then you may have had an encounter such as has not happened for centuries."

Kean stared at the man. "You sound like you actually believe in them."

"I would like to," Connelly admitted. "I won't deny it. I've spent many years delving into the facts, myths, and theories about them. Behind such myths, you know, there is always some grain of truth. And I've often wondered, how large a one for Them? Once men were fully convinced that They were real. Irishmen for hundreds, even thousands of years claimed to have often met with Them, fought with Them, even entered Their realms. Of course, such claims have lessened with growing modernity, as if the Sidhe have withdrawn farther and farther, like rare jungle beasts retreating deeper into the last jungles before the spread of civilization."

Kean shook his head. "I can't believe this. I was afraid to talk to you because I figured you'd think *I* was crazy. You really expect me to believe she's one of Them, and that They came out of Never-Never Land to steal her back?"

"I'm sorry. Perhaps I was carried away by my enthusiasm," the professor said carefully. "Mr. Kean, I believe we are both quite rational men. Of course I don't expect you to suddenly believe in supernatural beings. And I'm certainly not saying that I'm convinced they have manifested themselves here. However, I *am* saying that there is some undoubted connection between these . . . 'beings' you encountered and the vast body of folklore relating to the Sidhe."

"That's what we came to Professor Connelly to find out," Mac pointed out. "I think we should listen to him, Michael."

"You say you have no other clues," the professor went on. "Perhaps an investigation of this link, no matter how ephemeral, can eventually lead to them. Have you another choice?"

Kean eyed him searchingly for a long moment, then nodded in acquiescence. "Okay. I'll give you that. So, where do I start?"

"It would seem that this place she mentioned is the logical choice." Connelly opened the large and rather dusty old tome he had fetched down from the shelf. "Here, that's why I got this."

He flipped through its brittle pages carefully, stopping finally on one. He turned the book around toward them. Kean and Mac leaned forward to peer down at a flamboyantly and archaically drawn map of Ireland, marked out with topographical features and crowded with hundreds of elaborately scripted names.

"You see, this indicates various sites mentioned in the mythology," the professor explained. "That includes many supposed locations of the realms of the Sidhe that were parceled out to the various clans by Queen Danu."

His index finger moved across the map to stop on a spot not far inland from the central-eastern coastline.

"According to myth, the Dagda's Sidh is technically here," he said. "It's not very far away, actually. Just some thirty miles northwest of Dublin. There is a group of large, neolithic mounds there. Newgrange is the most famous."

"Why do you say 'technically'?" asked Mac.

"Because the Sidh was originally allotted to Dagda, b was stolen from him by a somewhat conniving son nam Angus Og. After being usurped, as it were, by his son, tl father mixed very little in Eire's affairs thereafter."

"A little boardroom shake-up," said Mac. "Happens e erywhere I guess. New regimes grabbing power from tl old."

"As you say," said Connelly. "Still, the Dagda's nam continues to be connected with the Sidh."

"And you think Caitlin Bawn might have something do with this place?" asked Kean.

"It could be. She implied she had been there. Perha she lived in the area. Perhaps she visited there. At lea there is a chance that someone might know of her."

Kean sighed. "It's better than nothing." He looked McBride. "We're going to check it out."

"We can send a team up right away," his friend replie

"No, not this time," Kean said decisively. "I'm not si ting around in Dublin any longer, going nuts waiting hear something. This I am going to go check out for m self."

"Are you?" said Connelly with great interest. "We then, there is a fine hotel near the town of Slane that I c recommend," he volunteered. "And if you wouldn't min I would like to accompany you. It's possible I might be further help for you in your . . . quest."

"I don't know, Professor," Kean said.

"Oh, but I wouldn't ask for further compensation," tl scholar added quickly. "And I would be most happy to further research. I might discover other facts that yc could use."

"It's not that," said Kean. "I'd be glad for your help, ar I'd pay you for it too. It's just that . . . well, you hear my story. Whatever's going on, it's pretty strange and could be dangerous too. I can't ask you to get involved something like that."

Connelly gave a broad, enthusiastic grin. "Mr. Kean, believe me, I would not miss this for the world!"

Kean nodded. He rose and thrust a hand across the table toward the man.

"Okay, Professor," he said as they shook hands. "Then welcome to the team."

20

Sunlight glittered in brilliant shards of silver-white on the broad, rippling surface of the river running by some quarter mile below.

Kean had paused with McBride and Professor Connelly on the graveled path above to look down on the water and out across the green, rolling countryside beyond. Starski and Garvey, their boss's inevitable twin shadows, were stopped some dozen feet behind. Their own gazes were more wary than appreciative.

The atmosphere of the place seemed lost on those two. But the sense of peace and timelessness appeared for some moments to hold the other three enthralled.

"The Brugh-na-Boyne," Connelly announced. "The famous Boyne River of the most ancient bardic tales. Standing here, it seems a place untouched by the centuries."

"I know what you mean," said McBride. "It is like walking back into the past. I can feel it."

"There are many places with such a feel in Ireland," the professor said. "Or there were. There seem to be less and less of them each year."

"Too bad," said Mac.

"Yeah, right," said Kean more curtly. "So, where're these mounds?"

"Just above," Connelly said.

They walked on westward along the path that paralleled the river, the two guards following. They passed by a number of other people walking back from a hillcrest ahead to a large car park behind. The broad stretch of parking lot was glittering too, but from sunlight striking the metal roofs of a sea of cars. The people they passed were clearly sightseers, clutching maps and brochures, loaded down with still and videotape cameras, chatting loudly and animatedly.

"At least they've kept the car park separated well here," Connelly commented as they moved along. "Not so obtrusive on the atmosphere of the old place. All that part and the museum are rather new, you know. Once, oh, not more than twenty years ago, one could come out the secluded lanes and across the open meadows to places like these, isolated still, all but deserted much of the time. It was only those really keen to make the journeys, those who . . . understood, who visited them. They were unspoiled, and they were also free."

"Free?" Kean repeated.

"No admissions charged, I mean. Oh, yes. Many of them were so, I recall. The soaring, windswept Cliffs of Moher; the high, raven-haunted ruins of Cashel; the seat of Eire's ancient high kings at Tara. All places for coming closer to the past. All become tourist . . . 'traps,' I think you call them now. There are charges for entering, cars and great tourist buses swarming in, marketplaces for fast food and cheap souvenirs clustered all around." He grimaced in distaste.

"That's the way it is, Professor," Kean said. "If people want to come from all over the world to see those places, why shouldn't someone, especially your own country, make a buck from it?"

"Maybe," said Connelly.

He eyed a group of several rotund adults and a clutch of unkempt children going by, all looking disappointed, mumbling, and shaking heads.

"I'm tired of old castles and smelly caves," one young boy was whining. "I want a place with rides! With an arcade!"

Another female child with them discarded a candy wrapper casually, as if the rest of the world's task was to clean up after her. The professor picked it up and glared after the people as they moved away.

"I only wonder how many of this lot really care?" he said with some despair.

They went on, climbing the path toward the high ground. As they grew nearer, a large form seemed to swell into view ahead. They came up onto a higher plain to see the form fully revealed before them.

They paused again to take in the impressive sight.

"Newgrange," Connelly announced with a note of pride. And then he quoted in ringing, lyric tones:

> "Behold the Sidh before your eyes.
> It is manifest to you that it is a king's mansion,
> Which was built by the firm Dagda,
> It was a wonder, a court, and admirable hill."

Before them rose a smoothly rounded mound, some twelve yards high and a hundred in diameter. Its sloping outsides were grass-covered, unbroken save on the south side. Here there was the black rectangle of an opening into the mound's base. It was framed by two upright stones capped over by a third.

The slope of the mound on either side of this opening had been cut away sheer and faced with walls of piled rock. A few feet before the entrance, a massive, long stone lay horizontal on the ground.

"That little piece was said by the old Irish poet MacNia when he first saw this," Connelly explained. "It's one of the finest passage graves in all of Western Europe. It dates back to 2500 B.C. As old as the Egyptian pyramids."

He led them right up to it. They stopped by the outer stone. Its front surface was deeply etched with large spiral-shaped decorations. Mac ran a hand lightly over one of them, tracing the whorls around.

"I'm touching something that's forty-five hundred years old," he said with awe.

"Yes," said the professor. "Those spiral decorations were very common then. But they've also persisted right to this day in Irish art. No one knows what their original meaning was. Something of a deeply mystical nature, most likely."

"Like the symbol of some kind of force, maybe," Kean said in a musing way. "Like . . . a tornado or something."

"Perhaps," said Connelly, eyeing him curiously.

"So, Professor, are you saying that these Sidhe folks built this thing?" asked Mac, gazing up at the mound looming above.

"No. I'm saying nothing for myself. *Science* says it was built by mortals, early tribes of pre-Celtic settlers. Its designated function was as a passage grave. That opening leads to a small chamber in the very center, with two other chambers, one on each side. It's surmised that the cremated remains—probably of kings and high chieftains from pre-Celt and Celtic times—were laid to rest within them."

"So then what's the connection of this place to the Dagda and his friends?" asked Kean.

Connelly shrugged. "That too is a matter of opinion. Perhaps the tales of the gods' connection to this place made it a sacred spot. Thus it would be the logical place for mortals to build their own holy places." He looked around him, adding more slowly, "Or perhaps there is a feel about this place, a sense of the power of the supernatural concentrated here that drew the people to it."

"You're kidding, right?" said Kean.

"No," Connelly said earnestly. "I believe there are such places in the earth, as do many others. They seem to be spots of fascination to man throughout the ages. Over the millennia we've built our churches and monuments upon them. We bury our dead and worship there, as if we are closer to our deities. Perhaps these *are* the points of contact between our world and others. Perhaps they truly are entrances to the realms of the Sidhe."

Kean sighed. "Look, Professor, could we just stick with reality? I don't see how this gets us any closer to Caitlin. Nobody at the museum back there knew her name or recognized her description. She sure doesn't *live* anywhere around here. If this thing's just a big grave, then where's this Dagda's house she mentioned supposed to be?"

"Well, once this whole collection of mounds—there are actually seventeen in this area—was considered the most famous site of fairy hills in Ireland. This one and two others called Knowth and Dowth were believed parts of Dagda's main residence, before they were excavated and proven to be tombs. But there is one somewhat smaller burrow over there"—he gestured southwest—"closer to the Boyne. It's called the Tomb of the Dagda, and it's never been opened. There was a Dr. James Furgusson, an archaeologist some years ago, who was convinced the Tuatha de Danann were real people. He felt that the proof of the Dagda's existence would someday be discovered within that very mound."

"Great," said Kean. "Well, maybe I'll just wander over there and check it out. Not that I'm sure what good it'll do. I'm just curious to see the place." He looked to Mac. "You want to come along?"

"Well, if you don't mind, I think I'll just hang around here. I'd like to check inside. Maybe I'll see the ashes of some ancestor."

"Sure," Kean said sarcastically. "Your ancestors were kings just about as much as mine were. But, suit yourself. Professor? Why don't you stay too? I'll just jog over and come right back."

"As you wish."

"You want us both to stay with you, don't you, sir?" Garvey said, stepping forward.

"No, that's okay," Kean said. "You guys can stay here with them."

"Remember last time, Michael," Mac warned. "You went wandering off in the countryside, got lost, and then met her."

"Yeah, well maybe I'm hoping it'll happen again," Kean said.

"Things are a little more involved now, sir," Garvey pointed out. "The people you're looking for are extremely dangerous."

"He's right, boss," Starski added in an unusual, unsolicited speech. "You gotta have some muscle with you."

Kean sighed. "All right, Stony. You come along with me. That's enough." He waved at the others. "We'll see the rest of you guys later." He signed to Starski. "Come on."

As those two headed back down the pathway again, a curious McBride led the way through the entrance and into the mound. A disinterested Garvey stayed outside.

Mac and Connelly walked in along a low corridor made of large, flat, upended slabs of rock set side-by-side, roofed over with more of the same. They were heavily decorated with spirals, diamonds, and curlicue designs.

"Likely this structure of stones was built first," Connelly explained, "then covered with dirt. But it was very exact work, aligned precisely with the sun." He pointed back up the corridor. "Above the main opening a smaller square hole was visible. "See there? At solstice time a beam of sunlight shines right through, along here, and illuminates the central chamber."

They came to it as he spoke. It was a cavelike space with two others through arches on either side. The air was heavy with a damp, earthy smell.

Mac peered in at a large basin carved from stone that sat on the floor of one chamber.

"No sign of anyone's leftovers there," he said.

"You mentioned ancestors," the professor said. "It's clear from your name that you've Irish blood. But what about Mr. Kean? Has he some roots here too?"

"Michael? Oh, you bet he has. Both of his folks were pure Irish. His dad was second generation." Mac looked over the stone carvings as he talked. "His grandpa and grandma came over—*went* over I should say—in the twenties. You'd never know it though from him. He wrote that whole thing off. Even changed his name's spelling to make it more readable. It was spelled C-I-A-N before."

"But pronounced the same," said Connelly. "I can understand that. But why is he so against his heritage?"

"His dad and granddad brought that on, I guess." Mac turned to the other man. "Look, let's get out. This place is getting claustrophobic."

Connelly led the way. Mac continued as they walked along.

"See, Sean and Patrick—Mike's father and granddad—were both laboring stiffs. Hardworking, honest, but never successful. Dumb Micks they were called. There was still some real prejudice back then. I know, my own dad got it too. He and Mike's dad worked together. Plumbers, painters, odd job men. Broke both their backs and spirits finally."

They came out of the mound back into the sunlight. Mac took a deep breath of fresh air before going on.

"Mike never accepted it. His old man was a loser, and he was never going to end up that way himself. So instead of taking crummy handyman jobs in those tenements where we lived, he went into realty and started selling them until he raised enough money to buy some himself. Within a few years he was one of the biggest real estate wheeler-dealers on the East Coast. It was only uphill from there."

"He became an entrepreneur," said Connelly. "Sounds as if he's to be admired."

"Maybe. Except he lost interest in everything but making money and bossing around the world. Little things like humanity just got in the way. I guess I was the one exception—the childhood friend he felt like he owed something to."

"That is too bad," said Connelly.

"It was. See, that's why I guess I'm glad he's mixed up

in this, crazy as it is. For once he's doing something for some other reason than greed."

"What reason? Love?"

Mac considered. "Love? Well, I don't know. I'd like to think so. She sure brought out some kind of real emotion in him." He looked down the pathway in the direction Kean had gone. "It's just nice to see him have a purpose without a selfish end. And that's why I'm still sticking with him."

"I only hope that he, and you, can follow it through to a successful end."

"You and me both, Professor," Mac said wholeheartedly. "You and me both."

The other two men had meantime traveled some distance away. They'd left the path to travel on past the car park, paralleling the river.

Starski this time walked close beside his charge on guard. Kean peered off intently toward the river as they went, finally spying the distinctively rounded peak of a hill poking above some trees near to its shore.

They made their way down toward it, pushing into a little wood of venerable oaks and stately rowan trees. In the center of the wood they came into a large glade, its center marked by a mound some twenty feet high and fifty yards across.

"No wonder this one's been left alone," said Kean as they strode up to it. "You'd barely know it's here."

"Listen," said Starski, stopping to cock an ear.

"I don't hear anything," said Kean.

"I know," the man said, openly amazed. "I don't think I've ever not heard so much in my life."

Kean smiled at the odd grammar, but then he really listened too. The glade was wrapped in a quiet that seemed preternatural. There was no rustling of winds in leaves, no song of bird, no whispering of the nearby river. The vast silence was almost a presence of itself.

Kean shrugged sharply as to throw the eerie sensation off.

"Never mind," he said briskly. "Let's just check this thing out and get the hell out of here. You go around it that way"—he pointed left—"I'll go right. Meet you in a minute."

"Boss," said Starski uncertainly, "I don't like letting you outta sight."

"Geez, Stony, the thing's only a few hundred feet around. Get going."

The big man nodded resignedly, turned, and started off his way. Kean headed off the other.

He moved at a slow walk, gazing up at the rounded hill above. It was like Newgrange, smooth and covered with grass, but with no sign at all of openings.

"Just what in the hell am I looking for?" Kean said aloud.

"Is it lost you are, maybe?" asked a voice.

Kean stopped abruptly, whirling around.

A figure stood some way behind him. He was far from threatening: a little man, lean and very stooped, dressed in a shabby grey wool coat and trousers; worn, dusty boots upon his feet and a battered cloth cap upon his head. A large scythe with a much-honed curve of iron blade was propped against one shoulder, looking almost too much for him to handle.

"Why, lad, you look as if you'd seen the Devil himself," said the man as he saw Kean's surprised expression.

"Sorry," said Kean, recovering. "But I've had too many people sneaking up on me lately."

"I didn't mean to be doing that," said the man. "I was just doing a bit of the trimmin' up, over there." He waved vaguely toward the trees. "Someone's got to keep things neat." He stepped closer. "You one of them from up there, are you?"

"I guess so."

"They seldom come down here from the big mound above. Too little to see."

Kean eyed the man more closely. He seemed elderly his face much lined and his bushy eyebrows white. Bu there was an ageless quality to his deep blue eyes, and also an intelligence. He stared back keenly at the American, a small smile on his lips.

"Do you know very much about this place?" Kean asked.

"Been about here all my life," he said. "A very long time indeed."

"Maybe you can help me then," Kean said hopefully. "Do you know a woman named Bawn? Caitlin Bawn."

The man's eyes narrowed. "Caitlin Bawn," he repeated in a considering way. He shook his head. "I can't say that I've heard a name like that."

"She's a blonde. Slim. Fairly tall. Around twenty. Very good-looking too, and with blue eyes like"—he stared into the man's own deeply colored ones again—"well, like yours."

"Sorry, lad. There's many a woman like that I've seen in my years."

"She might be with some men," Kean said more desperately. "One of them called himself Rury O'Mor. They dress in Irish clothes, old-fashioned ones. Cloaks and things. They carry swords. Maybe they're some kind of historical group. They might hang around a place like this. Have meetings here, or . . ."

The man lifted a hand. "Forget it, lad. There're none of them come around here dressed like that. And wouldn't they be put away for madmen if they did? Why no one's dressed like that for hundreds of years."

"I know that," Kean said. "I just thought that—"

"Now, you may have let the ancient air of this place go right to your head," the man said, interrupting again. "It happens sometimes to those of overly fanciful minds. They think they see all kinds of things ahauntin' about these mounds, 'specially on a misty Samhain eve. Terrible demons sometimes, and little fellows dancing in a ring as gaily as may be, their little red caps waggin' on their heads. Some say they've come under *pishogues* here—the fairy spells. Terrible visions they have then, of corpses, monsters, and headless fighting men."

"I'm not afraid of anything like that," Kean assured him. "I just . . ."

"Don't be so blessed sure of it," the other went on. "I knew a man not afeerd of the wildest night, 'til he had a terrible vision here. Never spoke of it, but an apparition of the worst kind it musta been. And now he'll not go out after dark. Very strange he's become. Even went to a priest to be sprinkled with holy water. It was no help, of course."

"Look," said Kean, trying to retain his patience, "the ones I'm looking for aren't part of a fairy tale. You people all seem to have that on the brain. These people are real."

"So you say," the old man replied gravely, fixing him with an intense gaze. "But be sure. For if it is some spirits you're seeking here, best beware, lad, since you might succeed in rousin' 'em. If I were you, I'd give it up and go right away."

"Thanks for the advice," Kean said dryly. "But I'm not through checking around here yet. This is very important to me. I'm giving this area a thorough shakedown before I give up."

He pulled a business card out of his pocket.

"Look, my name is Michael Kean," he said, passing it over. "You say you don't know anything, but maybe someone you know does. Pass the word around, okay? There'll be a big reward for any information."

The man squinted closely at the card, then looked to him. "Kean, eh? And a reward?"

"Right. A big one. I'll be staying close by, at the Ballivor Manor Hotel if anyone wants me. It's only a couple of miles from here."

"Ah, I know it well. Lord Ballivor himself lived there in the old times. I've visited it myself."

"Then, you'll pass the word?"

"Oh, I'll surely pass on who you are and what you're seekin'," the man assured. "Though it'll likely do you little enough good." He lifted the scythe down to clasp in both hands. "Well, I've got to be back to my cuttin' now. So, a good-bye to you. And may your quest not bring a curse on you, young man."

On this rather dark blessing he turned and started away. Somewhat taken aback by the parting words, Kean called after him: "Curse? What the heck are you talking about? Old man! Hey, old man?"

But the man seemed not to hear him now, moving back toward the edge of the glade, swinging his scythe out in rhythmic strokes at the long grass as he went.

Kean opened his mouth to shout louder after the man, but was stopped by another voice from behind him.

"Mr. Kean?" it said. "That you?"

He turned. Starski had just come into view around the curve of the mound. His big face broke into an expression of immense relief as he saw his employer's face.

"It is you, boss," he said. "Where have you been?"

"Where have I been?" said a perplexed Kean. "Right here!"

The bodyguard shook his head emphatically. "You couldn'ta been. I went all the way around this thing. Twice! I was getting kinda panicked the second time, I'll tell you!"

"You've had one too many punches to the head, Stony," Kean said dismissively. "I've been standing right here the last few minutes. I was talking to that old guy."

"What old guy?" said Starski, looking around.

"That one," said Kean, turning to point toward him. "Right there!"

But the old man was gone.

21

Kean walked on and on across the night-covered countryside.

The night was a bright one, with the moon near to full, and the meadowland stretched away open and flat and with seeming endlessness on all sides, its even carpet of lush grass gleaming dark emerald under the moonlight.

And then an object came into view ahead, not appearing from the distance, but swelling right up from the ground to abruptly loom starkly above him. It was an immense and smoothly rounded shape that he easily recognized. It was the Newgrange mound.

"Just what am I doing here?" he asked aloud. He looked down at his Rolex, its lighted dial revealing the time: 12:01. "After midnight? Why the hell are we still here?" He looked around him. "Stony? Stony, where the hell are you? Mac? Where are you?"

No reply. He was alone.

His last words had barely echoed away into the night when the sound of tramping feet came to him from ahead, growing louder very rapidly. He listened, and he heard voices growing in volume too, raised together in a song. But though its words came clearly to him, their meaning was still unintelligible:

"Feuch an rogaire 'g iarraidh poige,
Ni h-iongantas mor e a bheith mar ata"

Warily, he crouched down in the shelter of a bush that he suddenly found close by, peering ahead as some figures came into view from beyond the mound. They moved toward him, stepping in unison to the time of their continuing song:

*"Ag leanamhaint a gcomhnuidhe d'arnan na graineoige
Anuas's anios's nna chodladh 'sa' la."*

He saw now by the moonlight that there were six of them, all dark-cloaked men of long and pale hair, all carrying together a single large bundle on their shoulders.

As their song ended, they came to a stop, not four yards before him. They threw the bundle down unceremoniously on the ground, and he could see too clearly what it was.

The face of a corpse long dead looked up to the night sky. Its decimated body was cloaked in filthy rags. Its dried skin was cracked and drawn tight over protruding cheeks and jaw. Its mouth hung open to reveal a black, shriveled tongue. It stared with the shrunken, dulled orbs that were once its eyes. *Things* crawled upon its form so thickly that its surface seemed to writhe.

Kean stared at it, aghast.

"Isn't it lucky we met you tonight, Michael Kean," said one of the men. "Stand up now so we can see you."

He rose up to face them. "How do you know me?"

"And isn't it my own task to know all those who come about, rousing the spirits here?" the man said, stepping closer.

Kean stared more intently at him. The figure was taller, straighter, more majestic of bearing. The face was much younger and bolder of feature, but its look was still familiar, and so were its glinting blue eyes.

"I—I met you today," said Kean. "You were an old man!"

"So I appear to be for those who dare to invade my realm," the other said. "But to those of the Otherworld who abide here, it's the Chieftain Angus Og that I am. I gave fair warning to you to go away, but you ignored me. And by your continued disturbing of us, you've made yourself our slave."

"What are you talking about?" Kean said. "You can't do anything to me." He tried to turn, to step backward, but he was frozen on the spot.

"You can't withstand us, Kean," the man said. "You're in our power now. Lift up that corpse."

Kean glanced again to the abhorrent pile. "I won't," he said defiantly.

The man looked to the others. "Kean says he won't lift the corpse," he said.

And there came in reply from them a harsh, awful laughter, like dry branches scraping together in a sharp winter's wind.

Then, in a group, they rushed upon Kean. He tried again to run, but couldn't move. They grabbed him, threw him down, and held him tight, his face pressed to the ground.

They raised the corpse and brought it forward and heaved it upon him. The sunken, vermin-infested breast of the dead man was pressed against his back. The wasted arms were thrown forward around his neck.

The six pulled back from Kean and let him get to his feet. The corpse was draped upon him, its awful head lolling back, gape-mouthed and staring. Kean's own face was a mask of horror. He started to shake himself violently to throw the body off. His look of horror worsened as the dead arms somehow pulled in tighter about his neck, and the two bony legs rose up to clamp tight about his waist.

"You see the power we have," the being called Angus Og told him. "You refused carrying the corpse and were made to do so. So you listen to me now, Michael Kean: you'll obey me in what I'm telling you to do, for you've no choice in it."

"Why are you doing this to me?" he asked.

"It's your fair punishment from us. That wretched man

you carry was a great evil in your world. He was a wild, unruly man of charm and handsome face who could steal the heart of any maid who looked on him. He said he loved a girl, but he deceived her. He wanted no more than her father's wealth to waste away on gambling and drink. She found out he never meant to marry her, and she died from the shame and the sorrow of it. Now he's cursed to never find a quiet grave for his crime, and you're cursed to forever carry him about for yours."

"I haven't committed a crime," Kean told them desperately. "I helped a girl. She's still in trouble. I want to help her again."

"You betrayed a girl's trust and stole her away," the other sternly said. "You violated her life as you have ours. There'll be no mercy for you, Michael Kean. You're doomed!"

"*Nooooo!*" screamed Kean. He turned and rushed away, stumbling across the uneven ground with the corpse clamped on his back.

The six made no move to follow, letting him run on across the moonlit plain.

He ran for what seemed hours, or days, or years, though the night sky always stayed the same. He stumbled often, crashing to the ground, but the rotting corpse kept always firmly astride.

At last he came into a stand of withered trees. He plunged into the moonlight-streaked shadows beneath its bare limbs. In the depths of the wood he came upon a high wall that was in places broken down. An old, grey church showed within it, surrounded by scores of cracked, canted headstones. A dozen more dead trees stood about it too, no single leaf or twig on any of their crooked branches, and them stretched out like the arms of an ancient, threatening man.

He hesitated, staring in at this. And then a most terrible, rasping and rattling voice spoke up from close behind him.

"You must go in there."

He started, and the sweat broke out on his forehead.

"Who's talking to me?" he said.

"It's I, the corpse, speaking," the thing said, its awful tongue vibrating in the black cavern of its gaping mouth.

"You can talk?" Kean said, both intrigued and horrified.

"Now and then. But I speak now to tell you how to be rid of me. Take me in there, Michael Kean. Take me into the church and raise the flag in the middle of its floor and make a grave for me there. Then I'll rest easy and we both will be free."

Kean didn't argue. He climbed over the broken wall, made his way through the churchyard, and walked in through the doorless entrance to the church.

It was long deserted, bare inside, its corners and raftered ceiling festooned with cobwebs. Shafts of light from the moon struck through holes in the roof and made silver pools on the dark slate floor.

He went to the center of the floor and looked down. The slate piece there was massive, over six feet long and three wide.

"Bury me. Bury me now!" the dead voice whispered in his ear. "There is a spade to do it."

Kean looked around. There was an old spade lying nearby. Without delay he took it up. He shoved its tip into a chink between the stones and heaved.

It didn't budge. Soaked in his streaming sweat now, he shoved the spade deeper and tried again. His body tautened. He groaned with the strain.

But the slate moved.

He heaved it up a crack, shoving the spade beneath. He let go of the tool and grasped the cold slab with his hands, lifting it clear, shoving it back, revealing a yawning hole below.

Another corpse that was now more bones than flesh rose upward in the hole. It lifted arms and chattered out through grinning, lipless teeth: "Go! Go! This grave is mine. That one you're carryin' has no place here. Go out or you're a dead man. A dead man!"

At this it fell back into the grave again. Kean stared

down at it, eyes boggling in his head, hair standing stiffly like the bristles on a pig. His body trembled from cold sweat and fear.

A chill, cruel laugh came to him from the church doorway. He looked around to see the one named Angus Og watching him.

"You see?" the man said. "You cannot bury him. No grave will have him. It's for you to carry him through all eternity."

"No!" Kean screamed at him. "I won't! I won't!"

He began to swing himself wildly about, slinging the corpse hard against the walls. He slammed himself back upon it, crushing it. He rolled upon it on the flags. The dried body crackled and cracked grotesquely as its bones snapped apart. The skull popped under Kean's weight, shattering to bits.

Some pieces fell away, littering the floor. One leg dropped off, while the other hung on by shreds of flesh and strands of ligament. Most of the skull went, leaving only the jaws and shriveled tongue affixed to the twisted remains of spine.

But through all this, the two arms still hung on intact, their grip on his throat growing always tighter, tighter.

Finally Kean was exhausted, staggering back to crash into the stone altar. He leaned against it to stay erect, gasping heavily for breath, tugging at the choking hands to drag them free. They would not move.

"It's no good," Angus Og said, stepping up to him. "You can't win. You'll never be free of our nightmares, Michael Kean. So long as you stay in Ireland, you will never be free!"

The man laughed, a shrill peal of sound that reverberated deafeningly within the cold stone room. A stream of light—bright gold and red with blue streaks flicking through it—rose up to coil around Kean, enveloping him.

He was blinded, deafened, all but strangled. His last breath was rasping in his throat.

An instant silence and darkness descended on him at once.

He thrashed violently, tumbling over the edge and thudding to the floor.

He looked around him in confusion, peering into the sudden dark. It was the edge of a bed he had fallen from. He lay on a thick carpet. The furniture of a bedroom was visible about him, showing in the moonlight shining through a curtained window.

He got to his feet and switched on a lamp on a bedside table. A brochure lying there came into view. It showed an exterior view of a neat, symmetrical Georgian manor beneath the printed heading: Ballivor Manor Hotel.

He looked around the bedroom in the light; it all appeared quite normal. He looked at the bed. Its clothes were yanked apart by his struggles; its sheet was twisted into a knot where it had gotten around his neck. He looked down at himself: he was in pajamas. He breathed deeply in relief.

"Just a goddamn dream," he said.

A long, shrill peal of cold laughter came echoing to him.

He swung around toward its source. It was the window, opened, its curtains stirring in a breeze.

He rushed to it, threw the sash full up, and leaned out. Below him, in the graveled yard before the hotel, a figure stood in the moonlight, looking up to him.

It was the one called Angus Og, grinning at him.

"Have you had enough of me, Michael Kean?" the man said tauntingly.

"I'll get you, bastard!" Kean said with heat.

Heedless of his dress, caught up by anger, he charged out of the room, along a corridor, down a sweep of front stairs to the door. Recklessly he flung it open and plunged out into the night.

He stopped there, looking around him. The yard was empty.

"Where are you!" he shouted challengingly. "Come on. Come on, you! Face me now!"

The response that came to him was a clopping and jingling noise rising from down the road to the house.

Up through the trees along one side of its curving drive a long black coach of antique style came suddenly into view.

As Kean stood staring, it rushed toward him, its huge wheels rumbling as they rolled along. The six galloping horses that drew it strained sleek black bodies forward and thrust out long necks—all untopped by heads.

The driver was visible now, clutching the reins and urging the team along with cracks of a long whip. Like his steeds, this being too was headless.

Kean stepped back toward the shelter of the doorway as this massive apparition charged toward him. But he moved too late.

As the coach blasted by him, something was flung down toward him by its driver. It struck him fully in the chest and face, splashing across him in a great burst of heavy, dark liquid.

While he stood stunned by the unexpected blow, the coach rolled on, down the other side of the drive, back into the night. Before it faded away into the black, a faint, hoarse, gloating voice drifted back to him: "Never be free, Kean! Never, never be free!"

And it was gone.

He looked down at his chest, drenched through. The sticky liquid was dripping in slow, fat droplets from his face and thickening rapidly. From its quick coagulation, deep red-black color, and distinctive sick-sweet smell, it was most obvious what it was.

Blood.

Kean threw the pajamas top down on the dining table.

The great splotch upon it, now dried to a rust-brown, showed with startling vividness against the white tablecloth and made a most unappetizing contrast to the pleasant breakfast of rashers, scrambled eggs, and toast spread out there.

"*That* certainly wasn't a part of any dream!" Kean announced to his companions at the table.

He, Professor Connelly, and McBride sat in the dining room of the hotel. It was a bright place in the morning, lit by sunlight through large southern windows. Besides themselves, only a few other guests dined at the room's dozen tables. They all pointedly avoided looking at the rather loud American and his friends.

"All right, Michael, so you're saying that somebody drove a coach by and threw blood in your face," said a skeptical-sounding McBride. "But your shouting out there at midnight woke up half the hotel." He glanced around at the other diners. "P.O.ed them real good too. I heard all the complaints. A bunch of them looked out. They all say they saw you. *Nobody* saw a black coach pulled by a headless team."

"So you're telling me I'm having hallucinations now?" Kean asked.

"No, no," Mac said. "But . . . well, you have been getting pretty wrought up over this."

Kean got angry. "So, did I slit a chicken's throat for this blood or just slash up my own wrists?" He held both arms out to his friend. "Wanna check?"

"Please, gentlemen, be calm," the professor put in soothingly. "I think that we must accept that something has truly happened to Mr. Kean. These events, dreams or otherwise, were certainly not created by his own mind. They were foisted upon him by some power outside. And, once again, these manifestations are traditional ones of Ireland."

"What do you mean?" asked McBride.

"The meeting with the ghostly figures about the mounds, their charge to carry around a corpse, the desperate wanderings in the night, the waking dead—all these are elements from oft-repeated folktales. And there are few commoner superstitions here than that of the *coiste-bodhar,* that black coach you saw. It's been often described through the centuries: an immense, hearselike vehicle drawn by headless horses and driven by a *dallahan* —a headless man. If it rumbles to your door, don't open it, or a basin of blood will be cast into your face."

"Is there some point to that?" asked Kean. "I mean, other than to ruin some good pj's?"

"I believe the goal of all these . . . visions was the same," said Connelly. "They were meant to frighten."

"Frighten?"

"Yes. To scare you away. To make you give up your search."

"But that would mean we're getting close," said Kean with eagerness.

"It might," Connelly said more cautiously. "Your poking about at Newgrange might have aroused them."

"Then their little tricks will have just the opposite effect," Kean told him. "They've proved they're out there now, and I sure won't quit hunting them down."

"I think they may also have proven something else, Mr. Kean. Something much more significant for you."

"How do you mean?"

"That these incidents seem further evidence of the involvement of the Sidhe. The one who called himself Angus Og, for instance. He's that son of the Dagda who's said to rule the Sidh now. He has the nickname of The Disturber. That's because of his power to frighten cattle"—he paused here to add significance—"*and* to influence mortal dreams!"

"And he was using that power on me?"

"That power and more. I would say, if these beings are real, that these are their ways of interacting with our kind. Your meeting with that 'man' up on the mound, the nightmare, and that ghost coach are types of methods they've used to control or avoid man through the ages. Through such means they've managed to keep our world at bay—at least, until now."

"I don't know," said Kean, still stubbornly skeptical. "I say it could all be tricks. And I should know. I've paid guys to invent better illusions than that coach."

"And the dream?" asked Connelly.

Kean shrugged. "Maybe it was just a dream. Maybe I am psyched like Mac says. Maybe we're just dealing with a sneaky bunch of ordinary guys."

"And maybe we're not," said Mac. "Michael, I still think our best bet's to listen to the professor. Even in New York I had a feeling there was something not natural in this. Over here that feeling's gotten a whole lot worse. Why not humor me? What have you got to lose?"

"He has a point, Mr. Kean," said Connelly. "If it is a power of the Otherworld you face, then perhaps it is time for you to use a like force against it."

"How do you mean?"

"I mean that I am only a historian. But if you agree to go, I can take you to someone who might be of much greater help than I."

Kean looked from him to a hopeful Mac. He looked down at the bloodstained shirt beside his plate. He sighed and nodded.

"Okay, Prof. What the hell?"

22

"**Y**ou cannot continue resisting Matholwch and the other druids this way, daughter," Aisling said exasperatedly.

Caitlin's haughty, silver-haired mother paced the plain stone cell in which her daughter had been confined. It had been sumptuously appointed with comfortable bed, table and chairs for dining, wardrobe and chests for clothes, rich-textured tapestries and rugs for decoration. Still, it was a place of confinement, iron-doored and windowless.

The small, plump handmaiden to Caitlin named Caoimhe was at the open wardrobe, hanging out a fine, deep red gown, brushing it down meticulously for her mistress's wearing. The green dress that had come from Kean hung neglected on a hook within. Caitlin herself, wearing only a brown wool shift now, sat upon the bed, watching her mother pace with a defiant air.

"It's not resistance I'm giving to them, Mother," the young woman said. "At least, not to their magic spells. I think you know that better than any of the others."

Her mother abruptly stopped pacing to look at her. "What do you mean?" she asked sharply.

"Just that I know, Mother. I know it was you who sent Rury after me. Caoimhe told me that you watched my leaving in the imaging pool."

"She did?" The older woman glared at the maid who

looked away, flushing, brushing faster at the gown to cover her chagrin.

"She did, and I'm glad she did," Caitlin said in her defense. "Finding that out told me that you surely must have realized it was my own choice to follow after Michael Kean."

"I—I know nothing of the kind," Aisling bluffed uncomfortably. "Perhaps you were not carried bodily away, but you could well have been forced to follow. How do I know what enchantment he put on you when you met him by the stream? The imaging pool's magic did not allow us to hear you. He could have said anything."

"It's only fooling yourself that you're doing now, Mother," Caitlin said severely. "I hear it in your voice. Such self-deceit has never been a quality welcomed by our race. You're the one who taught me so. But much worse is the deception that you have practiced upon Rury and the rest."

"I deceived no one," Aisling forcefully replied. "I meant only to save my daughter."

"What you did was to nearly bring on a war," her daughter replied with equal force. "You might have harmed many."

"I? Well, what about you?" the mother countered. "It was your running away that began all this. Haven't you any guilt in that?"

"I have, and a most sore one at the thought that I might have been a cause of poor Kevan's death. But I had hoped to vanish away from you and be left to do as I wished. And I would have succeeded if you had let me go."

"How could I do that? My own daughter? What I did was only for your good."

"Was it? Or was it for your own? Our clan has never been very rich or strong. My marriage to Rury would change that. You would have a chieftain as a son-in-law. We would leave our little home for his grand one."

"Unfair, daughter," Aisling said indignantly. "It was

Rury who sought you, of all women, because you were the fairest choice to wed and he the most deserving of a wife."

"And it's for those reasons alone that I'm betrothed to him?"

"He loves you. Hasn't he paid the proper court to you over all these years? Hasn't he waited patiently for the time when you should feel ready to wed? No man's shown more kindness, more tenderness, more generosity to a woman. How can it be that you've no love of him?"

"And when have I had a chance to decide my own feelings for him?" Caitlin shot back. "From the time I was a girl, I've been promised to him. I knew nothing else. I was born too late for any of the life you elders had, when you were freer to go out of our Sidh. I saw nothing outside the confines of our own realm. I knew no other men but those of our own clans. I was fettered, Mother, to you, to him, to our narrow world and its rules."

"Our world is wonderful!" Aisling argued. "Full of beauty, free of pain and care . . ."

"It's not my choice!" Caitlin all but shouted, cutting her mother off. "Don't you see? For all the wonders of it, it was not freely picked by me. And because of that, it's no more than a prison to me as surely as if it had bars of thick, black iron."

Aisling shook her head in frustration. "How a daughter of my own could ever speak so!" she said. "To have a chance to marry such a man and only see it as servitude." She sighed resignedly. "Well, I can only believe that you truly are under some great and evil spell. There is nothing else that could so turn you against your mother and against your race. I'd hoped that coming here, that reasoning with you, might help your senses return. But if you will not listen, then I've no choice but to let them break the spell."

"No, Mother!" Caitlin cried. She sprang up and moved to the woman. "You can't do that. You know it is a lie. Look at me. Look into my eyes." She grabbed Aisling's arms tightly. "Mother, look!"

Reluctantly Aisling's gaze met her daughter's.

"You know you see no spell there," Caitlin said fervently. "You can't ignore the truth. You must speak out. Help me. Convince them. Tell them that their magic will not work on me. Please, believe me!"

Aisling looked steadily at her daughter, uncertainty flickering in her eyes. Then she steeled herself again, drawing up stiffly, saying coldly: "I'll never accept that. What happened to you is over. Finished. You have returned to us. And now you will be restored, whatever it takes."

Caitlin drew up stiffly too, her own look growing hard. "Then know that the only way they can wipe the defiance from my mind will be to destroy it altogether. Let that be on your head, Mother."

"Better that than continued disgrace to our clan," Aisling uncompromisingly replied. She gestured to the handmaiden. "Come, Caoimhe. We will leave Caitlin now."

"Yes, lady," said Caoimhe. She looked to Caitlin. "Oh, I'm so sorry. I . . ."

"Hush, Caoimhe," the elder woman said sternly. She rapped on the iron door.

It was opened at once by a young warrior. The two women went out. The door closed on Caitlin with a clang of finality.

The young woman's defiant look gave way to one of sorrow. She moved to the wardrobe. She lifted out the green dress, her only link now with the mortal world, and fingered it lovingly.

"Ah, Michael Kean," she said despairingly, "is it true that I'll never see you more?"

"Angus Og did what?" the Sidhe King Fionnbharr asked in dismay.

"He used the old tricks to frighten this Kean away," said the small, boyish-faced, and freckled man who stood before him in his great hall. "He felt it was the best thing he could do."

Rury, the giant warrior Angus, and Owen the druid sat at a table nearby the king, listening to the newcomer's report. Their own response was guarded. Fionnbharr's was openly hostile.

"And just who is Angus Og," he stormed, "to make such a move without speaking first to me?"

"My chieftain feels he does not need to seek out your permission first," the little man said with some hauteur, pulling himself up and puffing out his chest. "And he did not send me to you now to ask acceptance of his actions. He is a son of the Dagda, a brother to Bobd Dearg, a powerful leader among the de Danann in his own right. Are you meaning to give challenge to that?"

The king swallowed his anger with an effort, saying more soothingly: "No, no, Killian. It's too many battles we've fought among ourselves in the past. There's no place for them now. As the world's become of late, we must combine all our efforts just to protect ourselves."

"Angus Og agrees, of course," the man called Killian said, somewhat appeased. "It's why he took action to chase this interfering being away."

"Yes, I understand," said the king. "It's only that I would like to have discussed his methods first. There are things that are . . . well, too dangerous to try. Things that might arouse them or reveal ourselves too much."

"My chieftain is no fool," the little man said, bridling again. "He did nothing to harm the mortal, only to frighten him off. He used the same tricks that have been used often in the past, always with success."

"A thousand years ago, even a hundred, that was true," Fionnbharr said patiently. "Now the mortals are too close to us."

"You think Angus Og doesn't know how close they are?" the man returned. "His contacts with the mortals have become greater even than your own since they have

turned our Sidh into a place of curiosity to be swa
over by their kind."

"I only wish he would stay within his Sidh," the
said, "not go out in disguise and talk with them."

"That has become our only protection, Fionnb
said Killian. "You should well understand. You co
prefer he used the magic of Astray to keep them off?
surely would only bring their curious upon us in g
droves. They'd investigate as they've done elsewhere
haps start digging and—"

"Yes, all right," the king said, raising hands. "I u
stand completely. I suppose there's no harm done."

"Great good, in fact. My chieftain has managed to
guard on the mound when mortals do come around, a
find out something about their lives as well. It's ho
discovered who this Kean was and that he was se
Caitlin and Rury there. And that is the knowledge
sent here to bring you."

It was Rury who replied to this: "We much appre
it, Killian. Thank Angus Og for me. It *is* of great co
that this man has returned to Eire seeking Caitlin. I
being of great and dangerous powers."

"Who also knows far more about us than he sho
added Fionnbharr, shooting O'Mor a reproving look

"Well, none of that did him any good here," sai
little man, grinning. "My chieftain ran him ragged, s
him white, so he did. The *coiste-bodhar* had the poor
all asweat and trembling."

"And you say these ancient tricks actually succee
asked Owen.

"Aye. That they did. Next morning he and his lads
packed and speeding away from there."

"Back to this far New York of theirs?" asked Ang

"That we don't know. But they raced off throug
country westward in one of those iron vehicles. Ang
set my brother Kieran to following them, to be ce
where they'd gone."

"Is that a good idea?" said Rury with concern. "It could be risky."

"Ah, no risk to it," Killian said dismissively. "We did it so much in the old days, we're masters of the craft. There's no mortal who'll even suspect he's not the real thing. And my chieftain told Kieran to report what he discovers direct to you, Rury, as the party most interested in this."

"I thank him again," O'Mor said graciously. "And I deeply thank you and your brother for all your efforts too."

"Glad to help," the little man assured him. "Since we lost cousin Kevan, we feel it's only right to do our part. And we don't mind a chance of having a bit of revenge on this Kean, as well. It's only too bad there's not some greater harm that can be brought on him," he added more harshly.

"To do that might only be to bring the same on us," Fionnbharr reminded him. "The last thing we'd ever want is an all-out war against his kind. For all the powers we have left to us, I'm afraid we'd be no match at all for what they have become."

"Still," said the warrior Angus, "dying that way might be a better fate than being slowly strangled to death by their encroaching ways."

"The feeling of my own Angus exactly," Killian said enthusiastically.

"You both forget that it's not only warriors at stake here," said Fionnbharr. "It's our wives and children too, all deserving of a life. We've no choice but to keep protecting what we have."

"Aye, my king," the big man said, subsiding. "I understand."

"I too, though I don't like it," added the little one. "Well, I'll be going back now. And we'll all pray to Danu we've seen the last of this man named Kean."

With that a familiar cocoon of light rose to envelop him. His shape shrank and shifted within it, rising up as the light fell away to reveal itself now as a large blackbird.

With a loud caw for good-bye, it swept around on its

broad wings and flapped its way out through the doors of
the king's hall.

The blackbird, nearly as large as a hawk, winged its way
over the countryside.

Its sharp eyes were fixed downward as it flew, focused
on a black Mercedes limousine making its way along a
narrow lane right below.

Inside the limo were what had by this time become
Kean's only entourage. Starski was, as usual, behind the
wheel. In back rode Kean himself along with Mac, Garvey,
and Professor Connelly.

Kean looked out at the passing view as the car twisted
its way through the landscape. It was a more dramatic part
of the Irish country here, with rich, varied textures and
hues. Green swells rolled up on either side to higher hills
beyond, a soft brown when near, a misty blue in the distance. The closer meadows were billowing masses of grass
gleaming with the wet of a recent shower, swathed brilliantly across with crimson foxglove and purple heather.
The sky above was a deep, clean blue showing through
dark and drifting masses of cloud that threatened more
rain.

"Where did you say this was exactly?" Kean asked the
professor.

"It's Clare County we're in now," the man explained.
"In the west part of Ireland. It was part of the kingdom of
Connacht back in the Celtic times. That was Lough Derg
we've just come 'round, and Feakle's just ahead. Lovely
country, eh?"

"Yeah. Yeah, I have to say so," Kean admitted, looking
out appreciatively at it.

"See there"—Connelly pointed—"that's Slieve nan-
Or."

A higher peak had come into view, rising well above the
rest. Sunlight pouring through a rift in the overcast fell
upon it, making it seem to glow with a quality of burnished gold.

" 'The Golden Mountain,' " Connelly went on. "It's surely displaying itself for us today. You know, it's up there, the legends say, that the last great battle will be fought before the end of the world."

"You people have a lot of real cheerful legends, don't you?" Kean observed.

"Just part of the Irish soul," Connelly told him, "steeped in the sorrows and travails of a thousand lifetimes."

"And you love to make the most of it, don't you?" Kean said.

The professor smiled. "Of course! It's a national resource. What would a Joyce or Yeats or Synge have been without it?"

They rolled down now toward a town nestled in a fold of the hills below. They passed an idyllic set of little whitewashed cottages perched on a hillside above it, the landscape and distant mountain spread before them in stunning panorama.

"There's Feakle, below," Connelly pointed out. "It's where we leave the main road."

"Main road?" said Kean. "You call this cart track a main road?"

"It looks like a nice, unspoiled, out-of-the-way spot," McBride commented.

"Not so much now," the professor replied. "Those cottages we just passed are really modern tourist ones, inhabited mostly by British and Americans on holiday."

They entered the village, driving slowly through. It looked quaint and traditional, its shops and pubs as they had been for centuries. Some TV antennas and poles with electric wires were the only obvious evidence of modernity.

"I like this place," said McBride. "It's got a . . . a *comfortable* feel. It's like I already know it."

"Perhaps you did in some past life," the professor said. "A clan called the McBrides has been dominant in this part of Ireland since before the Normans came. Look there."

They were just passing a pub front. Above its red painted door and large windows was the typical long sign identifying the place as being "McBride's."

"A pub. Well, that's appropriate for you," Kean said.

"The whole area's peppered with old sites named for them," Connelly went on. "Ring forts, tower houses, castles, shops, and more pubs. Parts of the whole history of the family's life here are still about to be seen."

"I'd like to come back here and stay sometime," Mac said. "Really stay and look around, I mean. Maybe live here awhile."

"You know, maybe I would too," Kean said, and with such sincerity that Mac looked at him in surprise.

"Why, Michael, that's amazing," he couldn't help replying. "It's all so . . . so 'outside' for you!"

"Cute, Mac," Kean said, but not angrily. "I guess I've asked for that."

"Mr. Starski, would you just take that first turning right beyond the village?" Connelly now instructed Stony through the intercom.

The driver nodded and wheeled the big machine off the highway onto the side road.

If what they'd been on was a cart track, this was little more than a cow path. It ran like a ragged scar across the smooth cheek of the meadows, the deep red earth of it turned to mud by the rains and spotted with rusty pools.

The limo crawled along, only its power and Starski's skill keeping it from bogging down.

"How much farther on this?" Kean asked, rolling up a window to avoid the mud sprays being thrown up by the churning wheels.

"Only a mile or two," said Connelly. "I hope she's there. She's often out helping those in the countryside. No way to contact her. No phone, of course, or any other modern convenience. They interfere with the auras, she says."

"And you're really convinced this . . . witch lady can help us?"

"I say that she's worth the try. I've no scientific proof of her powers, Mr. Kean. I'm only saying her magic seems to work."

"What is she, exactly?" asked Mac.

"Part seer, part healer, part sorceress," Connelly said. "So far as I know, she may be one of the last of her kind. I suppose Biddy Early was the most famous of her profession in Ireland. She lived somewhere about here too, but that was over a hundred years ago. One story about her said, 'There used surely to be enchanters in the old time, magicians and freemasons. Old Biddy Early's power came from the same thing.' Perhaps that's true of Nelly Quade as well."

"And we're supposed to buy that?" Kean said skeptically.

"If you are 'buying' the possible existence of the Sidhe, then why not this?" the professor returned. "In any case, many locals believe that Nelly somehow taps into the powers and spirits of the earth. They say she dances with the fairies, hobnobs with the 'old ones,' communes with the dead, and all that. Ah, we're nearly there."

He leaned forward to the intercom. "All right, Mr. Starski, it's just ahead, across that hump of bridge and up the hill."

Starski looked at the narrow and battered stretch of bridge crossing a small brook swollen to car-swallowing proportions by the rain. He braked to a stop.

"No way am I crossing that wreck," he said firmly.

Kean peered out at it. "I agree, Stony." He looked at the rest. "Well, friends, looks like from here we walk."

23

Starski pulled the limousine as far off the road as he could. "Although, I don't think anybody else's gonna be coming *this* way," he said.

The five men got out. A wind was beginning to rise and it smelt heavily of rain. All of them pulled on trench coats before making their way through the muck and pools to the old bridge.

Garvey eyed the much-rotted supports and planks of it critically. "Better let me go first," he volunteered.

He made his way cautiously across with no problems. He waved an okay from the far side and the others followed him across.

On the far side the road began to slope steeply up. Because it was rockier and the drainage better, it was drier and the going much easier. They climbed upward rapidly, and near the top, Connelly pointed off to the left.

"There," he said. "Up there."

They could see the thatched peak of a cottage sitting off on the roadside up there atop a piled-looking mass of immense rocks. They made their way to the hilltop and circled around the outcropping to reach its yard. This was a small, fairly level patch, bare save for some scrubby grass tufts and one very ancient, very gnarled yew tree.

They stopped at the yard's edge, gazing speculatively across at the cottage.

It was certainly a sad-seeming place, looking sway-backed and sodden and most forlorn there alone on the barren tor. Its thatch was the dark grey of great age. Its windowsills were half-eaten away by rot. Parts of its stucco had fallen away to reveal patches of the brownish stone beneath, giving it the appearance of an old hound with the mange.

"I don't like this at all," Garvey said with misgivings. He looked to his boss. "Mr. Kean, I don't like you coming to a place like this with just Starski and me as cover. Why didn't you let me bring along some more men?"

"Because we'd have to explain what we were doing to them," Kean explained. "I told you before, Frank, the more who know, the more chance Lance will find out what I'm up to. I don't think I want the chairman to know I'm out visiting a sorceress, do you?"

"I just don't like working this way," the disgruntled security chief said.

The clouds had by this time welded their rifts into a solid, boilerplate overcast. A fine mist began to fall upon the men. The wind whipped up, scouring across the rocky hilltop and tugging at their long coats. It blew the fine mist stingingly into their faces and wailed mournfully through the branches of the treetops.

Kean turned his collar up against the wet and cold, saying pointedly, "Let's get inside, okay? If we can. Professor, you'd better go first."

Connelly nodded and led the way to the door. It was the typical split door of the old cottages, painted a bright red now much faded and badly peeling.

He rapped upon its planks. They waited.

No response.

He rapped again, and they waited expectantly.

Still nothing.

"Nobody home," said Kean.

"I recommend withdrawal, sir," said Garvey, looking around guardedly, as if expecting something to pounce.

"She's very old," said the professor. "Give her a bit more time."

He rapped once more. This time a shuffling sound could be heard within, moving slowly closer. The sound stopped. There was the clink of an opening latch and then a loud squeaking as the top half of the door swung inward on rusty hinges.

A face poked out. It was a quite ancient woman's face, finely seamed with a crosshatch of countless wrinkles, framed by a wispy mass of grey-white hair.

She stared out sharply at them with hazel eyes unclouded by age. As her gaze fell on the professor, her thin lips drew up to reveal yellow teeth in a welcoming smile.

"Ah, Mr. Connelly, is it?" she said in a cracked, dry husk of voice. "I knew it would be you coming"—she peered at the others—"and bringing friends too. Come in and welcome."

She unlatched the lower half of the door and moved back to let them in.

They passed through the door in single file. Starski, last to go in, heard a flapping noise behind and glanced around to see a large blackbird settling to a branch of the yew tree.

It met his eye with its own glittering one and gave a loud caw. He shuddered and hurriedly followed the rest inside.

They went through a small vestibule, past her, and into the dark interior. The group stopped there momentarily while their eyes adjusted to the light.

The cottage had only a single principal room. A door at one end opened into a small sleeping chamber. A stairway led to an open loft space above it, right up under the rafters. This seemed to be used only for storage.

The main room was a singularly gloomy and claustrophobic place. The only light came from a small turf fire glowing redly under the grate of a big, walk-in fireplace. The heavy smoke scent of the fire and the cloyingly sweet smell from some steaming concoction bubbling in a pot upon the grate intertwined with the room's great mustiness to produce an all but gagging atmosphere.

Plank shelves filled up the wall space. Plank tables crowded the floor, all crammed and stacked with a bewildering array of bottles, jars, pots, pestles and mortars, mugs and pitchers, bowls, boxes, odd pieces of iron and wood and brass, objects that looked most unpleasantly like dried bits of birds or reptiles or rats, and objects not readily identifiable at all—but no less unpleasant for that.

Herbs and weeds and flowers were suspended from the rafters for drying. The men ducked below a row of them as Connelly led them on in, through the maze of tables to a small open space before the fire. Old Nelly Quade joined them there, her stooped, scrawny form moving past them to ease creakingly down on a single rocking chair drawn up close beside the fire.

"Sit, please," she told them, indicating a pair of crude benches across from her.

Kean, Mac, and Connelly sat. The two others remained standing behind them, staring around. Garvey's gaze was filled with open dislike for the dark and cramped conditions. Starski's look was one of some uneasiness at the weird surroundings.

"Nelly, I've brought this man to you for help," Connelly said, indicating Kean. "His name is Michael Kean. He's from very far away."

She took a big ladle from a hook. "America. I know," she said in her thick brogue, stirring the brownish mass in the pot. "A man of very great wealth and power. A man of some arrogance too, I sense."

"Thanks," Kean said dryly. "The professor says you've got some power yourself. He says you may be the only one of your kind left."

She hung the spoon back. "It's possible, young man. I did have a cousin who had the knack too. Slaney O'Brien was her name. But she died some two or three years ago. *They* took her."

"What? Do you mean these Sidhe?" asked Kean.

"No. Evil ones. There are other powers at work in the world, you know. Much blacker powers too. But the Others have never been a danger to me."

Kean eyed her thoughtfully. "I can't help wondering—if you have such powers, why do you live this way? Couldn't you be rich?"

"That was a condition of my winning the knack from the spirits that offered them those many years ago," she said. "I could help others, but I was to gain nothing great from it myself, for that would make my power a selfish one. And I've not minded giving up those things of the world most others think so fine. It's no hardship at all giving up everything to gain something you truly love"—she smiled at Kean—"is it now?"

"It sounds good," said Kean. He glanced around him. "Though, I'm not sure you've ever had a real basis for comparison," he added with a burst of his old cynicism.

"Mr. Kean, careful now," Connelly warned. "We've come to ask Nelly for help."

"I just don't know how much good she can do for me," Kean replied. He looked to the old woman skeptically. "I mean, how could you know anything about Caitlin Bawn or Rury O'Mor?"

"Caitlin Bawn?" she repeated. She shook her head. "Ah, you're right there. I know nothing about her."

Kean began to turn toward the professor, an I-told-you-so expression on his face, when she spoke again: "But about this Rury O'Mor I surely have heard."

He looked back to her, surprised and wary at once. "You have? What do you know?"

"That years ago he fought a long, hard fight to save his wife," Nelly said. "Etain was her name. A fair woman of great beauty and great charm. The evil brigand Brasal stole her away to make his own. She wouldn't have him. Rury O'Mor hunted for years across all Eire until he found her, imprisoned within the villain's mountain. He fought the monster for her, and he won, but Brasal took the life of Etain too. A sorrowful tale."

"I've heard it!" Kean all but shouted in realization.

"You have?" said Connelly.

"Yeah. At some touristy thing. At that . . . um . . . Duncovey Castle. Somebody they called a bard was telling the same story."

"He must have been a most learned bard," said the professor. "I couldn't find any reference to O'Mor among my sources. You're certain it's the same one?"

"I . . . well, I wasn't listening all that close," Kean admitted, "but I think it was."

"It was," said Mac. "I remember too." He smacked his head with a palm. "Damn, I'm an idiot. The name should have rung a bell."

"Why should it have?" said Kean. "That story was from centuries ago. Why connect the two?"

"Because they may be the same," Nelly said. "The Rury O'Mor of the tale is a most handsome man. A great warrior. Tall, proud and blond, with a flashing grey eye."

"I guess that could describe him," Kean said. "He's not all *that* tall."

"The colors of his clan are a green-and-yellow plaid."

"He wore a cloak with those colors," Kean admitted.

"His close companions are a giant warrior, a lean and red-haired druid, and a small, cheerful man who can shift shapes."

"I guess that would describe them pretty well," Mac said this time. He looked to Garvey and Starski. "Right, boys?" Both of them nodded. Mac looked to Kean. "Right, boss?"

"I guess so," Kean said, but grudgingly, unwilling to accept.

"Nelly, how do you know all this?" asked Connelly.

"Not all the old tales have been written down in your books," she told him. "I've lived very long, and I've heard things known only to a few who truly are part of the old spirit of the land. Though," she added regretfully, "that's all but faded now."

"So you're saying this guy's still around from centuries ago," said Kean.

"Fifteen of them, at least, yes," she said.

"He's that old?"

"Oh, he's not so old," she said. "Not for one of Them. He's surely not among the ranks of the First Ones— Dagda, Morrigan, Nuada, and the rest. Their lives go back to the dawn of time."

"But he is one of these Sidhe?"

"Most certainly," she said. "And it's a rare occasion indeed for any mortal man of your time to have an encounter with Them. Especially an encounter of such a great kind as yours."

"How do you know about that?" Kean asked, suspicious again.

"Have faith, my boy," she said. "I read it in your eyes. I feel it from your head. You must believe in me, or I'll be no help to you at all."

"I'll take a shot at it," he told her. "It's not easy."

"I understand," she soothed. "You're only a mortal man living in a most ignorant age." She stirred the caldron once more with the ladle, sat back comfortably, and fixed her gaze on him. "Now you must tell me your own tale. Everything that's happened."

Kean looked around at his companions, took a deep breath, and began.

"So Caitlin Bawn was betrothed to Rury O'Mor," Nelly said at the end of Kean's tale. She sat forward to stir her pot again. "He chose someone at last. It took him long enough to find the one."

"The one?" said Kean.

"The tale goes that after Etain's death, he sorrowed long," she said. "To ease his grief and his loneliness, the king of the Others told him that any maiden among Them would be his choice to wed. Still so wrapped in his deep mourning was Rury that he vowed he'd love no other woman 'til he found one that could replace his lost wife. It would seem he chose this Caitlin."

"She said she had no choice about marrying him," said Kean. "She said it was arranged with her family."

"And so it would have been, as most marriages were made in the old days, with great ceremony. But, Mr. Kean, it is a very grave thing you've done to interfere in this."

"I didn't interfere with them," he said in exasperation. "Why won't anyone believe me? *She* ran away. She said she was a slave. She only wanted to be free."

"But now you've chosen to come find and rescue her. And why is that? Is it because of a true love you feel for her?"

"Love? No. I mean . . . Hell, I don't know," he said in some confusion. "What difference does it make? They took her against her will. I can't let that happen. I made a promise to her."

She looked shrewdly at him. "And have you never broken your word before?"

"I'm a good businessman," he said bluntly. "That's part of the game. This is different."

"Why is that? It would seem your business and even your life might well be at stake in this."

"Look, I'm not here for fortune-telling or psychoanalysis," he said, his patience lost. "Are you going to help me or not?"

"I could help you in one way that might be best for you," she said. "I have an herb you could take. Its power will erase her memory from your mind and cleanse all feeling for her from your heart. You'll be at peace. You can go home and be as you were before you met her."

"You might be better off to take it, Mr. Kean," Connelly suggested, "rather than plunge any deeper into this."

"No, Michael," said McBride, dismayed at the idea. "Don't listen to him. We've come this far. You can't let it go now."

"Mac's right," Kean said decisively. "I'm not forgetting her. And I'm not backing away. This O'Mor and his boys are terrorists, no matter what else you and the professor say they are. If they want a war, I'll give it to them. And I'm not losing this time. I'm getting her back from them, no matter what."

"Very well, Mr. Kean," she said. "I can see you'll not be turned away. I won't deny you my help in your search. But I'll do nothing against Them myself. I've no wish to do Them harm or to bring Their wrath on me."

"Just help me find out where she is," he said. "Any kind of hint or clue about her, or even about O'Mor. We don't know where to start. They could be anywhere."

"Aye," she agreed. "It's most likely they'd be in one of the Hidden Places, though there are many scores of those. But it may be I have a useful spell."

She took the ladle and stirred again at her pot.

"Ah, nearly done," she announced.

A curious McBride leaned forward to look at the bubbling grey-brown goo atop which floated some greasy, shapeless lumps. "Will that help us?" he asked her.

"No," she said, "that'll help me. It's stew for my supper. My own secret recipe. Would you be wanting a taste of it?"

"No thanks," he said.

She put up the ladle, rising from her chair. She crossed to a table, browsing through its clutter, finally taking up a handful of sticks.

She brought them back to the fire and sat down, holding the sticks up for the men to see.

They were slender, straight tree branches, an inch thick, neatly stripped of any twigs and all their bark.

"Yew rods," she explained. "With these I might just wrench an answer from the Other side. You"—she waved at Starski—"tall one. Fetch me the knife down from the shelf above."

Starski took a large, old carving knife down from a shelf

above the fireplace, handing it to Kean who passed it across to her.

She began to carefully carve at one of the sticks. She made a row of slanting notches, some long and some short, grouped in various numbers and combinations, running down the whole length of the stick. The men watched her with curiosity.

"These marks are Oghams," she explained, putting down the first stick and taking up another. "That's the writing from the olden times. Made up by the druids, it was, and only they could read it then. But there's great magic in it, and others learned its secrets, like me."

She put down the second stick and took up a third.

"One of these I've carved with Caitlin Bawn's name. On the second I've put Rury O'Mor's. This one will be an incantation to make the great powers tell us where they are."

"What's the fourth for?" asked Mac.

She put down the third and took up the last, saying gravely, "This will be a blessing meant to see that no harm falls on us for what we do."

"Definitely don't forget that one," Mac said fervently. "And be sure you spell everything right."

She carefully carved the last row of Oghams on the fourth stick.

If the men expected some elaborate ceremony for casting the spell, they were disappointed. After removing her pot of supper from the grate, she merely murmured a soft incantation under her breath, then lay the yew rods in the fire one by one, crossing each over the others.

The dried sticks immediately began to smoke and glow as the coals from the turf set them to burning. She made a swift spiral sweep of her hand above them, then the sign of a figure eight. After that she sat back and they all watched intently.

From smoldering the four twigs quickly burst into full flame. A grey smoke began to billow up from them in an amount amazing for four pieces of such small size.

Kean glanced around at his companions. Connelly and McBride were rapt. Starski stared in wide-eyed wonder and Garvey in hard-faced disbelief.

The smoke gathered rather than just trailing up the flue, rolling into a ball right above the grate. It grew darker and darker, forming a pulsing but now solid-seeming mass.

Nelly murmured something once again. Within the black cloud, lights began to show.

They were like sparks first, but holding place, not drifting upward. Quickly they grew from spots of red-gold light into streaks, thickening, lengthening, then forming in a line. Soon they made a horizontal rank through the center of the smoke, long and short marks of light in varied groupings, looking very similar to the Oghams she had carved.

Once fully formed, they hung there for several heartbeats in full view. After this they abruptly flared up in a last, brilliant burst of energy and flashed out of existence.

The smoke ball unrolled itself and flowed upward normally once more. It also thinned out rapidly, as the four yew rods that were creating it had already been consumed to crumbling, black remains, their own last glow dying out.

She looked around to Kean. "I have a name," she said to him in a triumphant tone. "Knockma!"

"Knockma!" Connelly repeated excitedly. "Of course!"

"What the hell's that?" Kean asked her.

"It's—" she began.

She broke off as a sudden gust of wind boomed across the roof, shivering the thatch.

The whole cottage vibrated from the blast's force. The rising black smoke, caught by a downdraft, was slammed back downward through the flue, puffing out into the room in a second fat cloud.

They all pulled back, staring at it in alarm. For this time the smoke had formed into a face.

It was a huge face, a monstrous face, evil and catlike.

Lights also burned within its blackness, but as two baleful eyes. A broad, fanged mouth opened and seemed to move in speech. A voice came to the watchers, hollow and piping like a winter wind wailing across a chimney top. It said a single word: "Beware!"

24

With that single word of warning, the head vanished as the smoke dissolved into tatters, drifting formlessly, harmlessly up into the rafters.

"My dear Lord," said a clearly unnerved Starski, crossing himself. "I signed up to protect you from just about anything, boss, but I don't know about this."

"Well, well," Nelly Quade said in a surprisingly calm tone. "So the Others do know what we're about."

Kean turned his still-startled gaze from where the apparition had been to her. "Weren't you just a *little* scared by that?"

"I was not," she said matter-of-factly, rising again, "and neither should you be." She shuffled to the tables and began once more to sift through the clutter. "The first thing you'll have to be learning if you're to go against them, Mr. Kean, is never to show fear. If they make you give way, they've won the advantage of you. Anything might happen then. Mr. Connelly, you might have given him a warning about that yourself."

"Mr. Kean is not one to be taking warnings, Nelly," the professor said frankly, "from anyone."

"Well, he'll take one from me, and like it," she said, moving to a new table and searching some more. "It's as with that coach-a-bower you saw. You should never give way to such on the road. Keeping your nerves—that's the trick of it." She took up a jar from the table and turned back to him. "Of course, that's not sayin' a bit of magic isn't useful too." She held it out. "Come take this now."

He got up and went to her, taking the jar. He examined it. It was a squat container made of crude pottery with a cork in its wide mouth.

"You leave that tightly shut until you've need of it," she admonished sternly. "Then you open it and scatter the powder out on the persons or things."

"What's it do?"

"Dispels the charm that may be hiding their true nature from you. If they're invisible and you know where they are, it'll reveal 'em to you. If they take on an animal's form, this'll bring back the true one. If they seem to mean good, you'll discover if they really mean you evil."

"Man, I know a few lawyers and accountants I'd like to use that on," said Mac.

From another table she took up a long canelike object, a gnarled and knobby length of black wood with a large lump for a head, and also handed it to Kean. "Take this as well. It's a blackthorn stick. It'll work as a charm for you. Wave it before you and you'll pass safely through enchantments set to bar or harm you. Very useful if you mean to go near Their realms."

"Thanks, I guess," said Kean, dubiously eyeing the stick.

"And now, it's time for you to go," she announced. "I've done what I can for you, and I'll have you here no longer, further rousin' Their ire against me."

"Yes, of course," agreed the professor, getting up. "We wouldn't want that. Mr. Kean, shall we go?"

Mac rose too, and Connelly began to lead them toward the door, but Kean hesitated, looking to her.

"Are you sure there's nothing I can do for you? I'll be glad to give you money or . . ."

She held up a staying hand. "Nothing at all. For to take any gain for my powers would make those powers vanish. And to do something for someone knowing there's no reward makes it the most valuable, don't you know?"

"I've been told that," he said.

"Be off with you then," she said, moving up to take his elbow and urge him toward the door. "Just remember, Their power to act in the mortal world doesn't extend far beyond the limits of Their Hidden Places. And except for this little battle They've had with you, They seldom venture out in force now. So it's when you come close to Their realms that you're in greatest danger."

"I understand," he said. "That won't stop me. If I have to go in to get her, I will."

"I know you will," she said. "I feel the strong will in you. It clutches at you, so it does. You can't be free of it until you win." She raised a finger to shake at him, adding warningly, "But think hard on what you mean to do, Michael Kean: it's a struggle like no mortal's seen for a thousand years you may be bringing on now. Be certain of the reasons you're entering it. If they're the wrong ones—you cannot win."

"I'll win," he told her firmly. "Somehow I will."

"Then good fortune go with you." She looked at the others gathered there. "And may it go with the rest of you as well."

They thanked her in return, made their good-byes, and went out into the yard.

The huge blackbird that had waited throughout their visit flew up cawing at their reappearance and flapped swiftly away.

The wind had faded somewhat, and the mist had died. Sun was again slashing through the overcast to spotlight areas of countryside beneath.

"Man, if these powers of hers are real, I should set up a clinic for her," said Kean as they headed back down toward the car. "Just think what it could do."

"Very little, I'm afraid," said Connelly. "No one would go to her save those who believe, and there are fewer and fewer of them left every day. No, she's a most endangered species in our world, Mr. Kean, like her whole way of life and that kind of cottage she lives in. All fast going the dodo's way."

Kean looked back at the forlorn little house, touched now by a ray of sunlight that made it glow hazily, like something from a dream.

"And I suppose it's guys like me helping it along," he said in a voice touched with regret. Then something else occurred to him. His gaze swung around to Connelly. "Hey, wait a minute. I still don't know where I'm supposed to go."

"You do," the professor said. "To Knockma. That's what her spell found out."

"Yeah. Right. But what's Knockma?"

"Long ago it was called Meadha. It was a Sidh parceled out with the others to the de Danann clans. It's upon a large hill some five miles west of Tuam, in County Galway. That's nearly due north of here, about sixty miles away—as the crow flies. Likely no more than a two or three hours drive."

"And we can find her there?"

"Or him, or most likely both. It's logical. They'd get the greatest help there. It is the Sidh of the king of all the de Dananns, after all."

"It is?" said Kean with interest. "The head guy, huh? And just who's he?"

"His name," said Connelly, "is Fionnbharr."

"Fionnbharr," said Aisling anxiously, "is it true this man Kean is in Ireland?"

She confronted the king in his main hall, where he was supervising a dozen leather-aproned cooks in the preparing of dinner. Various meats cooked on spits around the edges of the fire pit. Bubbling caldrons hung suspended on chains above the flames. Savory smells filled the air of the huge room.

Rury was there too, sitting at the tables with Angus and some two scores of other red-cloaked men of the Sidh who had gathered for a bit of pre-meal drink and talk with the

visitors. Aisling's voice brought him around to see the
woman moving upon Fionnbharr, the elderly druid
Matholwch in tow.

"Just how is it you know about that?" the king asked
her.

"He told me," she said, indicating the druid.

"We meant to keep it from you," Fionnbharr said, shooting Matholwch a glare, "and only for your own good. We
saw no need for you to worry."

"I didn't mean to speak," the old druid whined in his
defense. "She's a woman of great will and great persuasive
powers."

"So I've learned," said the king with a small sigh.

"And why haven't I a right to know something that
effects myself and my Caitlin?" she told him heatedly. "It
was all ended, you said. My daughter had been rescued
from this man and she was safe. But now he appears here?
And clearly in search of her?"

Rury left the other men and crossed the room to join the
discussion.

"Aisling, he hasn't found us," Fionnbharr said reasonably. "He hasn't even come close. He's only a mortal. He
hasn't the skills or powers to discover where Caitlin is."

"I don't know that at all," she shot back. "From what
I've learned from Owen, this 'mortal' of yours has powers
that even amaze him. With all his wealth, couldn't he buy
whatever other skills or knowledge he needs?" She looked
around to O'Mor. "You faced him, Rury. Can you tell me
in full truth that you don't believe this man might be a
threat?"

"I suppose he might have been that," O'Mor admitted.
"But it doesn't seem we'll have a chance to know. Word's
come to us that he's broken off the search. The tricks of
Angus Og frightened him away."

"The childish magic of that old prankster?" she said
disparagingly. "They're not enough to frighten off a child."

"Apparently they are," said the king. "Kean and his men
packed up and rushed away."

"And you know this for certain?" she asked.

"A shape-shifter followed them to be certain they left Eire," said O'Mor. "We've had no final word about that yet."

She shook her head in doubt. "I don't have faith in any of what you say. Maybe the man is much slyer than you know. I know of a few mortals clever enough from years ago." She looked to the king. "Fionnbharr should well remember at least one himself."

The king colored uncomfortably. "Maybe I do."

"So this Kean might well be playing tricks himself," she went on. "It only makes it all the more clear to me that we must act swiftly. I say we can take no chances. If Caitlin should discover this man is here, who knows what it would do? It might redouble her desire to get away, to go back to him. It might recharge the spell and make it impossible ever to lift from her."

"And just what would you like to do, my lady?" the king inquired.

"Make certain that she is cured as soon as possible. Have this Kean driven right out of her head. I've discussed a means with the druids. They say it can be done."

"Yes," Matholwch agreed, but reluctantly. "We do have a . . . a means that we believe would work. But it's a drastic one. A spell of considerable power. We've no idea how much it might do to her."

"What do you mean?" asked O'Mor.

"Well, it would surely wipe her memories of this man and his world out of her mind. But it might wipe her entire mind clean as well. She'd remember nothing. She would be like a small child."

"And as easily retrainable as one," Aisling put in bluntly. "She would soon learn where her true love and loyalty lies. It might well be preferable to have those things in her that have made her discontented wiped fully away."

"Along with all that which makes her Caitlin?" said O'Mor.

"I should think you would prefer that too," said Aisling. "She could become more the image of your Etain than she ever was. She would be exactly as you wish her to be."

"As I wish?" he said.

"Of course. You must only agree to let the druids begin," Aisling cajoled. "In just one day more Caitlin will be free again."

O'Mor looked to his king. "It's up to me, then?"

"She is your betrothed," Fionnbharr said. "The spell upon her affects you the most. You must decide what will be done for her."

He considered this, frowning in perplexity. Then he shook his head. "I can't do it," he said. "Not so simply. There must be other ways that can be tried first. I want to talk to her."

"I don't know, Rury," said Matholwch. "She still feels a great anger toward you. She sees you as the one who stole her away."

"You don't know that I can't reach her and bring her back to us," the chieftain countered. "Before I let anything else be done, I have to try."

"Very well then," the king said, much to Aisling's vexation. "Go to her."

Caitlin looked up as the bolt of the door clanged open and the iron panel swung back.

Rury stepped into her plush chamber, looking about him.

"It's not a bad-seeming place," he commented.

"It is a cell I cannot leave, and you have put me here," she told him bitterly.

"Caitlin . . ." he said, moving toward where she sat upon the bed. She looked away.

"Don't come near me," she said.

He stopped. "Caitlin, I don't mean you any harm," he told her gently.

"You've already harmed me more than I can say," she replied.

"What I did I only did for your own good."

She laughed harshly. "You sound like mother now."

"I meant to save you."

"Save me? Instead you've now condemned me to a life I can do nothing but despise."

"And that life includes me."

"As the chief author for my pain, yes!" she said in a harsh way. "I believed that you truly cared about me, that I had your respect. I believed that when you understood what I truly wanted, you'd leave me alone. Now I know you only wanted me for yourself, with no thought for my own desires or needs."

Sorrow filled Rury's eyes at this reproof. "You must believe I never would mean that. I'd do anything to keep harm from my own . . ."

He stopped here. She looked sharply up to him. "Your own what?"

"From the woman I love," he continued instead, "and the one who I thought loved me. Caitlin, don't you remember our many years together? Were the feelings I thought you had for me all false?"

She looked into his stricken eyes. Her own look softened. "Rury, I'm sorry," she said in less harsh tones. "For all that's happened, I do still have feelings for you. It's only that I . . . I'm not certain what they are. These newly awakened feelings are so much stronger! They've taken me over."

"*He* put them upon you," Rury said.

"No," she protested. "They must have been within me. Something penned up. A longing I never knew I had until I met him. But I'm certain they were there before. It's why for so long I made those delays, saying I didn't yet feel ready to wed."

"So, you don't love me."

"I don't know that," she said forcefully. "Don't you see? I've never had a chance to find out."

"And your love for him . . . ?"

"Is no more certain in me. He never declared a love for

me or any feelings at all. I may have felt something in him, but there was no time to discover more. You brought me back."

"This is where you belong, Caitlin," Rury argued. "Not out there. Your mind is confused now. I understand. But if you give it a chance . . ."

"I won't be as I was again, Rury," she told him with certainty. "I can never be your Caitlin again, knowing what I know now. The discontent will always be alive in me from this time out."

"I won't believe that's true. You can be rid of those other feelings if you try. You can return to being the woman that I . . . that I know."

She looked hard at him. "That you know, Rury? Or that you only *think* you know. One that has been created in your mind."

"I don't understand."

"I've come to wonder, how was it you chose me? After so many years of waiting, with so many to choose from, what brought you to me?"

"I finally found someone with qualities that attracted me," he said simply. "At last I was able to begin forgetting Etain."

"Begin forgetting, or begin replacing?" she said. "I know how much I look and sound as she did. My mother knows it too. She made certain you found out about it as well, didn't she?"

"She did," said Rury, somewhat taken aback, "but I . . ."

Caitlin rose up and stepped to him. She put her hands upon his arms and stared into his eyes.

"Search my gaze," she told him. "Search your heart as well. Is it truly Caitlin Bawn that you see before you, or the image of your lost Etain, somehow born again?"

He pulled away from her. "I'll answer no such foolish charge," he answered angrily.

"You have to," she persisted. "For both our sakes. Ask

yourself if I am truly the one you were risking yourself for."

"I'll listen to no more of this," he snapped, wheeling toward the door. "I'm leaving now."

"Leaving, or running from the truth?" she called after him as he went out through the door, slamming it behind him.

Outside it he stopped, standing white-faced and panting, glaring at the door as the guard threw its bolt closed.

"Is it all right you are, Chieftain?" the man asked him.

"Yes, yes. All right," he shot back. He turned to start away, but stopped again as he saw Owen coming toward him.

"Rury, I was looking for you," the man greeted. "I . . ." He stopped as he noted O'Mor's strained look. "Why, what's wrong with you? You look as if you'd been wrestling a boar."

"I've been battling much worse," O'Mor replied. "The things that I have heard from Caitlin! They cannot be coming from her own mind. They cannot!" He looked back toward the door. "Perhaps Aisling is right that something desperate must be tried."

"If you really believe that, then it should be tried very soon," the druid returned.

O'Mor looked sharply to him. "What do you mean?"

"The shape-shifter named Kieran just flew in," Owen reported. "He has been following Kean and his people since they left the domain of Angus Og." He paused, then added reluctantly, regretfully, "It seems they haven't left Ireland after all."

"Where are they then?" the other demanded.

"I'm very sorry, Rury, but they're here!"

25

"We really are glad you asked us to stay," said Kean, ". . . ah . . . say, what should I call you? Earl? Lord? Mr. Desmond?"

The man walking beside him laughed. "It does seem rather overly complex, doesn't it? I'm seventh Earl of Desmond, formally addressed as Lord Desmond, but I find that much too grand. My name is actually Richard Hopewell Wyndham Quinn. That's a bit much too. So please just call me Dick.

The speaker was a spare and sprightly man of middle height and late middle-age. His short-cropped but still thick and rippling hair was a steely grey, as were his emphatically bristling eyebrows. His long features had the same sharp-hewn boldness as his speech. In manner he was a brisk but gracious man.

He strode along with Kean and McBride through a spread of carefully proportioned and meticulously tended formal gardens. The exact patterns of the beds, mathematically subdivided into ornate patterns by a wide variety of flowers and shrubs, covered acres of absolutely flat land.

The garden's Age of Enlightenment rationalism provided an intriguing counterpoint for the massive sprawl of manor house that lay beyond it. This was a splendid monument to the Romantic era's flamboyant neo-Gothicism The soaring grey stone walls were pierced with ornate pointed-arch windows. A forest of lean chimneys decorated with individual, intricate designs grew from the tiled rooftops. A fantastic and grotesque assortment of gargoyles, animal heads, and masks adorned myriad corners of the encastellated gallery range. And above the four-storied main section of the house, a huge tower with crenellated top and high steeple soared up fifty feet more. In all, the Desmond manor house looked to be part castle, part medieval church, and part grandiose statement of great wealth.

"I really don't like horning in here," Kean said. "I usually like to pay my own way."

"Nonsense," said the earl. "When Professor Connelly called to say you were exploring the countryside in this area, I naturally insisted you must stay with us. We seldom get the chance to meet visitors out here. And the old place certainly has the space."

"I'd still like to give you something . . ."

Lord Desmond waved that away. "Won't hear of it. Don't need the money at all. The company will be payment enough. Love to hear what you're planning for your Irish park, you know. Heard about it some, of course. Sounds a great thing for Ireland. A great thing!"

"You don't have any problem with it at all?" Mac put in. "I mean, an outsider creeping in, grabbing up the virgin countryside, ripping everything off it, putting up his huge thing on it, and . . ."

"Jesus, Mac, that's enough," Kean said, sounding a little abashed. "You make it sound like I'm raping the man's daughter."

"Sorry," said Mac with a little smile, himself not abashed at all.

"I understand how some might think that," said Quinn. "But I'm certain you'll do the thing quite tastefully."

"Oh, quite," Mac said with audible irony, earning a glare from Kean.

"Besides, there's a need for new blood," the seventh earl went on, not noticing. "Gotten stale over here. You may very well commercialize the place. I say, why not!

Get more people to come and see what it's really like—the real wealth and scope of culture this land's got."

As he continued, he warmed to his subject—clearly a pet one—his words becoming more forceful, more eloquent.

"We've been the butt of the world's jokes for years. We're the provincial ones. The backward ones. The dreamers and the drunks. And one would think our history began in 1914 and revolved around nothing but the damned 'Troubles,' or that we've never been anything but the epitome of quaint, straitlaced 'Catholic.' They've got to be told of our arts and literature. They've got to learn of the Celtic heritage we've kept alive, and how much it's a part of all western civilization today. Too many are totally ignorant of that, including, I'm sorry to say, a great many of your Americans who like to think themselves Irish."

"Woo!" said Mac, finally embarrassed by this description. "I guess *I've* gotta say 'guilty' there."

"Maybe I do too," allowed Kean. "Nice speech, Dick. You sound like Professor Connelly."

Lord Desmond seemed pleased. "Do I? Well, I'll have to talk more with him. Interesting chap. Wish he'd stayed about."

"He just ran back to Dublin for a little research," said Kean. "He'll be back here in a day or so." He neatly segued subjects here. "But as far as experts go, you probably know more about this area than anyone."

"Should do," Quinn agreed. "Family's been living here since Norman times. Twelfth century. Some Norman blood ourselves. But we're all Irish now. No one stays an outsider here for long."

"I'm beginning to feel that already," Mac said.

"Yeah, I noticed you were picking up a brogue," Kean told his friend dryly. "So, Dick, your family built this place then." He stopped to look toward the imposing mass with open admiration. "Really my kind of place. Not for sale?"

Quinn smiled. "Sorry, no."

"I figured. When was it done, medieval times?"

"Heavens no," said the earl. "It was built in the 1840s. Cheap labor then, you know. Romantic age and all that. The old manor was Tudor. Very plain. The fourth earl wanted a castle. There was one here originally. Well, a tower house more like. Motte and bailey they were called. Stone tower on a mound surrounded by a wall and ditch. Still remnants of another one on the grounds." He waved off vaguely to the west. "Fourteenth century. Mostly fallen now."

"So you've got one of those here too," said Mac.

"Remnants of a lot of history on the grounds," he said, gesturing more broadly around. On the other three sides of the garden lay a countryside of meadows broken by clumps of trees for as far as they could see. "A friary, fifteenth century. A church, the same. Two ring forts. They're especially old. Oh, some Ogham stones too. Know about them?"

"We learned just recently," said Kean.

"These were gravestones I suppose," Quinn said. "Don't know for whom."

"What about this place called Knockma," Kean prompted innocently.

"Ah, the mound. Well, that's up there." The earl pointed southward, where the ground sloped uphill to a higher plateau. "You might just glimpse its top from an upper window. Right on the hill's crest in the center of a pasture. You can go up to see it if you like, and you're not afraid."

"Afraid?" said Mac, exchanging a look with Kean.

"All the locals are," said Quinn. "Won't go near the place. Fairies live in it, they think. Drive everyone off or send them Astray."

"Astray?" Kean echoed.

"Old superstition. Some fairy power to cloud your mind, send you far off course and away, lost. We've never had trouble of any kind ourselves." He gave a smile. "Of course, the Desmonds have had an affinity with them since the first."

"Really?" said Kean with interest.

"Oh, yes. Old Finvarra—that's the king of the fairies—apparently made some friendship pact with the first earl. Took the family under his wing as it were in exchange for his mound being left alone. It's due to his benevolent influence, they say, that our cellars never go dry and our wines' quality never deteriorates."

"And do you believe that?" asked Kean.

Quinn laughed. "Rather be a fool not to, eh? Never had a bad bottle or been without means to keep ourselves well stocked in seven hundred years."

"That does sound like a pretty good deal," Mac said.

They had passed out of the gardens by this time and moved into an open yard area close behind the manor house. Here a row of long windows and French doors allowed a view of the gardens to a large sunroom within. Just outside the doors, wrought-iron furniture filled a brick patio. Starski and Garvey waited there, sitting beneath an umbrella at a glass-topped table. They looked rather uncomfortable and out of place in the midst of the elegant scene.

"Well, gentlemen," said Quinn as they reached the patio, "I must go in and see to our dinner now. Will you come in?"

"I'd like to wander around out here a little more, if you don't mind," said Kean. "You too, right, Mac?"

The other swiftly followed his lead. "Oh, yeah, sure."

"Of course, go right ahead," the earl told them expansively. "The manor is yours." He gestured toward the two guardians. "Are you quite certain about your men? We certainly could find room for them as well."

"We've already booked them into rooms in Tuam," Kean said. "That's fine for them. I'm not going to put you out any more."

"If you're certain," said Quinn. He consulted his watch. "Six forty-five. Well, I'll see you in the lounge for drinks at seven-thirty then. All right? See you soon."

With that he set off briskly, entering the manor through

the French doors. Kean and Mac walked up to the table to join the other two.

"Okay, so why are we staying out here?" McBride asked.

"Just wanted a little time for us to talk alone," Kean said.

"Aren't you going to tell Lord Desmond what we're really up to?"

"Hey, you heard him. His family's buddies with the Sidhe. He just might not be too crazy about our poking around his mound and trying to roust them out."

"Does that mean you're not going to check it out?"

"Sure I am, but it's got to be done carefully. That's why we're waiting 'til Connelly gets back. I need to know everything I can about that place before we decide how to act."

"You aren't seriously beginning to think that there is something supernatural up there, are you, sir?" asked Garvey.

Kean looked to him. "What do you mean, Frank?"

"Look, Mr. Kean, I've kept my mouth shut about this for quite a while, but this search of yours, the means that brought us here, the whole way the operation is going is becoming more and more ludicrous."

"I'm not arguing that, Frank," Kean said reasonably. "But it's all we've got. Just bear with me, okay? Just do your own job."

"And how am I supposed to do that adequately?" the security man complained. "First you eliminate all my men, and then you send me off to stay five miles from you."

"You know why I did that. I'm damn lucky this guy's letting me stay here. Now I can pump him all about this place. I wasn't doing anything to screw that up. Besides, I don't really need you here, do I? If the Sidhe thing is a wild goose chase, this place is completely harmless."

"And if it's real?" asked Starski.

"Then how much can you boys protect me from a supernatural force? Quit worrying. I'll be careful. I promise.

And I've got my magic spells, don't I? Now, com'on, you got that detail map of the area, Frank? I want to go over the layout of the mound."

Reluctantly the security chief produced a large-scale map and unfolded it on the table. Mac and Kean sat down, and the four began to pore over it.

None of them took note of a faint rustling in the hedge of the garden flower bed closest by.

A small twitching nose poked out through the leaves toward them. Two pointed ears were cocked toward them, listening. A plump, white-tailed bunny was observing them carefully. It had, in fact, been tailing Kean and companions throughout their garden walk.

But with the men now around the table, their voices low in technical discussion of the map, the rabbit gave up its surveillance. It stole slowly, silently away from the patio until it had reached a safe distance, then shot off, arrowing southward, up Knockma hill.

At the top it shot right through a host of other bunnies munching the lush greenery on the empty hilltop in the early evening sun. It ignored them, streaking toward the mound.

A few feet from the base, the creature grew hazy, seeming to dissolve into the mound's side as it struck, vanishing from sight.

Only moments later, the rabbit was transforming to a man shape within the great hall of King Fionnbharr.

"Well, Kieran," Rury O'Mor anxiously asked the little man before the glow of shape-shifting had even died, "what did you discover? Is he there?"

"That he surely is," Kieran replied. "With several comrades too. One a very large fellow with a hairless head."

"Yes, I met that one before," Angus said. "It's Kean, all right."

That big warrior, the druids Owen and Matholwch, Aisling, and some twenty others of the Sidh had gathered with Rury and their king to hear the shape-shifter's report. Now Aisling spoke up most emphatically.

"You see? I said not to trust that man. Now there's no question that we must see this spell upon Caitlin broken very quickly."

"I'm sorry, Aisling, but our main problem here is with Kean," Fionnbharr countered. "Even if your daughter discovers he is here, we can prevent her from escaping to him. But if he believes she is in this Sidh, he may well come after her, no matter what."

"Yes, I think that's true," said Rury in a troubled way. "I am much amazed at his perseverance so far. Not what I would have expected for a villain. For all his seeming treachery, he has a strong will not unlike my own. He will not quit."

"Could you learn anything of what he's up to, Kieran?" asked Fionnbharr.

"Some," the little man said. "He seems to be only gathering knowledge now. I don't believe he's going to act immediately. He's going to await the return of another one of their lot named Connelly, who left them this morning. But I think he plans to act within a day or two."

"Act how?" asked Rury.

"He isn't yet sure. He seems to be studying the mound."

"He could do many things," said Fionnbharr, looking around at the rest. "We all know what mortals have tried against us in the past."

"Can't we defend ourselves?" asked one of the others of the Sidh.

"With the certainty that we won't be destroyed or exposed?" said the king. "That I don't know. It would depend on how much power this man has."

"We can't take such chances," said a second person.

"What else can we do?" said a third. "We know he can't be frightened away."

"No," said Owen, "but he might be eliminated. We might strike at him first."

"What, you mean attack him?" said O'Mor. "Go against him at Desmond Manor?"

"That you will *not* do!" Fionnbharr said adamantly. "We've had a pact with Desmond's earls for hundreds of years. They've always respected it."

"It doesn't seem they're upholding it now," said Angus, "letting this cunning wolf in through their gates."

"We don't know that they are any party to Kean's plans," the king said. "I tell you that we stay away from there."

"Very well," said Owen. "Then we simply get Kean away from that place somehow."

"Yes, then we be rid of him once and for all," said Angus, meaningfully tapping his sword hilt. "I've more than one reason to want vengeance upon him."

"Not that way," said Fionnbharr. "Violence and death would only bring others swarming about here. It must be something that stops him as a threat, but in a way that will not rouse the other mortals against us."

"Perhaps if we only take his mind then, not his life," suggested Matholwch.

"Of course!" said Owen. "We talked of wiping Caitlin's mind clean of him. Why not wipe his clean of us?"

"How?" asked Angus.

"I know how," said Fionnbharr.

Rury shook his head. "I do not like this. It smacks of cowardice. I'd much prefer battling this Kean head-to-head."

"Our first need here is to avoid a war," the king reminded him. "This seems our best choice." He looked to the old druid. "Matholwch, summon the Amadan-na-Briona to me. And see that the *pucas* come here too. We'll waste no more time. We act tonight!"

Kean awoke to the sound of a faint rattling.

He sat up in his huge four-poster bed and peered out into the darkness of the room. The manor's bedroom, like the place itself, was done in a large-scale, elaborate, medieval style. Lots of hulking, sinisterly shaped things loomed in the shadows of the huge space. But none moved or made a sound.

The rattle came again. This time he identified it. Pebbles were being thrown against one of the windows of the room.

He rose and went to it, peering cautiously out. He was on the second floor in the manor's rear. A figure was visible on the patio below, the body shadowed, but the face revealed in the moonlight. It was not the face of some apparition or dream this time but a face he knew well.

He quickly opened the window and leaned out.

"Professor Connelly," he called down softly, "is that you?"

"Yes," the other replied.

"What are you doing back here now?"

"I came back early," came the response in a hoarse whisper. "It's very urgent, Mr. Kean. I've discovered that they're going to act tonight."

"Who?"

"The very ones we're seeking. But you and I can act first, if you'll come with me."

"Act how?"

"No time for questions. We must go at once. Come down and meet me here."

"I'll get Mac."

"No. It can be only us two in this. If you wish any chance to save Caitlin Bawn, come alone!"

"Save Caitlin!" Kean said excitedly. "Wait there. I'll be right down!"

Hurriedly he donned pants and shirt and shoes. In two minutes he was slipping out of the room, creeping down through the silent, dark house to its front door.

Upon the bureau in the bedroom he left behind him lay a small clay jar and a gnarled black stick, both forgotten in his headlong haste.

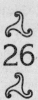

26

Kean slipped outside and started around the house.

From behind a hedgerow beside the walk a massive black form suddenly loomed up, blocking his way.

Kean started back, raising his hands defensively.

A familiar voice came to him: "It's just me, boss."

"That you, Stony?" Kean said, peering close at the shadowed figure.

"Yeah. Garvey and me decided we couldn't leave you without a guard. We decided to take turns coming here to keep watch."

"I should have figured. Well, just *stay* right here. I've got something to do."

He started around the big man, but Starski moved to block him again. "No, boss. Garvey said I wasn't to let you out of sight."

"Look, Stony," Kean said, trying to be patient, "I appreciate it. Really. But this is too important and I'm in too big a rush. You stay right here, don't move, don't follow, or I'm going to fire your ass! Understand?"

"Yes, boss," Starski said in a wounded tone.

"Good boy," said Kean, ducking around the man and trotting on into the night.

He swiftly rounded to the back of the manor, looking around for Connelly.

"Professor?" he called softly.

"Here," whispered the other, stepping out from the

pool of black beneath a fat rhododendron bush. "Follow me."

The man started off at once. Kean ran to follow, catching up as they left the gardens and started away westward into the manor grounds.

"So what's going on?" asked Kean, moving at an all but jogging pace.

"I discovered they're sending some of their forces out tonight," the other said, the rapid pace he was setting keeping him just ahead. "When they do, they'll open up the Sidh. We'll discover its entrance."

"Where are we heading?"

"No more talk," Connelly hissed. "Keep silent. And hurry. It's nearly time!"

The two went on at a near run across the field. Beyond it they plunged into a stand of trees. It was dark within, lit only by stray strands of silver moonlight slipping down through small gaps in the trees. A gloomy scene, and uncomfortably similar to the one in Kean's recent dream.

Once Kean looked sharply around as he moved through the wood. Had he caught a glimpse of a movement in the underbrush to one side? But he peered intently as he continued on and saw nothing more.

Beyond the trees they came out into the open once again. Ahead of them now lay a large ruin, bathed in the moonlight. It was the old tower house Kean's host had spoken of. The ragged top of the tall, half-fallen structure showed high against the sky. A low and crumbling stone wall circled it.

Without pausing, Connelly led the way on, through a gap in the wall. They came into what had been the tower's open yard, now littered with fallen stones. Kean stopped there and looked around.

"What are we doing here?" he asked.

"What do you mean?" asked the other, pulling up some way ahead and turning toward him.

"I thought the Sidh's entrance was up at the mound. We're nowhere near there."

"No, we're not," Connelly agreed in his still-soft, still-hoarse voice. "But then, we wouldn't want you anywhere near there . . . when you're found."

Kean looked hard at the professor. "What the hell do you mean?"

"Only that I'm afraid you won't be finding the Sidh entrance this night."

"You mean they're not coming out?"

The other grinned. "Oh, they're *already* out!"

At that the form of the professor seemed to break away. A ragged fracture showed first at his forehead, like a crack made in a hard-boiled egg, running down through the center of his face. The two halves of it fell grotesquely apart. The fissure continued down, his body dividing, each side collapsing outward onto the ground, there to instantly dissolve away.

What was left standing was certainly not Connelly anymore, but it still grinned widely at Kean.

In general appearance it seemed to be some morbid kind of clown. The body was lean and lank to an absurd point, awkwardly constructed, knobby of joints, with immense hands and feet. The clothing was a voluminous shirt of nearly fluorescent green-and-yellow stripe, covered over by a baggy, vividly purple, hooded cloak. Both garments were in tatters, flapping around and barely concealing the skinny limbs. Through holes torn in the hood, long ears—flopping and hairy like a dog's—poked out.

All the features of the thing's head were, in fact, of bizarre proportion. The too-broad mouth was filled with gaped and mismatched rows of teeth. The face was all but chinless, this contrasted by a thick, enormous thrust of nose. And the eyes were immense, like porcelain saucers in the night, their silvery pupils shifting wildly.

In total the being evoked an image of a kind of deranged Goofy, and might have been laughable if not for the sinister implications of its appearance there.

"Wh-who are you?" Kean said.

"Just a friend! A friend!" it told him, the whisper replaced by a high, singsong voice. It raised an arm and held a hand out toward him. "Now, let me touch you, and we'll be friends for always."

Kean drew himself up defiantly. "You're not scaring me away. I'm not backing off this time. I'm not afraid of you."

"Fine, fine," it told him. "Then it'll be easier." It stepped forward. "Only a touch. Only one touch is all it needs."

Kean looked at the long fingers of the hand stretched out toward him. He decided that standing his ground this time was perhaps not the wisest thing. He began to back away.

From beyond the wall behind him, two other forms leapt into view, clearing the stones in a bound to land in the yard.

Kean heard a low growling. He glanced around toward it. Two immense dogs stood there now, like Great Danes, but broader of build. Their sleek hides were a glowing blue-black. Their eyes were sparks of crimson fire, and their teeth were rows of sharply glinting points.

Those teeth showed well as both dogs snarled and stepped up on either side behind him, blocking his line of retreat.

"No escaping now," the clownish being told him. "Don't struggle. Make it easy for us both. Just the touch, and you'll care about nothing anymore." It stepped closer. "That's not a bad thing at all. To be free of the troubles of the world. Always happy. Always smiling." It stepped forward again. "Come and let the Fool of the Forth touch you."

"I—I've heard of you," said Kean, fighting without success to keep from looking into the swirling pupils of the eyes.

"Of course. So welcome me," it cajoled. "It's a greater kingdom I'm calling you to now. A kingdom the sane don't understand. Free of the awful master that men call reason. Free of desire, of fear, of responsibility. You'll be left alone.

You'll do only what you want. You'll be free, free, free, free, free . . ."

Kean stared, frozen, motionless, all but completely mesmerized.

The being moved closer, its outstretched fingers only a yard away.

Another figure leapt over the stone wall. It dived immediately down atop one dog, taking it by surprise. The beast yelped as the two went down together.

The clownish being was distracted. It broke off eye contact with Kean to look. Freed of its spell, Kean looked around too.

It was Starski—having ignored Kean's threat and loyally followed after his boss—who now rolled with the growling, snapping hound upon the ground. Both the big man's hands clutched at the beast's throat.

The second animal leapt into the fray, its jaws closing on Starski's right forearm.

"Stony!" yelled Kean, starting toward him.

"Get away, boss!" the big man yelled back. "Just run!"

Kean looked back toward the clown as it lunged forward to make its touch. He ducked away. The hand missed, its owner staggering past. Then Kean was off, running for the ruined tower.

The being recovered and pursued. It moved swiftly for something so awkward-looking. Kean went into the ruins, searching for a way through. It was a bad choice. He found his way blocked by the remains of stone walls rising on three sides. The advancing Fool closed up the fourth.

Kean's eyes fell on a narrow, circular stairway in the one intact corner of the tumbled, shelled-out ruin. It wound upward without obvious gaps.

"Now I know why they always go up," he murmured, and ran for it.

He reached the stairway and went up as fast as he could. Some of the stone steps crumbled beneath his feet, but he went on, leaping upward, heading for the top.

If he'd thought his move would discourage his pursuer,

he was soon proved wrong. Without hesitation it started up after him at a brisk trot.

In the yard below, Starski continued his battle with both dogs. He now had a big hand to the throat of each, trying to throttle them. The beasts thrashed wildly to get free, clawing at him with their feet. The man hung on, huge body tensed with strain, teeth gritted as he tightened his grip.

Kean reached the stair top. He found himself suddenly in the open, standing on the one short section of the tower's battlements left. On one side there was nothing between him and a drop of fifty feet to what had been the building's bottom floor. On the other only a flimsy rail made from rusty pipe guarded against a like fall to the yard.

The clownish being came up the last stairs behind him.

"Give up now," it advised. "You've no wish to be hurt. Just come to me."

"Like hell," Kean said and backed away along the rail, moving toward the last intact corner of the tower's remains. The being went after him.

Below, one of the hounds violently tore free of Starski's viselike grip on its neck. It lunged for the man's own throat in an attempt to rip it away.

Starski put a foot up against its belly and shoved. The beast was jerked backward, its jaws snapping shut on empty air.

As it tumbled away, the big bodyguard used the opportunity to grab the other hound by a hind leg with his freed hand. He got his legs under him and rose upward to his feet. With a grunt of effort he pressed the heavy, struggling beast overhead in both hands to hold it at arm's length above him. Handling it like one of his opponents from the wrestling ring, the Stone Man pivoted to whirl the beast around, then released it, sending it flying toward its twin.

The two hounds crashed together. Both hurtled backward to crash against the stone wall. They collapsed there in a heap, loosened stones avalanching down on them. Both beasts lay motionless, seemingly stunned.

The bodyguard swung around from them, gaze searching for his boss. A rattling of loose rocks falling from above him brought his eyes upward.

Silhouetted against the moonlit night sky was Kean, atop the tower, backing away from the advancing, menacing figure.

Starski headed for the tower at a run.

Up above, Kean had backed to the end of his length of platform. The bit of rail rounded the corner of the tower, then stopped abruptly where the battlement had fallen away. Kean stopped too. He looked down from the height.

"Only death that way," the being said. "You don't want to die. No other choice but me." Its grin spread wider as it slowly closed with him.

The only choices for Kean did seem to be to jump, to stand passively—or to attack. To attack meant that he most surely would be touched. But the consequences of that touch were unknown. That left attacking the most reasonable alternative.

The clown's hand reached out. One finger was extended to point right at Kean. It was only inches away now.

Kean crouched to spring.

A figure loomed up suddenly from the darkness behind the clown. Massive arms shot out to enwrap the being's waist.

It was Starski again, yanking the being up completely off its feet.

It shrieked in surprise and kicked out. The toe of its huge foot struck Kean's chin. He was knocked backward, striking against the rail, toppling over it.

He grabbed out desperately and seized the rail. It gave, its slim pipe bending, one support bracket tearing loose from the crumbling stone. But still it held. Kean dangled, hanging from one hand.

The faithful bodyguard, seeing his boss go over, was enraged.

"I'll kill you!" he shouted at the clown.

Hoisting the being higher, he swung it out over the rail. Struggling to free itself, the Fool wrenched its shoulders hard around. It swung a lanky arm out as far as it could, bringing a hand around toward Starski's head.

One fingertip touched the big man's temple. At the same moment, Starski heaved the clown outward.

The being fell, screaming out its fear, absurd clothes billowing about it.

Kean, now clutching the bent rail with both hands, watched the clown arch out and down to slam onto the yard.

There was an unpleasant thud. The scream was cut off. The angular body lay for a moment sprawled and broken amid the fallen stones.

But then a faint golden glow rose up from it. The light grew stronger, enveloping the figure. Its form grew hazy within the glow, then seemed to dissolve away.

Within seconds the strange being's shape was gone. The golden light exploded into a bloom of tiny lights that spread up and out and faded away like dying sparks.

No trace of the Fool of the Forth was left.

Kean began pulling himself up, hand over hand, along the rail. Soon he was high enough to throw a leg up over the tower's edge. With that help he managed to lever himself onto the battlement, rolling away from the edge to safety.

He got to his feet, peering around in the darkness.

"Starski?" he said. "Where are you?"

An odd, faint, frightened whimper came back to him. He stepped forward, seeing a huge lump ahead on the platform.

He moved closer, looking down. It was Starski lying on his side, legs pulled up and encircled by his arms.

Kean knelt by him. "Stony, what's wrong?"

There was no answer.

With a look of puzzlement, Kean gently rolled the man

back, revealing his face. He stared down in shock at his bodyguard.

Starski's face was slack, all expression wholly wiped away. Saliva dribbled from one corner of his sagging mouth. The eyes that stared up at Kean were blank, staring, and as emptied of their personality as if the mind behind them had somehow ceased to be.

"Stony!" Kean said, shaking the man hard. "Stony, listen! Talk to me!"

All that came back to him was a long, low, tortured cry of pain.

The morning sun revealed a dramatic scene unfolding in the graveled parking area before Desmond Manor.

An ambulance was pulled up close before the manor's front door, and a stretcher bearing the strapped-down form of what had been "Stone Man" Starski was being carried forth by two straining attendants.

At a discreet distance, a knot of black-and-white-clad servants of the manor—looking much like a penguin flock —stood watching curiously. Nearer to the ambulance stood Mac, Kean, and Garvey, watching as their stricken companion was loaded into the vehicle.

McBride was the only one showing great distress. Garvey was as impassive as usual. Kean's expression was hardened by anger.

A Vauxhall Cavalier rolled up the drive and into the parking area just as the attendants were swinging closed the ambulance's rear doors. It drew up beside Kean's group, and a worried-looking Professor Connelly emerged to watch the attendants climb into their own vehicle.

"What happened?" he asked as they started the ambulance and roared away. "Who's that?"

Before answering him, Kean stepped up close and eyed the man up and down most searchingly. "That is you, isn't it?" he demanded.

"Of course," said Connelly. "I've just driven out from Dublin. What do you mean?"

"Something looking a helluva lot like you showed up last night and conned me outside on a wild goose hunt. Real clever move too. It was just about the only way they'da got me out alone. We went out to an old ruin, and then the 'you' changed into this scrawny, wild-eyed nut."

"My God!" said the professor. "More ancient magic. What did he do?"

"He wanted to touch me. That was it. He said that he was called the Fool of the Forth."

"The Amadan-na-Briona," Connelly said. " 'He whose stroke is, as death, uncurable.' A most awful figure of the Otherworld. Some say that he is the worst of them all. That touch of his can steal all reason."

"I found that out," Kean said grimly. "The hard way. But Stony found out harder. That was him they were taking away. He came out to rescue me, and he did. But he got touched instead."

"And this touch—it worked on him?" the professor asked.

"It's like there's nothing left inside," said McBride, tapping his head. "He rocks and cries and shivers like a scared baby. He won't do anything else."

"Poor man," Connelly said in dismay.

"He wouldn't move at all afterward," said Kean. "Just lay there, up at the top of that ruined tower. I stayed out there with him all night. I couldn't move him. I was afraid to leave him there."

"This morning, when we found out they were missing, we went out searching," said Mac. "Lord Desmond and some of his people helped. Took us 'til noon to find them. Took two hours more to get poor Starski back here."

"What did you tell the earl had happened?" asked Connelly.

"That we went out walking, explored the ruins, and Stony hit his head," Kean supplied. "I didn't think he'd buy much else. He was still pretty upset. Thinks it's his fault for having unsafe ruins. His wife really got shook up. He's inside trying to comfort her."

Connelly shook his head. "Things have escalated much more quickly than I thought. To send such a creature after you. To try to harm you that way . . ."

"Yeah, well, they took their shot," Kean said fiercely. "They missed it. Now, I'm going to take mine!"

27

The servants of the manor had by this time all returned inside, leaving Kean and his three companions alone in the drive.

Connelly looked about him as if to be certain no one was eavesdropping, then asked conspiratorially, "Just what do you mean by 'take yours,' Mr. Kean?"

"I mean that I'm not putting up with this bullshit anymore. I'm tired of being on the defensive. I'm tired of getting beat up by them. And I'm tired of their goddamn tricks. I'm sure they're here now. And I'm sure they're in that mound. So somehow I'm finding a way—any way—to get at them."

"I might have one," said the professor. "Though I'm not certain how much it will help you."

"Tell me."

"Why don't we stroll up toward the mound," Connelly suggested. "I think you ought to see it. It will help explain."

He led the others off the drive and across the manicured lawns southward, toward the slope upward to the mound.

Garvey trailed a few steps behind, still stoically doing his job of guardianship, but alone now.

"I went through all my sources on Knockma and Fionnbharr," the professor explained as they walked. "At first there didn't seem much that would help. Then I came upon the remnants of a tale once told to Lady Gregory. She researched folklore in the countyside of western Ireland along with William Butler Yeats. This was during the Irish Renaissance, back in the 1920s, and they were trying to compile—"

"Yeah, yeah," Kean said impatiently. "I don't need the background. Just, go on."

"Excuse me," the professor said with a touch of indignation, his lecture having been thus rudely curtailed. "In any case, she traveled about collecting stories from the peasantry in this area of Eire. And it seems a very old farmer of Galway told her one about Fionnbharr. According to it, the king's Sidh was once attacked by mortals—successfully."

"It was?" Kean said with great interest.

At this point they reached the limit of the tended part of the manor grounds. Talk was suspended while they climbed a low wall of piled stones that marked the boundary. They began to move uphill through unmowed wild grasses that swished about their ankles. Connelly went on.

"The story was a rambling and fragmentary one. Possibly a remnant passed from father to son, from who knows how far back. Perhaps an ancestor was a participant. From what I could gather, the incident took place some three hundred years ago. That's recent history for Ireland. King Fionnbharr was out wandering in the countryside, as the Sidhe apparently did more freely then, and he came upon a most striking woman."

"That seems to happen a lot here," said Mac with a glance at Kean.

"I understand what you mean," said Connelly, "but this situation was exactly reversed from yours. It was *he* who was of the Sidhe, and *she* who was a mortal."

"Still an interesting coincidence."

"Ah, but there's very little of coincidence when you're delving into the realms of the Otherworld," Connelly pointed out. "In fact the stolen woman motif is a very common one in tales of Fairy. It's almost as if certain events or relationships are destined to be played out again and again. There's much of fate at work."

"Fate or coincidence," Kean prodded. "What was the deal here?"

"Oh, yes," said the professor, recalled to his subject again. "Well, in this case Fionnbharr glimpsed the lady dancing at a party. It was in the manor of another lord nearby. The king was captivated by the loveliness of the lass and he stole her right away. He made one error, though—the young woman was a bride. He'd actually stolen her from her own wedding feast, out from under the very nose of her new husband, the manor's lord. That lord, needless to say, was a bit incensed."

"I guess I can see why," said Mac.

"An invisible voice—the tale doesn't say whose—told him where to seek his bride. He gathered an army of workers and soldiers and marched upon Knockma. They fell to work demolishing the mound. A great breach was excavated in one side. When it had gone far enough, needless to say, Fionnbharr capitulated. He gave back the bride."

"So the lord won," said Kean.

"Yes and no. She returned to her world, but unfortunately still under the deep trance he had thrown on her."

"What happened to her?" asked Mac.

Connelly shrugged. "The storyteller didn't say. Perhaps she stayed entranced from that day out. But the lord did win her back." He pulled up, looking ahead. "Ah, there it is."

They had come up onto the top of the hill. It was flatter there, a large, open pasture of lush grass. In the center the familiar shape of a mound rose up. It was near to Newgrange in size, but slightly more rounded and steeper of side.

Across one side of the slope there was the time-softened remnant of what might have been a trench, like a long-healed wound in the otherwise even, unmarked face of the mound.

"See there," Connelly said, pointing. "That's what remains of the cut they made. It was claimed by the old farmer as proof of the Others' existence."

Mac looked at the scar, at the mound, and then around at the empty hilltop. It seemed abnormally quiet and extremely isolated there. The civilization of normal men seemed far away.

"Is it safe here?" he asked with a certain anxiousness. "I mean, *They* wouldn't try anything now?"

"In the daylight? With all of us here?" said Connelly. "Highly unlikely. And so far as we keep our distance from the mound, we shouldn't be viewed as any threat. If we moved closer . . . well, who knows?"

"Excuse me," said Garvey, stepping forward, "but are you saying you think there's someone inside that thing right now? Hiding underground?"

"Not precisely," the professor replied. "It's very hard to explain. You see, the tales of what a Sidh is like vary widely. They're confusing, vague, and often contradictory. Few mortals have entered and returned to speak of them, after all. Sometimes it's a fabulous underground palace; sometimes a part of a whole, vast, Irish Elysium called Magh Mell or Tir n'Aill or Tir na n-Og; sometimes it's a more localized domain. But in all cases the mound or hill or lake or grove that is the entrance opens into a realm not really subterranean, but of a world 'elsewhere,' coexistant with ours."

"Like Alice down the rabbit hole," said Mac.

"Yes. And perhaps such more modern tales of wonderlands indicate a longing still in us for those 'Other' places that once were better known to mankind."

"Kid stories!" Garvey said derisively. "Fairy tales! What you're talking about isn't possible."

"We're not dealing with our reality in there," the professor countered. "In an Otherworld, who knows what's possible?" He looked toward the mound. A light of mixed longing and eagerness shone in his eyes. "Just think . . .

to actually go in. To learn firsthand about Them. To see the beings of legends!"

"Maybe you'll get a chance, Professor," said Kean. He looked to McBride. "Okay, Mac, I'm going to need some help from you again. Big help too. You're going to have to go on a mission for me."

"A mission? Where?"

"No more talk here," Kean said. "It makes me nervous being so close to that thing. Let's wait and talk down below. Come on."

They turned away from Knockma and started back down the hill.

They didn't realize that they were being watched by several pairs of eyes.

A large, round shield of silver, polished to the smooth sheen of a mirror, hung on the wall of King Fionnbharr's great hall. Within its depths it magically displayed a shimmering image of the world close outside the Sidh, just as Aisling's imaging pool had done.

Fionnbharr, Aisling, O'Mor, Angus, and the two druids stood grouped around it, watching the four mortal men vanish from sight as they went below the hill's crest.

Owen swept a hand before the shield making the image fade away. It was left to show only a reflection of the room and the faces of those who stood before it. The reflected expression on the face of the king was one of rage.

"Not only did the cursed man survive the Amadan-na-Briona," he said, "but he then has the brazen arrogance to come right up here."

"He's surely proven his evilness once again," said Owen, "destroying yet another of our race."

"The Fool *was* trying to destroy him, Owen," O'Mor fairly pointed out.

"I feel very badly about this," Fionnbharr said. "It was my own choice to send the poor being out there. After so many centuries of life, I cause him to be destroyed. Strange and terrible as his power was, he didn't deserve to die."

"What about myself?" old Matholwch said sorrowfully. "My own magic it was that put the likeness of that mortal upon the Fool to trick Kean. And so I helped him to his doom as well."

"But who could have known it would end that way?" Angus put in. "The Amadan's touch has never failed."

"*I* should have known," the king said angrily. "It's I who've warned you often enough about the new dangers waiting out in Their world."

"All of you are ignoring the main thing here," Aisling said testily. "That man out there is extremely powerful. He defeated the Fool. He also defeated the two *pucas* sent to help."

"It was his guard who did that," said O'Mor.

"Yes," Angus agreed. "A formidable man. I regret his strength and courage being wasted that way. No warrior so brave should meet his end by the loss of his mind. Better if I could have met him in fair combat. That would have been a fight!"

"It doesn't matter how Kean survived," Aisling persisted. "The truth is that he did! And each moment he continues surviving makes him a greater threat to my daughter. Something has got to be done!"

A small, brown thrush fluttered into the room, landing on the floor nearby.

"Ah, here's Kieran," said Fionnbharr as the glow of the shape-shifting rose about the bird. "We'll see what *he* knows."

In moments the transformed little man was approaching the group.

"Did you overhear anything to interest us, Kieran?" O'Mor asked.

The other shook his head. "Likely little more than you might have guessed. The 'touched' big one was taken away somewhere. To have someone try to remove the madness, maybe."

"No chance of doing that," said Owen.

"That Connelly—the one who seems like a bard or druid to them—has returned," Kieran went on.

"We saw him," said Fionnbharr, "in the mirror. What did they speak of?"

"They talked about this Sidh. Kean is certain now that we are here."

"Is he?" said Aisling caustically. "Well then, Fionnbharr, your try at Kean surely accomplished one thing well. It totally betrayed us to our enemy."

"Careful, woman," the king shot back. "You are trying my patience now."

"She is right though," Kieran said. "He knows, and he is determined to act against us."

"How can he do that?" asked Owen.

"I didn't hear."

"Did you hear anything else?" asked O'Mor.

The little man hesitated.

"Come along," the king demanded. "Hold nothing back."

"Very well. The Connelly person told him . . . well, he told him about your own little, ah, 'trouble' with that mortal girl."

"The man found that tale?" Fionnbharr cried, clearly much mortified. "Curse my own weakness doubly for ever doing that. It means now he'll know that we've been vulnerable."

"Is he planning to act on this knowledge, Kieran?" O'Mor asked.

"That I don't know. They went back down the hill to the manor. That man who seems a guardian suggested they get into that black metal vehicle of theirs before they talk more. It worked. They sealed themselves inside and all sound was cut off. So I left Killian down there to keep watching them and flew here to report."

"The man could do anything," Aisling ranted. "His resources seem limitless. A thousand men he could bring upon us. More! We've no choice but to act against him first."

"That we will not!" said the king. "Any further act by us against them will only serve to make things worse. We don't know that Kean will or can do anything more. We must simply wait to see. In the meantime I will not risk any more of my people in this. Do you understand?"

"Certainly I understand," Aisling hotly returned. "I understand that you are frightened by him. I understand that you intend to sit here and just wait for him to come. And when he does, just what will you do then? Throw Caitlin to him as you did that mortal wench?"

"Is it cowardice you're accusing me of now?" he thundered. "It's not your good or Caitlin's or that of any one person among us I'm thinking of. It's the protection of us all."

"Well, if the choice of inaction is your means of protecting us," she returned, "then we'd best be starting to look out for ourselves."

She turned on her heel at this and stalked away, out of the hall.

The others stood looking after her, seeming relieved to see her go.

"I always end up with a great churning in my stomach when I speak to her," said the king.

"Fionnbharr," said O'Mor thoughtfully, "there was no truth in what she said, was there? I mean, you wouldn't turn Caitlin over to that man just to avoid a greater conflict with him, would you?"

"How can you even suggest that?" Fionnbharr said in surprise. "I deserved my defeat all those years ago. That woman was my own hot-blooded mistake. I was arrogant. I brought danger on my people."

"So have I," the other returned. "It's my rescue of Caitlin that's brought Kean here."

"You ignore a great difference: I was returning a mortal I had stolen to the mortal world. Caitlin is one of our own. We would never give her up."

"Are you so certain? Had the choice been yours, you would have left her out there with Kean, wouldn't you?"

"I didn't say so. Perhaps I would have weighed the risks. I might have considered gains and losses. None of that matters anymore. You took the chance and won. She is back among us now."

"Then I can depend wholly on your help?" O'Mor asked bluntly. "You promise it?"

Fionnbharr put a hand on his chieftain's shoulder and spoke assuringly. "Rury, I know what you feel for her. If it means keeping her from the hands of a monster, I will do whatever must be done."

"Including going to war?" asked O'Mor, eyeing him keenly.

Fionnbharr met the gaze for a long moment, consideringly. Then: "We must all pray to Danu it never comes to that," he hedged.

In the meantime, Aisling had arrived at her daughter's cell.

She was admitted by the guard to find Caoimhe there. The two young women had been seated together on the bed, deep in conversation. They started and looked up guiltily as the older woman came in.

"What's going on?" Aisling demanded suspiciously. "What kind of conspiracy is this?"

Caoimhe stood and moved away to a corner, looking frightened. But Caitlin stood up to boldly confront her mother.

"She has told me what has happened, Mother," the daughter said. "I know that Michael Kean is here."

"Traitor!" Aisling cried, incensed. She stepped toward the cowering handmaiden, raising a hand to strike.

But Caitlin stepped before her mother, raising her own hand in defense.

"No, Mother," she said warningly. "You'll not harm her. She's no traitor; she's the only friend I have left. The only one who believes me, who knows the truth."

"She is doing you no good to bring such knowledge," Aisling said, dropping her hand, but still glaring at Caoimhe.

"Of course she is. She brings me hope. Hope that I may yet be freed. And hope that you might finally see the truth. Doesn't his coming so far, going through so much, convince you?"

"It convinces me that he is an even more obsessed and more ruthless villain than I'd thought. All the more reason you must be protected from him."

"No, Mother. He's only come to rescue me. He is a good man."

"No one believes that," her mother said tersely. "Your mind is still deranged." She sighed. "Why would Rury not listen to me and have the druids wipe all those foolish ideas from your mind?"

"You asked Rury to do that?" her daughter said in shock.

"Of course. You've clearly no idea what the truth is anymore. Then at least he and I would not be forced to deal with the problem of you while we are also dealing with the mortal."

"Dealing with him?" Caitlin said with alarm. "What do you mean? You won't try to harm him?"

"Oh, didn't Caoimhe tell you? That's already been tried by our king. He failed. But I won't!"

"Please, Mother, don't," Caitlin pleaded.

Aisling was unmoved. "And wait until he finds a way to reach you? Never, child. I fear Kean's power, and I don't trust Fionnbharr. Therefore I have to act to protect you myself. It is my right."

"What about *my* rights?"

"I told you, you are not capable of knowing what they are."

"What do you mean to do?"

"I have a friend. A very old friend. She's agreed to help me." Aisling smiled. There was chilling cruelty in it. "She's quite anxious in fact. I've asked her here to see you."

There was a clacking as the bolt of the cell was drawn.

"Ah, likely that's her now," Aisling announced.

"Mother, who is this?" Caitlin demanded fearfully.

As if in answer, the door swung open. Caitlin stared in horror at what was revealed.

"Oh, Mother!" she cried. "No!"

28

"**Y**es. I understand," Kean said into the teleph
"Yes, I'm certain you've done everything you poss
could."

He stood at a massive desk of dark oak to use the ins
ment. It was at one end of an enormous gallery room
stretched well over a hundred feet along an entire sid
the manor. The outer, northern wall was lined with
leaded windows of stained glass. The inner wall was i
with three elaborate fireplaces spaced evenly to heat
whole area. Between the fireplaces sat ponderous b
shelves filled with antique tomes. Dark portraits of g
faced ancestors hung on the walls above, and above th
over twenty-five feet high, the arches of carved w
vaulting supported a barrel roof.

Halfway down the room behind Kean, Connelly and
Earl of Desmond sat before a fire blazing in the cer
fireplace. The two men sat forward, poised intently
their tapestry-covered easy chairs, their snifters of bra
forgotten on the tables beside them as they openly ea
dropped.

"Well, I appreciate it," Kean was going on. "No. N
ing more but see he's comfortable. Right. I've taken
of things. Tomorrow. Yes. Well, thanks again. Good nig

He hung up the phone and went back to them.

"How is Mr. Starski?" the professor asked.

Kean sat down and took up his own drink. "Still noth

hey can do," he explained grimly, taking a big swig. "No evidence of trauma, the doctor said. No sign of any damage at all. They still can't get any positive response from him."

"Poor man," said the earl.

"He was a good guy," said Kean. "A good friend too." He paused and then added musingly, "I guess I didn't realize *how* good."

"He was also an employee, Mr. Kean," Connelly pointed out. "What he was doing for you he was doing for duty's sake."

"It was more than that," Kean said sharply. "Stony wasn't loyal just for money."

"Of course not," the professor soothed. "I only meant that what happened to him wasn't your own fault."

Kean shook his head. "I don't know about that. But I do know I'm going to take care of him now. I'm having him sent home tomorrow. I'll get the best treatment I can for him there. Neurosurgeons, shrinks, any kind of specialist it takes. Maybe they can do something."

"Perhaps," said the professor, but not very heartily.

On this cheerless note, Lord Desmond finished his brandy and set down his glass.

"Well, gentlemen, sorry to excuse myself so soon, but I must see to my wife." He got to his feet. "She went to bed early, you know. Severe migraine. The stresses of the day and all."

"I understand, Dick," said Kean. "And, look, we'll be out of here tomorrow. You don't need us around any longer, causing her more headaches."

The earl waved a negating hand. "Wouldn't hear of it!" he said emphatically. "I insist you stay. It was my own damn fault, not warning you about the ruins."

"There are just some things you can't warn anyone about," Kean said. "There's no blame on you. We're big boys."

"It helps to hear you say so," said Desmond. "Well, good night to you both, gentlemen."

He went out of the gallery, leaving only the two before the fire.

Connelly sipped at his brandy. "Are you certain you shouldn't have told him?" he asked. "I mean, about what you intend to do."

"He'll find out quick enough," Kean answered. "And I don't think he's gonna be so hot to let me stay on here afterward." He drained the last of his drink and got to his feet. "Well, I'm off too. I really need some sleep after last night. And Mac should be back here early if things go okay."

"That means staying up all night."

"Hey, they'll get enough double time to cover losing some sleep. I'm not wasting one more day."

"You know that I don't approve of this," the professor told him frankly.

"Yeah, I figured. So, why stay on?"

"I thought I might protect things as much as possible. Minimize the harm."

Kean eyed him searchingly. "Are you sure that's it? Are you sure you're not curious too . . . to see what'll happen?"

"I suppose," Connelly answered in all honesty. "I can't say I'm not intrigued by the notion of an encounter with Them. And at the same time, I don't know if I really want it proved. That might bring on more loss than gain—for Them, for us, for Ireland, even for the whole world."

"I don't care about any of that," Kean said callously. "I'm getting Caitlin back, and *nothing* is stopping me this time. So maybe you'd better just stay out of the way, Professor."

With that he turned and strode away, out of the gallery.

He left Connelly looking after him, his face drawn in a troubled frown.

"Alas for all that's been before," the professor murmured, "and may never be again."

He took a deep draught of his brandy.

Kean, meanwhile, was finding his way through the rambling house, up a sweep of staircase and down a length of corridor to the door of his room.

He looked up and down the shadowed hall before he went in. It was empty. The manor was silent.

He entered a room even more heavily shrouded in darkness. The tall window had its curtains pulled against all but a pale glow of moonlight. A single, small lamp on a table by the door did little to dispel the host of crouching and looming shadows that crowded the far reaches of the big space.

He pulled off the cardigan he wore, leaving himself in trousers and shirt. He was beginning to unbuckle his belt when a noise from the bed reached him.

It was just a faint creak, but it was enough to bring him swinging around in alarm.

He peered toward the bed. He could see nothing but shadows within its canopied area. His eye fell upon the blackthorn stick on the dresser. His expression hardened with determination. Stealthily he moved to it; noiselessly he took it up. Cautiously he crept across the room to the bedside. He grabbed a bed curtain and yanked it back, raising the stick threateningly.

A figure there lifted arms defensively. A voice spoke: "You wouldn't strike me with that, would you now, Michael Kean?"

He lowered the stick, staring in astonishment. The figure revealed in the faint light was that of Caitlin Bawn.

"Caitlin!" he said.

"Michael," she said, now beaming delightedly. "I'm so happy to see you once again."

She sat with legs curled under her in the middle of the big bed. He put down the stick and sat on the bed's edge to see her better. Her long hair hung unbound about her shoulders. She wore the green dress he had bought her.

"How did you get here?"

"A friend released me. She couldn't stand to see what they meant to do."

"To do?"

Her look of joy turned to one of pain at the thought. "Yes. Most cruel they meant to be. To wipe my mind clean. To erase all memory of you. And my own mother in it too." Tears welled up in her eyes. "I'm alone there. I'm an enemy to them now, Michael. There's only you left in the whole world to protect me. Will you do so?"

She looked so miserable he slid closer to her, enfolding her in his arms.

"I will," he promised her. "That's why I'm here."

She put her arms around him and drew close in a comforting embrace. Her head dropped down upon his shoulder.

"I knew you would. I knew it when I learned you'd come to find me. You meant to get me away from them, didn't you?"

"Any way I could. I promised."

Her head lifted from his shoulder and she looked at him. "Then it's a great gift of thanks that I've come to give you in return," she said, and pressed her lips to his.

It was an ardent kiss, a long kiss, her clutching him tight against her and him not struggling to get away. When they pulled back from one another, he was breathing heavily, and his face was flushed with the warmth she had generated in him.

"You're very welcome," he said wholeheartedly.

He looked down at her face, so close to his. Her eyes glowed with the bright azure light of her arousal. She panted softly, her red lips slightly parted. Her white cheeks were rouged by her own risen heat.

"I never thought to see you again," she said in a voice grown low and husky from emotion.

"You wore the dress I got you," he noted. Although somehow it seemed to be clinging more tightly to her lithe body now, accentuating all its most sensuous lines and curves.

"Yes. I had to bring it. It was the only thing of you I had there. I wanted nothing from them. I only wanted you."

She pulled him into another kiss, falling back on the

bed, drawing him down with her. This time she held him even longer, hugging tighter, moving her body to bring his whole length pressing against hers.

It was he who broke the kiss, with some little effort, pulling back and taking a deep breath.

"Woo!" he explained in an appreciative way. Then in an attempt at more reason, he added, "But, look, should we be doing this right now? I mean, won't They be coming after you again when They know you're gone? Shouldn't we get out of here fast? Put distance between you and Them?"

"No. No," she said in a passionate tone. "I'll not be denied this. There's a great hunger in me. It will be satisfied."

She moved on him aggressively again, pushing at him with surprising strength to roll him upon his back. Instantly she was astride him, kissing him hungrily while her fingers went to the buttons of his shirt.

He lifted hands to grab hers, pushing her away.

"Whoa, here," he said in protest. "This isn't right."

"Why are you fighting?" she asked him. "You want this as much as I. I feel your body stirring against mine. I feel your heat."

"Jesus, why wouldn't it be stirring?" he said. "But what about your courtship thing? All that premarital chastity? All the years before even touching? All that?"

"All that means nothing now," she said. "I'm not of them anymore. I'm free of them. And to prove it, I will break any bond left. My union with you will do it. It will prove that I am wholly yours."

"It will?"

"Yes." She fixed him with a gaze of fiery intensity. "You will have me truly this way. Have me now!"

Still astride him, she sat up. In a single, swift move she swept the dress up and over her head, casting it away to whisper to the floor. In the faint light he could see her body above him as a smooth, sensuous white form, her hair a flow of burnished gold.

She began to lean down toward him again. His hands came up to her shoulders, stopping her.

"All right," he said. "I want this too. But let me be certain it's safe first. All right?"

He rolled sideways, gently lowering her onto the bed, sliding away from her. "It'll just be a second," he assured her as he did.

He moved away from her into the darkness. His shadowed form crossed to the window. He parted the curtains to peer out.

"Nothing there," he said.

She watched him move on around to the door. It opened as he checked outside. It closed. There was a click of the lock.

He started back, but stopped with the sound of a thump.

"Ow! Damn bureau," he muttered. "Can't see in the dark."

He moved back across the room to the bedside, going slowly as if feeling his way to avoid more collisions.

She lifted arms toward him. "Come back to me," she said. "I'm afire for you."

"Are you, really?" he said.

One of his hands lifted out over her. The fingers moved and something fine and glittering sprinkled down upon her left forearm.

There was a sound of sizzling and a smoke rose from her skin there, as if it were truly afire. She gave a shriek of pain and drew her arm back, slapping her other hand over the spot.

"What did you do?" she cried. "You've burned me!"

"I just used some of this." He lifted what he held in his other hand into view. It was a crude pottery jar, its stopper removed.

"What is it?"

"Just a little magic of my own. It's supposed to show the truth. But it shouldn't be dangerous to you, if you *are* Caitlin Bawn."

With a snarl of rage she lunged out, trying to grab the jar away. He stepped back, sweeping the open jar out before him. The move cast out all the remaining powder in a broad fan, sending it cascading over her, covering her form.

Immediately her whole body was convulsed. She fell back thrashing upon the bed while her flesh seemed to smolder and burn away.

"God!" said Kean, looking most dismayed at the horrendous effect he'd wrought. He cast his gaze about as if seeking some means to quench the blaze that engulfed her.

But the fire extinguished itself in seconds. The figure ceased convulsing. The smoke drifted off.

Kean moved closer, peering at the form.

It sat up suddenly, and he stepped back again, his look changing to one of revulsion.

The form of Caitlin Bawn had been entirely burned away. The new figure revealed was still unclothed, still female, but that of an ancient hag. Her limbs were shriveled, their flesh wrinkled and ghastly white. A body that might once have been voluptuous was wasted to sagging masses of skin. Hair that might have been a thick flow was a sparse and ratty bush of grey. And a face whose bone structure spoke of once-great beauty was now cadaverous, its red lips grotesquely bright against the chalky complexion.

She drew herself up to sit again, bony legs drawn under her, bony arms clutching together defensively across her chest, glaring at him.

"Just what are you?" he asked.

"The Leanhaun Sidhe I'm called," came a rasping whine of voice. "What you would call the Fairy Mistress."

"Another one of Them sent out to get me."

"How did you know?" she asked.

"I don't trust anything in Ireland anymore. And I knew Caitlin long enough to think I knew her character. I couldn't buy her throwing away her morals just like that.

So I decided to test her out. She flunked. And just what little special talent have you got? Or were you just some kind of a distraction?"

"It's the love of mortal men I crave," she told him. "I disguise myself as mortal women they desire, seek them out, and offer myself to them. If they consent, then they become my slaves. Only by finding another to take their place can they escape."

"What if they don't escape?"

"Then they waste away. I absorb their own vitality, you see. It brings youth and a great beauty to me. They die young, but they die without complaints. For in return I bring an inspiration to their minds. They live a life of passion and brilliance, like a great bonfire, burning brightly before dying out."

"I'll take your word for it," he said. "Especially the passion part."

"You cannot judge by what you see now," she said with indignation. "You nearly accepted my embrace moments ago. You can't deny it."

"Okay," he admitted. "You put on a good show."

"In years past I had my pick of mortal men," she told him proudly. "It was many a fine, handsome painter and poet I was muse to then, and my own beauty was as none you can imagine. It's only now, with ourselves grown so separate from you, that I have so wasted away. A hundred years and more it's been since I've sucked in to myself the sweet life force of any man. It's why I seized this chance to come to you, though," she added disparagingly, looking him up and down, "it's no great artist that you are, nor so handsome, and not such a young man."

"All right," Kean said, "enough of that. Now I want to get some information from you." He took up the blackthorn stick from beside the bed and pointed it meaningfully at her. "And no more tricks. You're not getting away from me without talking."

"You've no need to threaten," she said coolly. "I'm already bound to do as you ask. Why do you think I've spoken to you so far, when I might have simply vanished away?"

"What do you mean?"

"That by your refusal to accept my love, it's you who've made a slave of me. Give me something to cover myself with now, and I'll give answers to anything you ask."

"All right," he agreed.

He picked up the fallen dress from the floor, looked at it, then shook his head. "Not this," he said.

Instead he fetched his own long flannel robe and tossed it to her.

"I thank you," she said, slipping it on. "Even such as we feel the night's chill when there's nothing between it and our own skin."

He sat down on the bed's edge. "Tell me about Caitlin first," he demanded. "How is she?"

The woman's answers came truthfully but most economically. Though bound to reply, she gave away no more than she had to.

"She is well enough."

"Nobody's hurt her?"

"Nothing's been done to her."

"And she's here? I mean, she's in that mound?"

"She is in the Sidh of Meadha. What you call Knockma. Yes."

"Can you tell me how to get in there?"

"I cannot. No mortal can enter a Sidh unless we open it to you."

"And they won't let her come out."

"They are protecting her within it. They are keeping her safe from you."

"Safe? I don't want to hurt her."

"You stole her away. You used force to try to keep her."

"I used force to save her from some lunatics," he argued. "And I didn't steal her away. It was her idea. She followed me."

"Of course," the woman countered. "You put a spell on her."

"What is with this spell crap!" he said angrily, getting up to pace the room. "Goddammit, I haven't got any magic like that. I'm just a normal guy. A 'mortal.' She wanted to come with me. She wanted to escape from you. Why can't you believe me?"

"Why would a Sidhe woman wish to leave our world for yours?" she asked, clearly skeptical.

"How the hell should I know? Why don't you ask her?"

"It's not my place to ask," she said. "What I've done I've done only at the request of her mother."

"Her mother? So she *is* in on this too? You meant that?"

"Aisling only wants what's best for her daughter."

"Yeah? Well, that's what I want too," he said. "And I'm going to get it." He pointed the stick at her like a sword. "You've tried to scare me, make me crazy, suck my life away. Well, I'm not screwing around with you anymore. It's showdown time, my way!"

"What do you mean to do?" she asked, fear in her voice for the first time.

"Nothing to you. I'm letting you off. You go free, but only if you promise to take back a message to Them."

She looked relieved but puzzled. "What message?" she asked.

"You tell Them if They don't let her go, I'm coming to get her. Tell Them They've got 'til tomorrow—at dawn!"

29

"Liam O' Grady saw what?" Lord Desmond said, looking up from his account book.

"Equipment, sir," said the slim, stately, and black-suited man who stood at the study door. "Mr. O'Grady rang up to inquire if you were doing some form of construction or excavation on the estate."

The earl had been at work at his desk in the manor's study when the servant had interrupted. He now gave up the accounting to fix his whole attention and a puzzled stare upon the man.

"Just where was it that Liam said he saw this equipment, Delancy?"

"On the south Tuam road apparently, sir," the man supplied. "I gathered he was passing along there somewhat earlier this morning on the way to town when he noted the equipment leaving the road and entering the grounds."

"Is that so?" said Lord Desmond skeptically. "And do you happen to know from where he was calling?"

"Well, from the sounds behind, I would judge a drinking establishment of some type, sir."

"McCormick's Pub in Tuam," said the lord. "He never misses an opening. Not a man to be relied upon for information, Delancy."

"Exactly why I didn't disturb you about it earlier, sir," the other replied.

"Well, we're not involved in anything using equipment

just now, so he's clearly mistaken. Was there something else?"

"Yes, sir. Cook wondered how many would be at luncheon, sir. It's just past eleven now."

"I've really no idea," he said. "That fellow Kean and Professor Connelly went off somewhere early, it seems. No idea where. Don't know when they'll be back. A bit rude, actually, not to leave word. I can understand Kean—an American after all. But not the professor." He shook his head. "Still, there you are."

"I'll see places set for them, just in case, sir," Delancy said and withdrew.

The seventh earl went back to his work. But in less than a half an hour the servant was returning, apologetically poking his head in through the study door.

"Ah, sir, sorry to disturb you again."

"What, lunch already?" Lord Desmond asked.

"No, sir. It's your wife, sir. It seems she went out into the gardens to pick fresh flowers for the table . . ."

"And?" the lord said, a bit testy at what seemed a frivolous interruption.

". . . and she says she heard a strange sound."

"Strange sound?"

"A sort of rumbling, sir. She seemed rather alarmed by it. She came right back inside."

He sighed. "Yes, well, she has been rather highly strung since the unpleasantness yesterday. Don't want anything else alarming her." He put down his pen and got to his feet. "Tell her I'll see about it myself, Delancy."

"Very good, sir."

The Earl of Desmond slipped on a houndstooth walking jacket, left his study, and made his way through the labyrinth of cavernous rooms to the rear French doors. He selected a stout walking stick from a stand there and went out into the gardens.

Here he paused, listening intently. A sound was indeed audible. It seemed to be coming from some distance but was quite clear—definitely a low rumble, like the roll of thunder, but constant.

He turned slowly to place its direction. It came from the south, up the Knockma hill.

"What the devil?" he said.

He set out at a brisk walk, leaving the formal grounds and heading upward through the long grasses of the slope. As he went, the sound grew louder. Then it was joined by a second sound, similar but this time fluctuating, rising in volume for short bursts. The nature of the sounds was identifiable now as a pair of running engines, one of them being revved.

"Machinery?" he muttered, striding ahead yet faster. "But we aren't doing any kind of work on the grounds now . . . are we?"

The answer to that came as he topped the rise and looked across the hilltop toward the mound. He stopped to stare in bewilderment.

A large lorry, a passenger van, and two transport trucks were drawn up not a hundred feet from the mound's base. A small, tracked, shoveling machine had already been unloaded from the flatbed of one transport. A large-wheeled, mechanical earth-scooper was just being backed down from the other. Some twenty men in workmen's overalls worked around the equipment or unloaded tools from the lorry.

"Bloody hell!" said the seventh lord, and he stalked in toward the site.

He spotted Connelly to one side, out of the way, apparently observing the activity. Nearer to the mound, by the worn remains of the old cut, stood Kean himself, flanked by Mac and Garvey. With animated gestures toward the mound, he was explaining something to a burly man in leather coat and cloth cap, who listened with a certain bemused expression.

Lord Desmond stalked straight in toward Kean. Observing his approach, Mac pointed him out to his boss. Kean broke off his explanations and swung to greet the lord. He put on a broad, friendly grin, but it didn't totally hide an uh-oh-I've-been-caught look of guilt.

"Dick, old boy," Kean said heartily. "Good to see you!"

Desmond ignored the greeting. "What in blazes do you think you're doing here?" he demanded.

"Nothing very much," Kean said reasoningly. "We're just going to do a little bit of digging."

"On my property? I haven't given you permission to do anything like that."

"Yeah, I know," Kean admitted readily. "And I didn't think you would either. That's why I just brought the stuff in to do it anyway."

The lord stared at him in astonishment. "What impertinence!" he said in outrage. "What utter gall! Do you believe you can just go anywhere and do whatever you like?"

"Well, I did hope we could," Kean said. "I thought maybe we could slip in and do the job quick without your noticing. It won't take long."

"To do what?"

"He wants to dig a trench into the mound," said Professor Connelly, who had by this time joined them.

This further confused the lord. "I still don't understand. Is this some kind of archaeological thing?"

"You might say so," said Kean.

The lord looked to Connelly. "And are you a part of this, Professor?"

Before Connelly could reply, Kean answered for him: "The professor's just along to protect the mound. This little project's all my baby."

"Your 'project' is an invasion of my land," Lord Desmond said. "An insult. And after I offered my hospitality to you."

"I appreciate that," said Kean. "But this is too important. You've got to let us go ahead. We won't do any damage. I promise. We'll fix the whole thing up afterward like it'd never been touched."

"That is utter madness," Lord Desmond shot back.

Kean stepped closer to the lord, putting a friendly hand

on his shoulder. His voice became cajoling. "Look, Dick, I can make this worthwhile to you if you just play along. Money's no object. What would it take for you to feel good again?"

The lord angrily shrugged off the hand and stepped back. "I don't want any of your money!" he said in towering indignation now. "I want you and your machinery off my land. Instantly! Or I assure you I will call in the authorities!"

Kean looked both dismayed at his failure and uncharacteristically left at a loss for what course to take next. It was McBride who now jumped into the fray.

"Oh, come on, Lord Desmond," he said. "This thing's on your land, but it's a historical site too, isn't it?"

This somewhat nonplussed the lord. "Why, yes. It is."

"Then we don't really need your permission to do some excavating here. Just the government's."

Kean looked around to his friend in surprise at this new ploy.

"Are you saying the Office of Irish Antiquities has granted you rights to dig here?" the lord said.

"That's right!" Mac blithely lied.

"You're not archaeologists! This isn't an authorized expedition!" the lord challenged.

"Who says?" Mac countered. "With the clout Mr. Kean has over here, we can swing anything."

"And you have the necessary papers to prove this?"

"Sure! Well, not with us. But it's all set up. Check it out if you want."

"That I will!" said the lord. "That I most surely will!" And he turned and strode away, heading back to the manor.

The others looked after him as he started down the hill. Kean then looked to McBride.

"Mac, that was brilliant," he said appreciatively.

"He will check, you know," said Connelly. "He'll find out that you have no right to be here."

"Yeah," said Mac, "but we've been having to deal with

your government people for four years now. The way their bureaucracy works, it'll take him a while to find out anything. Days is my guess."

"And by then we should be through and out of here," said Kean. "Really brilliant, pal." He shook his head. "Just shows my own screwed-up state of mind that I didn't think of it."

The leather-jacketed man moved up toward Kean again.

"Sir, could you be finishin' tellin' us what we're to do now?"

"Right," Kean said briskly, returning to business. "Get the equipment up here and I'll lay out the area. We can get this baby opened up before nightfall."

The man headed off to pass orders to the drivers of the shovel and the scoop.

In moments the machines were rumbling in to the base of the mound, taking up positions on the edge of the ancient trench.

Kean used stakes and line to lay out the parameters of the dig.

"We stay just in here," he told the machine operators and a crew equipped with shovels and wheelbarrows. "Go easy for now. Keep it neat. Save the sod. Pile the dirt for refilling. I'm not out for destruction. Just a trench. Just enough to show 'em I mean business."

"Show who?" asked the burly man curiously.

"The fairies, pal," Kean said. "Now get your boys to work."

As Kean's workers were setting to their dig, the old Druid called Matholwch was stepping back from the image of it in the magic shield, shaking his head.

"Such metal beasts they have in service," he said in alarm.

He had watched the gathering forces outside the Sidh in company with King Fionnbharr, O'Mor and his friends, and Aisling. The Leanhaun Sidhe, her wasted body now modestly clothed in a long green gown, was also with them.

"Can't the magic of the Astray be used on them?" asked Angus.

"That can be used to confuse a peasant shepherd or lone traveler," said Owen, "but it'll not work on so many."

"To use such magic would only be to convince them the more that we're here," added the king. "It would bring them on us in yet greater force. And the machines you see there are as nothing compared with what monstrous others the mortals have created. Rury can tell you I speak the truth in that."

"There are indeed many great and terrible devices in their world," O'Mor admitted.

"You see?" said the king. "Not all our magic is enough to stand against such forces if they are fully brought against us."

"We must still stop this Kean somehow," said Owen. "Certainly we can keep that one man out of here."

"I'm not certain that you can," said the Leanhaun Sidhe. "That man is most determined, and he is most vital, magic or not."

"Quiet," Aisling said to her angrily. "If you had used the great skills you claim to have, we would have been done with him. You failed. His being out there is much your own fault."

"Not hers," said Fionnbharr pointedly. "Yours, Aisling. After I warned you not to interfere. After I decreed we would stay away from Desmond Manor. Still you send her there."

"At least I tried something," Caitlin's mother returned defiantly. "I didn't wait like some rabbit cowering from a weasel in its hole. I told you to stop him. Now it is too late. I say only a direct attack can destroy him now."

"You want us to go out and give battle to them?" a disbelieving Fionnbharr asked.

"To save Caitlin," she said stubbornly, "yes."

"Must she be saved from anyone?" the Leanhaun Sidhe

asked. "Michael Kean says he was not the one who stole her away. She chose to go."

"What's that?" said Fionnbharr.

"He lies," Aisling said quickly. "What else should we expect? He is treacherous, as indeed are all mortals."

"He could have enslaved me," the Fairy Mistress pointed out. "Instead he chose not to make me hostage or do me any harm. He let me return."

"Just to warn us," Aisling argued. "Just to let us know he had worse in mind for us. I say he not only wants Caitlin; he wants us destroyed!"

"Rury, you know him best," said Fionnbharr. "You saw his world. You spoke to him the most. Do you truly believe his intent is so evil?"

"Why?" O'Mor asked suspiciously. "Are you seeking some reason to deal with him? Are you looking for an excuse to turn her over after all?"

"I'm seeking the truth," the king said tightly. "I will not bring our people to destruction in a conflict that is only a misunderstanding."

"He broke a bond to me," O'Mor said with force.

"His treachery did destroy poor Kevan," Angus put in.

"And I saw that man steal my daughter away," Aisling added in a bald-faced lie. "If you do nothing, Fionnbharr, then you will be less than a king to us. Less than a warrior. You will not even be a man."

"By Danu!" the king stormed. "It's not another such insult I'll tolerate from you, Aisling."

"Still, Fionnbharr," said O'Mor, "we must act, or we may as well simply surrender to them."

"Yes, yes," the king accepted grudgingly. "But there must yet be other means than open warfare." He looked to the two druids. "Owen, Matholwch, you must have some powers that would work."

The two druids exchanged a searching gaze. They nodded. Matholwch looked to the king.

"There is a spell we can use. You know of it, my king.

We can deny him. Frustrate him. Perhaps force him to quit."

"Of course!" said Fionnbharr. "The perfect thing . . . if this Kean doesn't know the counter to it."

"We can only try," said Owen. "But there's another problem too. The spell can only be spun out in the dead of night. In the old times, that lord had nothing but men to do his work. It went very slowly. There was time. But with the speed of these machines . . ."

"Yes," said Matholwch. "They could well burst through the outer shield before nightfall."

"Then find some way to slow him down," Fionnbharr said.

The older druid considered. "Very well," he allowed. "I think that can be done." He looked to the younger druid. "Owen, will you help me?"

"To confound Kevan's murderer," said Owen, "anything!"

"Then fetch the Great Caldron here," the old druid ordered.

Obese, slow bubbles boiled up from the black liquid within the immense vat, rolling the oily ooze.

The caldron of softly gleaming, hammered bronze sat upon a tripod of thick iron legs erected over the central fire. The metal vessel, some eight feet across and shaped like a giant wok, filled nearly the whole space enclosed by the hearth of the circular pit. Its rim came within inches of the pit's sides.

A hearty fire was blazing beneath the pot. Half a dozen men were constantly tending it, taking care to feed it in a balanced way to keep the heat on the caldron uniform.

Matholwch stood upon the hearth at one side, ignoring the heat welling up from below to feed ingredients into the viscous mass.

Powders, liquids, bits of vegetable and animal and mineral alike were one by one dumped in to be swallowed by the black morass. These things were being handed up to him by Owen, who stood down beside a table on the floor behind. The table was loaded with such a vast and varied array of vials, bins, and bizarre objects as would have made Nelly Quade most envious.

Some way back from the fire pit stood Fionnbharr, O'Mor, and the others, fascinated.

"I've seen this done before, of course," the king observed to the rest. "Manannan MacLir it was who worked up the spell to help me then."

"Really?" said O'Mor, impressed. "Manannan himself? And what is it that's happened to him? I've not heard of him lately."

"Ah well, he went off and vanished somewhere in the mortal world again. A most dangerous thing to do, but he can't be stopped. He assumes a mortal guise and uses the name of Gilla Decair, you know. Anyway, Matholwch seems to be doing the thing quite well this time."

In fact, it seemed that the old druid was just completing his work, and with first signs of success for his recipe.

After a last bundle of dried heather had been tossed in, the ooze had begun to boil yet more vigorously. Matholwch now hurriedly stepped down from the hearth. He and Owen backed a few steps away.

All watched intently. The mixture in the caldron began slowly, ponderously to turn. It picked up speed as it went, revolving faster, its surface drawing into a spiral that grew tighter, tighter, spinning inward to the center of the pot.

From that center, a point of the liquid lifted up. Like a cone it rose at first, but then it lengthened, drawing out into a dark, whirling, sinuous snake formed of the thick goo.

It writhed and stretched upward, drawing the liquid out from the caldron into its whirling coils.

The serpentine creation lifted up to touch its upper end against the roof. Lights like flares of lightning flicked within it, and a sharp crackling sounded in the room.

The atmosphere in the great hall began to dim, as if light were also being sucked away. The fire died to a dull, ruddy glow. The air became heavy with an acrid scent, oppressive with humidity. The watchers breathed heavily, their exposed skin glistening with started sweat.

"By Danu, send it out, Matholwch," said the king. "It's suffocating us."

"Not yet," said the druid.

He watched the snake of blackness intently until the last of the liquid was sucked up into it. Only then did he lift a long yew rod and point its silver tip toward the ceiling.

A slender ray of blue-silver light flared out from the tip, touching a spot in the ceiling's center, right above the caldron. At the light's touch, the solid-seeming ceiling pulled back, like an iris dilating, opening a yard-wide hole.

The top end of the black creation wavered close about it tentatively, like a live creature examining it curiously. Matholwch shifted his rod. The ray of light dropped down to play up and down along the thing's length.

"Go forth," the druid entoned as he did this. "Rise up and spread yourself upon the sky. Find, gather, and impregnate its forces with your own energies. Draw the forces your mating gives birth to upon those mortal men. Go!"

As if released from a tether, the black serpent instantly shot upward, slipping through the hole, vanishing from sight. The hole swiftly closed beneath it.

The light from the yew rod died. The old druid lowered it, turning toward his king.

"Now," he said, "we need only wait for *It* to come."

30

Outside, in the mortal world, the sun had passed midafternoon and was beginning its slide down the last quarter of the sky toward evening.

The mortal workers had only been at the laboring for some three hours now, but the trench their machines were helping to create had already assumed impressive proportions—a dozen feet wide, fifty long, two yards deep. And it was growing deeper rapidly.

At Kean's direction, a neat, surgical incision—like a scalpel's cut across a swollen belly—was slashing deep into the smooth side of the rounded hill, threatening to lay it open. The removed turf exposed the red-brown earth, showing it in startling brightness against the contrasting green, making it seem all the more a gaping wound.

The men toiled on. So intent were they on their somewhat exacting task, however, that they were unaware of the ominous darkness that began to boil upward in the sky all around the hilltop. Dense, grey-black clouds lifted from every side, like gathered armies joining, forming one great host, surrounding Knockma hill with a solid ring, rolling up and in, closing together to shut the blue sky off.

The men first became aware of the change when the sun was swallowed, casting them in sudden shade. They all looked up. The clouds were in a clear circle halfway up from the horizon to a point straight above. There the last, rapidly shrinking patch of blue sky showed.

"Looks like a storm comin'," said the foreman. "Could be bad."

"Keep them working," said Kean.

"I never saw a storm come in from all sides," said Mac wonderingly, "or move so fast."

"It can't," said Connelly with alarm. "I think it's Them."

"Them?" echoed Kean.

"Of course. They have the power to raise storms. At least localized ones. There are many cases of their being used to confound enemies."

"Well, it's not confounding this one," Kean said with force. "A storm's just a storm. It can't stop us. Some wind. Some rain. How bad can it be?"

"Have you ever heard the expression 'famous last words,' Michael?" said Mac.

He looked up again as the last opening, like the iris of an enormous eye, shrank closed.

They were engulfed in an abrupt twilight. A wind whipped up from nowhere, swirling about the hilltop in booming gusts. The air temperature radically dropped.

The workmen paused in their labors to look about nervously.

"They don't like this, Mr. Kean," the foreman told him.

"Pay 'em double, then," Kean snapped back. "Just keep 'em at it. I want this finished before night!"

After the wind came rain. No initial sprinkles or mist, just an instant downpour. It came down hard, then harder, torrents of rain sweeping in thick curtains across the open hilltop. And the wind shifted, seeming somehow to blast straight in at them from all sides, driving in the rain to soak, to sting, to blind.

Kean tripled the pay, and they went doggedly on.

Rusty streams of mud ran from the cut like thickly flowing blood. Men splashed knee deep in gathering puddles, slipped and fell headlong on the slippery ground. Their bodies thick-plastered by red muck, they moved ponderously. All individual identities were lost.

Kean quadrupled the pay.

Thunder rumbled about them, making the whole hill vibrate. Blue-white lightning crackled down, one jagged spear plunging to earth only yards from the shoveler.

Its driver leapt out, leaving the machine to run on, slam into the end of the cut, and stop there, still running, big wheels churning uselessly in the slime.

The other men cowered, looking about for more lightning strokes. The angry foreman approached Kean.

"Enough!" he cried to be heard through the tumult of wind and thunder and rain. "We've had it!"

"Five times!" Kean yelled back. "Five times normal pay!"

"Not ten times. Not a *hundred* for this risk!" The foreman signaled to his men. "Come on, lads, get into cover."

They abandoned equipment, tossed down tools, and ran for the vehicles, clambering into van, truck cabs, and lorry.

Kean stood looking after them, seething with rage and frustration. McBride put a soothing hand on his friend's shoulder.

"Forget it, Michael," he advised. "The guy is right. There's nothing you can do. Let's just get out of this ourselves."

With no other choice left, Kean agreed. He and his companions moved away from the excavation toward the vehicles.

The van and the truck cabs were already filled with men. The four went on to the lorry, climbing into the open back to find shelter in its big storage area.

They stood there, at the open doors, water streaming from them as they stared back out into the tempest they had escaped. Rain drumming on the metal roof created a constant roar. The intervening, near-solid screen of water made the mound a vague mass of grey-green.

"It'll stop soon," Kean pronounced optimistically.

"Jesus, Michael," said Mac, pushing back the hair the wind and rain had plastered against his face, "you sound like Charlie Brown at a rained-out ball game. Look at that! We'll likely float away first."

"It just can't rain that hard for very long," Kean said stubbornly. "It's gotta stop soon!"

But for hour upon hour, it continued to fall steadily. And as evening came on, the foreman appeared at the back doors of the lorry.

"Look, Mr. Kean," he said, "it'll be dark soon. There'll be no more working today. Me and my boys, we want to go in to town, get some hot food, find a place to sleep."

Kean sighed resignedly. "Yeah. Go ahead. Charge everything to me. But be back up here at first light, rain or not!"

"What about you, Mr. Kean? Aren't you going with us?"

"I'm staying here. Go on. Take off."

The foreman went to pass word to his men. Soon the few from the truck cabs had crammed themselves into the van with the rest, and the vehicle was heading off down the hill, vanishing into the rain.

Kean looked around at the three remaining.

"You guys can go too, you know," he said. "Desmond's likely not going to give you free room and board tonight, but you can go into town. The limo's down below."

"You really mean to stay up here—by yourself?" Garvey asked.

Kean nodded. "All night. I'm not letting Them think they're running me off with this little trick. They've got to see I'm staying, sticking it out. They've got to know I'll be back at Them as soon as I get a chance. Maybe then *They'll* give it up."

"Okay," said McBride. "Then I'll stay too."

Kean put a hand on his friend's shoulder and gave a little smile. "Thanks. I figured you would."

"They might not give you another chance," Connelly pointed out. "This storm might just keep up."

"They can't keep it going forever," Kean said with certainty. "They can't have that kind of power. Hell, if They did, They'd be ruling the world by now. This thing's got to run out of steam sooner or later."

"So you'll wait until it does and go right back in," said the professor.

"That's right."

"And if this cut of yours doesn't work? If They don't surrender?"

"I'll go deeper."

"How deep?"

"I'll level the goddamn thing if I have to," Kean said fiercely.

"You would be so ruthless?" Connelly said, dismayed. "You could destroy the Sidh."

"They wasted my penthouse, didn't They? I've gotta prove I'm as ready and able to use massive force as They are."

Connelly sadly shook his head. "I had hoped it wouldn't come to this. I'm sorry, Mr. Kean, but I cannot be party to your quest anymore."

"You know why I'm doing it," Kean said. "You know I haven't got a choice."

"I'm really not certain. So much has been put at stake. So much could be lost here, both by ourselves and Them. I don't know if it can be balanced by the life of this one woman."

"You're not going against us, are you?" Kean asked. "You won't help Desmond?"

"I'll do nothing against you," Connelly assured. "I promised you I'd keep your confidence, and I won't betray you. But I won't stay here. I just can't stand to watch it anymore. Do you understand?"

Kean nodded. "I guess so." He put out a hand. "Thanks for your help. And believe me, I really didn't want this."

"Are you absolutely sure?" Connelly asked him as he took Kean's hand and shook it.

The professor shook hands with Garvey and Mac as well, turned up his trench-coat collar against the rain, and clambered from the lorry, sloughing out into the storm. He didn't look back.

Kean watched him out of sight, regret showing clearly

in his face. Then he shrugged it off and turned to his head of security.

"Well, Garvey, how about you?"

"You're still my chief, sir," the man said flatly. "Naturally I'll stay."

"Hey, boss, do we get our pay quintupled too?" Mac said with a smile.

"If we win this one, you can have whatever you want," Kean told him.

"I'll settle for a cozy, quiet cottage over here," the other said sincerely. "After this, I am definitely retiring."

"A cottage?" Kean said. "How about a pub?"

"Don't tempt me, Michael," Mac said, licking his lips at the thought. "Times like these, I sorta miss a little ole stiff drink."

And so the three waited, turning the lorry's rear compartment into their encampment for the night. Garvey fought his way out through the storm, returning with food and blankets and a thermos of hot coffee foraged from the nearby town.

"It's really crazy," he said as he doled out the largesse. "The storm seems to be centered on a spot around this hill. It's dry as a bone two miles away from here. It was quite a show to watch when I was driving back. The lightning's lighting this place up like Baghdad under an air raid."

"You still think all that supernatural stuff is garbage?" Kean asked him.

"It's some special effects, however it's being done," Garvey answered. "I don't know what's gotten crazier, all these things that are happening, or you."

"That's being pretty frank, Frank," Mac said in surprise at the man's unusual openness. "If you think the boss's gone nuts on us, why stay on?"

"Not my part to question the one in charge," the man said, sitting down cross-legged and unwrapping a sandwich. "I've had plenty of bosses in the government who seemed lots crazier. So long as I work for them, I just carry out orders."

"And who can ask for more than that?" Kean said.

McBride only "oomphed" noncommittally and bit into his own sandwich.

Once they'd eaten, Mac and Garvey found spots on the lorry's floor to stretch out for some rest. Kean too settled down in the blankets for a doze, but he lay awake, staring into the dark and rain, trying to make out the mound. It remained only a black, enigmatic shape, seemingly devoid of life.

Inside the mound, the scene was vastly different. Fionnbharr and his people were gleeful at the storm's success. They were watching the two druids preparing for their second spell.

"The storm spell will be dying out soon," Matholwch explained as he once more worked with Owen. "This one must be spun out by then."

This time the two were using a much different method to create their magic. Rather than a concoction of ingredients, this spell's assemblage seemed more one of construction.

At one side of the fire pit, the tables and chairs had been moved aside, clearing a large area of the hall's stone floor.

Matholwch was slowly walking around and around in the space, drawing the silver-shod tip of his druid rod lightly across the floor. It left a faint groove scratched into the stone. He moved in constantly shrinking circles, carefully, precisely laying out a huge spiral.

Owen moved behind him. From a golden ewer he poured a stream of thick, silver liquid out along the line. It formed a thin and even bead that began at once to glow with bluish-white light, as if it were a long, coiling, fluorescent tube that was being laid there.

"We must tap into the power of the Sidh itself," the older druid explained as he reached the center point of the spiral and stopped there, awaiting Owen. "We must concentrate it and direct it at one point. Like a tool it will be. The thread to bind our hurt."

He stepped out of the way as Owen reached him. The younger druid poured out the last of the liquid in a small puddle at the tight curl of the spiral's heart. The two then carefully high-stepped their way out across the coils of the spiral to fetch the rest of their materials and carry them back in.

Most painstakingly the druids erected a simple structure over the spiral's exact core. It was a tripod of slim silver rods some three feet high. Most of the rods' lengths were down below the crossing point, forming legs. Only some six inches of them thrust above.

Satisfied with the tripod's stability, Matholwch and Owen came upright beside it. The older druid reached within his robes and drew out a clear crystal, smoothly polished, shaped like an egg save for a more sharply pointed top.

Matholwch lifted it to show around. "This," he announced with a flourish, "will become the needle."

He placed it firmly in the crux atop the tripod, point upward. He and Owen moved back again to stand outside the spiral. Both lifted their rod tips to point toward the stone.

"We call upon the power of our world," Matholwch said in ringing tones. "We invoke the magic that shapes it, binds it, keeps it safe. Come into this place now."

The coils of the spiral began to glow brighter. From the outmost curve more intense flares appeared, like rhythmic pulses of energy, running inward, intensifying as they sped toward the center. Upon reaching there, they gathered in the pool below the tripod, forming into a bubble of near blinding glow that swelled upward until it touched the crystal egg.

The egg seemed to absorb the power, glowing now itself, but with a light more concentrated, controlled, and transformed to an intenser blue.

"Go out from there and find the place of danger,"

Matholwch ordered. "Seek out the rent in the shield of our Sidh."

At this, tendrils of light began to grow out from the crystal, like the root system of a tree sprouting and growing rapidly. But these roots of light grew upward, stretching toward the ceiling at one side of the hall, touching it, the tendril tips flickering across as if feeling the way, then penetrating, slipping through.

Outside, the storm had faded away to a fine mist. But it still served well enough to mask the mound and conceal the excavation from the gaze of the sleepless Kean.

He couldn't see the faint flickers of blue light, much like Saint Elmo's fire, that crept up from the mud within the pit to rim its lips, sides, and bottom with the eerie glow.

All unaware, the determined Kean sat staring on throughout the night.

Dawn found McBride awakening to see his friend sitting hunched cross-legged in the lorry's open doorway, a blanket wrapped around him and over his head like a hooded cloak.

Stretching muscles cramped by a night on the metal floor, Mac crawled back and around Kean to see his face. He was awake, but the effects of the long night were very visible. Kean looked haggard, with black circles beneath the red-rimmed eyes that still stared fixedly out toward the mound.

The mist had also ceased now, but only to be replaced by a dense fog. Even in daylight, hilltop and mound were deeply shrouded by the billowing grey.

"Want some coffee?" Mac asked. "There's still some left."

"Yeah," said Kean gratefully, shifting his own stiffened limbs and grimacing.

Mac poured a steaming cup and held it out toward Kean. But as Kean's hand stretched toward it, he was distracted by the rising sound of an engine.

"They're back," he said. The coffee forgotten, he clambered from the lorry, vigor seemingly restored.

Mac shrugged, poured the coffee back, and followed Kean out. Garvey, who had arisen some little time before, was already outside. He'd just ceased his morning limbering exercises to stare off toward the sound.

The air was very heavy, very dense with the odor of wet earth and grass. The saturated air, so filled with fog, was almost like a liquid medium. All sounds seemed muffled, all actions slowed by the atmosphere, as if they were at the bottom of the sea.

The van came into view, ghostly at first through the greyness, coming clear as it rolled up close to the lorry and stopped. The workmen climbed out, looking rested and chipper, in contrast to their boss and his comrades.

"All right, Mr. Kean. We're back," the foreman said. "At your price, truth to say, none of the lads wanted to stay away. Have we work to do?"

"Damn right," Kean said briskly. "We go on with it, same as before. I want that hill opened up. So let's get back there, get those machines going, and—"

"Mr. Kean," Garvey interrupted, staring off, listening intently, "another vehicle's coming."

In seconds they all heard it: a motor sounding from the direction of Desmond Manor, growing rapidly louder. Soon a big Land Rover was topping the crest of the hill, rolling out across the field toward them.

It pulled up near the van. Two men got out. One was Lord Desmond. The other . . .

"Oh, God, no," moaned McBride.

It was Lance Larson who strode through the wet grass toward them, his expression that of a man very, very put out.

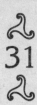

31

"**M**r. Kean," Lance said in a severe tone as he reached them. "There you are at last."

"Lance!" said Kean with poorly feigned enthusiasm. "How are you doing?"

"All right, finally. I've found you. Do you know that I've been looking for you for days?"

"Have you? Well, I've been on some . . . errands."

"Errands?" He looked over the rumpled, damp, and haggard man before him—a far cry from the dapper and dominant Kean of yore. "You leave New York under most questionable circumstances. You carry on some kind of secretive operation over here. You disappear from Dublin, leaving no word. And now this! I'm informed by the Irish government, thanks to Lord Desmond, that you're here, apparently engaged in vandalizing his estate!"

"So, you got quick action after all," Kean said to the seventh earl. "Thanks, Dick."

"You *should* thank him," Lance said. "He agreed to let me deal with you, rather than have the Irish authorities come here. Who knows what kind of scandal we might have had then?"

"I don't give a damn about any scandal," said Kean.

"No. Clearly you don't!" Lance shot back. "You didn't care in New York when you ran out on that little mess. And you don't care here, when you're all but creating an international incident. But your colleagues care, Mr.

Kean. Oh, yes. They care a great deal. As do your investors, the finance board, and the directors. Especially the chairman himself cares. And he was more than a bit upset when I informed him of all this."

"Yeah, and I'll bet you tattled to him with extreme reluctance," Mac said sarcastically.

"Just how could I not tell him?" Lance said defensively. "You commandeer a corporation work crew, bring it here, and use it to deface one of their historical sites? Their government is astounded! Outraged! They think that you've lost your mind. They're threatening to pull out their backing, renege on a multibillion-dollar deal because of you. That's why I'm here. I'm doing damage control."

"How are you doing that?" Kean asked.

"I'm defusing the situation. And you, Mr. Kean, are the fuse. The only way to save the Irish project now is to unplug you from it. I mean, all the way."

"You can't do that!" Kean said.

"Of course I can," Larson said coolly. "You've made it very easy with your wild antics these past weeks. Nobody trusts you anymore. Between the board back home and the government here, you're being disenfranchised even as we speak."

"I don't suppose *you're* going to get too hurt in this," Mac said.

Larson gave a little smirk. "Actually, as savior of the situation, I expect to do quite well."

"You're fired, Lance," Kean told him.

The other smiled outright. "That's very funny, *sir*. Actually, I believe *I'm* firing *you*."

"Look here," Desmond said testily, "your corporate squabbles have nothing to do with me. Now, what about the damage to my mound?"

Larson's smile vanished. "Certainly," he told the earl soberly. "I'll see that it's completely repaired." He turned to the foreman. "Your crew will do it."

"No!" said Kean. "I'm not quitting now. These guys are working for me!"

"Not anymore," Larson told him.

Kean appealed directly to the workmen. "Stay on with me. Just today. I'll give ten times your pay."

The men hesitated, looking at one another.

"You don't work for him anymore," Larson told them. "He won't be able to pay you. If you want to keep your jobs, you'll do as *I* say."

"Right," the foreman said. "We'll fix it all right up, sir. Just as you wish."

"Let's get a look at the damage, then," said Larson.

"Right ho, sir," the foreman said. "This way." And he led them toward the fog-shrouded mound.

The others, including a helpless Kean, followed him. Kean pleaded with Larson as they went.

"Lance, listen. Please. Just give me one day. I'm almost finished!"

"Finished with what?" Larson asked curiously, peering ahead through the fog. "Exactly what is this bizarre little enterprise of yours about anyway?"

"Only an excavation. Very simple. But," Kean added meaningfully, "it could be a real discovery."

This caught Larson's attention. He looked to Kean with new interest. "Have you got some angle in this?" he asked avariciously. "Is there something big here?"

"Goddamn right," said Kean, grasping at straws. He moved closer to the man, his voice cajoling. "It could make you big too, Lance. So big you can't imagine. Just let me go ahead. I know it's gonna work. Just let me make the trench a little deeper, and—"

Larson pulled up suddenly, staring ahead. "Trench?" he said. "What trench?"

Kean's gaze jerked around from Larson and looked ahead as well. The mound was now clearly visible through the last thin screen of grey. He stared, then he ran forward.

"No! No!" he said in anguish as he reached the mound's base. "It can't be."

The others came up behind him. He stood at the edge

of the place marked for his trench. But he stared now at an untouched, grassy slope, showing only the faint indentation of the old, long-healed cut. All sign of his own incision had vanished as if it had never been.

"You haven't done anything here yet?" said a surprised seventh earl.

"Yes. We have. We worked for hours here," said Kean. "We had a trench cut. A big one."

"And I suppose it filled itself back in," said Lance sardonically.

"It was here," Kean said. He looked to the workers. "You guys dug it. You saw it. Tell him."

The foreman and his men exchanged gazes again. Some looked confused, some dumbfounded. Many looked afraid. "Well, I don't know now, sir," the bewildered foreman said uncertainly. "It was confusing here, what with all the rain and wind. I'm not sure *what* I saw. Maybe we dug a trench here . . . and maybe we didn't."

"It doesn't matter," said Larson. "There is obviously no trench now. No damage I can see at all." He grinned with satisfaction. "This is even better than I'd hoped." He looked to the earl. "It seems you should be most grateful, Lord Desmond. I've stopped Kean in time and completely saved your mound."

"Apparently so," the earl accepted. "But I want these men and that equipment out of here immediately!"

"Absolutely, Lord Desmond," Larson agreed. He turned to the foreman and snapped, "Get your gear loaded and move out of here. Right now!"

"Aye, sir. That we will," the foreman said, and he and his crewmen set briskly to it. They looked most anxious to be quit of the haunted hill.

"I trust, Lord Desmond, that this will convince you to tell your government not to turn against our entire venture just because of the behavior of one man," Larson said.

"Yes, I suppose I might do that," said the lord. He looked to Kean. "But I do hope you'll see that something is done for Mr. Kean. I don't understand quite what happened. He did seem all right before this."

"He'll be taken care of, I assure you," said Larson.

"Goddammit! I'm not crazy!" Kean said angrily. Then controlling himself with an effort, he said more reasoningly, "Look, I've got to level with you. I've got to go on with this. A woman's life could be at stake."

"A woman?" said Larson. "How?"

Kean hesitated, then plunged ahead. "Well, there's a . . . a group of people. They're holding a woman prisoner here. I've got to force Them to set her free."

"People?" said Larson. "Here? You mean, under this mound?"

"They live under there, somehow," Kean said awkwardly, aware of how strange it must sound. "They have . . . powers. The Sidhe They're called. Lord Desmond, you know about Them."

"Mr. Kean," said the earl, taken aback by the statement, "those beings are spirits. The stuff of fairy tales. Some few peasants may still believe in Them, but They're certainly not real."

"But you told me before . . ." Kean said. "I mean, I thought maybe you believed."

"Only as one believes in not stepping beneath a ladder, to avoid bad luck. Nothing more. Mr. Kean," he added in a tone of sympathy, "the spell of Ireland is strong. It can effect a susceptible mind. If you've somehow been deluded . . ."

"I haven't!" Kean told him with force. "Look, what I'm doing here has been done before. A lord came here to dig this mound up, in the eighteenth century." He pointed to the faint impression. "The mark's still here. That's proof."

Lord Desmond shrugged. "I've heard the tale, of course. Some madman in the third earl's time, it was. Came here, much like you did, over some obsession with a girl."

"Seems that madness was infectious, Earl," Larson said with smug amusement, eyeing Kean.

Kean lifted a fist as if to swing at him, stepping forward. Mac moved in to block his friend as Larson stepped quickly back.

Kept from reaching the man, Kean snarled at him: "You stupid bastard. I *know* They're real. I've been fighting Them since New York. They trashed the tower. They stole this woman back. She's one of Them. A Banshee. I tracked her here. I know she's inside."

"I'd calm myself if I were you, Kean," Larson said sharply. "All this is doing nothing but making a stronger case for your instability."

"He's telling the truth," McBride said in staunch support. "I saw Them too. I know what They can do."

"Wonderful," Larson said caustically. "The word of a notorious drunk verifying that of a crazy man. There's a pair for you. Better watch it, McBride, or they'll be putting you away too."

A glowering Mac moved out of Kean's way. "Go ahead and hit the s.o.b., Michael," he advised.

But Kean tried more logic. "Garvey's seen Them too," he said. "He can verify." He looked to the security man. "Can't you, Frank?"

Garvey looked from Kean to Larson and back, his expression one of perplexity. He opened his mouth to speak.

"Don't!" said Larson, lifting a staying hand. "You don't have to cover for Mr. Kean's strange activities anymore, Garvey. I know you were only doing your job for him, but that's over now. You work for the corporation, not him. The chairman wants you back home, doing your job as security chief again."

Garvey considered this. A look of open relief came into his face. "Yes, sir," he said briskly. "Thank you, sir." And he stepped away from behind Kean to stand by Larson.

"Frank!" said a shocked Kean. "You're turning against me too?"

"Sorry, Mr. Kean. I wasn't ever really with you. It's like I said before: I do whatever I'm told to . . . by my boss. You're not my boss anymore."

"Well then," said a pleased Larson, looking around at the workmen loading up, "it seems we're finished here. We can go." He looked to his onetime boss. "Kean, are you going with us?"

"Go to hell," said Kean.

"In spades," Mac added.

Larson shrugged. "Suit yourselves, boys. But if you want to salvage anything from this, I suggest you pack up and go home at once. And I'd drop all of that crazy story if I were you." He looked Kean up and down again and shook his head regretfully. "You know, it is too bad. What a waste. The proud and powerful Michael Kean, King of the Castle. I actually admired you. And you just threw it all away. For what?"

On that parting shot, he turned and strode off toward the Rover.

Garvey obediently followed after his new master. Lord Desmond turned to follow too, but then paused to look back.

"You know," he said to Kean, "if your tale were true—if those beings *were* living beneath that mound—you still wouldn't have reached Them this way."

"What do you mean?"

"Just that it seems you didn't learn the entire tale. You see, that lord had his men dig deep into the mound's side every day. However, the fairy folk apparently had a special power. For every night the hole would be magically filled in again."

"But that lord won," said Kean. "He dug a hole in deep enough and the Sidhe gave up."

"Only after the lord learned a little trick," said the earl. "You see, salt apparently has some antimagical property. When he sowed it into his dig, the fairy spell no longer worked. When They saw They couldn't defeat him, They capitulated, or so the story says. Well, good-bye, Mr. Kean. I'm truly sorry for the way this has turned out."

He strode off after the others, back to the Rover, and the three got in. Larson gave a jaunty good-bye wave to

Kean as the lord started the vehicle and drove them off, down the hill toward the manor.

They left a rather desolate- and defeated-looking pair of figures watching them go.

"Salt," Mac said in a bleak way. "Now he tells us."

"Damn!" said Kean, a new resolution firing his voice. "We're not licked yet."

He moved briskly toward where the workmen were packing up, a puzzled Mac following. The van, full of workmen, was just pulling away, followed by the lorry. One truck, with the scoop loaded back on its flatbed, was preparing to leave. Kean approached the second truck, where a driver and helper were moving the big-wheeled shoveler up a ramp onto its back.

Kean stopped and stood watching them maneuvering it up the ramp until the other truck had started away. It was only Kean, Mac, and the two workmen on the hilltop now.

Kean called to the driver: "Hey, you. I want you to leave the shovel."

The man braked it halfway up the ramp and looked to him in surprise.

"Leave it? Are you out of your head?"

"Apparently. But I need the machine. Leave it, and I'll pay you."

"We can't," the man said. "What'll we tell them? We'll lose our jobs."

"No you won't. You can tell them I stole it from you. Tell them it broke down. Say anything. Just leave that thing behind."

The driver looked at his fellow worker. "Whaddaya think, Mickey?"

"I don't know, John," the other said doubtfully. "It's still a risky thing. It'd have to be well worthwhile."

Kean pulled his wallet out and went through it, drawing out a handful of traveler's checks.

"I've got eleven hundred bucks' worth of these," he said, and looked to Mac. "What about you?"

McBride checked his own pockets. "Four hundred fifty," he announced.

"We'll sign them all over to you," Kean told the men, "just to 'forget' that thing here for a while."

"Fifteen hundred and fifty," John said, "and in American dollars." He looked to his friend. "What do you say about that, Mickey?"

"I say back that hunk of metal back down off of there and let's be off to the races!" the other cried.

It was only minutes before the shoveler was back on the ground and the truck with the two suddenly richer workmen rolling away.

Kean wasted no time in approaching the machine and climbing up into the operator's seat.

"So, you're gonna dig the hole yourself," said Mac.

"That's right," said Kean, settling himself behind the controls.

"Can you work that thing?" Mac asked.

"Hey, how hard can it be?" he answered, fiddling with the levers and wheels. "I'll figure it out. And then I'll tear back into that hill. It may not be neat, but it'll sure be one big hole."

"What do I do?"

"You, my friend, are going into town."

"Into town?" said Mac. "What for?"

"Can't you guess?" said Kean. "For salt, of course!"

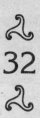

32

Inside the mound, the people of the Sidh watched Mc-Bride depart from Knockma hill, leaving Kean alone. They watched the single man struggle to understand the controls of the shoveler and then send it in, in a new attack upon their mound.

As Kean had predicted, the hole he dug into the rounded slope was far from neat. But it was certainly a hole, and growing rapidly larger as Kean gained mastery of the machine.

"Given enough time," pronounced Owen after examining the unfolding scene in the imaging shield, "I say he can do it. He can break through."

"Given enough time," said Fionnbharr. "But how much does he have left? The others all seem to have abandoned him. He can't go on alone."

"He seems to be doing just that quite well," pointed out Aisling.

"Even I am surprised by his tenacity," said O'Mor musingly. "It's hard to believe that he'd go so far against us without help just to reclaim his stolen prize."

"Perhaps it's not for greed or lust or revenge that he's coming against us now," said Angus, marveling too at Kean's persistence. "Perhaps it's something else that's driving him."

"Something else?" said Fionnbharr. "Like what?"

"Like love?" suggested the Leanhaun Sidhe. "I did see it in his eyes. For her . . . not me."

"Nonsense," Caitlin's mother answered sharply. "Foolish old crone. He's as mad as he is villainous. He doesn't know when to stop. So I say to finish it for him. He's all alone. Even our brave king should have no more reason to fear him. One of you great warriors can just go out and destroy him."

"No," said Fionnbharr. "It's still possible his death might rouse the others again."

"Cautious to the very last, my king?" Aisling accused.

"I agree with the king," Matholwch said. "How do we know what could happen? And why should anyone go out against him now? It will be simpler to just thwart his efforts again. That will harm no one. He's clearly very tired. Once more should sap the last strength from him. He'll have to give it up."

"What about the storm?" asked Owen. "Should we also raise that once more?"

"Why not?" The older druid looked at the toiling man pictured in the shield and smiled. "Make certain he accomplishes the least and with the most difficulty. Then, with pain and exhaustion followed by the utter futility of his task, we will most surely finish him."

"I hope so," O'Mor said fervently. He too looked at the image of his adversary in the shield. "Give up, Michael Kean," he said to it as a prayer. "Please, just give it up!"

But Kean continued to work at the hole, like a tough, starving mongrel worrying a huge bone, chewing off bit after bit.

And he went doggedly on even when the black ring of clouds once more lifted about him, and sharp wind blasted and tore at him, and driving rain soaked him and stung his face, and strokes of lightning cracked to earth close by his machine.

Through one hour and then another he toiled with the shoveler, scooping ever deeper into a ragged hole running with red-brown muck, laboring to keep contro¹ of the machine on the slanting, slippery ground.

Then the black limousine appeared, heaving up into view over the crest of the hill, crawling forward across rain-slicked grass and through spreading puddles. Caught once in a deeper pool, the car's huge engine hauled it free, dragged it on, tires spinning frantically, to get it within fifty yards of the mound before it finally bogged down.

The engine revved to a useless roar trying to pull the limo farther. After a few moments, it shut down. Mac climbed out and waved to Kean for help.

Kean threw his own machine into idle, climbed down, and sloughed across to Mac.

"Sorry I took so long," the other yelled to him through the storm. "Went to three towns finding the salt. And it was no picnic getting back."

"Never mind!" said Kean. "Let's just get the stuff up there!"

Mac nodded. He moved around the car and opened the trunk. There were two huge bags of heavy plastic nearly filling the space.

"Rock salt!" said Mac. "Biggest I could get! A hundred pounds each!"

"Okay. Let's get one!"

They each grabbed an end of the top sack and wrestled it out. Hampered by the weight and the spongy ground, they staggered toward the mound.

Several times they stumbled, one or another falling. Each time they struggled on. The plastic bag fast grew slippery from rain and hard to hold. They dropped it often, their hands growing cramped from trying to keep a grip. Then, halfway to the mound, both men hit a particularly boggy patch of sod. With the extra weight, their feet sank in. Both went headlong, splashing down face forward.

They rolled and sat up, both slowly and wearily, both streaming with rain and plastered with mud. Mac spat out a mouthful of muddy water and sat panting, looking at his friend as Kean immediately took hold of the bag again. Mac didn't move.

"Come on! Come on!" Kean snapped at him. "Help me."

"Give me . . . a minute," Mac gasped out, still getting breath.

"No time," Kean said fiercely, trying to wrest the bag up alone. "I said move! Those sons of bitches aren't beating me this time. I'm getting Them. I'm showing Them. I'm taking down that O'Mor."

"Getting Them?" said Mac with sudden realization. He brushed the hair and rain from his eyes, looking searchingly up at Kean's intent, glowering face and teeth gritted in a savage grimace. "Taking down O'Mor! That's what it's about, isn't it?"

Caught by the words, Kean stopped and looked from the bag to his friend. He seemed puzzled. "What? What do you mean?"

"I mean that I was right before," Mac said with growing heat. "It's not about her. It's really about you and that O'Mor, isn't it? Another guy you've got to beat. Another contest you've got to win."

"No, Mac . . ." Kean began in protest.

"Shut up, you lying bastard," Mac shouted back in rage, struggling to his feet. "Last time, you convinced me. I really believed you'd changed, that you weren't out for yourself this time."

He came erect and stood, legs set wide to brace him against the tempest, face thrust out boldly and belligerently toward his boss as he went on: "Good ol' guillible Mac," he said bitterly. "And I went right along. Well, not this time, pal! You want to play this game out, you're doing it alone. I'm not your fucking stooge here anymore!"

He turned on this and stalked away into the rain.

"Mac!" Kean called after him. But the man kept on, quickly fading away into the storm.

"Mac," Kean said again, softly, regretfully.

Then his gaze dropped back to the bag of salt. His face

once more hardened with resolution. He grabbed the bag and began again, alone, to drag it along, walking backward to haul it over the sodden ground. The rain-slicked grass gave him some help, and he moved steadily toward the mound.

Inside the Sidhe king's hall, they watched his progress closely.

"What's that he's doing now?" Angus inquired.

"What's he dragging along?" asked Owen.

"I can't read the Sasunnach writing," said Matholwch.

"I can," said Fionnbharr, "a bit." He moved in close to the shield. He peered at the big letters on the bag, half-masked by mud.

His mouth moved as he sounded out letters. Then he recoiled in shock.

"My good Danu. It's salt!" he cried, and turned to them. "He's learned the counter charm."

"Quickly, Owen," said the older druid, "we must cast the spell again. If we don't close before the salt is used, we'll lose our chance."

They both moved at once toward the spiral scratched in the hall's floor.

Outside, Kean at last reached the mound's slope. He started upward, still backward, digging in his heels and using his back and arms to wrench the bag higher, foot by foot. His muscles were pulled taut, vibrating from the strain. But he moved upward.

Inside, Owen began his slow walk in along the coil, pouring out his thin strand of liquid light. The gazes of the watchers went back and forth from his agonizingly slow process to that of Kean on the mound. The race was truly on.

Kean reached a point higher than his cut. He began to sidle crablike sideways, cautiously moving the sack, making for a spot right above the crudely scooped cavity.

Owen reached the center of the coil. He poured out his last puddle of glowing liquid at its heart.

Kean reached his point too, centered right above the

top side of the slanting hole. He hauled the sack into position on the edge.

The two druids moved to set up the silver tripod speedily.

Kean tried to rip the bag open with his fingers. The plastic was too thick.

Matholwch pulled the egg-shaped crystal from within his robe and set it on the tripod's apex.

Kean fished frantically in his pockets for something he could use.

The druids lifted their yew rods. The spiral's coils began to pulse with light flares running toward the core.

With a cry of triumph Kean drew an object forth—a Montblanc Meisterstuck Solitaire fountain pen. Unceremoniously he yanked the cap from its elegant, pinstriped gold casing and rammed the finely engraved, platinum-plated, eighteen-karat gold point into the sack. Again. Again. The tough plastic dented but stayed intact. The gold nib began to bend.

Light was collecting at the spiral's center. The crystal began to glow.

Kean drove the pen in again with the power of both arms. The point snapped, but it also punctured through. He jerked the pen around, opening a wider hole.

The light within the crystal egg was an intense blue now. Tendrils of light began to grow up toward the ceiling.

Kean shoved one finger, two, then his whole hand into the puncture, tearing it farther. He shoved in his other hand.

Matholwch raised his druid rod and directed the light tendrils toward the exact spot on the ceiling. They lifted to it and began to slip through.

The edges of the hole below Kean started to glow with the magic healing energy.

Kean saw the glow. Desperately he wrenched the tear wide open with both hands, heaving the bag upward at the same time. It ruptured, the crystalline rock salt exploding from within. He swung it before him, spilling the salt, spraying the salt, showering the salt into the excavation, sending it sprinkling down all across the hole.

The glow that had begun there instantly disappeared. Within the Sidh's hall, the tendrils of light snapped back from ceiling to egg like released bands of stretched elastic. They shot all together back into the egg, raising the blue glow's intensity to a near-blinding height.

The reversed power seemed to overload the crystal. It exploded, spewing out a spreading blossom of tiny, glistening shards.

Most of those in the room about the spiral ducked under the blast, escaping all the effects but a harmless shower of fine crystal particles.

Matholwch was not so lucky. A flash of the released power from the egg shot to the point of the old druid's lifted stick before he could lower it, crackling down its length to strike him. The startled man was lifted by the blast of sizzling power, flung backward, and cast down hard on the stone floor to lie scorched and smoking from the force of his own spell.

"Now, I've got you," Kean snarled, sliding back down the slope.

Inside the Sidh, Owen and Angus were rushing to the stunned druid's assistance. O'Mor and the rest were watching the shield's image of Kean climbing back aboard his shoveler.

"He's going to do it," King Fionnbharr said in alarm as Kean started up the machine. "He'll keep coming now."

"Then kill him," Aisling said flatly.

"No!" said the king.

"Look what he's done to Matholwch," said Owen. He helped Angus to gently lift the moaning, badly burned old man. "We'll take him to his chamber, and I'll see to him myself."

"He didn't cause the druid harm on purpose," said the king as the two men carried Matholwch out. "He only meant to block the spell." He shook his head. "This man is too determined. He's willing to face pain, danger, even

death to get at us. I can't believe it is only for evil intent.
What can he gain?"

"My daughter!" said Caitlin's mother.

"One woman," the king said. "Would he go to such
lengths for that?"

"For true love he would," said the Leanhaun Sidhe.

"There are too many questions in all of this," Fionnbharr told them. "I say he has won the right to be fairly
heard."

"What?" Aisling said in outrage. "You'd let that mortal
into the Sidh?"

"He'll be coming in himself soon," the king pointed out.
"Allowing him in will stop his breaking the barrier and
exposing our realm to the outer world. It's only him, now.
Let him come and answer our questions. Perhaps we can
still settle this peacefully."

"I've doubts of *that* being so," said O'Mor. "Still, I am
tired of hiding behind tricks and sorcery. We faced him in
his sanctuary after forcing our way in. It's fitting that he
now face us in ours."

"Then we will open the shield barrier," Fionnbharr proclaimed.

At this a glowering Aisling stalked away, out of the great
hall.

Soon she was entering the chamber of Matholwch,
where Angus and Owen were already seeing to the old
druid.

Angus was carefully stripping off the man's scorched
robes while Owen looked through the druid's shelves of
magic ingredients for the means to produce an efficient
treatment for the burns.

"Owen, you must help me," she said.

"My lady, please," he said impatiently. "I must see to
him." He poured dried leaves into a mortar and began to
crush them with a pestle.

"This will not wait," she insisted. "They mean to let that
villain in. He will surely try to win Caitlin away. With his
spell still on her, she will not argue."

"It's true what she says, Owen," put in Angus. "Fionn-bharr may then give her to him to preserve our peace."

"Then where will your Chieftan O'Mor be?" said Cait-lin's mother. "Owen, our only chance now is that you use the magic on her."

Owen paused in pouring the crushed leaves into a bowl. "What? Erase all her memory?"

She nodded. "The spell will be destroyed. All feeling for him will be gone. She will deny him, reject him. How then can the king find any excuse to let him take her away?"

"Perhaps," the druid said cautiously, still unconvinced. "But didn't Rury say he was against such a drastic choice?"

"Only if there was no other left," she argued. "And there is no other now. We are at a desperate point. The time is short. There is only one way that Rury's betrothed, the woman he loves more than his own life, can be saved for him. You and Angus are his clansmen, his most loyal friends. Don't you have to act to help him now, just as you always have?"

Owen looked to Angus.

"I say we do," the big warrior grimly said.

Owen nodded. "Yes, you're right. Angus, you go along with her now. See that Caitlin is readied. I'll come as soon as I've put a healing salve on Matholwch."

"Come then," said Aisling briskly, and headed for the door.

Angus followed her, but paused to look back to Owen. "I really don't like doing this, you know," he said.

"Neither do I," said the druid. "But it's for Rury. Go."

Outside the mound, meantime, Kean was forging ahead with his machine.

The storm had abated to only a light shower. The wind had died away. Without the gush of mud and water from the hole, his going was easier.

"Come on. Come on. Show yourselves," he growled as he backed out with a new scoopful of dirt. "Show your-selves, or I'll eat right on through."

As if in reply to his demand, the mound began to change. He had dumped his load of dirt and was starting back in toward the hole when he noticed it. He stopped the machine to stare.

The opening in the slope and the slope itself were fading away.

In moments they became like a stage scene drawn on a scrim, no more than a ghostly image superimposed on a field of grey-white.

He got down from the machine and gingerly approached. He stood peering through the softly shimmering surface of the mound for a while, then tentatively thrust a hand through. It touched nothing solid.

"Here goes nothing," he said, and boldly stepped on through.

He was instantly swallowed up in a realm of fog.

Thick billows of it swirled around him. But it seemed to be much lighter straight ahead. He went forward.

He walked for what seemed a great distance through the void. Still, the light before him grew no brighter.

"How the hell big can this place be, anyway?" he murmured.

His answer to that came in a few paces more. Abruptly he stepped out from the band of fog, leaving it rising steeply behind him like a solid wall. Ahead of him now lay a strange, new, wondrous land.

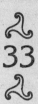

33

For an entire land it indeed appeared to be.

A whole countryside rolled far away to the horizons. It was made of emerald-grassed meadows, fields of vividly hued flowers, and woods of bright-blooming trees and great oak trees and trees heavy with a myriad of fruits. The air was richly fragrant with the blended odors of the abundantly growing things.

A flowing river ran through the bountiful landscape, its sparkling music as it flashed across its pebbled bed blending with the songs of brilliantly plumed birds that soared overhead, forming a single, joyous symphony.

A warm, golden light fell from what appeared to be a perfectly real sun to bathe this supposedly underground paradise. And what seemed to be a most authentic azure sky with drifting silver clouds stretched impossibly over it.

"Now I really do know how Alice felt," said Kean, staring in astonishment at the scene.

Some way ahead, atop a broad, low hill, sat a fortresslike construction—a great circular building of burnished white-silver walls surrounded by a palisade of gleaming bronze. There was a troop of men drawn up before the house, mounted on golden horses with crimson manes. Light flared sharply from the spears that each one held.

Kean eyed the fortress, clearly the place that he must go. But he also looked with a certain concern at the armed men.

"Do not fear, Michael Kean," said a man's voice from nowhere. "The warriors before you are the Riders of the Sidhe. They will not harm you. Come forward, if you'd confront us, and enter our dun."

And so Kean steeled himself and marched boldly ahead, across the plain, up to the bright fortress.

As he approached the men, he saw them watching him with the glinting gazes of chill, blue-silver eyes. They were an even more imposing and colorful troop seen close. Their looks were high and lean and cleanly handsome, their hair a flow of yellow bound with a band of gold. Long green cloaks clad their lean, muscled bodies over white shirts embroidered with red-gold thread. Large brooches fashioned in the shape of a spiral were fastened at their throats.

Each had slung on his back a shield of silver with a rim and boss of gold. Each clutched in his hand a sleek, wickedly barbed spear covered with rings of gold from heel to socket. The rings jingled when a horse or a rider moved.

But for all their intimidating look, the troop of horsemen parted obediently as he approached, opening an avenue to the front entrance of the dun, where huge bronze gates stood open.

Kean passed between the rows of riders, his face set in as stalwart a look as he could muster. He marched without hesitation up the slope of the dun, through the gates, and into a grassy yard.

The single structure within the palisade loomed up before him. He examined it as he approached.

Smooth walls of silver rose three stories to a peaked roof that rose two more above. The roof seemed to be thatched with the huge, pure white wings of birds. Square, gold-shuttered windows pierced through the upper portion of the wall at regular intervals, and directly before him a large doorway gaped open.

He took a deep breath, passed through the opening, and entered King Fionnbharr's great hall.

The vast space was crowded now with several hundred

people. They sat at the many tables re-formed in their concentric rings about the central fire.

They were a most handsome people as a whole, largely slim, fair, and elegant of feature, richly dressed in flowing, colorful cloaks and gowns. Their hair was long, loose, plaited, or caught up with ornate jewelry. Much other ornament of gold and jewels and bright enameling was in evidence, adding to the sumptuous texture of the scene.

A wide passage through the tables had been left from the door to the center of the room. There, before the fire pit, Kean saw a silver-haired man of noble demeanor clearly waiting to meet him.

He strode on forward, up the passage, looking unflustered by the many scores of bright and searching gazes that followed him in.

He reached the cleared inner space about the hearth, stopping there to face the waiting man.

He eyed the man's tall, splendidly garbed figure up and down, then looked over his own still-wet and mud-caked form.

"Sorry," he said. "I'm usually better dressed."

"We understand," was the response. "We have watched you, Michael Kean. We know what labors you have undergone."

"Okay," he said, keeping his voice level and controlled, "so you know who I am. Now, who are you?"

"My name is Fionnbharr," the other said. "I am king to all the Tuatha de Danann of Eire. I am also ruler of this Sidh." He gestured around him. "These are my people—the Sidh's inhabitants."

Kean looked around him. "It's quite a place," he said with unhidden awe. "I expected some kind of underground cavern. How do you swing this? I mean, it's like we're outside. How can it be real?"

"It can't, in *your* world," the king replied. "But within this one, we have our own reality. Much of it is an illusion, you see, created and sustained by tapping into the supernatural energies existing here."

"Here?" said Kean. "Where's that?"

"In a realm that exists . . . well, shall we say 'beside' your own mortal one. Certain places on the earth—haunted or sacred places, you might say—are doorways into this other world. Our Queen Danu found those doorways for us long ago, helped us set up our hidden palaces beyond them, and gave us means to shield the doors. Through magic, we can live in a real-seeming land of beauty, harmony, and peace, free of all want and pain."

"Sure knocks virtual reality into a cocked hat," said Kean, his business sense surfacing, even now. "Man, what an A-ticket ride this'd make!"

"Our land is our sanctuary," the king pointed out. "It is much threatened by the encroachment of your world already. It's for that reason we invited you in. You seemed most determined to break through our protecting barriers. Why?"

"You know why," Kean told him. "I want Caitlin Bawn."

"Caitlin Bawn?" Fionnbharr repeated blankly.

"Don't give me that," Kean shot back. "I know she's here. Nothing better've happened to her or . . ."

"Or what?" said the king. "Remember, you are here alone."

"Yeah, but if you meant to kill me, you already would have," Kean returned. "I think you brought me in because you mean to deal."

"Very shrewd of you. We want no trouble from mortal kind, *if* we can avoid it."

"You know how you can," said Kean. "I'm only here for one thing: I came to save her."

"Save her?" said another voice, which then gave out a derisive laugh.

From out of the mass of watchers arose one familiar figure who moved out to stand beside the king.

"It was *I* who saved her from *you*, my friend," said Rury O'Mor.

"So, you are here," said Kean. "I guess that settles if I

got the right address. But you're the one who's got it backward, pal. I'd say you're the bad guy here."

"You're a liar, Kean," O'Mor said harshly. "We've seen your kind of mortal at work in Ireland for two thousand years now, trying to destroy its land, its beliefs, its people. And you're one of the worst of them. I know what you intended to do here. To ravage the land. To destroy the Sidhs of our kind."

"Hey, I didn't know you were living here," Kean said defensively. "I wouldn't do that now. To tell the truth, I . . . I'm not so sure I could do anything to this country anymore. Too many things have happened to me. There's too much to rethink."

"Ah, he's a master at the fine speaking, with a silver tongue," O'Mor said derisively. "Listen to him now, trying to convince us he's no villain, but just one poor, innocent man. But it was this one man who stole Caitlin away. He imprisoned her in his fortress tower, surrounding her with armed men. And he betrayed his word to me."

"I had to," Kean argued back. "I'd already given one to her." He turned to address himself to the entire throng. "Look, all of you, it was *her* choice that I met her. *She* was the one who followed *me* to New York. She said she was a slave here. She wanted to be free. She said she needed protection"—he pointed to O'Mor—"from this guy!"

"That seems hard to believe," said Fionnbharr. "Rury is no tyrant. He loves her. They are betrothed."

"By whose choice?" said Kean. He looked to O'Mor. "She must have told you the truth. Why don't you believe her? I only wanted to save her from your making her a prisoner."

"Caitlin Bawn is one of us," said the king. "She is surely no prisoner here."

"Then why isn't she here with us right now?" Kean challenged.

That had an effect on them. Those in the watching crowd exchanged wondering looks. There was an undertone of concerned muttering.

O'Mor supplied an answer. "You know well why she's being kept safely away from you. Because of your cursed spell."

"I'm telling you, there isn't one *on* her!" Kean said with force. "Face it, O'Mor, she just doesn't love you."

"Oh?" said the warrior. "And I suppose you then wish to claim her for yourself?"

"Yeah," Kean said boldly. "Yeah, I guess I do."

Fionnbharr looked around him at the crowd. "People of the Sidh, it is very much the fates of all of us at stake in this. What do you say?"

"This mortal sounds most sincere to me," one man said.

"And yet, we mustn't be distrusting the word of our own O'Mor," said another.

"There seems to be no way to decide which one is speaking the truth," a perplexed woman put in.

"It is Rury O'Mor and that mortal alone who are in conflict over this," said another. "It should be decided between them, not involving the rest of us at all."

"Hey, all right," said Kean. "I'll buy that one. It *should* be just between the two of us, O'Mor. How about a rematch?"

"You would agree to do that, here?" asked the surprised warrior.

"Seems fair. Last time *you* did it on *my* home ground."

"But this fight would be no game, no illusion. It would be real. It would mean real death."

"I guess so," Kean accepted, then stepped toward the other man, adding pugnaciously, "but I've got a few scores to settle up with you. You kicked my tail before. You killed some of my men. And you wiped my friend Stony's brain clean."

"You killed my own friend Kevan," O'Mor returned as aggressively, stepping toward him. "I've debts to repay too."

They squared off toe-to-toe, the two men glaring uncompromisingly into each other's eyes.

"Very well, then," said Fionnbharr to the other Sidhe. "It seems these two have decided. Let's be about it."

As those in the great hall were moving to prepare for the combat, Caitlin was being tied down upon the bed in her own chamber.

It was Angus who was doing the tying, and even that burly warrior was having trouble containing the struggling girl. But at last he stepped back, breathing heavily from the fight, leaving her bound and immobile.

"I'd as soon have wrestled a mad boar," he said.

"Thank you, my friend," said Owen. He was carefully laying out some objects from a case on Caitlin's vanity. Aisling watched him closely, curiously.

"You're certain this will not damage her?" the woman asked. "At least, not permanently?"

"Besides wiping her mind clear of all memory, she'll be quite unharmed," he assured her. "Administering the potion will be the only hard thing. Getting her to swallow it, you know. It's why I have this."

He held up a long, slim, curving length of rolled, golden pipe. To the lower end was fixed a wide, spatulate spout. The upper end flared into a wide funnel.

"Nasty-looking thing," said Angus.

"Most efficient though," said the druid. "After that she'll be unconscious. When she awakes, she will be as a newly born babe in knowledge."

"Ripe for my shaping," said Aisling gloatingly. "Good. Then get on with it."

"You can't do this, Mother," a frightened Caitlin cried as Owen began to mix his ingredients. "Why are you? Why?"

"For your own good," Aisling told her, watching the druid pour a powder into a gold flagon. "For your good, Rury's good, and mine. Now relax, my daughter, and in a few moments you'll have nothing to fret over anymore."

Owen added a drop of dark red liquid to the mix. It sizzled, and a yellow puff of acrid smoke arose from it.

Caitlin stared wide-eyed.

Back in the great hall, Michael Kean was just reentering, escorted by Fionnbharr.

Cleaned up now, he was clad in a deep green tunic and leather boots like those of the Sidhe men.

The two moved through the tables to the central space where Rury O'Mor waited. The tables there had been moved back farther, opening a wider area about the fire pit, hemmed in by the crowd. Some objects had been laid out beside Rury on the hearth.

"I'll explain this to you as you once did to me," said O'Mor to Kean. "But this time things will be much simpler."

He took up one of the objects from the hearth. It was a belt and sheathed sword.

"This is, of course, a real sword," he said. He buckled the heavy belt about Kean's waist. The long scabbard hung at his left side. "It is a very good one."

"In fact, it is my own," said Fionnbharr.

Kean drew it out. The slender, polished blade gleamed redly in the fire's light. He hefted it and swung it experimentally. "Nice balance."

"Of course," said the king. "Goibniu, greatest blacksmith to the Sidhe, made it for me himself."

"Goibniu," said Kean dryly. "Sure. Then how can I go wrong?"

O'Mor lifted a round shield, slipped it up over Kean's left hand, settling it on his forearm.

"Does that feel all right?"

"I'm not all that sure how it's *supposed* to feel," said Kean, lifting it before him. "But I guess it's okay."

"Now," said O'Mor, taking up a shield himself, "I know you have the fighting skills. There will be no tricks here. No monsters. No other challenges. It will be just you and me."

"Got it," Kean said.

The warrior met his gaze and said solemnly: "Michael Kean, I ask you as you asked me before—are you certain you wish to go through with this? You could just walk away."

"I didn't come this far for that," Kean said unwaveringly. "And I really don't have anything else to lose."

"Before, even with your great advantage in the points, you could not beat me," the warrior reminded him.

"I've learned a few other things since that time," Kean said with all the bravado he could muster.

"So be it then," O'Mor said resignedly and stepped back.

The king stepped up beside Kean. A gold chalice was in his hands. "We know you have been much wearied by your toil," he said. "We would not have you go into a fight with any disadvantage in strength. Here, drink this." He held the chalice out to Kean.

Kean sheathed his sword and took the chalice. He looked at the golden liquid within, sniffed at it experimentally, then took a swig. His eyes grew wide.

"Woo! Some shot!" he said. "In-vig-or-at-ing!"

A flush of new energy was visibly coming into his face. The drawn look, the weary eyes, the attitude of fatigue, were swept away.

"It helps to keep us young and without sickness," the king explained.

"You'd have one good market for that out there!" Kean said, handing the chalice back.

"Ah, but it has potence only within the magic aura of the Sidh," said the king.

"Just as well," said Kean. "There're too many living too long out there already." He took a breath, pulled himself up into a heroic pose, and again pulled the sword from his sheath. "So okay, let's ring the first-round bell."

O'Mor drew his own sword. The two moved out into the center of the open space, faced off, and struck a defensive stance.

Fionnbharr looked from man to man to check their readiness. Then he very simply said, "Begin!"

They circled, feinted, and charged in together, weapons

striking out. The hall was filled with the clang of iron on iron as the two fought furiously, swinging out with both their swords and shields.

But it was quickly clear that O'Mor had the best in this. With real weapons he was a master fighting man, and Kean lacked even the edge supplied by his state-of-the-art game. He was clumsy with the ponderous sword and shield, swinging too slowly to effectively parry O'Mor, much less strike back efficiently at the Sidhe warrior.

Within a few minutes he had been nicked a half-dozen times. Blood streamed from slashes on thigh, arms, shoulder, and forehead. Why O'Mor did not finish the seemingly hapless man came clear when locked together in a clinch, the warrior pleaded: "Give it up now, Kean. Haven't you yet learned? You cannot win."

"Like hell," Kean said fiercely, shoving O'Mor back free of him and leaping to the attack again.

But that tactic was no help either. O'Mor sidestepped, sweeping his shield around as Kean went by, slamming the American across the back, and sending him staggering on to crash into the hearth.

Kean toppled forward, landing across the stone wall on his stomach, his head hanging over the embers of fire.

O'Mor moved up swiftly behind him, his sword lifting to strike down.

Kean rolled, bringing his shield around in time to knock the sword away. It clanked down harmlessly against the hearth, raising sparks.

But Kean had no chance to get up as O'Mor's sword rose to strike again. He couldn't even return a cut, holding up sword and shield to defend against the torrent of swift, savage blows that pounded down upon him, hammering him back.

Little by little he was being bent backward over the hearth by the relentless attack. His arms were aching from the pummeling. His head was steadily being pressed down, down toward the glowing coals.

And while Kean struggled against destruction, Caitlin struggled too.

She was throwing her head violently back and forth as Owen lowered the gold tube toward her mouth with one hand. In the other he held the flagon, filled with a vile green brew.

"I can't do this!" he said exasperatedly. "Angus, help me."

"I don't like it," the big warrior said, but obediently he moved up to the bed.

He grabbed the top of Caitlin's head in one hand, stopping its movement. His other hand came up from below, closing around her jaw. The two immense hands all but swallowed her face.

"Don't fight," he told her. "I don't want to hurt you."

And using only the least necessary force, he pulled her mouth open.

Owen immediately forced the tube's flat end in through her lips. It passed over her tongue, sliding to the back of her throat. There was nothing to stop the potion's free flow into her now.

Aisling watched the operation, nodding in satisfaction.

Owen lifted the flagon, positioned its spout over the tube's funnel end, and tilted the vessel to pour.

The green stuff oozed out toward the spout's edge. A single first drop hung glistening from the lip, ready to fall.

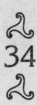

34

A hand swung in from one side, slamming a ceramic jug hard against the druid's head. The jug shattered, his head snapped sideways, and he toppled like a tree, taking the flagon and its awful contents down with him.

A startled Angus turned about. He saw the door was open, its guard unconscious on the floor. The little servant Caoimhe, who had just struck the druid, was now moving in to draw the gold tube from Caitlin's mouth.

Before the nonplussed man could act to stop her, another hand shot in from his other side to seize his sword's hilt and yank the weapon out in a swift move.

He wheeled back that way to find the point of his own blade was at his chest.

It was being held by the Leanhaun Sidhe.

"Release Caitlin," the old woman told Caoimhe. "Quickly."

"You can't do this!" screamed Aisling as the servant moved to unbind her daughter.

"I can," the crone replied, "for such true love as I felt between these two. I can't see it denied."

The untied girl rose from her bed with Caoimhe's help. She looked at the stunned Owen moaning on the floor, at the puddle of spilled potion steaming beside him, then up to the Leanhaun Sidhe.

"I thank you," she said wholeheartedly.

"Now, Caitlin, you must move like the very wind," the

old woman said. "The one who sought you for so long is at this moment in the great hall."

"Michael Kean?"

"Yes, but you must help him. Tell them what it is you truly want. Tell them the truth. Go now."

"They won't believe her," Aisling spat out. "They think she's still beneath a spell."

"Mother, you are right," Caitlin said. "So you will have to come with me!"

With that she grabbed Aisling by the long plait of hair and, with her unleashed anger powering the slender young woman, dragged her wailing mother out.

"We'll wait here awhile longer, large one," the Leanhaun Sidhe told Angus with a grin, "just to be certain she has her chance. So, don't move."

He eyed the point held rock steady before his heart. "To be sure, I won't," he readily assured.

In the great hall, Kean had drawn upon some inner reserves of his own power and made a bold drive upward against O'Mor.

In a skilled move that brought gasps of surprise from the assemblage, he whipped his sword across to catch the other's blade, forcing it aside.

In the second's respite gained, Kean heaved upward from the hearth with a massive effort of back muscles, ramming forward with his shield.

O'Mor staggered back, disengaging from him, and looking a bit surprised.

"I think I'm getting the hang of this, pal," Kean said. "Let's try again."

They came in at each other and began a new exchange more savage than the last. But this time Kean, face drawn in lines of fierce determination, gave as well as he got, parrying, swinging, thrusting out, even managing to clip the lobe of O'Mor's ear.

The Sidhe warrior broke off the fight, backing away, lifting a hand to feel the cut streaming hot blood down his neck.

"Kean," he said, this time with great surprise, "what spirit is in you?"

" 'The spirit of total desperation,' " Kean said, quoting O'Mor's own words. "You said once that only when I had something worth fighting for would I have the will to win. Well, a minute ago, when I thought you had me, I realized that, dammit, I've got that will now!"

"That we'll see," growled O'Mor and charged in again.

But Kean drove in hard too, as if truly fired by a whole new energy. He knocked O'Mor's swings away and smashed him into retreat with a series of massive blows.

When O'Mor came in to grapple close with him, their shields and swords locking together, Kean countered by thrusting his head forward, slamming his skull into Rury's face.

Recoiling from this, the warrior went off balance. Kean stepped in, giving O'Mor a powerful shove backward.

O'Mor staggered back a few steps, colliding with a table as its occupants quickly scattered from the way. He struck hard against the table and hung against its edge, guard lowered, for a moment vulnerable.

Kean leapt in. A cut from his sword forced O'Mor's shield down. His own shield swung left, slamming Rury's sword from the way, then back to the right, delivering a slapping blow to the side of Rury's head.

The Sidhe warrior rolled sideways from the table, crashing to the floor.

Before O'Mor could recover, Kean was over him. The American's foot came down on the wrist of the warrior's sword hand, pinning it. Kean's own sword lifted over O'Mor's head for the final stroke.

The blade paused there, held high, glinting redly from the fire's light. Kean's battle-heated gaze met that of the downed O'Mor. Only a fearless resignation to his fate showed in the proud Sidhe warrior's eyes.

The blade fell, not in a swift death blow, but slowly, swinging harmlessly down to the American's side. Kean stepped back, releasing the warrior.

Cries of astonishment arose from the watching people. O'Mor sat up, staring in disbelief at the other man.

"You could have killed me," he said.

"That's right," Kean said. "And I didn't."

"What are you doing?" asked Fionnbharr, moving forward.

"Proving something," Kean told him. "Proving I didn't come here to show I'm the tougher guy or to get revenge." He looked around at the others. "Don't you see? I have thrown the rest of my life away to get here. All of it. I found one thing worth giving it up for. Isn't that enough to make you believe me? Or do I have to kill him too?"

"It is more than enough," said a voice.

Everyone turned to see that Caitlin Bawn had entered the hall. They watched in surprise as the determined woman hauled her protesting mother by the hair through the rows of tables and into the central space.

Caitlin hurled her mother down upon the stones at Fionnbharr's feet and stood over her threateningly.

"My mother sought to destroy my memory," she said to the crowd. "She convinced the druid Owen it was to protect me, but it was really to hide the truth."

"Destroy your memory?" said a shocked O'Mor, climbing to his feet. "Caitlin, believe me, I didn't want that to happen."

"I know," she said. She glared down at Aisling. "It was her doing, as so much of the rest has been. None of this would have happened had she not caused it. So now, Mother," she said in hard tones, "it is time for the whole truth at last. You will tell them."

"I don't . . ." Aisling began.

"Tell them, Mother," snapped Caitlin, "or I'll make no plea to the king to save you from punishment for what you've done."

"All right," the woman said defeatedly. She looked up to Fionnbharr. "I . . . I knew that my daughter had left us on her own. I knew she'd freely chosen to follow Kean. Her servant saw the truth, but I silenced her."

"Go on, Mother," Caitlin said, prodding her with a foot. "The rest of it."

"I lied to Rury O'Mor. I told him she had been stolen away by force. I sent him after her. I did all that, but I did it for Caitlin."

"You did it for yourself, Mother," her daughter said uncompromisingly. "Sending Rury after me I might have forgiven, but not all of the rest. And you've lost my love for it."

At this the beaten woman hung her head and shook with broken sobs.

"Well, it seems we truly owe an apology to Michael Kean," Fionnbharr said, looking to the man. "I only hope he understands why we've acted as we did."

"You thought you were protecting yourselves and your own," said Kean graciously. "I can't fault you for that."

"You surely are a man of great benevolence," said the king.

"*There's* something I never expected to be called," Kean replied.

O'Mor moved to Caitlin. "So it's true. You feel no love for me."

"I'm sorry," she said regretfully. "I tried to make you believe."

"I was a foolish man," he said, "deluded by my pain and loneliness. It was so easy to see in you a replacement for my lost wife." He lifted a hand to lightly stroke her cheek. "You were so much her image." His hand dropped away. "But now I understand that in spirit you are most certainly not her. You are Caitlin Bawn. You are your own person. And I would never seek to hold you to me."

"Well, Michael Kean, it appears that you have truly won what you sought," said the king. "I can now give Caitlin's hand to you."

"I'm sorry, my king," said Caitlin emphatically, "but I do not *wish* to be given to him."

They all looked to her in astonishment.

"But wasn't that what this was all about?" asked O'Mor.

She shook her head. "You don't really understand yet, do you?" she said. She looked around her at the watching people of the Sidhe. "None of you do. This isn't about love. It's about freedom. I was a captive here. I had no choices in my life. When I met Michael Kean, he represented another world to me; a chance to escape this closed and narrow realm of ours and live life as I wished."

"But we've chosen to shut ourselves off from that world," said the king. "We know how it's become. We know its threat."

"*You've* chosen to shut us all away, from fear," Caitlin replied, "yet I survived out there."

"As did my comrades and I," put in O'Mor. "We overcame our terrors and we discovered means to prevail."

"We fear what we don't know," she told them all. "But we could learn. And maybe there's no choice for us now but to do that. Yes, the centuries have changed things. There are many evils and much ugliness out there. But it doesn't have to be that way. Maybe the only way to preserve what we have left from the mortal world's ravages is to enter it, understand it, and use our powers to help it change again, to something better this time."

"So, you used me for a chance to get out of here?" said Kean, who had been standing frozen and looking stunned through all of this. "Was that it? You don't feel anything else?"

She moved to him, speaking with great warmth: "Oh, Michael, I feel a great deal for you. There's much affection in me. Much gratitude. But I don't know that it's truly love. I want the freedom to learn that too, for myself. We had so little time together. It's more time that I hope you've won for me here"—she looked to Fionnbharr—"if my people are willing to let me go."

The king considered. He looked around him at the gathered Sidhe.

"Caitlin is right," Fionnbharr pronounced. "If we've

learned anything through this, it's that there is no hiding anymore. The mortal world has become too close. Keep up our fearful ways, and we may risk it all. We have to find a way to deal with them."

"Then, if Caitlin wishes it, let her be the beginning of our return to that world," said O'Mor. "She's taken the first steps already."

"I could be that," she said, "but not alone." She looked to Kean. "Would you guide me?"

"If it would give me a chance to be with you, of course I would," he said. "I want to know more about you, your people, and my own world too. I know now there are a lot of things out there you can't ignore."

She beamed in pleasure at him. "It's most happy I am to hear you say that, Michael Kean. Together we might create a world where the Sidhe could move freely as we once did. Together we might make both realms a paradise."

A roar of acclamation went up from all the crowd.

A lone, bedraggled figure stood on Knockma hill staring at the mound.

Bill McBride, still caked with red-brown mud, stood in the last drizzle of fading rain. His gaze moved over the ragged hole gnawed into the mound's side, over the shoveling machine left abandoned yards before it, over the empty salt sack lying on the slope above.

There was no sign of Michael Kean.

"Did you get what you wanted then, Michael?" Mac said aloud to the empty hilltop, "or did 'They' get you?"

He gave a sigh and turned away. But the sound of a voice stopped him.

"Mac!"

He turned back toward it. A ray of sun from a golden sunset was lancing through a rift to bathe the hill, sparkling brilliantly from the wet grass, surrounding the mound in a haze of light.

Out of that haze two figures were walking.

"Michael!" he shouted. "Caitlin!" And he rushed forward to meet them.

As he reached them, his gaze was drawn to something just beyond. Through what seemed a shimmering image of the mound's side, he caught a glimpse of scores of bright-clad people, looking out toward him. Then the mound had grown solid again and they had vanished away.

"Michael," he said in amazement. "I thought I saw . . . I mean . . . They are in there?"

"They are, Mac. Just like the professor said. A whole world."

"I came back," Mac said contritely. "I realized I just couldn't abandon you. But you were gone."

"I went in there," Kean said.

"And you got Caitlin," he said, grinning at her. "You won!"

"In a manner of speaking," she said, smiling in return. "They let me go. But without the help of Michael and of you, I'd be a prisoner still. Now I'll be free to live in this world, and with their blessing."

"Jeez," said Mac. "There must have been some dealing in there. How'd it all happen?"

"I'll tell you later," said Kean. "Right now we've got some work to do."

"Some clothes first," she said. Kean was back in his own mortal clothes, but she was clad in a long shift and cloak of her people.

"No problem," Kean said. "Oh, and I've got a certain green dress of yours."

"You saved it from the Leanhaun Sidhe!" she said delightedly. Then her eyes narrowed suspiciously. "And just how did you do that, by the way?"

"I'll . . . uh . . . tell you that later too," he said quickly. "First we're going to have to figure out how to get a mortal identity for you. I hope I've still got the connections to swing it."

"We'll do it somehow, boss," Mac assured. "We may

have to walk from here, though, with the limo bogged
down."

The three walked toward the black car. They found that
the pool it had been mired in had miraculously dried,
leaving it on dry sod.

"Nice to have the magic on your side," Kean said. He
opened the door for Caitlin. "Shall we go?"

She paused at the door to meet his gaze searchingly.
"You don't have to do this, you know," she said with earnestness. "You've given up your life here. Do you remember that song?"

"The one you were singing when we first met? How
could I forget?"

"It ended:

> "But since that day his chase did stray,
>   The hunter ne'er was seen,
> And legends tell he now doth dwell
>   Within the hills so green.

"That could be you, Michael. You could stay in the Sidh
and become immortal too. It has happened before."

"Not a chance," he said, ushering her into the car. "It's
real nice, but way too dull in there. Besides, I may have
lost it all, but I didn't say I couldn't win it back. Hell,
that's where the fun is. If you want to see a real battle, just
wait 'til I get home. Lance Larson's not gonna know what
hit him."

"That I believe," she said.

"Want me to drive, boss?" Mac offered.

"You let me do that," Kean said, ushering him into the
back as well. "Have a rest, my friend. I feel great. Better
than I ever have."

"Me too," said Mac, resting his weary body back. "And
without even wanting to have a drink."

Before closing the door, Kean looked back toward the
mound. "Looks like Knockma's going to have a new scar,"
he said.

"And a new legend to be told in the centuries to come," she added. "Good-bye, my people. I will see you again."

Kean closed the door and climbed behind the limo's wheel. He set the car off, rolling down from Knockma hill, leaving the mound silhouetted against the blue horizon and the setting sun.

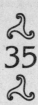

35

The elevator's door slid open. A most nattily dressed Michael Kean and a Caitlin Bawn now in smart business suit strode from it into his penthouse.

The damage from the battle waged there had been long erased. The room was as before, save for one thing: circular stairs no longer rose to corner turrets above. Instead of the destroyed turret having been replaced, the other three had been taken down. The grandiose roofline of Kean Castle had been replaced by a more low-profile one.

"Do you really think it went well?" Caitlin asked.

"Yeah, I do," said Kean. He crossed to his desk and set a briefcase down upon it. "If we can just get that final backing, we can pull it off."

He gazed at a large artist's rendering set up on an easel beside the desk. It depicted a place labeled simply as Irish World. In scope and intent it was a much more modest enterprise than the gaudy mammouth of before. It was also a much more intriguing place for that. The computerized thrill rides of a high-tech theme park had been replaced by re-creations of the true historical Ireland. An authentic farmstead, an eighteenth-century town, a Celtic hill fort, and other scenes from through the ages were pleasingly scattered across a green space surrounding a castlelike hotel that looked genuinely medieval. The name of Kean did not appear anywhere.

She moved up behind him, looking at the rendering too.

"You will succeed," she said to him. "I know. I've seen how quickly you've recovered after only these few months of being back. I'm most amazed."

He turned to her and smiled. "Thanks. You're moving pretty fast yourself. They all think you've been in the business world for years."

"I have a good teacher," she said, taking his hand.

"Maybe," he said, putting his other hand upon hers. "But I'm learning some things too. Like that you can play the game and still do the right thing."

They were interrupted as the desk intercom came to life.

"Mr. Kean," it said, "this is the lobby. There are three gentlemen here to see you. They haven't an appointment, but they were quite insistent."

"Who are they?" he asked.

"Old friends, they say. From a group called the . . . ah . . . S-H-E-E? I'm sorry, but I don't know that acronym."

He exchanged a wondering look with Caitlin. Then to the intercom he said, "It's okay. Send them right up."

In moments the elevator opened again. Three men in very dapper business suits indeed stepped out into the penthouse. With their modern dress and neatly barbered hair, Kean and Caitlin took a moment identifying them.

"O'Mor?" Kean said to the blond one.

"And Owen, and Angus," the chieftain replied.

They greeted one another warmly then. Kean looked over the Sidhe men's outfits.

"Nice threads," he said, impressed. "Make you look very Big Town."

This was no overstatement. The gawky druid Owen now looked like a staid and most successful stockbroker. The massive form of Angus had been disguised and shaped by the skillfully cut suit into more elegant lines. O'Mor, with his boldly handsome looks, gallant air, and golden thatch of locks, was the image of another Irish-American media star about to make his run at a senate seat.

"There are those among us skilled in the making of clothing," O'Mor explained. "And we've been doing some research to prepare."

"Why did you come?" Kean asked.

"With Caitlin well established, we thought it time a few others ventured out," the chieftain explained. "We three had the most experience here."

"Experience," said Owen sardonically. "I suppose that's a way of putting it."

"What do you boys want to do here?" said Kean. "I mean, do you have anything in mind?"

"Well, I want to know about how your machines work," said Angus. "For a start, I'd like to see over this marvelous building of yours."

"No problem," said Kean. "I'll have Stony show you around."

"The big man?" Angus said with surprise. "He was touched by the Fool."

"I guess that's not as permanent as it used to be," said Kean. "The 'miracles of modern medicine' and all that. Anyway, he's my security head here now."

"I'm glad," said the big warrior. "I'd like to meet with him again"—he smiled—"to talk."

"*I'd* like to get into this Wall Street place of yours," said the druid. "I want to see if any of my own skills might be of use there . . . if that's allowed."

"I'm sure we could work something fairly legal out," Kean said casually. "I wouldn't mind having a real financial wizard on the team."

"For myself, I wish to understand how a modern chieftain rules," said O'Mor. He turned to Caitlin and took her hand. "And I'd like my own chance to get to know Caitlin Bawn, as herself," he added, giving her a smile.

She smiled in return. "I would like that too."

Kean hastily stepped up close beside them, saying heartily: "So, Rury, tell me, how's everybody back home?"

This succeeded in drawing O'Mor's attention back to him. "Very well," the chieftain said. "Fionnbharr sends his greetings to you with us. And how is your own other companion, Mr. McBride?"

"Fine. In Ireland, actually. Got a nice little place there, in Feakle. He's sober. Thin now too. Says he loves exploring the countryside."

"So he's left your company?" asked Owen.

"No. He's doing liaison work over there for me. A real ball of fire. Lined up lots of Irish companies for the new project. Professor Connelly's been helping in the planning. Even got Lord Desmond to help too."

"This is what the new park will be like," said Caitlin, directing them to the easel.

All of them moved to look at the rendering.

"Very nice," said O'Mor. "It all seems real."

"I believe I've actually visited there," said Angus, closely eyeing the hill fort.

"It'll be built in a completely new locale," Kean explained. "The Irish government ended up dumping that whole other scheme. They liked this better. It fits in to the landscape and doesn't screw up a few square miles of virgin countryside. That castle in the middle's already there, in ruins. It gets restored. No trees or historical sites get bulldozed. And best of all, there's not a Sidh anywhere nearby. Caitlin made sure of that."

"We haven't quite got the money for it all yet," she said regretfully. "Michael's tried hard, but many of the old investors wouldn't come back."

"Not commercial enough," Kean said scornfully. "Not enough animatronics and video games."

"So, you need more wealth," said O'Mor thoughtfully. He looked to the druid. "Show him, Owen."

The druid took a leather pouch out from his coat. With a flourish he untied and upended it. A half-dozen gleaming, thick, irregular coins clinked out onto the desktop.

Kean picked one up and hefted it. "Heavy!"

"Gold," said the druid. "Armorican staters from the trove of Brian Boru. Worth several hundreds of your dollars apiece, I understand. And there are many, many thousands more where those came from."

"Thousands," repeated Kean. He looked to them with a grin. "Well, gentlemen, it looks like we are destined to have one very nice partnership. Shall we all have dinner to celebrate the linking of two worlds?"

Owen and Angus exchanged a look.

"Well," said Owen, "in truth, Angus and I would like to be off and look around your town. You see, last time we saw most of it rather, ah, hurriedly."

"That's great," said Kean. "I'll set Stony up to guide you. He'll love that." He looked to Caitlin and Rury. "Just the three of us then?"

"Surely," she said. "And afterward, could we stop in the park too? There are some swans there I'd still like to feed."

"Fine with me," said Kean. "Shall we all get going?"

He led the way to the elevator and opened up its door. As they entered, Angus and Owen moved to the back. Kean and O'Mor stood before them, close at Caitlin's either hand, their sides just touching hers. They exchanged a glance and a challenging little smile above her head.

Angus and Owen looked at the close trio interestedly.

Angus looked at Owen, one bushy eyebrow raised.

Owen looked to Angus, seeing the questioning eye.

He only grinned and shrugged.

None of the men could see the confident and amused smile on the face of Caitlin Bawn, shut from all view as the door slid closed.

NOTES

The powers and characteristics I have attributed to the noble Sidhe are the ones of tradition. They have been gleaned and gathered over the years through my research into Irish myths and legends and my travels in that country.

I wrote this because, as in other of my books, I want to give some idea of the depth and richness of true Celtic beliefs still existent today, though largely unknown to Americans, even those of Irish descent. The true nature of the banshee—a well-known but misunderstood being—seemed a fit candidate for examination.

Ireland is still one of the few places where the Celtic culture that spawned the Banshee may still be experienced today. Untouched by Rome, somehow surviving British and Christian cultures overlaid upon it, it still influences Irish life and arts. In that green land, the beliefs in the old ones and their powers does still exist, and one can still find the lonely, haunted places where the magic spirit of the Otherworld feels very close.

But, alas, as W. B. Yeats said, "As life becomes more orderly, more deliberate, the supernatural world sinks further away." With the continued encroachment of the rav-

ening beast we call modernity, even that last bastion of the
Celtic world may someday be lost to us.

I list below the approximate pronunciation of some of
the more difficult Irish words:

Aisling	Ice-ling
Bobd Dearg	Bove Derg
Caoimhe	Kee-va
Cian	Ke-an
Connacht	Kon-akt
Darvrach	Darv-rak
Fionnbharr	Fin-var
Kieran	Kee-ran
Lough Derg	Lock Derg
MacCumhal	Mac-Coo-al
Matholwch	Mat-olk
Meadha	Mee-a
Seamus	Sha-mus

Here is a glossary of those words that might benefit
from a bit of further definition:

Amadan-na-Briona—The Fool of the Forth. Many in
Ireland used to believe that all those not "bound by reason
to the wheel," as it were, had met this being in some
shoeugy spot. They were thus, as in other cultures, held in
some awe by the rest of the populace. It is from this that
the term "touched" for such special people came into being.

Angus Og—A son of the Dagda, and one of the principal characters in the ancient cycle of tales about the beginnings of the Sidhe. He took control by trickery of the
Newgrange Sidh that had been allotted his father, and is
famous for his prankishness.

Astray—A Sidhe power, still believed in by many, to
disorient mortals and send them off wandering and lost.

The invisible force that does this surrounds the Sidh and is part of its protection.

Biddy Early—This seer and healer did actually live near the town of Feakle. Fantastic claims for her abilities are made to this day. Lady Gregory visited the remains of her cottage in the 1910s.

Brugh-na-Boyne (Brew-na-Boyne)—A spot on the famous Boyne River in eastern Ireland associated with many legends. It is said to be home for the Dagda and Angus Og.

Cashel—An immense cathedral complex atop a rocky hill. It is not far from Tipperary, in County Limerick. Definitely worth seeing.

Celt (Kelt)—A member of a tribe, traceable back to Indo-European roots, which once inhabited most of Europe. Though much overlooked, their heritage did have a significant impact on the western civilization of today. Only when one is referring to a certain Boston basketball team should the word be pronounced with a soft C sound (i.e. Seltics).

Cliffs of Moher—Spectacular 700-foot high cliffs on the west coast of Ireland near Galway and Shannon Airport. Another must-see for tourists.

Coiste-Bodhar (Costa Bower)—Later anglicized into "coach-a-bower." It is a black coach, often a hearse, drawn by headless horses and driven by a headless man. (See *Dallahan.*) If it rumbles past you or your door, it is a sign of very bad luck, probably death. It is an apparition similar to this that Scrooge encounters in Dickens's *A Christmas Carol*.

Dagda—A sort of father figure, earth god in the Celtic pantheon. One of the original beings to learn the magic powers of Danu, he helped establish the Sidhe in Ireland and figures in many of the old tales.

Dallahan—A most gruesome Sidhe creature. It traditionally has no head or carries it under one arm. Often it is seen driving the black coach called the coach-a-bower. (See *Coiste-Bodhar.*)

Danu—The powerful goddess who provided the Sidhe with their magical powers and became a queen to them. (See *Tuatha de Danann.*)

Dun—A large hill or man-made mound on which the ancient Irish hill forts were constructed.

Feakle—A picturesque village in County Clare some thirty miles south of Gort. Quaint and comfortable cottages actually can be most reasonably rented by tourists there.

"Feuch an rogaire . . . chodladh 'sa' la"—An ancient Irish poem quoted on pages 226–227 of the manuscript translates as follows:
"Look at the rogue, it's for kisses he's rambling,
    It isn't much wonder, for that was his way;
He's like an old hedgehog, at night he'll be scrambling
    From this place to that, but he'll sleep in the day."

Leanhaun Sidhe (Lee-an-awn Shee)—The Fairy Mistress. This poor creature of the Sidhe is cursed with an insatiable thirst for the vitality of young men and a need to get it to sustain her own magical youth and beauty. But if her lovers are wasted away by her desire, so do they gain great inspiration from her. It's said that down to recent times this malignant fairy has played muse to most of the Irish poets. Perhaps this is why so many were famous, but died young.

Newgrange—One of the most impressive neolithic burial mounds in Europe. It is located about thirty miles northwest of Ireland, and is near many other Irish historical sites, such as Tara. (See Tara.)

Oghams—A form of writing said to have been invented as ceremonial script by Celtic druids. It consists of slanting lines in various numbers and combinations to represent different letters—somewhat like Morse code.

Pishogues (Pi-sho-gees)—Fairy dreams. They may be visited upon mortals by the Sidhe in an attempt to frighten or influence them.

Knockma—Originally called Sidh Meadha. It really is considered to be the home of Fionnbharr, king of the fairies. Located five miles west of Tuam, it may be visited. In truth, it is the Kirwan family of Castle Hacket on Knockma's north slope who were said to be under the king's special care.

Samain—The most important Celtic festival day, when the Otherworld become visible to mankind and the forces of the supernatural are loosed on the mortal world. It was celebrated on the eve proceeding November first, and is the basis for our modern Halloween.

Sasunnach (Sass-unn-ak)—Simply, an Englishman, but often spoken by the Gaels as if it were some form of an insult.

Shoeugy (Sho-gee)—The rath, mounds, glens, and other such places dotted thickly over Ireland that are believed to be haunted by the spirits of the Others. Many believe strongly in this to this day in Ireland and strictly avoid such places.

Sidh (Sith)—Residences of the Tuatha de Danann, provided by Queen Danu's magic and parceled out to various clans by the Dagda. Each is a barrow or hillock that acts as a doorway to an underground realm of inexhaustible splendor and delight. Unfortunately, these *cannot* be visited by tourists.

Sidhe (Shee)—The name under which the Tuatha de Danann were popularly known to the Irish peasantry. The name *Aes Sidhe* or "People of the Hills" became shortened to the *Sidhe*. It is from this that the term "Banshee" (i.e. Ban-woman, Shee-Sidhe) was derived.

Slieve-nan-or (Sleeve-nan-or)—The Golden Mountain, located in County Clare. The word *slieve* simply means "mountain," and is used plentifully on maps of Ireland.

Tara—The ancient seat of the high kings of Ireland, and a most sacred site to the Celts. Its remains can be seen today on a windswept hilltop some thirty miles northwest of Dublin. A most scenic place.

Tir-na-nog—"Country of the Young." The dwelling place of the fairies or Sidhe. There are many and conflicting stories about its location and nature—as should be expected of a magical place of another plane of reality seldom seen by mortals of our world. Some say it is a double place, existing at once within the Sidhs and on an isle said to exist far out in the Atlantic. It is known also as *Magh Mell* (Ma Mell) or "Land of the Living."

The Troubles—A reference to the war between Irish and British for Ireland's independence. Begun with the Easter rising of 1916, it continues in Northern Ireland to the present day.

Tuatha de Danann (Too-a-ha-day-Don-an)—Another name for the Sidhe, it means "children of Danu" and was assumed by these beings in honor of the mystical Queen Danu who gave them their magic powers.

I also enclose here a bibliography of some of those reference works that I have used to write both this and many of my other Irish-based novels.

I recommend especially the works of Lady Gregory for those interested in the true basis for Irish folklore, myths, and superstitions. It was she who did much to paint a picture of the real beings known to us as the Banshee.

Gregory, Lady Augusta. *Gods and Fighting Men.* New York: Oxford University Press, 1970.

Gregory. *Visions and Beliefs in the West of Ireland.* New York: Oxford University Press, 1970.

Harbison, Peter. *Guide to the National Monuments in the Republic of Ireland.* Dublin: Gill and MacMillan, 1970.

MacCulloch, J. A. *The Religion of the Ancient Celts.* New York: Folcroft Library Editions, 1977.

MacManus, Seumas. *The Story of the Irish Race.* Old Greenwich: The Devin-Adair Company, 1983.

O'Faolain, Eileen. *Irish Sagas and Folk Tales.* Dublin: Ward River Press, 1983.

Ross, Anne. *Everyday Life of the Pagan Celts.* New York: G. P. Putnam's Sons, 1970.

Squire, Charles. *Celtic Myth and Legend.* North Hollywood: Newcastle Publishing Co., Inc., 1975.

Yeats, W. B., ed. *Fairy and Folk Tales of Ireland.* New York: Macmillan Publishing Co., Inc., 1973.

ABOUT THE AUTHOR

KENNETH C. FLINT is a graduate of the University of Nebraska, with a master's degree in English Literature. His interest in the mythology of Ireland began in graduate school and led to the writing of eight novels based on the tales of the heroes of ancient Ireland. His latest novels, *Cromm, Otherworld* and *Legends Reborn* all interweave Celtic myth with a contemporary setting. He is currently working on a new novel.

Centuries ago, druids and mages could sense ancient lines of power that traced the earth like a ghostly, binding web.

Untended for eons, such energy can take on a life of its own, drawing ambitious dark forces toward a devastating confrontation.

OTHERWORLD

A Dark Fantasy

Kenneth C. Flint

When Robert Cassiday begins to investigate the death of his best friend, little does he know the ancients are watching. And now, out of the darkness, out of Celtic legend and modern power, comes a menace from the darkest corners of human myth, a cruel new order hungry for a door into our reality and ultimately for dominion over our world...

From the author of the bestselling Amber series and from one of the genre's most popular humorists, a fantasy novel that posits that anything worth doing is worth doing well—especially if it's the end of the world...

BRING ME THE HEAD OF PRINCE CHARMING
Roger Zelazny and Robert Sheckley

Most people don't know the world ends every millennium. Generally nobody notices except for the forces of good and evil, who vie for control of the universe every thousand years.

Azzy Elbub, demon, is out to win the Millennial Evil Deeds Award for the year 1000, given to the being whose acts do the most toward reshaping the world. Azzy wants to create a "Frankenstein's hero" to send off on a doomed quest to wake up a sleeping princess. The plan, if it succeeds, will end with the princess stabbing her princely rescuer, then committing suicide—an evil deed indeed. Azzy is backed fully by the Powers of Darkness and is even given a credit card good for anything in Hell he might need. However, since he is competing for the Millennial Award, the Powers of Light are permitted to send an observer, and Azzy is stuck with the angel Babriel. And that's only the beginning of the end....

Bring Me The Head of Prince Charming
A rollicking romp through heaven and hell.

"A distinctive, richly imagined setting."—*Dragon*

The Death Gate Cycle

by Margaret Weis
and Tracy Hickman

Ages ago, sorcerers of unmatched power sundered a world into four realms—sky, stone, fire and water—then vanished. Over time, the magicians' descendants learned to work spells only in their own realms and forgot the others. Now only the few who have survived the horrors of the Labyrinth and crossed the Death Gate know of the presence of all four realms—and even they have yet to unravel the mysteries of their severed world.

Follow Haplo the Patryn as he traverses this segmented universe through the Death Gate, learning about his extraordinary world and the role he plays in its ultimate destiny.

❑ Volume 1: Dragon Wing (28639-0 * $4.95/$5.95 in Canada)
❑ Volume 2: Elven Star (29098-3 * $5.50/$6.50 in Canada)
❑ Volume 3: Fire Sea (29541-1 * $5.99/$6.99 in Canada)
❑ Volume 4: Serpent Mage
       (08310-4 * hardcover * $20.00/$25.00 in Canada)